[DON'T?]
STAY IN
YOUR LANE

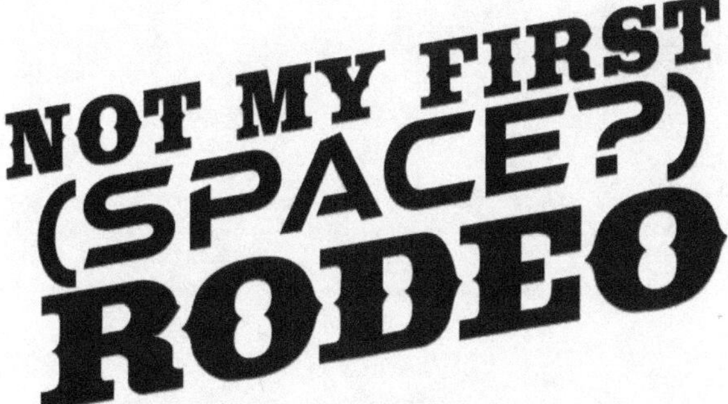

NOT MY FIRST (SPACE?) RODEO

BOOK TWO

(DON'T?) STAY IN YOUR LANE

M. TALON

Podium

Podium

[DON'T?]
STAY IN
YOUR LANE

CHAPTER ONE

THE IMPORTANCE OF CULTIVATION: DOES LEAD BEAT JADE?

A breath of air blew through the courtyard of the Jade Blossom School. The gleaming white marble steps in front of us led up to a green-and-gold gate from which hung brass-bound wooden doors. I stood at the front of the party, Sage and Grandpa behind me, with Bill and Bob bringing up the rear.

Between us and the doors were three men and two women arranged in an arrowhead formation.

The man at the point of the arrow wore long, flowing white robes and a red sash. His jet-black hair was long, too, and hung loose past his shoulders. His jade-colored eyes narrowed as he took in me and my party.

"How dare you profane these halls?" he demanded. "I, Master Li of the Jade Blossom School, will teach you to respect your betters. Any of my students could beat you with no more than a single pinky. The students at my school have trained for years to even have a chance of advancing to the first rank. And you, you outsiders without a trace of cultivation in your bodies, you dare come here and ask us for our most sacred treasure. I tell you no. The Elixir of Heaven shall never be yours."

"Yeah, okay, I guess that's our answer." I unslung the grenade launcher from my shoulder and raised it casually. "Time for Plan B." I fired off a shrapnel grenade.

The grenade arced over the head of Master Li and his disciples. It landed just below the gate. The disciples turned to look at it for a moment, as if waiting for the delayed explosion.

Master Li's mouth gaped. He lifted an arm to point at us. His sleeve was ridiculously big, hanging from his wrist in a long, silken loop. "Fallen Leaf Disciples, end them!" he shrieked.

The woman to his right stepped forward and beckoned with one elegant, golden-clawed hand. A bevy of students wearing gi with orange sashes appeared in the courtyard to our right.

"Did I just not notice them?" I asked Grandpa. He was, after all, our team ninja.

Grandpa shook his head. "Pretty sure they just spawned in. How long's the fuse on that grenade?"

"About another two seconds."

Sage cast Mucking Out the Stalls under the Fallen Leaf Disciples' feet just as our fragmentation grenade went off in a thunderous roar by the gate. The explosion sent a wave of shrapnel down the stairs, little pieces of metal raining to the ground close to where the cultivators stood. A blast of air ruffled their robes. From here, it was impossible to tell if the grenade had done any damage to the doors at all.

Master Li howled. "Students of the Flowing Wind, attack!"

The man to his left stepped down, slowed by Sage's muck, and a squad of blue-belted ninjas appeared on the other side of our courtyard.

"Bill, Bob, let's clean these up!" I shouted. I lobbed my second grenade at the gate and stowed the launcher in my inventory. Then I Quick Drew my gun and fanned down the hammer.

Six shots left the barrel so close together I could barely hear the individual retorts. I didn't bother to aim, just pointed in the direction of the blue-belted ninjas. I was shooting flechette rounds. As soon as they got within ten feet of a person, each bullet exploded into a dozen heat-seeking darts.

The ninjas stumbled back away from us as Bob and Bill went to work. Bob used his Babel spell to disrupt their coordination, then followed up with Lost in Translation.

He'd picked that up a couple of missions back. It was a nifty little spell that caused enemies to go into an enraged state for thirty seconds, attacking whoever was nearest.

I made sure to stay away from its area of effect as the disciples tore into each other like a pack of angry tigers. Speaking of angry tigers, my attention was diverted as Master Li swore an oath to the heavens and called upon the patron spirit of the Jade Blossom School.

I would have assumed their patron spirit to be something floral in theme, but apparently it was a heavenly tiger. Li reached skyward as a bolt of lightning dropped from the clear sky to the ground where he stood. I blinked away the afterimage. An enormous white tiger, tall as a man, stood in Li's place.

"No fair!" Sage shouted. "He's tripled his hit points!" She and Grandpa had made quick work of the Fallen Leaf ninjas and their mistress. Only two of the ninja students still stood, and Sage had her T-Shirt Cannon pointed at the ninja mistress, who was lying on her face in the courtyard with Sage's boot on her back.

"Just try it," Sage purred. "I'll wrap you up before you can say 'pressed cotton.'"

Grandpa had used his ability to teleport behind an enemy and deliver a Crippling Blow to great effect. He and Sage had only taken a couple of points of damage each.

I turned back to my other side, where Bob and Bill were cleaning up the blue-belted ninjas. Only the tiger and his two disciples remained.

It also left my other grenade. I had been counting down the seconds. The fuses were longer than I liked, since theoretically someone could have picked it up and thrown it back at us, but we were working with the materials we had.

"Brace!" I shouted as the second grenade exploded. This one sent flames rocketing down the steps. The blast wave knocked one of the two remaining senior disciples off her feet.

I charged over, activating my Fastest Gun in the West ability to cover the distance in an eye blink. She had taken a lot of damage in that fall. From her knees, she raised her hands heavenward, praying for the spirit of the wind to intercede.

No time for that, with a giant tiger only ten feet away. I emptied six rounds into her, reloaded, and dumped another six. She fell forward onto the steps.

"Looks like lead beats jade," I quipped. I was hoping to earn a new skill from the system based on my scintillating wit. It hadn't happened yet.

I ducked as the tiger leapt at me. The last disciple glanced at the scene before promptly skedaddling up the steps. I swore. "Get him! I'll keep the tiger busy! Don't let him get to the vault!"

The two grenades should have gotten the ironwood doors open. From our earlier scouting of the Jade Blossom School, we had learned all about its defenses, most notably the ironwood doors. They were impenetrable by normal means. Blades would only scratch them. Fire would do little more than mar the surface.

We'd conducted experiments on similar boards, using a knife to scratch just enough to get under the outer coating. Then we were able to apply an alchemical solution that burned hot enough to make the ironwood literally explode.

My first grenade had scratched the door in a hundred different places and applied the solution. The second one was full of thermite. I knew it had worked because of the explosion of ironwood that had knocked the disciple at my feet off her balance.

Bill, Bob, Grandpa, and Sage scrambled up the steps past me. Meanwhile, the tiger prowled the courtyard below, lashing its tail. I didn't know whether it still had Li's intelligence, but even a stupid tiger is dangerous.

"Well, Master Li," I said, choosing rounds from my gun belt and loading my gun manually since I apparently had the time. "You haven't been very friendly to strangers. Your sect could take a few lessons on hospitality from, well, basically anyone else in all of history. We tried asking nicely, you know. We needed that heavenly elixir, and we told you so. But you didn't have to lose your whole sect over it. Pretty sure those vaults are brimming with cultivation treasures and growth items. This isn't the first Wuxia mission we've faced, Brother Li."

The tiger yowled at me.

"Yeah, well, I'm not sorry. From what I can tell, you guys are just the book one assholes. If it hadn't been us, it would have been some other adventuring party come to blow your school up and steal all the treasures. Nobody here looks like a protagonist to me. You'd probably all be stuck on silver, or whatever your third level up is, forever."

I aimed my gun as the tiger crouched to spring, and as the animal leapt into the air I fired an incendiary shot. My bullet struck it in the chest and lit the beast's fur on fire. It took fifteen points of damage right away.

I had been putting points into my strength on my last couple of level-ups, and my bullets were starting to pack a punch. Of course, the tiger was level eight, and I was only level four, so this might take a little while.

I ducked and the flaming tiger sailed past my head. It hit the steps hard. I fired another round into its flank. This one we had made special from materials we had gathered earlier in this mission. It was brass wrapped around a heartwood core, and the sage who had helped us with the recipe guaranteed it would do extra harm to a spirit animal.

Sure enough, Tiger Li went down to **[350/500]** hit points. We only had two incendiary rounds left, and I was holding on to the other one for emergencies. I fired a couple of truesilver rounds. They'd been more effective against the werewolves we had encountered in the previous mission, but the tiger didn't seem to like them.

In chat, I asked, *How's it going?*

Found the Tears of Eternal Youth and the Elixir of the Heaven, Grandpa reported.

There's so much good stuff here! Sage said. I could imagine the excitement in her voice. *I found a sack of holding and I'm stuffing everything into it!*

Sage, your inventory is infinite, I replied as I threw a couple of fragment rounds at the tiger. I reloaded and then booked it across the courtyard as the tiger charged at me, snarling.

I ducked behind a pillar, causing the tiger to overshoot and slam into a wall. I fired six rounds into its flank, then used my Roped Into It ability to throw a line over the top of the pillar and shimmy up it.

I perched on the edge of the parapet surrounding the courtyard. The tiger was at a bad angle now, but I'd be able to get him as soon as he moved.

Who cares about my inventory? That's boring. This is cool, Sage said. *I found a flying carpet!*

Great. Get on it and come pick me up, I replied. *We're on a timer here. The Great Son of Heaven is dying, and if we don't get the elixir back to him by sunset, we'll fail the mission.*

We're on it, Grandpa assured me.

The tiger snarled, clawing at the column I had just climbed. I used Trick Shot to put another spirit poison round into it and was gratified by the dismayed yowling as the tiger's health ticked down.

We're on our way, Grandpa said. *Heads up. We're coming out fast.*

I'm up on the wall to the left. The tiger's just below me. He's angry, but not dead yet.

Understood. A moment later, my party burst out of the ruined doors and flew down the steps past the bodies of the fallen members of the Jade Blossom School.

Literally flew. Sage was sitting at the front of an eight-by-ten oriental rug that hovered about four feet off the ground. She whooped and hollered as the rug answered her bidding. Grandpa was right behind her. Bob and Bill hugged the back of the rug, curled up like pill bugs.

"Come get me," I shouted.

"We can't. It only goes this high," Sage yelled back.

"What kind of stupid flying carpet is that?" I stood up and checked the distance. Time for a Tarzan moment. I used my Roped Into It skill again, lashing it to a pillar on the far side of the courtyard. Thirty feet was the extreme range. Then I sprinted to the edge of the parapet, threw myself off, and cancelled Roped Into It at just the right moment.

Grandpa caught me as I tumbled into the middle of the carpet. "Finish off the tiger!" I yelled at Bill and Bob, but they were too busy trying not to fall off.

We zoomed out of the doors of the Jade Blossom School. "I can't believe we failed to kill the sub-boss!" Sage shouted over the rushing wind.

"Well, we'll lose a lot more if we don't get back to the emperor's son in time," I said. "So, just keep flying!"

CHAPTER TWO

RUNNING A GUILD: PERSONNEL MANAGEMENT AND YOU

There had been a lot of changes to Threshold in the last two months. The ramshackle buildings and makeshift tents had been replaced by real buildings erected by the various crafters of our coalition or one of our allies.

We kept to one sector of the great portal room. While the whole place was circular and most of the portals were hard to tell apart, there was one enormous unopened portal three times bigger than all of the others that everyone designated as "North." From there, we went clockwise around the circle.

Our sector was located between seven and nine o'clock. We sometimes ventured into the five or six o'clock or the ten and eleven o'clock regions for portals, but mostly we stayed fairly close to home.

Our coalition had grown to over a thousand people. I no longer even knew half of their names. But the center of the Misfits Guild was still Mama Grace's restaurant, though it was now housed in a long barn that stretched nearly one hundred feet along one of Threshold's streets. The outside was painted bright red, and each end had a quilt-like design painted over the door.

It was two stories high. The bottom floor held the enormous dining hall, a spacious kitchen, and multiple different crafting rooms. Upstairs were bedrooms for the crafters and anyone else who was not currently on a mission or working a farming zone.

Out back was a bathhouse. We'd put that in two weeks ago, and I was proud of our contribution. My team had fought a pair of dragons and brought back their steaming hearts to serve as power sources for our crafters. The waste heat was used for the baths. I'd already spent several glorious hours soaking in a hot tub of suds.

We stepped into the restaurant and found an empty booth at the back. Rosa appeared, spotted us, and hurried off to tell her mother. They both emerged a minute later, bringing drinks and platters of good homemade food.

"How did it go?" Mama Grace asked.

"Great!" Sage exclaimed. "I got a flying carpet and the cutest little cloud pet. But I couldn't take it out of the mission with me. I had to give it to the Princess of the Sun. That was all right, though. She married the emperor's son. And they're going to fix everything so the cultivation schools have to be opened to everyone, not just the elite."

Rosa laughed gently. "Sounds like you really got into this one."

"It was great! Shad didn't kill a tiger, and I fought a whole army of ninjas at once."

I helped myself to some of the delicious cornbread muffins. "Is Juana here?" I asked around a mouthful.

Rosa smirked at me. "No, she's not. She'll be sorry to have missed you. She went to one of the farming levels. Our quotas have been down, and she wanted to make sure our people are all right. Don't worry," she said as I struggled to chew the muffins so I could get another word in. "I had a message from her that everything's fine. They just were pushing themselves too hard and needed to take better work rotations. She should be back in a few hours."

"More importantly," Grandpa interjected. "We,"—he gestured at me, him, and Sage—"just hit level five and the brothers made level four. We're staying ahead of the curve."

"Did you get anything good?" Rosa asked, diverted.

I held up a hand. "Hold on just a second." I had just received a priority message from Veda, our sponsor and the guild backer.

I opened it. *Very important I see you at once. Come up immediately.*

I sent back a message. *We're talking with Grace and having a meal. How urgent?*

Drop everything and come. I have to handle some things on my end. We'll talk when you get here.

I looked at Grandpa. He nodded, having received the same message. "Sorry, we've got to run," I told Mama Grace. "Veda sent for us."

"Surely it can wait until you've eaten."

"She says it can't."

Grace looked at Sage. "You want to stay here, honey? You can eat and take a bath while your grandpa and Shad go up to the Hub."

Sage shook her head. "Nuh-uh," she said. "What if Veda has a present for me? Maybe *she* remembered it was my birthday." She rolled her eyes at me.

"Okay, look, I didn't forget it was your birthday," I said. "It's just the system clock rolled over while we were in that mission, and the times didn't match up at all. I already said I'm sorry, *and* I said happy birthday to you."

"Not good enough, Shad."

"All right, we don't have time for this. Veda wants us right now. Bill, Bob, you can come or stay or . . ."

The brothers looked at each other. "Uh, yeah, so about that," Bill said.

I got to my feet and slid out of the booth, letting Sage come out so that Grandpa could slide over and get up.

"Look, we really appreciate how you've been helping us get leveled and geared up. We've learned more running missions with you than we would have any other way."

"But what he means to say," Bob interjected, "is that you're insane, Shad. We like you, we really do, man, but you're going to get us killed. We can't keep up with you three."

"And honestly," Bill said, "we don't really want to." He held up a hand. "We're okay still running missions. Just, we need partners who match us a little more."

I looked at Grandpa and Sage. "Are we really that bad?"

Sage shrugged. "They're like the fifth group to have said so, so I guess we are," she said.

I hadn't thought I was taking that many risks, not with my sister and Grandpa along, but in order to beat the missions, in order to do what needed to be done, you couldn't go halfway on things.

Grandpa slid out of the booth and nudged me. "Come on, we don't want to keep Veda waiting."

All the way up the elevator, I stewed over what Bob and Bill had said. "We're not crazy. We just get things done."

"It's all right," Sage said. "If they'd been more on it, we could have killed that giant tiger when we were on the flying carpet. There were at least thirty seconds when it was still in range of their guns, but they were too busy being fraidy-cats. We'll find someone who has a little more drive."

I looked over her head at Grandpa. Bob and Bill weren't the first miners to leave our team because they couldn't keep up. Our first partner, Frank, had said much the same thing when he left.

We still spoke with Frank regularly. He had taken over one of our coalition's mining levels and was supervising all the teams that worked there. He was doing brilliantly. They hadn't taken a single casualty in the month and a half he had been leading, and their production rates were through the roof.

"I'm not crazy. We're not crazy," I said again.

"Just take it easy, Shad," Grandpa advised me. He turned to Sage. "Well then, young lady."

She stood up a little straighter. "Yes?"

"What is it you'd like for your birthday?"

That brought me back to reality in a way Bill and Bob hadn't. It was Sage's birthday. We had been involved in this crazy scheme for almost four months now. We had been kidnapped from our home on the Arizona Strip, brought to an alien construct beneath the surface of Ganymede, and thrown into one insane simulation after another. Our lives were at risk almost every day as we competed to earn soul coins and other resources that would enable us to, what, keep playing this stupid game?

Back when this had all started, the alien artificial intelligence that we all called "the system" said there would be a chance for some of us humans to claim ownership of the Reality Engine behind all of this. Veda, our sponsor, told us there was a three-phase process of exploiting the Reality Engine, and that we were only in phase one. She also said that the locals, meaning us, never made it to phase three.

This was no place for a twelve-year-old girl to be risking her life in one ridiculous scenario after another. Me, on the other hand? I had to admit the past four months had been some of the best of my whole life. Maybe that meant I was screwed up.

The thing was, at least I felt like I *could* protect Sage, could protect myself. I didn't wake up in the middle of the night in a cold sweat anymore hearing a baby cry and knowing there was nothing I could do about it. I got to spend all day with my sister and my Grandpa.

I'd always had a wild streak. I used to indulge it riding a dirt bike I'd managed to buy when I was fourteen and then kept running with bailing wire and a lot of elbow grease. I'd ride that thing up the side of bluffs on paths a goat wouldn't take. I'd race along the edge knowing that one wrong turn would mean plummeting straight down dozens if not hundreds of feet. Helmet? Nobody on the Strip wore a helmet. Those were for town people who came out on weekends to drive their fancy side-by-sides. Not us local kids.

My abuela used to scold me, but even she had given up eventually. She died shortly before I went into the Army. I wished she could have been here with us and been rehabilitated like Grandpa, but on the other hand, I didn't think she'd have made the transition as easily as Grandpa and Sage had.

Abuela had been not quite a pacifist, but close. Her Catholic beliefs in just war doctrine meant she didn't approve of most of the military actions of the last fifty years or so. She had tried to dissuade me from enlisting, but Grandpa had put his foot down, one of the few times I'd ever seen him outright contradict my abuela. They had been married for probably forty years at that point, and I still remember how shocked she looked when he told her that it was none of her business and I was going to do what I was going to do.

I shook myself out of my reverie as we made the now-familiar journey up from Threshold to the Hub. Sage kept her nose pressed against the invisible force field almost the whole time. I had to admit, the view didn't get old. Jupiter hung below us, round and ruddy, a hundred times bigger than any full moon I'd ever seen. It was almost worth everything just to see that up close.

"What do you think Veda wants?" I asked Grandpa, trying to get my mind off other things.

"No way to know. Hopefully she hasn't sold us to some other conglomerate."

"Surely not."

"They could have made her an offer too good to refuse," Grandpa said. "We'll wait and see. Might as well sit back and relax." From his inventory, he pulled out a box of cold fried chicken that Mama Grace had pressed into his hands as we left. He chewed appreciatively, offering me a piece. I took one of the drumsticks. "We're going to have to interview again," he said. "Not looking forward to that."

"Who in the Coalition isn't already teamed up?"

"There's a couple of pairs, but I'm not sure any of them match our strengths and weaknesses."

"Neither did Bill and Bob," I pointed out. "We could really use someone who's got better heals than just Sage's Raise Your Spirits. And more area damage would be nice, unless Sage can whip me up a bunch more grenades."

"I told you, just get me the mats," Sage said, her attention still focused on Jupiter. "Besides, what's wrong with my heals? I've kept you alive so far, haven't I?"

"Sure," Grandpa said. "But more healing would always be better. Right now we have to plan our fights out pretty well. And one mistake could be deadly."

"Shad hasn't even come close to dying in six weeks now," Sage said. "We're good, Grandpa. We're really good."

"Well, we'll see what Veda has to say."

We docked at the Hub and followed a glowing ball of light to the quarters Veda had rented for us. They always looked about the same. I'd heard from other mission runner teams that their sponsors went all out on fancy suites with all sorts of luxuries, like chairs that massaged your back while you sat on them. Veda bought us the budget model.

I wasn't complaining. There was still plenty of space for us to kick back for a day or so, relax, see the medical professionals of the Hub to make sure whatever we were doing in the Reality Engine hadn't caused some sort of soul damage. I really wasn't clear what they were talking about there, and I wasn't sure I wanted to ask too many questions.

The last couple of times there had even been packages of Earth entertainment we could watch, brought in fresh from home. I was pretty sure the movies and shows had been censored, since there were no news shows available, and the dramas offered were conspicuously lacking any reference to current events, like, say, ten million humans being abducted by aliens.

I knew Earth governments understood some of what was going on. We had received one communication from the Joint Chiefs of Staff months ago, but I didn't know what they were telling the rest of the world. Had the Reality Engine Exploitation Committee announced what they were doing, or were they only talking with the heads of state?

Someone would have had to come up with an explanation for why people had just vanished, especially since we had taken a chunk of Earth with us. In our case, it had been about a hundred-foot-radius circle chopped out of Grandpa's ranch and the nearest couple of vehicles and outbuildings. Mama Grace had brought along a big piece of her old restaurant. If someone had been taken from the middle of a busy city, that would have made a noticeable dent.

Veda wasn't here yet, which wasn't a surprise. She almost never met us in person. Usually her projected presence was already waiting. We filled up at the room's buffet and took a seat.

Sage started playing a Spider-Man cartoon movie that had been included in the latest media package. "Why don't you watch something educational?" Grandpa suggested. "You've missed four months of school. You might try to catch up a little on your learning."

Sage rolled her eyes. "There's nothing they've got to teach in school that I'm going to find useful," she said. "What, I'm going to study Earth history? Really? Or algebra? I think we're a little past algebra, Grandpa. Besides, it's my birthday. I get to do what I want."

Veda appeared in the middle of the room. She was wearing a yellow sarong-like outfit today along with a halter top, with her hair piled up in two conical spikes on her head. She was an objectively pretty woman, maybe even beautiful, and looked fairly human. But somehow I could tell she was an alien. I would have said it was the pheromones, except she wasn't really here, so I couldn't be smelling any. Could I? Maybe their projections included smells. I had never noticed one way or the other.

"Thank you for coming," she said. "I'm sorry to have called you up so abruptly. I know you just finished your last mission, but I wanted us to be able to strategize in person. Phase two opens in three days."

CHAPTER THREE

RETRAIN AS A CAREER COUNSELOR AND IMPACT LIVES!

Phase two?" Sage jumped up from her seat, scattering a plate of fruit and cookies all over the floor. "I thought it was still at least months away."

Something Veda had told us about phase two way back at the start of this whole adventure was bugging me. I shook my head. "No, no way. You said phase two couldn't start until we had lost enough of Earth's miners to make room for the outworlders. You said something like fifty percent. That would mean we had less than five million humans left here, and I know that's not the case. I'm not in touch with everyone, but we've been talking. We have a good picture of what's going on."

My coalition had a secret weapon, in fact. One of our members, Arjun, had a class, Mycroft, that let him compile vast quantities of information. He also had a skill that let him trade that information with other similar miners through the system. The last I had spoken to him, he had the personal information, skills, and affiliations of a million and a half miners in his database. I had no idea how one mind could hold all that, but I assumed the system was helping him out somehow.

"I would know if we were taking losses like that," I insisted.

"You're right." Veda dipped her head. "In fact, you humans have been taking losses far less than we projected. Since arriving four months ago, you've only lost 423,000 miners beyond those who died in the initiation."

Four hundred and twenty-three thousand people dead. That was an enormous number, almost half a million. Yet my heart swelled with pride because it could have been so much more.

One big advantage we had was that several of the remnants of Earth's various armed forces were now cooperating. We were coordinating who used what portal and avoiding conflict as much as we could. "So then how is phase two starting?"

"Your numbers were so good, actually, that several of the big conglomerates who usually show up in phase two petitioned the Reality Engine Exploitation Committee to allow them to start phase two early. They pointed out that even though you humans aren't dying, you also don't have as many mission-capable miners as most species. You seem to be a lot fonder of working together in groups than the last few Reality Engine exploits have seen. So you've got more people farming, fewer running missions."

That matched what I knew. "So that gives the big conglomerates an in?"

"Exactly. For their mission running teams, anyway. There aren't slots available for their farmers, so they're going to have to make deals with you human miners or with your sponsors." Veda grinned. "We are potentially in a really good spot, Shad. I know we only have two fully mission-capable teams in your coalition, but with all the farming and crafting, we're going to be able to sell supplies and consumable items to the people coming in. I hadn't expected that before. It's not my family's usual strategy to make money off of phase one. I've got a plan drawn up. What I'm thinking is we coordinate with a few allies and work on taking an early phase two objective. If we can hold it for a month, we'll have more than made back my investment and paid off a lot of your coalition's debts. Also, being up front with you, that will renew my company's phase two license, which will let us stay in business. It's probably my second-most important goal after making my money back."

"You told us before that phase two isn't deadly. That if you die, you just respawn," I said. "Is that true?"

"It is."

I sat back on the couch. That was something, at least. We'd made it through the dangerous part.

"How about party size?" Grandpa asked. "Is that going to work differently?"

"It'll be like when you worked together to claim a farming level. You'll have individual squads who can be managed by the officers in charge. The party size will increase to fifteen, which can be split into three squads of five."

"Are we on track for levels?" Sage asked. "I knew we should have pushed harder! We could have made level six, but Grandpa wanted us to be careful."

"Actually, in phase two, levels are equalized. You'll earn XP, but only in the background. It can be cashed in at the end, when you either return to phase one levels or progress to phase three."

"That doesn't seem fair," I complained. "We worked hard for those stat points."

"You'll keep those as your baseline. Offworlders have a complicated formula that basically works out to them being stronger than you, but not by much. Their real advantage will be in having better gear. Some of their backers could buy my company and still have money left for breakfast. Anyway, the larger bids will feature multiple teams, but there's no discount for less than a full party, so you'll want to recruit other mission runners or convince some of your farmers to join the team."

"Bid?" I asked.

"So for phase two, some of the portals that were offering missions will now be tuned to the new phase two maps. These are going to be bigger even than what you saw in farming zones, and much more diverse. The Exploitation Coalition is negotiating with the Reality Engine right now over how many maps it will open and what kind of stakes are to be provided."

Veda gestured, and my system pinged with an information packet. I held it in reserve to look at once she was done talking.

"We're hoping that since we have more eligible human miners than usual, the system will be inclined to be generous. Once we know how many maps are open, each team can put in a bid for entry. It'll be based on team composition and a lot of other factors. An all-human team should be able to make it in with a smaller bid than what the outsiders are going to have to do."

We drank that in. "Does the Reality Engine have a preference for locals?" Grandpa asked.

"Kind of. There's all sorts of conspiracy theories about that. Anyway, I want you to put together a bid proposal. We'll run it through my systems and see what kind of suggestions we can get. The initial maps are going to be blind bids. Nobody knows what to expect and nobody can see anyone else's bids until they've been awarded. The system gets to do the awarding," Veda explained, "with a few vetoes and legacy slots that the Exploitation Coalition will be able to use."

"Vetoes?"

"Not on individual bids, more like on rule sets. That's another of the bids going on, but that'll be at a much higher level and we aren't going to get a look in. What I'll do is attach our team proposal bid to a couple of different rule set bids and then whichever we can afford, we'll buy into. There's almost always a battle royale map," she told us, "and I don't think that plays to our strengths. We're going to look for more like a capture-the-flag or perhaps a take-a-point-and-hold-it rule set. Something we can build up. I'm hoping we're successful enough with our initial foray that one of the larger companies will offer to buy us out. That's when we can really make some money."

"And what happens to us when we do take the buyout?" Sage asked, leaning forward and clasping her knees.

"I'm not going to accept any offer that leaves you here in debt," Veda said simply. "Your coalition, I don't owe as much to, but I'll make sure they're not shafted in any way. At the very least, I will negotiate a buyout that gives them a favorable contract for supplies. They won't be forced into running anything dangerous."

"You said phase two, nobody dies," Sage said, shrugging. "So how bad could it be?"

"You need to take it seriously," Veda said. "I'm going to have you all on a very strict schedule of coming up here for medical and psychic evaluation."

I snickered at that. "What, we're going to have Miss Cleo read our palms and tell us our future?"

Veda frowned. "I don't know that allusion. There must be a translation issue here. We have very sensitive systems and trained specialists who can analyze what kind of damage you've been taking to your psyche. You won't die in phase two, but you're going to think you have." She leaned forward, her voice deepening as she spoke. "Respawns hurt. Not just physically. You're going to be in situations where your brain deep down believes you are about to die and that there's nothing you can do about it. And then you're going to wake up somewhere else and be asked to do it again."

"Shell shock," Grandpa said.

"What we call PTSD now," I agreed, sitting back on the couch. The Army had been starting to take PTSD seriously in the past couple of years, but based on the experiences of some of my colleagues, I knew they'd still had a long way to go. I wondered if dealing with the aftermath of ten million humans disappearing had changed their perspective. "You're saying you can prevent it?"

Veda shook her head. "No one can prevent it, but we can monitor you and make sure that we intervene if things get too bad."

"Is that part of what you've been doing already?" I asked.

"It's included in the package," Veda said. She seemed a little hesitant, probably because they were doing something shady with our brains that I didn't want to ask about. "So, let's get to work and start planning strategies. I'm going to call up a list of some of the most common rule sets and we can list them in your preferred order. You're going to need to recruit more people, either from your guild or some of your associates. If their sponsors are willing to let them work with me, I'm willing to work with them."

"Oh wait!" Sage jumped up. "We reached level five last mission, and I finally got my class evolution! I have to tell you about that."

"Wonderful!" Veda clapped her hands.

Grandpa had gotten a class evolution at level three. His Tomahawk Ninja class had evolved to Last War Chief. He'd kept all his abilities and gained some buffs for allies, as well as a couple of tactical skills. It had also enabled our coalition to double in size immediately. That plus the coalition upgrade tokens we'd been picking up in missions had been key in letting the Misfits Guild grow.

Sage had been angry at level three, then incensed at level four, not to get a class evolution. She'd pouted for days. I had been more relieved than she was when she finally got it at level five.

Sage displayed her character sheet for us all to see, a nice trick possible here on the Hub. "I'm a Barrel Racer now!" she exclaimed. "I've kept everything else, but I have a Three-Barrel Race skill that lets me designate two points on the battlefield and teleport between them and my starting location at will. And I've upgraded my T-Shirt Cannon. Now it can take rounds I craft with my reloading press. There's still a stupid long reload time, but I've got decent AoE damage at last!"

"That's excellent. You should still be looking for more area damage and healing abilities to supplement your own. Or add team members who can do those things. Just because you won't die doesn't mean you should neglect healing. The respawn timers can be brutal. Now, let's focus on our plans for phase two." Veda projected several images into the air. "We'll go through our options and then list them in terms of your favorites."

CHAPTER FOUR

STAT CHAPTER

This isn't a real chapter; this is for readers who may wish to see our heroes' current stats and abilities list. This entire chapter can safely be skipped if that's not important to you!

Level 5 Stats

	Shad	Sage	Grandpa
Cha	12	17	6
Dex	14	9	14
Int	4	8	3
Sta	15	12	13
Str	5	5	13
Wis	6	5	7
HP	150	120	130

Abilities cheat sheet. Not all abilities and skills may be listed here.

Shad, Class Evolution: Ride for the Brand

High Noon: In a one-on-one duel, you always get the first shot.

Quick Draw: Instantly call bonded weapon to hand, up to 50-foot range.

Trick Shot: Target an opponent and fire. Shot will connect even if opponent is behind cover.

Barrage: Empty all currently loaded rounds at once. Each round has a 15% buff to damage.

Call 'em Out: AoE reveal of enemies/taunt. Cooldown: 5 minutes.

Bluff: Use to boost skill at persuading targets to believe what's being said.
Test Your Mettle: When below 30% health, you receive a 100% boost to health regeneration.
Never Bring a Knife to a Gun Fight: Force opponents in melee range to drop their weapons.
Loyal: Bonus to soul coins when with long-term party.
Fastest Gun In The West: Cover 100 feet in 1 second and knockback.
Roped Into It: Conjure a rope and use it to swing up to 40 feet.
Sharpshooter: When above and more than 10 yards away from an enemy, accuracy is increased by 50% and damage by 35%.

Grandpa, Class Evolution: Last War Chief

Shadow Step: Teleport behind an enemy.
Scalp: Apply massive head damage.
Counting Coup: Shadow Step behind, then damage an enemy for 1 point. If not previously damaged, 2 points. Cash in 4 points for **Coup-de-Grace**, which instakills enemies below 25% (not bosses).
Blur: Harder to hit when moving.
Pub Dart Champion: When one thrown weapon hits, the next three go to same spot.
Crippling Blow: From behind the target, damages enemy and then applies a **Slow**. Also generates 1 point toward **Coup-de-Grace**.
War Chief's Aegis: Bless allies. More details will be revealed.

Sage, Class Evolution: Barrel Racer

Cowgirl Cheer: Buffs allies. 5% buff to dodge chance and damage done for all party members in range.
Lasso: Pull in and trip an enemy.
Eye-Spy: Reveals information about enemy weaknesses.
Raise Your Spirits: Cleanse and HoT (heal over time). Can be used on multiple targets at once.
Mucking Out the Stalls: Turns a large area into difficult terrain. Any target who gets the created muck on their bare body gains the **Stinky** debuff.
Tame: Lasso now has a charm aspect.
Three-Barrel Race: Teleport between three locations at will.
Item: T-Shirt Cannon: Shoots various constricting or damaging shots.

CHAPTER FIVE

OFF THE RESERVATION

We spent hours strategizing with Veda before she at last excused herself. "All right, we have a decent set of frameworks here. You tell me what allies you can round up, and I'll file our plans once those are done. In the meantime, there's plenty for me to do."

She disappeared without further formality. I stretched and yawned. "Guess we might as well get a good night's sleep," I said. I stood up to go use the restroom.

While I was in the facilities, a message popped up from a new contact. That surprised me. Usually, I could only receive messages from people I had previously met. This one simply said, *Ames: Can we talk?*

Who are you and what do you want?

Trying to keep a low profile. Meet me here in twenty minutes. Come alone. The message blinked and then vanished from my logs. I got a ping on my mini-map for a location not far away.

I washed my hands and popped out of the bathroom. Sage disappeared in after me. "I claim the shower," she said brightly.

"Okay, I'm going out to look for a birthday present for you," I said. "Don't wait up. You can have it in the morning."

"Sure!" She closed the door.

I stepped over to where Grandpa was sitting. He was staring at a baseball game that had come up in the latest package from Earth. It was spring training by now, and the Diamondbacks were looking good.

I lowered my voice and told him about the message.

"Ames? I recognize that name. Hang on." He thought for a minute and nodded. "Wasn't that the colonel that the Joint Chiefs told us about a couple of months back?"

I tried to remember. "You might be right. He didn't send you a message?"

Grandpa shook his head. "Nope."

"Think I should go?" I asked.

"Sure. I don't see what harm could come from it, here on the Hub. Let me know what he says," Grandpa turned back to the game.

I felt a bit adrift. If it *was* Colonel Ames, the ranking US Armed Forces officer here in the Reality Engine exploit, it felt like Grandpa should have a message for him.

I left, heading for the appointed rendezvous. It was in a section of the Hub I hadn't visited before. Overhead, what felt like it must be half a mile up, an enormous glass window stretched the whole length of the great cylinder. Through it, I could see Jupiter. There were little shops and stalls all along the corridor here, offering various alien wares and delicacies to other aliens. The shopkeepers shot me unfriendly looks as I went past. I didn't think this was a section that catered to miners.

The address given turned out to be a small park full of green and red plants. They looked similar to Earth plants, with grass like leaves growing from the ground and odd alien trees with thin purple trunks that twined around each other, then radiated outward into yellow-leaved branches. The effect was quite lovely.

In the center of the little park was a bench. A man sat with one arm draped along the back of it, facing away from me. I stepped in front of him. He had no system tag displayed. I didn't know how to hide that information myself. Either he had gotten an upgrade somewhere, or he knew a few secrets I didn't.

"Did you send me a message?" I asked.

The man nodded. He didn't stand up. He was wearing civilian clothes, tan slacks with a blue dress shirt and a loosened tie at his neck. No hat. If this *was* the colonel, he was being unexpectedly informal. Maybe that's why he was sitting like that, so I didn't feel a need to salute.

"Thanks for joining me, Williams," he said. He moved his arm off the back of the bench and gestured for me to sit down. I did. "I've been wanting to speak with you and your grandfather for some time, but I am attempting to keep a low profile here."

"You are Colonel Ames, yes?"

He nodded. "I am."

"Then the Joint Chiefs put you in charge."

"Not precisely, as you know. I've heard all about your squabble with Waters." He raised a hand as I started to speak. "Don't worry. Like I said, I heard all about it. Waters is no part of any plan of mine, but I would very much like it if you and your grandfather were."

"Why'd you call for me and not him?" I asked.

"Because I am certain I am being watched, and I suspect he is as well. But the watchers are automated systems, and if we do not meet directly, it may keep them from flagging us for a higher attention."

A creeping sensation of dread filled me. This sounded like it was about to turn into secret agent bullshit. "What do you want?" I asked, maybe a little too brusquely, considering I was a lieutenant and he was not just a colonel, but also the ranking military officer for the nearest half billion miles.

"I want you and your team to keep doing what you're doing," Ames said. "I've got channels back to Earth. We have allies here, even if that's hard to believe."

"Don't trust them," I said at once. "Everyone here has got their own agenda. Even our sponsor wants us to do things for her that may not be for our benefit."

"We aren't trusting anyone," Ames said mildly. "Believe me, the US Army is used to working with people who are out for what they can get. Has your sponsor told you that phase two is about to start?"

I nodded. "We were just having a meeting about that now."

"Good. I thought that was the case, based on the timing. How much latitude are they giving you?"

"She wants us to build a team out of our allies and present it to her. The team ought to be able to take an objective and hold it for the first month. That's her goal."

Ames nodded. "Sounds like she has reasonable expectations. I want you to raise them considerably. We aren't just going to make a profit here. We're going to take a stand."

"What?" I didn't understand what he was getting at.

"When you get back down to Threshold, you'll be approached by another group with an offer. They will have the funding to back it. You're going to need to do more than take a point and hold it. We're going to need you to construct an entire outpost."

Veda had used that term briefly when talking about what the larger corporations that would end up owning phase two would be working toward. I still wasn't sure what an "outpost" was, but the implication was she could never hope to afford such a thing.

"I don't even know if our sponsor knows how to go about that."

"Not a concern." Ames lifted a hand. A message popped up in my queue, blinking. I didn't look at it yet. "That's an information package that will have all of the details on outpost construction. Share it with your grandfather. I know it's not his area of expertise. Fortunately, we have a logistics officer—don't we, Lieutenant Williams?"

I felt myself turning red. "I was only a corporal back on Earth. I don't have any command experience. Mostly I was just a guy moving boxes around."

"Well, then I guess it's time you earned your rank, Lieutenant."

"Sir." I gathered my courage. "What's the point of all of this? Our sponsor is trying to help me and our team only because we're helping her. She's willing to help our friends out as much as she can, but this sounds like you're asking us to go a lot further."

"I am, soldier. I'm asking you to go all the way." Ames had a grim smile. "It isn't going to be easy. Once the galactics realize what you're doing, they'll come for you. I'll be straight: We need to have a human-owned outpost at the end of phase two. That's the only way we'll get representatives into phase three, which is where the real deals are made. That's where they're going to decide who owns our solar system. You realize what happens when all of this is over?"

I nodded. I had picked up that much from Veda. "They move a couple quadrillion aliens into this Reality Engine."

"Right. And Earth becomes the most backwoods reservation you've ever heard of. I know where you grew up, Lieutenant. I've seen your family background. You know what that means. Imagine all of Earth being treated the way the United States has treated your native kinfolk. Shoved off into the worst pockets of land. Any time someone finds gold or oil, there'll be a well-backed businessman there to swindle them out of it."

He let that sink in. I knew very well what he was talking about. Then he said, "Well, we're going to do our best to make sure that's not the case. We're not going to be able to claim this Reality Engine for ourselves. That's not in the cards. But we might be able to claim a piece of it. That'll get us a seat at the table. Not much of one. We'll be like Rwanda at the UN, getting a few pity invites to cocktail parties and an aid package thrown our way now and then. But that's still better than not being at the party at all."

He stood up. "It was good to meet you, Lieutenant. Convey my regards to your grandfather. I've read his profile. Tell him I know he'll do what's right, and that I have faith in his willingness to take decisive action."

I watched as Ames strode off and disappeared, my mind full. It took an effort not to salute as he went, but we were being undercover here and neither of us was in uniform.

Ames seemed like everything Waters hadn't been. Patriotic. Forward-thinking. Decisive. But I wanted to know what was going on. Who were his allies? Were they just using us humans for their own game, or was there a chance we could wrest a victory out of this massive shitstorm?

I wandered the station for a while after that, thinking about everything Ames had said. My mind whirled. Over the last few months, I had gotten almost comfortable with being part of a coalition, taking risks, doing what had to be done. I was making a difference.

Now we were being recruited into a much bigger fight, and I wasn't entirely sure how I felt about that.

I finally stopped at one of the stalls and bought a present for Sage. I couldn't resist. The whole booth was western-themed, shaped like a wooden saloon door with a counter over it. Behind the counter was a row of glass whiskey bottles. Sombreros, cowboy hats, and preposterous Indian war bonnets like those from the worst Hollywood movies hung from the roof of the booth. On the counter was a cow skull, complete with horns.

When I stopped, the sales clerk, who looked like her ancestors had been snakes but possessed arms and legs like me, took a look at me and hissed, a long tongue protruding from between her lips. "You are one of the human minersss," she said.

"I am."

"You look like a good candidate for advertissssssing."

She pointed at some posters on her back wall. One of them showed John Wayne from one of his cowboy movies. The other was Roy Rogers atop his horse. "You interested in advertisssssing deal?"

"I might be," I said. "Assuming there's good coin in it."

"Best," she said and smiled with her wide, lipless mouth.

I pointed at a pink cowgirl hat next to a bright green sombrero. "And that. My sister will love it."

I came away with the pink hat, a pocketful of SoulCoin credits, and an advertising deal with her booth. This time, the Indian had gotten the better of the pale faces.

CHAPTER SIX

A NOOB'S GUIDE TO OUTPOST BUILDING

A*Beginner's Guide to Constructing Your Phase Two Outpost, Section 1.1: Introduction*

Interview conducted by Colonel Jefferson Ames, US Army.

Interview subject: Ostrichka Corporation Representative Sitska, after four rounds of something called Proximin Ale in one of the Hub bars.

You know you guys are fucked, right? Nobody who has a chance of constructing an outpost needs to know any of this. They've already been doing it for longer than your species has been out of the caves or trees or stagnant swamp pools, wherever it is you crawled out of. You look like the monkey types. Is that right?

Well, doesn't matter. These techniques get handed down from parent corporation to child corporation. Sometimes somebody comes up with a refinement, but it's pretty much the same strategy.

Anyway, fine. Step one is picking a good location. What's good for almost all of them isn't going to work for any of you because they're going to target you right away. So you're going to have to choose a spot they don't care about that much. It's still got to be worth your time though.

There's basically four tiers of resource generating locations. Alpha tier, forget about that. Those belong to the big boys. Beta tier, if you could take and hold one of those all the way through to the end of phase two, you'd be in good. You won't be able to. They might let you hold on to it at the beginning, at least for a while. That'd give you a pretty decent income. After that, they're either going to buy you out or send in an overwhelming army that you can't possibly defeat.

Delta tier, those are probably worth your time, but you'll never be able to grow it big enough to sustain the sort of outpost you'll need to make a serious phase three entry bid. And gamma tier, they'll let you have a gamma tier node. No question about that, because nobody wants them.

*So there's your answer. Anything you can hold on to, you don't want. Anything
you want, you can't hold on to. Like I said, you're all fucked.*

I played through the introduction in the "building outposts for noobs" guide
that Colonel Ames had sent me for a third time. I had already given Grandpa a
copy as well as a rundown of the conversation we'd had. Like an idiot, I hadn't
thought to record it.

Grandpa was perusing the guide, looking serious. I'd taken a quick look myself.
There were dozens of chapters covering all sorts of different scenarios and rule sets.
Way more than I'd be able to study in the next couple of days, especially since we
still had to recruit the rest of our team. I'd checked with Bill and Bob, and they
were in. Juana was working with Arjun to put together a list of candidates for us.

"Ames's the one who put this together," I said. "And he still sent it to us?
Seriously? Why not just send us a greeting card that says, 'Congrats, you're screwed'?"

"There's good information in here," Grandpa said. "Just have to get past all of
the depressing parts about how we are doomed to lose and our species is going to
spend the next ten thousand years as serfs, peons, and zoo exhibits."

"We should bring Veda into this." We were sitting in the elevator on the way
back down to the surface. Sage had downloaded a bunch of media onto the birthday
present Veda had given her. It was basically a space iPod that let her watch shows
wherever she was. She was sitting back in her seat and giggling at some teen drama.

Grandpa and I were taking advantage of the mostly empty elevator to strategize. "I don't think we should tell Veda," Grandpa said.

That surprised me. He was usually a straight shooter, and I would have expected
him to say we should lay our cards on the table.

"Ames is right about a lot of this. All the aliens have their own agendas. Veda's
been mostly straight with us, but there's still plenty she hasn't revealed. I don't
want her to know just how much Ames is entrusting us with."

"The aliens have got agendas, but so does he. I am a little burned out on that
whole patriotism bit after our encounter with Waters."

"I get that," Grandpa said. "I really do. But Ames isn't wrong. When the aliens
are done here, they're going to pack up this circus and leave. Then a hundred trillion or one quadrillion or however many aliens move into the neighborhood. What
happens to us puny eight billion Earth folk then?"

"I don't even know how much a quadrillion is, but it sounds like a lot." I knew
how many zeroes were in the number, but I couldn't picture it, couldn't reason
from "billion" to "quadrillion."

"You two grew up with me, out on the Strip. You know what it's like to have
nothing. Me, I grew up on a reservation. That's even worse, because it's nothing
and the stink of that nothing follows you everywhere. You get off the res and try

to make a life for yourself and all anyone around you says is, 'There's that Indian off his reservation again,' or tells you to get back to it. One of the reasons I didn't go back after marrying your abuela, I wanted your mom to have a chance to be more than just another reservation kid. Not that the Strip's a whole lot better off, but at least I had land that was my own."

The talk was getting gloomy and I was feeling worse. "All right, but what I don't like is that Ames is foisting some mysterious other teammates on us sight unseen. What if they come in and try to start bossing the show around? What if they do something that's going to hurt our friends? Our plan was that just those of us who've trained for this would go into phase two. For this outpost"—I tapped my head as I looked at the very long table of contents in the "how to build an outpost" guide—"we're going to need everyone. The whole guild and then some. I don't know if I want to bring Grace and Rosa into this sort of situation."

Grandpa's eyebrows raised. "What about Juana?"

"She can take care of herself." I shifted uncomfortably, aware he was teasing me. "Look, you heard what Veda said. Death might not be permanent in phase two, but it leaves scars."

"I know. I'd spare them if I could, but what else have we got to live for?" Grandpa asked. "We can't go home."

That had been an unpleasant revelation when Veda informed us that attuning to a soul coin meant we were now technologically bound to a Reality Engine or Reality Engine–derived technology. We might be able to go back to Earth, but it would take the help of some very expensive alien prosthetics.

Same for Mama Grace and everyone else in our coalition. Everyone else on Threshold. Most of them didn't know that yet. They were still dealing with digging out from underneath twenty years' worth of debt that the Reality Engine Exploitation Committee had foisted on us all.

"Before we can get out of here, we've got to negotiate buyout packages for everyone who has put themselves into our coalition," Grandpa said. "We owe them that much. It will be easier to do if I'm in a position of strength. Whatever Ames's up to, it's going to leave us in a stronger position. Besides," he said, "the first six or seven steps are pretty compatible with what Veda wanted anyway. All we have to do is get these new players on board, then write up a proposal and send it to her."

He leaned back in his seat and folded his hands across his chest. "And that, my dear boy, is exactly what junior officers were invented for. I suggest you start working on the proposal now. You can finish filling in the details once we've met our new friends."

I groaned. "I should never have let them promote me."

"Cheer up," Grandpa said. "At this rate you'll be a captain by your next birthday."

"Oh yeah? I haven't seen a board of promotion around here."

"Between me and the colonel, I think we can probably swing it." Grandpa closed his eyes and pretended to snore.

I spent the rest of the elevator trip down studying the first couple of chapters in *A Beginner's Guide to Constructing Your Phase Two Outpost.*

There was no point in getting ahead of myself. The outpost guide itself mentioned that until you had completed step four, you really didn't need to worry about the more advanced steps.

So I focused on the first four. It wasn't that bad, honestly. We needed to select a location that we could claim and guard. The higher the resource spawn rate of a location, the better our income would be, but we'd also need to spend a correspondingly large amount to defend and exploit the location. Too valuable a resource node would attract attention from other players. They would try to take it away from us.

The defenses that we would need to protect our node from the Reality Engine–spawned opponents—I mentally tagged them as "creep," like in a couple of the MOBA-style games I had played a few years back—would also help defend us against the enemies. I decided I would refer to them as "champions."

Ames's guide was quite thorough and depressing, and it tended to use Army-style phrases to refer to enemy combatants and their capabilities. I thought I would translate everything into something a little more readable.

In fact, the more I read, the more I thought this reminded me of a tower defense game. We needed to build up our defenses, kill attacking spawn, collect resources from them, and use them to strengthen our defenses—and also to pay off our miners and backers. Put that way, it didn't seem so intimidating. I started to make notes. We were going to need more than just the initial attack team. Building an outpost would cost a lot of money. If we could put our crafters to work right away, then have them sell what they made back to the aliens coming in to take a piece of our engine, we'd be able to build up a war chest to supplement whatever Veda and the colonel got us. But I didn't want our crafters to equip our enemies *too* well. This was going to be a delicate balance.

By the time we were back, I had a few good ideas, which was, of course, why Juana was waiting at the elevator station to derail everything for me.

CHAPTER SEVEN

WHY TO SORT YOUR APPLICANT LIST BY STARCRAFT LADDER RANK

What have you been doing, Shad?" Juana demanded.

I had never seen her look flustered before. Her face was red and her braid had started to come apart, with strands of dark hair falling across her face.

"Me? Haven't done anything yet."

She let us step off the elevator platform and down into the surrounding empty space. Threshold was full to bursting. There were people bustling about everywhere, more than I had ever seen here at one time, but even so, people gave the platform a wide berth. It was just good etiquette, not crowding the space elevator. We merged into the crowd.

"We got a system notification about an hour ago that the member cap had been raised to eight thousand thanks to an anonymous donation of several coalition level-up tokens. We've also got enhanced communications abilities, including a dozen custom channels that the coalition officers can use to address different categories of guild members. Like a 'general emergency' channel that goes out to everyone, but only officers can send out messages," Juana said. "And then we started getting applications. Lots of them. So I'm asking again: What did you do?"

Colonel Ames had implied he was sending a few people to join us. I had assumed maybe a dozen, tops. "How many applications?" I asked weakly.

"I don't even know. I'm having Kirin and Arjun go through them. They'll present me with priority lists once they're done. Meanwhile, I've been dealing with requests to meet from several other important coalitions. Something is going down. Do you know what it is?"

"Uh, yeah. Phase two starts in a couple of days."

Juana swore. I had never heard her use language like that before. Usually she made me feel guilty when I dropped too strong a curse word in Mama Grace's restaurant. "All right," she said. "Let's talk on the way back to the restaurant. I don't have a whole lot of time before the meeting. I was hoping you guys would be heading back down. That's why I was waiting for you. Phase two starting . . . What does that mean for us?"

I tried to collect my thoughts, glancing at Grandpa. I sent him a quick message. *How much should we tell her?*

Everything, eventually, he replied. *But for now, let's keep it simple.*

"There's a lot going on here. Some of it we will have to fill you in on later," I said. "Short-short version, we need more people because we're going into phase two hard and we have to make our mark. This is where we start paying off our debts. This is how we'll be able to help our people."

Juana shook her head. "We're doing fine right now. We've got the farming zones under control and we've doubled the number of crafters our coalition can support. I told Kirin and Arjun to prioritize applications from crafters with unique skills."

"And we're still going to want those," I said, "but we need people capable of fighting, too."

"I don't want to put our people at risk," Juana said.

"They'll be less at risk because in phase two, death isn't permanent. You respawn," I explained. "The more people we get into phase two, the safer we all are."

I had several niggling doubts about that at the back of my mind, but there was no need to get into that just yet. "Look, we still have to actually make our plans, but we're going to need to recruit some more people like me and Gramps," I said, gesturing at ourselves.

"And me," Sage declared, looking up from her handheld entertainment device indignantly. "Don't forget about me."

Juana laughed. "No one can forget about you, sweetheart. All right, what next?"

"The more alliances we can make with other coalitions, the better chance we have of really cleaning up here," I said. I still had a lot of the outpost building guide to get through, and I knew there would be a point of diminishing returns where we had no hope of holding a node valuable enough to pay all of us, but that point was a ways off.

I had already considered plans for taking multiple smaller nodes, holding on to them as long as we could to build up a war chest, and then concentrating on keeping just one. But until we knew the rule set and had an idea about the strategic layout, I wasn't going to commit to any single strategy.

"In phase two, we'll have crafting materials too. I'm not saying we abandon our farm zones, certainly not at once, and not until we know for sure what phase two is going to do for us, but we need to be ready to pivot. Everyone in the coalition will get a briefing about what they can expect in the next few days." I made a note to myself to figure out what those briefings would look like, or maybe to foist some of this back onto Grandpa. My action items were getting pretty long.

I kept up my conversation with Juana, Grandpa interjecting his two cents now and then, until we got back to the restaurant. Juana looked torn. "I've really got to get to this meeting. There's six of us local coalitions, and we're meeting with a representative from the Free Human League. He says they kicked out Waters and are reforming. I'm interested in seeing if we can work with them. They still have a foothold in some of the most profitable farming levels."

I nodded. "Go on. We'll fill you in when we get back." I stepped into Mama Grace's restaurant.

I was not prepared for the chaos I found there.

Mama Grace was in the kitchen, shouting loudly enough that I could hear her from the door of the dining area. All the tables had been pushed together into three long work surfaces. There must have been forty different coalition members running back and forth, carrying everything from stacks of brown paper to boxes of salvaged plastic zipper bags to trays of steaming food that had just come out of the kitchen.

"Just follow the instructions," Mama Grace was shouting. "No innovating. Do what the sign says. If you can't figure it out, ask your team lead. I'm busy in here."

We pushed our way through the throng. I noticed poster boards tacked to the wall with sets of numbered instructions on them. They looked like steps for making packaged meals out of Mama Grace's concoctions.

I saw now that the three long super-tables were being used as primitive assembly lines, with food and wrappers being deposited on one end for guild members to bundle up and then push along to the other end where they were carefully labeled and packed in big boxes.

"What's all this?" I asked a coalition member I vaguely knew. Emma was one of our farm team members who usually managed a squad of seven farming miners. She was standing at the head of one of the long tables, supervising.

"Not now, Shad," she snapped. "We've got a deadline and a lot of meals to pack."

"We should go into the back room and see if we can find Arjun," Grandpa said.

"Yeah, I'll just pop my head in the kitchen real quick and meet you there." I pushed through the throng, stepping out of the way of a woman carrying a tray heaped high with sliced meat, and entered the kitchen.

It was even worse in there. It felt like 120 degrees. A dozen coalition members were standing over the stove or in a corner or along one section of the countertop, peeling potatoes, chopping onions, and slicing fruit.

Mama Grace ran about being everywhere at once. She touched a pot boiling on the stove, then leapt across the kitchen and passed her hand over a roast. "What's going on?" I asked.

"Bad time, Shad," she panted. "I've got to keep my concentration up for this." She looked exhausted.

"Yes, but—"

"We got a contract from one of the off-world conglomerates. They want as many basic buff meals as we can possibly provide them, with a bonus if it's at least five thousand by the end of the day. They said they'll renew the offer for as long as we can get them the finished products. They're paying us four times what I've been able to charge the local miners."

That pulled me up short. Mama Grace's meals had kept the coalition afloat until we had managed to diversify our income streams a bit. She was easily almost as profitable as my team was, and she never had to face anything worse than a raw onion or a dull knife. If she was quadrupling her take, with an unlimited new market, we had to take advantage.

"Which conglomeration?"

"I don't know. Spectra, Astra, something, something."

I sent a quick note to Veda to see what she could find out.

"Now get out if you're not going to help. You don't have any useful skills, so go away," Mama Grace told me. "And don't let Juana come back either. I told her she's not allowed inside the restaurant until I'm done. She keeps distracting me."

Mama Grace's other daughter, Rosa, was in one corner of the kitchen kneading loaves of bread. She shot me a look of despair. I gave her what I hoped was a fully sympathetic shrug and backed out of the kitchen.

The back room was more full than I had ever seen it. Apparently anyone who didn't want to catch Mama Grace's attention was crowding in here to work on their own projects.

Arjun and his manager/helper, Kirin, were all the way back in one corner, huddled over a mundane-looking pad of paper and a couple of pens. I pushed my way through the crowd toward them.

"Where's Dwight?" I asked. I would have expected to see our master crafter in here, hard at work on gear to equip the coalition.

"He's out back trying to rig up a massive bread oven for Mama Grace," someone told me. "And keep your head down or you'll get a task of your own. She's got a bee in her bonnet for sure."

Grandpa had taken a chair over to the small round table where Arjun and Kirin were working. I swiped another chair from a crafter who had foolishly gotten up to fetch something from the other side of the room and carried it over to join them. Sage sat in the corner playing with her new entertainment system.

"Louis has just been explaining matters to us," Kirin said. "We'll get that applicant pile re-sorted by mission runner capability as quickly as possible. He and you together can approve any applicants to the coalition that you like the look of. Dwight is looking over the crafter types."

Juana, Dwight, and I were the official stakeholders of the coalition. There were another ten members with the power to give secondary approval to any applicant. It required at least one stakeholder or two secondary approvers to let anyone in.

"Just a second," I said. "I've been thinking about phase two. Arjun, we're going to need some specialized skill sets here and I'm hoping you can help me find them."

He looked up, his eyes briefly meeting mine before he fastened his gaze on a point just past my head. "What do you need?" he asked. I thought he sounded eager, but sometimes it was hard to read him.

"First on my list"—I tapped the pad of paper in front of him,—"are people with a serious eSports background. On Earth, I mean. Champions would be great. Somebody who's won a couple of tournaments. Strategy games would be best, things like StarCraft or even Civilization. Did they have Civilization tournaments back in the day? I don't know if they did. That would be ideal, but basically if there's anyone with an eSports background, give me their information so I can contact them."

Kirin frowned. "eSports?" she asked. "Like professional video game players?"

"Exactly. Phase two requires a very different set of skills than phase one. Sage and I have a lot of hours playing games between us, but almost none in a real-time strategy or base builder kind of game. I could use some help with my strategy going forward. Let me know what you can find."

"Right," Kirin scribbled down a note on the pad in front of them. "What else?"

"I don't know yet, but I'm certain there's going to be other specialists we need. I'll tell you as soon as they come up."

"And I suppose those requests will have priority, and that as soon as you do think of them, you're going to need them immediately." Kirin had just a bit of a sarcastic edge to her voice.

I shrugged. "Pretty much. Hey, think of it this way. It'll keep you here in Threshold helping Arjun, and not in a phase two mission getting killed over and over again while we try to figure out the ropes."

Her eyes went wide.

"I've finished sorting the new applicants list like you want," Arjun said. "I'm pushing the top hundred or so candidates to both of you right now."

I got a ping from the system as Arjun's information packet transferred over to me.

"Thanks," I said, then turned as Grandpa stood up. "What is it?" I asked him.

"I just got a message." His tone was very noncommittal. "Says it's from an old acquaintance who needs to talk to us. I think you should come for this, Shad."

I rose at once. If someone was contacting Grandpa without already being on our contact list, there was a good chance they were part of Ames's team.

"Sure, I'll come along," I said. "Sage, you good there?"

"Uh-huh," she said, her head buried. Oddly, it didn't look like she was watching any kind of normal show. The people on-screen looked a little like superheroes, but the action was cutting back and forth way too fast. From above her and behind the display, it was hard to get much of a look at what she was viewing, so I left it at that.

"I suggest you go out the back door," Kirin said.

"What back door? Not through the kitchen?"

"No, we had Dwight install a door before Mama Grace caught him. We figured we needed a way to get in and out without getting tasked on to team meal prep." Kirin pointed and I saw that there was indeed another door at the far side of the room. I thanked her and ducked out the back.

CHAPTER EIGHT

IS THE PLURAL MONGEESE OR MONGOOSES?

I'd be complaining that Ames's men are making us meet them on their turf if it weren't for the fact that the restaurant is not exactly a quiet place to meet right now," I said as Grandpa and I trudged through the streets of Threshold. "But they could at least have offered to meet somewhere in between."

The location was just about on the opposite side of Threshold from us. If we were down by seven o'clock, they were up around two, and on the far outskirts of the town, in the outer ring facing the portals.

I hadn't ventured through this side of Threshold very much. Most of the other miners I saw were South Asian or African. There were dozens of different coalition symbols painted on walls or floating above doors. I didn't recognize any of them except for the signs of Glorious Morning of the New Dawn faction. They were, as far as I knew, one of the largest player factions. While they didn't particularly like cooperating with the rest of us here on Threshold, they did listen to advice from the remnants of the Chinese military.

Since we at least had communication open with the Chinese military, I felt like we had an understanding with the Glorious Dawn. Of course, the understanding was basically, "You steer clear of us, we'll steer clear of you." Now Grandpa and I were walking through their turf.

We stopped in front of a small, nondescript building. It looked like it had been built out of a cargo container with a tarpaulin awning over the open door. I didn't know how anyone would have managed to bring a cargo container into the Reality Engine with them. That had to weigh a lot more than any ordinary human's weight limit. All of the stuff from Earth had come in through the initiation chamber, whatever people had the presence of mind to grab. At the time, nobody had class buffs to strength yet. So seeing a cargo container was weird.

Grandpa stood outside and called, "I'm Louis Twofeather. Somebody here ask to see me?"

We got an immediate reply. "Come on in, both of you."

Grandpa stooped and ducked into the cargo container. I followed. "Close the door," the same voice said. I couldn't see anything in the gloom.

Grandpa closed the door and immediately light flooded the room.

Five men sat on top of metal crates at the edges of the room. They wore US Army camo uniforms, modern ones, not relics or surplus-store castoffs. One of the men was cleaning an M4. They had removed their rank markings and name tags. I didn't know if I ought to salute or not, but Grandpa didn't, so I followed his lead.

Grandpa sauntered over and took the single metal folding chair in the tiny room, leaving me to stand awkwardly. "So," he said, looking them over, "I'm guessing you came in with Ames."

One of them nodded. "We did."

"I'm also guessing you're snake eaters."

The man cleaning an M4 looked up sharply. There was a tense feeling in the air, like a fight was about to break out, but I wasn't sure why. I tried to guess what made Grandpa think these men were special forces. Was it because they didn't salute? Or maybe he'd just met enough in his time to have developed a sense for them. I had run into one or two special forces during my time as active duty, but they didn't tend to hang out and fraternize with a logistics corporal.

I felt suddenly tongue-tied, like these guys were going to measure me up and find me wanting.

"Does it matter?"

"Not really," Grandpa said. "Just figured if we're going to be working together, we oughta know each other's competencies."

One of the men stood up from his crate. He laced his hands behind his back and began talking. "We're going to be working alongside each other. That doesn't necessarily mean together. We've got a common goal, I believe."

He shot us a challenging glance. Grandpa nodded. "Take and hold an outpost in phase two. Reasons why are a little unclear, but it's for the good of humankind."

"Reasons are because it's our orders," the man cleaning an M4 shot back.

"Now then, Lieutenant, we can look for more reasons than that in a situation like this," Grandpa said. The man's eyes narrowed. Grandpa laughed. "Or did you get a field promotion too? Should I have said 'Captain'?"

"No need for rank here," the one on his feet said. I guessed that meant that he was their highest-ranking officer and that he wasn't a major like Grandpa. My brain was busy telling me that this was worse than secret agent shit. This was going to be more military brass bullshit.

"How many missions does your team have under their belt?" Grandpa asked. "I don't mean back home, I mean here."

The men looked at each other. "We've run several."

"Well, my granddaughter has over two dozen under her belt. She's level five. None of you are higher than level three. That's the only rank that really matters here. I'm sure you've all seen some shit. You've made a difference. You've got experiences you can't tell us about. Back home, that's fine, but we're not back home anymore. The only experience that matters is with this Reality Engine. That's why the colonel put me and my boy here in charge of this project. So, are you in or are you out?" Grandpa asked.

The men exchanged a glance. The one I was pretty sure was their commander said, "I wouldn't take that insolence from anyone, not even a superior officer, if I didn't know your record, sir." The "sir" sounded a bit forced. "But you've seen some things, too. If we're all agreed on the objective, then we'll work with you."

"We're agreed on the first objective," Grandpa said. He held up his finger. "We take and hold a viable outpost in phase two that will let us have a bid accepted for phase three. We're still learning what exactly that is, and I'm not convinced that even your colonel knows that for sure. So, to hedge our bets, I've got a couple more objectives." He held up two more fingers. "Keep our current sponsor in the game. She's willing to play ball. She even stuck her neck out for me and mine, and if we can do her a solid, I think she'll prove to be an asset."

"It's humans first," the other man said coldly.

"Humans first, last, and always," Grandpa agreed. "But that doesn't mean only. How about you boys? You got any kind of sponsor we should know about?"

They shook their heads. "We're on the basic system contract. Colonel didn't want us to get entangled with any aliens."

"Good, though it sounds like he's got some behind-the-scenes diplomatic thing going. We'll leave that be for now. All right, and the third objective is we take care of my people. Got a coalition of good sorts, mostly peaceful folk, crafters and the like."

"We're not interested in dead weight," the man cleaning the gun stated.

Grandpa's eyes narrowed. "You ever fast-rope, son?"

"I don't see what—"

"Have you ever jumped out of a fucking bird?" he snapped.

"Of course. So?"

"Was the crew chief dead weight?"

I thought I saw where Grandpa was going, but I enjoyed seeing this side of him. The gun cleaner looked taken aback. "What?"

"Was the man that tied your fucking rope to the fucking helicopter dead fucking weight? Was the crew that fueled the bird dead weight?"

"I—"

"Shut your filthy mouth, boot, and don't speak while the adults are talking." Grandpa turned to the one who seemed like he was in charge. "Now, you boys on board, or not?"

The soldier considered. He looked my grandfather over, then me. At last he nodded. "Colonel knows what he's doing. We're in."

"Good, then let's get down to business. Shad, you've had a little time to look over that information. What are you thinking about the initial strike force? We need to get a proposal to our sponsor here in the next few hours."

"Uh, right," I said. "We have a team of five. Plus you five. Ten. We'll be looking for more likely recruits to fill out that third squad."

They shook their heads. "Don't need it. We're a match for a dozen."

"I'm sure you are," I said. "But we're putting together a whole party. No discount for going undermanned. We"—I indicated Grandpa and me—"will review those new applications and see who looks like they're worth a risk."

"Might be better to go with ten we can trust, rather than bring in more possible traitors. We heard what Waters did to you."

I had to admit the unnamed captain had a point there. I turned to Grandpa, deferring to him.

"We need all the bodies we can get," Grandpa said. "Our sponsor's digging into their backgrounds."

"And the rest of your people? The . . . noncombatants?"

I stepped back into the conversation. "Once we've gotten through the initial setup stage, that's when we're gonna need a lot of grunts. The farm teams will come in handy then. They'll help us set up defenses and start using what we find there."

"Let's worry about stage one first," Grandpa said. "So we need another five, for the third team, then we submit the list of names for our bid. Right." He rose from his chair. "Time for you all to join up."

They looked at each other. "What do you mean?"

"Shad, toss 'em an invite." He stared them down, and one of the snake eaters was the first to look away. "You're gonna be joining our coalition."

They looked like they were about to object. But Grandpa held up a hand. "Nope. No lone warriors. We've gotta be able to work together. Anyway, it's not so bad. You'll get a twenty percent discount at the restaurant."

"This is ambitious," Veda said.

We had just sent her our bid proposal, and she had surprised us by initiating a request for a video conference. Previously, she'd said those were far too expensive, and that if we needed to speak to her in person, we'd have to make the trip up to the Hub.

That wasn't too onerous. We had to visit the Hub every seven to ten days anyway to be looked over by the alien proctologists and shrinks to make sure we were handling our transition to the Reality Engine. I still didn't know what they were watching for. Were they worried we were going to grow tentacles?

Now we sat in one of the small rooms in the upstairs of Mama Grace's restaurant. Bunk beds lined the walls, but we had found an empty chamber and shut the door so we could have some privacy.

Sage sat cross-legged on the floor studying her entertainment system. I was a little concerned how much time she had spent watching videos on it since Veda had given it to her, but I knew she wouldn't let it distract her once we got to work again. She'd told me that the most recent batch of videos actually contained some shows that supposedly portrayed life on the Reality Engine for us abductees. I was curious, but really didn't want to see Hollywood's idea of soul coin mining, so I hadn't asked more.

"You want eight different sorts of auto-turrets. Six self-targeting mods. Three different base wall upgrades—" Veda looked up from the list, shaking her head. "This is way overkill for holding a gamma node."

"No, it's not," I contradicted. "It's exactly what we need. We're going in with almost no backing. We'll look like easy prey to any of these galactic consortiums you've been telling us about. We've got to be prepared for them to hit us hard and fast. Our only chance is to get solid defenses set up."

"You might be right, but I can't possibly afford this. I've already indentured my future. I've got mortgages on top of my mortgages. My family is in storage because I can't even afford the basic upkeep fees for the Reality Engine where they live. I'm tapped out."

"I know. You've been a good partner for us," Grandpa said. "And so we're willing to come to the table with you. Our coalition has funds. You know that. You've been taxing our income, you know we're doing okay. Well, we want to buy in on this bid." He sent her a figure.

Veda's eyes went wide. "That's got to be everything you've made in the last two months."

"Pretty close. But Mama Grace picked up a catering contract, and it looks like we're going to be clearing a nice profit there," I said. "We believe in this, Veda. It's our best shot out of the mess we're in."

I still felt bad lying to her. The money had come courtesy of our new team members, who had joined up and then disappeared, promising to be ready on opening day.

They had given us names so generic I felt sure they were fake. Like with Ames, they must have found a way to convince the system to display false information, because there was no way that they were really named Smith, Jones, Brown, Black, and Smith. Grandpa had assigned them all to one squad and called it Team Mongoose. Because, he had said, when I asked him if he was crazy, "Mongeese very famously eat snakes."

I left it at that and decided to make sure if they asked that I told them just who had come up with that idea.

We had added Bill and Bob back to our team. Nobody was thrilled about that situation, but the brothers had agreed they were willing to give phase two a try, especially since death wasn't permanent. Then we had grouped our five new recruits into a single squad. Grandpa and I were willing to shake things up and have them moved around between teams if we decided it was necessary.

"We can afford it," Grandpa said persuasively. "The party we've put together can take a node, and with this matériel, we can hold it."

"I suppose so," Veda said. "Your proposal says that you want to rank one of the capture-the-flag rule sets highest."

"We do," I said. "Based on your projections, those are the most similar to games we have experience with. Tower defense games, base builders, that sort of thing." It was also the most common variant and the one that our *Beginner's Guide to Constructing Your Phase Two Outpost* briefing covered in the most depth.

"Then I'll submit the build," Veda said. "I just hope you know what you're doing." She ended the connection abruptly.

"So do I," Grandpa said to the air. "So do I." He stood up. "We'd better get a good night's sleep. It's going to be a big day tomorrow."

CHAPTER NINE

WELCOME TO PARADISE, POPULATION NOT YOU

A *Beginner's Guide to Constructing Your Phase Two Outpost, Section 2.7: Location, Location, Location*

Interview conducted by Colonel Jefferson Ames, US Army.

Interview subject: Hua'Laona Gough, Purveyor of Fine Footwear and Former Phase Two Elite, at the Hub's most exclusive club, over two bottles of Rayellen Champagne.

I don't know what you're trying here. I thought you were inviting me out for a nice dinner. I only agreed because I do so like a smaller male.

What's that? Oh, my glory days. Well, don't mind if I do. Yes, I captained four different phase two teams that had been assigned a two percent chance of returning profitably and came back with buckets of soul coin every time. No, I won't tell you my secrets. What kind of girl do you think I am?

Yes, yes, go ahead. I'll take another glass.

Well, the really important thing is, of course, location. There are so many factors that go into choosing the right location. I don't just mean what level of node. I'm going to assume you already understand the type of node you're going to be able to take and hold.

There's so much more to it than that. You've got to look at the map and make some snap decisions in the first six or seven minutes of the level opening. You'll be able to tell a few things right off. Node quality, how far you are from other nodes, and some rough information about other resources spawning near your node. Those will be your crafting materials of various sorts, your rare spawn mobs, that sort of thing.

The map probably won't tell you what they are or how high-quality. You have to purchase upgrades for that, and most phase two teams don't bother. They just assume they'll scout resources manually and take over any enemy outpost they need to get hold of what they want.

So, yes, you want to consider those when picking your location. You also need to think about who your neighbors are going to be. If you're lucky, the rule set will provide you with information about who's in your sector. That'll let you make some intelligent decisions, assuming you know what the rules are talking about. Obviously, you won't, because you Earthlings are new to this whole thing. You're just the cannon fodder. Oh, don't take it that way. I don't mean anything personal. You look like you'd . . . Well, never mind. The point is, you need to think about the neighborhood.

My heart hammered as I stepped through the portal. It looked like any of the mission portals I had entered since coming to this Reality Engine months ago, but I knew better. This was where things would get interesting.

We didn't know what to expect. Veda had given us her best guesses, but admitted that she was basing them on very little. And yet I was still surprised to find a wooden deck creaking under my feet, white sails billowing in the wind overhead, and the cry of a gull somewhere off to my left.

Sage inhaled. "The sea!" She got excited any time our missions involved big bodies of water. Can't blame her. She was a desert kid and had never seen an ocean before coming to the Reality Engine.

I looked around to check that my whole team had made it. We were on a wooden sailing ship, complete with a parapet deck behind us and three tall masts festooned with various ropes and sails. Sailors in white and blue uniforms ran around the deck. I was no sailing expert, but this looked to me like a Napoleonic-era ship, based on a couple of movies I'd watched. I wondered if there were cannons down below.

My team was scattered over the whole deck. "Map!" I shouted. "Where's the map?" Our first steps were straightforward. Pick our target node, get to it, claim it, and hold it for the initial period. During that time, our allies outside could send in supplies, but not people. Juana's teams would be busy hauling crates and boxes of cargo over to the portal to ship through for us while we claimed the node.

Once the node was ours, we'd be able to bring in our backup teams and erect defenses, but first we had to stake a claim.

"Over here!" Sage yelled brightly. She was up behind the big steering wheel, pointing up the steps to the top deck area. I hurried over, Grandpa joining me as I climbed the stairs.

There was a big paper chart laid out on a table on the rear deck. A man in a gold buttoned coat with a big hat stood beside the table. I assumed he was the NPC captain of this boat and was just grateful that the Reality Engine wasn't going to make us sail the damn thing ourselves.

The map showed a whole bunch of different islands, ranging from tiny specks to shapes about the size of my fingertip. "Is there a scale on this thing?" I asked.

"How big is that?" I jabbed a finger at one of the biggest islands. It was long and skinny, shaped a little bit like Cuba.

The NPC spoke. "Ah, that'd be the pirate island of Hispana. You don't want to be going there. The crews that land there all end up fighting to the death over its treasures."

"Yes, but how big is it?" I asked.

"Oh, a league or two across, and twenty the long way."

I assumed that a "league" was something on the order of a mile. That meant even the smallest islands had to be at least a quarter of a mile in diameter.

There were different levels of resource nodes picked out along the map as color-coded dots. The map didn't have a scale, but it did have a helpful legend. Gold was alpha tier, blue was beta tier, red was delta tier, and purple was gamma tier. X's and skulls marked spawning locations of valuable beasts, and other symbols stood for resource-gathering locations.

Dashed lines on the map ran between islands, indicating that what were currently separate landforms would be connected by sandbars at low tide. Right now, all the nodes were on their own islands. The legend on the map indicated tides were on a forty-eight-hour cycle, which was of course nonsense if talking about Earth, but would make for very interesting gameplay.

Grandpa said, "I've sent a list of everyone else that's going to be in this sector to Veda so she can start running an analysis. What do you think?"

I pointed at a red delta-tier dot not too far from the edge of the map. It was equidistant between two gold alpha nodes, with a smattering of purple gammas and a single blue beta in the nearby vicinity. At low tide, all eight nodes would be connected together on a single giant island.

"That one," I said.

"Explain," Grandpa prompted.

I pointed to the ship symbol on the map. "That's us, so we can realistically expect to get about this far in the next two hours." I drew a circle around the boat. "I found the ship's speed in the rule set. Everyone gets a basic level-one vessel to start, and we can upgrade it later. Our top speed is ten knots." I managed not to say *per hour*. I wasn't a seaman, but at least I knew that much.

"Those two alpha nodes are far enough from each other that no team is going to try to claim both of them," I said. "If we're in between, then any attempt one of our neighbors makes at dislodging us will be seen as a threat by the other big power. Hopefully they'll respond."

"That's a lot to hope for," Grandpa said mildly.

"The other delta-tier nodes I see are in worse situations." I pointed out the ones we could reasonably reach in a short time. "Look, they're all surrounded by blue nodes. Anyone going after those beta nodes will snap up a delta in the process. The alpha node teams might not bother, at least not right away."

"You're making a solid case," Grandpa agreed.

"We'll have a chance here. We'll need to try to secure one or two of these gamma nodes if we can. I like how close these two resource patches are. If we're lucky, we'll be able to do serious harvesting. Remember, we have a strong farmer and crafter backline, and the galactics don't. We can't compete with them head-on, but we can corner a market and get an economic win. Probably."

Grandpa nodded. "I'll back that," he said. "Captain, set a course for this island." He tapped my selected node.

"Aye, aye, Commodore," the NPC captain said. He shouted something to the sailor at the wheel, and the ship turned hard to starboard. I think. It might have been port. I was clearly going to have to brush up on my nautical terms here.

Fortunately, the NPC sailors did a great job of sailing the ship. I was pretty sure you couldn't actually steer a ship like this so directly into the wind, but they did it anyway.

My guess was that the Reality Engine was taking liberties. The rule set had given the ship's speed in straight-up knots, without any elaboration on whether that meant upwind or downwind.

Soon we were approaching our chosen island. Sage had scaled up the mast, and she was clinging to the top and peering out. She yelled "Land ho!" and then swung down on a rope, dropping to the deck and giving us a "Ta-da!" in triumph. Her cheeks were tinged pink. "Can I have a pirate hat?"

"Maybe later," I said. I directed our team into two boats, with Team Mongoose in one, and Team Ragtag in the other. Grandpa had let the other newcomers name themselves.

Our team, Team Twofeather, split up. Sage and I went with Team Mongoose, while Grandpa, Bill, and Bob clambered in with the Ragtag squad.

Team Mongoose complained when they saw Sage. "You can shut it," I advised them. "She's the only one here with a healing spell. Not to mention she has about eight times more experience with Reality Engines than any of you do." The commanding Smith gave his men a glare to back me up. Since he was taller than the other Smith, I had my system tag him as "Tall Smith" and the other as "Short Smith."

The sailors lowered our boat over the side, and as it hit the water, I touched the oars. The boat immediately began moving forward.

"Whoa," I said, taking my hands off the oars. The boat stopped. "Okay, one of you get the tiller or rudder, whatever that thing is, and steer," I said. "Make for the closest bit of sand you can see."

"Looks like rocks over there," one of the Smiths pointed out. "Try to avoid that," he told Jones, who had taken the big steering stick at the back of the boat.

I grabbed for the oars again, and we raced in toward the shore of the island. A dazzling white-sand beach, thick, dense green jungle, and a black volcanic cone sticking up from the middle of it. It looked like the perfect example of a desert island. There was even a pair of palm trees at the nearest edge of the jungle, their trunks crossing each other to make an archway over a narrow path beneath. It looked idyllic.

We saw no signs of life as we came ashore. The boat ran aground, and we hopped out and pulled it farther up on the beach as Grandpa's boat nosed in to shore.

"All right, we've got to get to the node claim point," I said. It was on my mini-map now, blinking at me. I pointed and pinged it on the map. "That way. Everybody keep your eyes open for trouble."

According to both Veda and the noob guide, phase two NPC opponents didn't usually start spawning until a node had been claimed. We kept our eyes open any-way as we raced for the point. No sense getting sloppy.

The node capture point was on a hill that stuck out of the surrounding jun-gle. No trees grew on the black volcano cone. Instead, it was littered with giant obsidian boulders. At the top was an enormous stone head like the ones on Easter Island, except that this head was carved to resemble a snarling orc. I had seen sev-eral of those aliens on the Hub, and it disturbed me to know that there really were creatures in the galaxy that looked like that.

"That's the capture point," I shouted, pointing at the statue. "Gramps, do the honor!"

"Fine by me!" Grandpa charged up the hill and placed his hand on the statue. "And don't call me Gramps!" he yelled back as the statue shifted and melted, its features rearranging into a likeness of Grandpa's face with a feathered bonnet on top of its head. "That's more like it," he said approvingly.

A timer appeared over the statue's head. **[24:00. 23:59:59. 23:59:58.]** According to the noob guide, it would tick down for a whole day until it reached zero. At that point, we would be able to begin erecting defenses. Until then, we were vulnerable to attack from any other teams.

Another counter started under that one. **[Soul coins earned: 1]**. It ticked up to "2" when the timer reached **[23:58:59]**. One coin per minute during the ini-tial claiming phase was the base rate for delta nodes. A beta-level node would give ten times that, an alpha node, a hundred times, but a gamma produced only ten coins an hour.

I pulled up my chat and sent a message to Juana, who was coordinating the team's back-in threshold. *Start sending the defense supplies through.*

As soon as we claimed the node, it became a portal. I knew from the guide that any material sent to us from our coalition would come out here. We wouldn't be able to use it for twenty-four hours, but that was all right. We had plenty of work to do before then.

"Spread out and patrol," I said. "We can expect the first wave to spawn soon. Call it in and coordinate with each other. This statue is our fallback point. Remember, if you die, you respawn, so don't be too cautious, but remember that it'll take time for you to get back here." We would eventually be able to build player respawn points that worked faster, but until then, anyone who died would come back on the deck of our ship. It would take time for them to get back into the action. "Whatever happens, we protect the node. We can't do anything else in the game until it's claimed."

"Why not just stand here and wait for whatever's going to attack, instead of going out there?" Bill asked.

"Because that lets the NPCs mass up and launch a bigger attack. If we take them out as they're spawning in, it'll be easier on us." I tossed out assignments, leaving three of the new recruits, Annie, Mitch, and Lakshmi, to defend the point.

"You've got your assignments. Let's roll."

CHAPTER TEN

WHERE'S THE BOTTLE OF RUM, YO HO?

Veda had bought me another upgrade for my map skill. This one would reveal the location of enemies so long as they were not using some sort of camouflage ability. My mini-map was big enough to reveal the entire island if I chose to zoom out that far.

I activated my new Sense Enemies skill and watched three clusters of red dots pop up on the map. "Okay, we've got spawn." I pinged everyone the locations. "I suggest we hit the nearest group together, then split up and take on the other two."

"Sounds good," Grandpa agreed as we moved out. The closest group had spawned on the beach about a hundred yards from where we had left our boats. I briefly worried that they would destroy the boats, which would leave us unable to return to our ship unless we were dead. But as we stepped out of the jungle and into the brilliant sunlight, it was clear the enemy wasn't that smart.

"More zombies?" Sage asked in disgust.

"These are clearly pirate skeletons," I said. Backing me up, the system announcer proclaimed:

[Avast, Mateys! You've been boarded and keelhauled by Admiral Scaggers and his skeleton crew! Defeat them within one hour, or they'll claim your island for their own!]

There were a dozen of them, wearing tattered sailor outfits and wielding rusty cutlasses. Or, in the case of the skeleton with the enormous black captain's hat and eyepatch, a brace of pistols. None of them had more than **[60 HP]**, except for the one labeled "Cap'n Black," who had 150 health. He also was providing a buff to the other skeletons, called Shiver Me Timbers, which made them immune to any crowd control effects we had.

I marked the captain on our team map with a skull. "Take him down, then we'll worry about the rest." It didn't seem like we needed much more organization for a group this basic.

We rushed at the skeleton crew. Grandpa Shadow Stepped in behind the captain, hit him with Counting Coup, then stepped behind another skeleton. Whenever he got the first hit on one of the smaller skeletons, he took almost half the creature's health with one blow.

I fired a Barrage into the captain, sending all six shots from my cylinder straight into his skull. I reloaded with normal .44 Magnum rounds. I had almost a hundred special rounds in six different types, but I was saving them for something that seemed like more of a threat.

Team Mongoose swarmed into action. One of the Smiths, the short one, dropped a wall of sandbags a little ways down the beach. They formed a waist-high semicircle. Brown called up a machine gun from nowhere. Either it had been in his inventory, or the machine gun itself was a skill. He set it up and threw himself prone on the beach behind the sandbag wall, firing away into the mass of skeletons.

"Watch friendly fire!" I shouted. Even if we would respawn, I didn't want anyone getting killed this early.

"It's fine. His rounds only hit enemies," Tall Smith called to me as he threw a smoke grenade into the mass of skeletons.

Grandpa hit the pirate captain with Coup-de-Grace and yelled triumphantly as the skeleton collapsed at his feet. "I knew it! He's not a real boss! My ability worked just fine on him."

That was good to know. Several of our abilities specifically said they did not affect bosses. I had found that any sort of elite creature that was one of a kind, whether or not it was labeled as a boss, seemed to count, which was really annoying sometimes.

On the other hand, a mob that was merely in charge of a lot of other lesser minions usually could be hit, and the pirate captain was no exception. We downed the rest of the skeletons in a matter of seconds.

"Cease fire!" I shouted, and we converged on the piles of splintered bone and scraps of cloth that had been the skeleton crew. Sage bent down, picked up the captain's black hat, and admired the skull and crossbones. It vanished into her inventory.

Over our triumphant discussion, the system announcer blared, [**Wave one: 33% cleared. Time remaining: 45 minutes.**]

I checked how much time we had left on our node claim timer. Sure enough, it was down to [**23:45:03**].

So we had an hour to clear the first wave. I didn't know if that meant we'd also have an hour for the second wave and so forth. I wasn't going to be making any guesses just yet.

"No loot," said one of the newcomers, a man named Aaron Jackson, who had asked us to call him "Ice Spice" for reasons that I didn't ask.

"We're not expecting any. Leave them and let's split up."

I sent Grandpa a private message. *I can take the newbies and Bill & Bob. Mongoose will listen to you.*

That's why you'll take them, Grandpa said. *Team Mongoose respects me, or they think they do. They don't respect you and Sage yet. I need to know if you can win their trust, or at least keep them in line. Meanwhile, I'd like to get an idea of what Aaron and Lara can do.*

Acknowledged. So Grandpa took the brothers, Ice Spice, and Lara, the last member of Ragtag, and headed for the farthest group of spawn. The plan was that Team Mongoose, Sage, and I would handle the closer group, then join Grandpa's band.

We split up, Grandpa and his team heading deeper into the jungle, while I led Team Mongoose farther up the beach. "Is there a cooldown on that machine gun nest?" I asked as we went.

"Twenty minutes on the gun and sandbag wall both, but we can only conjure it six times a day," Brown told me.

"All right, let's get a look at the next threat before we use it then. By day, you do mean a twenty-four-hour period, yes?"

"The timer also resets if we sleep for at least four hours," the shorter Smith told me.

"Good to know. I doubt we'll be sleeping during the next twenty-four hours, but still good to know."

I kept an eye on my map in case any other red dots showed up. While I didn't expect any more spawn until the end of this wave, there was always the possibility that other miners or the galactics might appear. I wanted us to be ready if that happened.

There was a rocky promontory between us and the next spawn location. "Anyone have any kind of spying abilities?"

Jones stepped forward. "I've got a drone, but it costs five soul coins for each use."

"Well, then use it," I said. "We are not going to be hurting for soul coins, not if we do this right."

"Sure thing," he agreed.

"How about a roger on that?" I snapped.

He shot me a quick glance. I couldn't make out his thoughts. "Roger," he said.

I wasn't sure how much of Team Mongoose's attitude was disrespect and how much was just a more casual approach to missions. Special forces types had a certain reputation. We weren't using our military ranks, but Grandpa had put me in charge. I'd been a corporal back on Earth, and my promotion to lieutenant still didn't feel real. It was hard to get used to ordering anyone around.

Jones popped out a drone, which looked to me more like a mechanical falcon. After it spawned, it perched on his wrist while he gave it directions. Then it rose into the air and hovered like a drone before hopping over the rocks and making a swoop along the cove beyond.

"Huh." Jones scowled, his eyebrows knitting together as he watched the drone feed. "It looks like a bunch of pigs walking around on hind legs wearing loincloths with feather headdresses and war paint. They've got javelins and what look like bows and arrows." He turned back to me, looking upset. "What the hell is this stuff? Is this what the aliens think of us humans?"

I was too used to the nonsense by now to be offended. "This is all dreamed up by some sort of alien artificial intelligence that's older than our solar system, if I understand it right, and then translated through other alien artificial intelligences programmed by people who don't consider any human worth giving the time of day," I said. "Of course it's racist. Don't read too much into it. We're going to get down there. We're going to slaughter them. We aren't going to try to understand their culture. Anything interesting, strategically speaking?"

"They've got a cookpot boiling over a fire and a couple of those statues that are carved to look like a bunch of animal heads on top of each other. You know what I'm talking about?"

I nodded. "Sure. Gotta assume that any of those might be the focal point of an ability of some sort." I checked our clock. Thirty-seven minutes to go, and I wanted to leave time to be able to help Grandpa. "Right, here's what we're going to do."

I sprinted up to the row of boulders, vaulted past them onto the beach, then ran full out for the cannibal pig camp, assuming my team was right on my heels. My drover's coat flapped in the breeze behind me. The sun was warm, but the garment felt as comfortable in this heat as it did in twenty below zero.

The system announced:

[Admiral Scaggers's loyal allies, the Cannibal Pigs of Greenfeather Mountain! Defeat them to deal the admiral's invasion a swift blow!]

I shouted as I approached the camp, revolver in hand. As soon as I was in range, I cast Call 'em Out and then turned tail and sprinted back toward the rocks.

Team Mongoose and Sage stayed behind me, ready to act. All four of Team Mongoose had M4s out and would fire as soon as I was out of the way.

Sage cast Mucking Out the Stalls on the beach just past me, catching the first six or so pigs in the wet sand. I dove into a slide as I approached the team so Team

Mongoose could fire shots over my head. I slid past them, one leg out like a runner trying to steal third, then rolled over and started firing.

The pigs were stuck in the mud, and despite the stereotype, they did not look happy about it. A couple of them threw their javelins toward us. One sailed right past my neck and pinned the corner of my coat to the sand. I reloaded and shot that pig a couple of times in the head for his insolence.

Team Mongoose was busy turning the pigs into Swiss cheese. We dropped them all, dark blood staining the white grains of sand.

I got up, pulled the javelin out of my coat, and examined the hole. "I'm going to have to pay Rosa to fix that as soon as we're done with this first phase," I lamented. The hole was big enough for me to get three of my fingers through.

"Right." I checked the progress. It now said [**Wave one: 66% cleared**]. "Let's head for the other team and help them out."

CHAPTER ELEVEN

THE IMPORTANCE OF TIME MANAGEMENT

I sent a message to Grandpa. *Finished here. What's the situation?*

Got another set of skeleton pirates, but these ones had a chance to dig in before we got there. The so-called admiral is with them, so I assume we defeat them and then we're done. They've got a gun boat pulled up on shore.

A what? That didn't seem era-appropriate.

Like our landing craft, but with a small brass cannon in the front of it. It's got a decent range. We lured five of them out and took them down. I was considering just charging in now.

We'll be there in five minutes, I said. *Want to hold up?*

I think we will. There was no way of telling from the plain text, but I wondered if the new recruits weren't performing up to Grandpa's expectations.

We crashed through the jungle, not much caring about noise. I checked my mini-map regularly. No new red dots appeared. We could see the little green dots for Grandpa and his party and made right for them.

They were concealed a little ways back in the forest, peering around palm trees to study the enemy setup. I poked my head out.

This crew had a pirate boss—the "Admiral Scaggers" that the system had mentioned—and his sidekick, a Ghostly Cockswain. The cockswain was giving all the others a buff to their ranged damage, and these skeleton pirates were armed with muzzle-loading long guns. I couldn't quite make out the details from here, but they looked like wheel locks to me, not flintlocks. They were probably slow to reload and not very accurate, but they'd pack a heck of a punch.

"What's the operational plan?" I asked.

Grandpa turned to Team Mongoose. "We haven't had a chance to see you fellows take the lead. What would you suggest?"

Smith, the tall one, who I was pretty sure was at least an O-2 like me, peered out, then ducked back behind cover with the rest of us. "Anything wrong with just charging them head-on?"

"That would probably work," Grandpa agreed. "The thing is, we might take the opportunity to get a better look at some of their capabilities. We've got more waves coming before we've claimed the node. I'm gonna assume we'll see more of these guys."

"Then I think we need to use your team as bait while we sneak in behind them and knock them out," Tall Smith said at once. "How often can you use that trick to get them all to pay attention to you, Williams?"

"It's back off cooldown now," I said.

"What else have you got? We need to understand each other's capabilities if we're going to work together," Tall Smith said.

Grandpa grinned wickedly. "Indeed we are. So why don't you share your ability list with us and we'll share ours with you?"

Tall Smith blinked like he hadn't been expecting that. The five men Colonel Ames had landed us with had been pretty reticent to share much about their capabilities. "We can just tell you," Tall Smith said.

Grandpa sighed. "Now, I get that there are things you are hiding from us. I don't rightly understand why. We're all on the same side here. I assume the colonel's given you some secret orders, but for as long as you are going to be working with my team, we need to work together. Shad, Sage, send them over."

I pulled up my abilities list and sent it to the men. Sage stuck her tongue out but followed suit.

The other two newbies sent their info without being asked. I'd already seen their skill lists before. They weren't particularly impressive. Neither one had a very coherent class. Ice Spice was a Self-Taught Self-Defense Specialist with moves like I Know Kung Fu, which gave him a thirty-second ability to fight unarmed in melee and actually inflict some serious damage, and another one called 3 a.m. Martial Arts Movie Marathon, which sounded like it gave him a different batch of martial arts skills for a five-minute period but had a three-hour cooldown.

Lara was a Soccer Mom class with a Minivan ability that could teleport her entire current party out of battle space. That seemed like it'd be situationally very useful. Her offensive moves included School Run, which let her get in and deal crippling blows to three different enemies before disengaging, and I Brought Oranges for Everyone, which was actually a grenade-lobbing move like our buddy Deputy Young had.

Tall Smith blinked. His eyes went distant for a minute. "Thanks," he said. "Yeah, I'm getting the idea for a plan now." He did not share his own sheet.

"Captain Smith," Grandpa said, his tone dangerously cold. "I will now make it an order. You and your men share your skill sets with Shad and me immediately." There was no room in his voice for questioning him.

Tall Smith's jaw muscles worked. I could see the men glancing at each other and knew they were having a private conversation in chat. The seconds ticked by. They were getting dangerously close to insubordination.

Finally, Tall Smith said, "Understood, sir." A moment later, an information pack pinged on my system.

"Good. I'll take a look at that at my convenience. Now, it sounded like you had a plan," Grandpa said.

"Yeah." Tall Smith was definitely ruffled now. "Right, so it's pretty clear those guys have a ranged move. The ones we fought earlier were mostly melee. I'm wondering whether they can switch back and forth. So what I suggest is we drive in hard and scatter them, then take some time to see what moves they're capable of. Everyone here ought to be able to take one hit. If you take more than that, get out of combat by any means necessary."

"I can keep people topped off," Sage offered brightly. "And my team buff is powerful enough now to cover everyone here. It's not just limited to my original party."

"Then cast that as we start," Tall Smith said. "Williams, I want you to charge in and do your 'pay attention to me' move. Lara, I want you to lob some grenades at the group as soon as they're focused on Williams. I've noticed a few cases where sonic damage will break a crowd control, and it would be good to know if the skeletons suffer from that limitation."

That was good to know. We had used plenty of crowd control with Frank, and I'd never noticed that. I filed it away for future reference.

"After that, pay attention to how much damage they take from which abilities. Don't use any AoEs," Tall Smith continued. "We want to be clear about who did what damage. We'll debrief after the firefight."

That made sense to me. I could have suggested a few refinements, but Grandpa seemed to be interested in letting Tall Smith do the leading here.

"On your signal, then," I said.

"Go!"

Sage cast Cowgirl Cheer on all of us. I ran ahead of the group, though I didn't use my Fastest Gun in the West move yet. I wanted to save that for getting out of trouble, if necessary. Its range had increased as I leveled up, and I could now charge a hundred feet in a straight line. The upgrade was nice, but I still had to be careful where I was pointing to make sure I ran along a clear path and not into a tree. That had happened once in a previous mission, and it had hurt a lot.

The pirates looked up as I ran toward them. The admiral raised his arm and brought it down in a sharp motion. On his cue, a pair of skeleton pirates in their beached landing boat jumped to the cannon. They began wheeling it around to point it in my direction.

I ran into the middle of the group and cast Call 'em Out as the rest of the pirate grunts aimed their muskets at me.

A barrage of small orange grenades landed all around, instantly exploding. I hadn't expected Lara's skill to create a literal orange scent, or the cloud of acrid smoke that arose. The combination made me cough and my eyes water.

Some of the skeletons looked disoriented, turning to seek the source of the grenades. My crowd-control skill hadn't worn off, so this must be one of those effects that Tall Smith had mentioned. I would have to see if we could figure out the rules later.

I turned away from the skeletons and fired a Barrage at the pirate admiral. We needed to get him and the cockswain down, and then the rest would be fairly easy pickings.

The admiral was armed with a flintlock pistol and a rapier. Although he was staggering backward from my hits, he pulled out the pistol and fired at me. The slug caught me in the arm. I staggered back, the pain burning. My eyes were already watering from the smoke, and now I could barely see. I took twenty-five points of damage just from the one hit.

Sage cast Raise Your Spirits on me and a cool wash of relief flowed over me, easing the pain and restoring my health. The heal-over-time aspect started ticking my HP upward.

Admiral Scaggers dropped his pistol and swung his rapier at me. Grandpa Shadow Stepped in behind him and used Scalp, knocking his hat off. The skeleton admiral whirled on him, rapier coming within inches of Grandpa's hunting jacket.

Grandpa Shadow Stepped away to another of the skeletons, and I put another six rounds through the admiral. He was hurting pretty bad now, down to **[10/150]**.

One of the Smiths came in behind him with a KA-BAR knife and ran it across the admiral's nonexistent throat. That did the trick. The admiral's health bar disappeared and he collapsed.

All of the other skeletons lost the buff the admiral had been providing. I turned to look for the cockswain just as the skeletons on the beached boat fired their cannon.

The cannon shot blew through the middle of the melee, knocking one of the pirates out of the way and nearly hitting Jones. The ball carried on past and struck Ice Spice, knocking him back on to the sand. My ears rang. I aimed at the gunner skeletons and shot one, dropping its health from full to nothing in two seconds flat. The other one was struggling to reload, a heavy cannonball in its bony hands.

Grandpa Shadow Stepped up and Scalped it, then hit it with his Take No Prisoners move. He didn't use that very often because he was usually more mobile, preferring to dance around the battlefield and deliver a little bit of damage to a lot of different targets. But when he needed to drop a single damaged enemy fast and didn't have enough coup points to cash in, Take No Prisoners dealt a lot of damage really fast. It required him to have one of his axes in each hand, then hit the target three times with each.

By the time he was done, the second gunner skeleton was a pile of broken bone shards.

"Help!" Sage was shrieking. I turned to find her.

She was standing over Ice Spice, who lay on the ground with one arm and half his torso blown away. "My heal's not working!" she exclaimed. "He's still going down!"

"Potion! Quick!" I shouted, running over to her. There were still three skeletons up. The Mongeese ran around dealing with them.

"I can't!" She wrung her hands. Ice Spice lay on the sand, his blood leaking out. His eyes were rolled back in his head, and he was convulsing. His health bar was ticking down. Ten points left. Nine. Eight.

I grabbed a potion, then hesitated because I had just noticed the debuff on him. It read [**Shrapnel**]. The effect was [**This wound cannot be healed while Shrapnel is present. Time remaining: 15 seconds.**]

I swore. He wasn't going to make it. "Can you hear me, buddy?" I said, grabbing his remaining hand and squeezing. "Hold on. It's gonna be all right. You're gonna respawn right back on the boat and we'll send someone for you. It's all right. You did good."

I held on as tight as I could as his health trickled down to zero.

[Victory! You have defeated Admiral Scaggers and retain control of this island. Lick your wounds, savor your victory, and prepare for the next round of invaders!]

The battle was over. When I regained control of myself, I stood up. Sage was quietly sobbing. I put an arm around her shoulders. "It's all right, Sage. He's not really dead."

"I know, but it feels like he is. I was trying to heal him and it didn't work." Sage rubbed her nose as she sobbed.

"That was good intel," Tall Smith said, walking back to us. "Now we know those cannonballs apply a nasty debuff that we can't afford. We'll have to target any cannoneers first."

I restrained myself from calling him all of the names I was secretly thinking. He was right to be so matter-of-fact. Ice Spice wasn't really dead. In fact—I checked. He'd be back with us in five minutes.

We had twenty-two minutes remaining on our timer and the wave was one hundred percent clear. I noticed something else. "Hey, look," I said to Grandpa. "It's asking if we want to start the next wave now."

"So it is," Grandpa said.

"You think if we do that, it'll make us able to take the node any faster?"

Grandpa looked around at the beach, the piles of broken bones, and the looks on all of our faces. "Everybody, grab a drink and a snack," he said. "I'm going to start this up in five minutes so we can find out what's going on. Leave a message for Aaron to get back here as soon as possible." It took me a minute to remember he was talking about Ice Spice. Grandpa didn't like gamertags; he'd grumbled about it in passing before.

We had left the boats beached, but Ice Spice would be able to recall one from the ship. "Now let's see what else we can do," I concluded.

CHAPTER TWELVE

HOW MANY MEN CAN FIT ON A DEAD MAN'S CHEST?

Starting the next wave before the timer ran out did not advance our capture of the node point. That was still ticking down from twenty-four hours at a rate of one second per second.

Instead, our timer to clear the second wave read **[01:16]**. The leftover time from wave one had rolled over to wave two.

"I wonder if that stacks?" I said, excited. "That could be really useful." I was already thinking of ideas. We could get four waves ahead and then take a couple of hours of downtime, get some big cooldowns back.

"Let's clear this wave first, then meet back at the node point and have a quick discussion," Grandpa said to me. "What do you see?"

I checked my map. "Three spawn points, same as before," I said. "Looks to me like they're slightly bigger." I marked them so they'd show on everyone else's map.

One wasn't too far from us. We decided to tackle that one as an entire group. Jones pulled out his drone and sent it out to scout.

"Cannibal pigs again," he said, "and this time they've got some lizardfolk with them. The lizards don't have any weapons that I can see. Big sharp teeth and claws, though."

We agreed on a pincer movement tactic for this one and sent Team Mongoose to sweep around to the far side of the camp.

Then Grandpa, Sage, Lara, and I crept up closer. Lara was looking very uncomfortable. She had just seen a man bleed out and die in front of us, and even I was having trouble believing that he'd be back. I didn't blame her for being a little nervous.

Team Mongoose signaled when they were in position. "Let's do this," Grandpa said, and we charged in.

I had Lara throw a barrage of her orange grenades before anyone else stepped in. The citrus-scented smoke clouds went off again. I had a hunch it was those that had broken my crowd control and not any kind of sonic damage. Plenty of games had mechanics where you'd lose focus if line of sight got broken. After all, I would stop concentrating if someone threw smoke bombs into the middle of my camp, too.

The pigs and lizards seemed confused for a few seconds, especially once Team Mongoose started firing into their camp. Some of the lizards dropped to all fours and went charging into the brush. Sage cast Mucking Out the Stalls where they were going and tangled them up, then Lassoed one of the pigs who wasn't standing in a cloud of smoke and had him run around and attack the others.

I stepped in closer to get a decent shot. I could feel something sharpen as I did, and a minute later I realized the totems were staring at me. There were three of them, each a six-foot-tall stack of four nonhuman heads on top of each other. They looked like the pigs and lizards here in the camp. The bottom totem on each pole opened its mouth and began spouting gouts of fire.

I jumped back. "Ah! Look out!" The flames passed inches from me. I shot the nearest pig and dove for the brush. "Take out the totems!" I yelled, and Team Mongoose started shooting them. One by one, they blew up into clouds of splinters.

That enraged the pigs. They started charging around the clearing, swinging their stone axes and javelins at anything that moved, including each other. The lizards weren't so angry, or reckless. They were still sniffing around the brush after us. I shot one as it charged Sage. She laughed and had her tamed pig take out another lizard.

We cleaned up the enemy camp pretty fast. The enormous cauldron bubbling on top of the fire smelled suspicious to me. The pigs and lizards hadn't done anything with it, but I was concerned that each spawn wave was going to get successively harder, and that we might find out what it was for sooner or later.

After that, we split up to go clean out the other two camps. This time, Grandpa sent Team Mongoose off to clear a camp on their own with no instructions except to report back anything that they thought we should know about. We took Lara with us to the closer camp, leaving the rest of Team Ragtag to guard the node.

The next spawn was located deeper in the jungle. We slogged up a heavily forested, vine-covered hill. I had to pull a machete out of my inventory and start hacking through the vines to cut us a path.

We were almost on top of the spawn point before I spotted the enemy. There were only three red dots and I hadn't been able to tell what they were on the map, but as we approached the bottom of the hill, I noticed three piles of mossy boulders in approximately the right location. I pointed them out to the team.

Sage used her Eye-Spy ability. "Rock trolls," she said. "They're immune to fire, poison, drowning, and any kind of edged weapon."

"So what's that leave?" I asked.

"Sonic," Lara said cheerfully. She pulled out a stash of her orange grenades.

"Ice. Most of my bullets. Old age," I added as I thought about it.

"How about the boom rounds?" Sage suggested.

"We've only got ten of those," I said.

"They won't do us any good if you keep them in your gun belt the whole fight," Sage retorted.

"All right, I'll give it a try." I switched out my load to include two of Sage's boom rounds. We'd used them two missions ago and they had made an impact, that's for sure.

I looked at Lara. "Toss your grenades in to wake them up, then I'll take my shot. After that, we assess." She nodded brightly. "Ready? Go!"

I was glad to see she was doing better. Ice Spice had messaged the whole team after respawning, assuring us that he was okay, that it had hurt to die, but coming back was fine, and that he was on his way back to the island now. That had lifted my mood, and I'd noticed Lara also had more spring in her step since.

Lara threw the grenades, and they rained down around the three piles of boulders. I held myself ready as they exploded.

The boulders stood up. It was like watching a rock fall in reverse as each pile became a coherent, humanoid-shaped lump with rock arms, rock legs, and small moss-covered rock boulders atop the large shapes of their bodies.

Sage giggled. "They're like evil rock snowmen!"

The orange grenades had done some damage. The rock trolls had [120 Max HP] and they were down to [105/120] each.

I took a deep breath and pointed my gun in their direction, then squeezed off one of the boom rounds.

My shot landed in between the three of them and exploded a chunk of forest about twenty feet in diameter. Bits of tree rained down all around us. There was a crackling sound, and then smoke began to rise from small fires started around the edge of the circle.

The inside of the circle was just bare dirt. Even the plants and fallen leaves had been blasted away. Piles of loose stone lay scattered all about. I checked our progress bar. It said, [Wave 2: 55% cleared].

"They're not all dead," I warned and looked around.

"There." Sage pointed.

One of the rock trolls had [5/120]. It was trying to pull itself back together, which was a bizarre sight. Individual rocks rolled toward each other, and when they touched, they stuck together.

"Uh-oh," Sage said. "They've got a regenerate ability!"

"Well, shit!" I really didn't want to have to use another of my boom rounds. They were expensive and, as we had just seen, very effective.

I turned my revolver's cylinder to a different chamber and fired a normal round at the largest chunk of rock I saw. It hit and did two points of damage, chipping away a flake of stone from the troll's head.

I fired a couple more times, then reloaded, returning my boom round to my gun belt. It took ten shots directly on the re-forming troll to knock it out completely. I was literally chipping pieces of rock away with each round. Finally, it was dead, and we were at sixty-six percent complete.

How's it going? Grandpa asked Team Mongoose.

We're finishing up here. Meet you back at the node.

"Should we go check on them?" I asked.

"They say they're fine." Grandpa shrugged. "Let's go. We'll meet them back at the node."

I hesitated. I was starting to have an idea. "What about starting the next round immediately? I think we could clear three or four rounds pretty quickly. Earn ourselves a chunk of time."

"Then do what? Take a nap?" Grandpa scratched his head. "You've got a plan here, don't you."

"Not quite, but it's starting to form. I feel like we've got an opportunity here. Need a target to aim at, though." I holstered my gun. "I'll work on the thought while we get back to our node."

CHAPTER THIRTEEN

HOW TO BE AN EFFECTIVE PIRATE

We made it back to the node before Team Mongoose got there. They let us know they had finished without an issue, which the system had already informed us of.

We had cleared wave two with forty-five minutes to spare. That meant we had nearly two hours before we'd have to finish wave three. It wasn't enough time to take a break, or do anything else, but maybe we could keep this rolling.

The miners on guard duty at the node hadn't just been standing around. Once we started the node claiming process, we'd messaged Juana to start sending our gear through. Annie, Lakshmi, and Mitch had hauled everything off the node's receiving circle and sorted it into piles.

There were big heaps of crates and boxes scattered all around, all full of the gear Veda had sent us to use once we got our node fully converted and were able to start putting up defenses.

I picked up one of the crates and was shocked to discover it was eligible to go in my inventory. We hadn't brought any of this stuff through with us because none of this gear could be stashed in our inventory, at least not on the Threshold side. It was tagged as "support materiel" and trying to store it gave an error message, so it had been brought down on big floating pallets from the Hub and delivered to our staging area. Then our coalition delivered it through the portal to us.

Now, though, it showed up as "eligible to store." I tossed it into my inventory then brought it back out again, and a grin spread across my face. If we could put this stuff in our inventories once we got into the zone, that would save us a lot of effort. Our whole strategy was built around how much support gear we could get here and how quickly. The crate I held was labeled as containing one autonomous self-targeting defense turret, continuously reloading as long as it was connected to an active defense network with a base rate of fire of one shot per five seconds.

The other crates had everything from the building blocks of the defense network we would need to erect to a couple of boxes containing the starts of various buildings.

Veda had a lot more stashed back on the Hub for us. She was waiting for the price of shipping it down to Threshold to be more reasonable. For the first couple of days of phase two, space on the elevator was at a premium.

I stored the crated-up turret in my inventory, picked up another of the boxes, and stored it as well. Then I walked over to the other side of the hill, pulled them out, and dropped them.

"What are you doing?" Sage asked, looking curious. "I thought these didn't go in inventories?" She picked up one of the crates herself. It vanished. "What do you know?" she said. "Rules must be different once it's in a portal."

"Yeah." My mind was racing. "That gives me some ideas."

I sent Juana a quick message asking her if all of our supplies had come through. She replied back, almost at once, that they had, was there something else we needed, and how was it going?

It's fine. Fill you in later, I said. My mind was racing. I didn't know if what I was thinking was possible, but I did know the next couple of steps we would need to take.

As Team Mongoose emerged from the brush, looking tired but all in one piece, Grandpa said, "Now is probably a good time for us to take a break and start laying out the defense network. I know we won't be able to get it online just yet, but—"

"Hang on," I said, holding up a hand. "Sorry to interrupt you, sir, but I've got an idea."

He looked at me, eyebrows raised. "What's that, Shad?"

"This is more of a Lieutenant Williams idea and less of a Shad idea, sir," I said, formally stressing the command structure between us. "If I may suggest something?"

He nodded. "Go ahead."

"There's a lot of variables involved here. I don't know if it's even going to be possible," I said, "but I think I've got an idea for how we can get a jump on the competition."

That got everyone interested. They clustered around me, waiting for me to speak. I gave them a quick overview. Grandpa was nodding, and Sage grinned maniacally. Even Team Mongoose looked impressed.

"The first step we need is to gain a couple more hours. I think we should trigger the next three waves and clear them as fast as we can. Then we'll see if my idea is even feasible. I want to send a couple of quick messages while we're clearing waves."

"All right," Grandpa said. "Let's do that."

We left Ice Spice, Lara, Bill, and Bob to guard the node while Annie, Lakshmi, and Mitch got to come with Grandpa, Sage, and me to clear waves. Grandpa wanted a chance to see what the other three new recruits could do. He hung back and gave them suggestions while I took the lead, rushing into camps with Call 'em Out, catching everyone's attention, and letting my team clear up the resulting mess.

While we cleared camps full of skeleton pirates, cannibal pigs, and a new variant that had just popped up, sea monsters coming ashore to try to eat us, I sent a furious slew of messages.

To Veda, I sent: *Can you tell anything about the other teams in our sector? I don't have access to the full map right now.* That would be one of our early upgrades. Right now, we could only see the level map from our ship. One of the improvements Veda had sent along would give us a map table in our outpost.

I can pull up a list of who, but not where they are.

I should be able to check locations myself soon, I told her.

All right, I'll send you the listing.

Also, let me know which of them I should not piss off.

What are you planning, Shad? I could practically hear her alarm in her texts. *I thought we went over the strategy and everyone was agreed.*

Yeah, well, you know how it is once you get boots on the ground. Plans change.

We had not yet mentioned to Veda that we were trying to take a delta node instead of the gamma node she had planned on. At some point we were all going to have to sit down for a nice long chat.

We tore through the waves of spawn like a machine gun through cheesecloth. I wondered if this was supposed to be a challenge or not. Certainly, it seemed like there would be plenty of time leftover for players to interfere with each other during this phase.

The fourth wave was equally easy, but the fifth wave changed things up a bit. We had five spawn points this time, not just the usual three. We tackled the first spawn point as a group to make sure things hadn't gotten too much harder, and found our old friends the skeleton pirates. They had four officers with them this time and two different gunboats. Now that we knew to target the cannoneers first, it hardly counted as a challenge. I used another boom round to blow up both boats, we charged in, the skeletons died. Then we split up to clear the rest of the spawns.

Grandpa, Sage, and I were standing looking over the last camp, which held a bunch of the pigs. I paused. "Grandpa? We should have enough time for an attempt at my idea after this, but first I've got to find out which nodes are being taken by whom, which means getting to the map on the ship. I don't want to waste everyone's time if there's not actually a good opportunity here." I took a deep breath. "Fastest way over to that ship is right through that camp." I nodded at the group of cannibal pigs.

Sage's eyes went wide. "No, Shad. No."

"It's not real," I assured her. "Besides, I'm going to be sending people into combat knowing they have no chance of surviving. I need to know what it's like."

Grandpa nodded. "All right," he said. "Just make sure we're going to get a camp clear before you let them finish you."

I grinned at him. "You and Sage could clear this camp with one hand tied behind your backs, Grandpa." I looked through my inventory and found what I was looking for. It was an early attempt at a fragmentation grenade Dwight had made. Problem was, it had ended up weighing about ten pounds. Too heavy to lob unless you had trained in shotput, which I hadn't. It would, however, make a nice bang.

I took a deep breath. "See you on the other side," I said. I leapt out of cover, sprinted toward the camp, and ignited the fuse on the bomb.

So, interesting fact about phase two. Death doesn't hurt. You blink, and you've respawned. Dying, however, is a bitch.

When that bomb went off, I felt my body being torn to shreds, the metal ripping through my flesh and bone, the shrapnel tearing me to pieces. Then, nothingness.

When I opened my eyes, I was on the deck of the ship. I took a deep, deep breath. That was not fun. I sent a message to Grandpa and Sage right away. *I'm all right. I'm back on the boat. It didn't hurt,* I lied to Sage.

Don't ever do that again, Sage replied. *I just saw you blow up. This was a stupid plan, Shad.*

I didn't reply as I climbed the stairs to the poop deck and shouldered in next to Captain NPC.

The map lay in front of me, covered in different icons and markings. Our ship was indicated on the map just off to the side of the island we had claimed. In the middle of the island was the Misfits Guild logo, a pair of barbecue tongs crossed with a tomahawk.

The two nearby alpha nodes had both been claimed. I checked their sigils against the list Veda had sent me, and identified them very quickly as large galactic conglomerates. Happily, neither of them were Sicaris Corporation. We'd had unpleasant dealings with them previously. Both, however, were on Veda's list of *Please don't piss these guys off; they could eat us all alive for breakfast.*

They weren't who I was really interested in, though. There was a beta node not far from us. I had seen it on the ship map before, when we first came through, and had briefly considered making a bid for it. But Grandpa and I had already planned out our delta node strategy and I didn't want to change it up on the fly. It had been a tempting target, though.

Sure enough, someone had claimed it. I looked up their icon. The company was known as TriStar Unlimited, and was in a list Veda had labeled *Nobody likes these guys, but they have a strong backing. If you piss them off, we might survive.*

That was good enough for me. I double-checked the distance, consulted with the captain, and sent Grandpa a message. *It's on.*

CHAPTER FOURTEEN

A GUIDE TO FINDING BARGAINS AT GARAGE SALES

I had nothing to do for fifteen minutes but stand around and wait. I stared out across the waves toward the island until my eyes hurt. Finally, at last, I saw our two boats sailing toward the ship. Grandpa, Sage, Bob, and Bill were in one boat, Team Mongoose in the other. That just left Team Ragtag on the island.

It was a calculated risk. We had over five hours until the next wave had to be cleared. Theoretically, Ragtag shouldn't even have to do anything, just stand there and look pretty. If one of our rival teams decided to try to attack us, though, they'd be in big trouble.

I was making a gamble, but one I thought could pay off big. The NPC sailors hauled the boats up into their hoists as Grandpa and Sage climbed up to join me.

Sage was wearing the hat she'd stolen from the first pirate captain we'd killed. "Are we ready?" I asked.

"No sense wasting time," Grandpa said.

Sage put her finger on the beta node island. "Set course for Sage Point," she ordered the NPC captain.

The captain saluted her. "Aye aye, Captain Sage."

Wind billowed in the sails. The helmsman turned the wheel, and our ship set course for the other island.

"Did you hear that?" Sage exclaimed in delight. "He called me 'Captain'! It must be because I stole the hat. I got a promotion now. Do I have a title?" She dove into her menus and emerged again a moment later, looking disappointed. "I don't. That's not fair. I want to know how to get the title. I need an achievement." She looked up at the sky overhead and addressed the system. "I want a pirate captain title. Do you hear me? Make me an achievement for that."

"Don't go changing your class now, Sage," I said. "Not when you're doing so well as a Barrel Rider."

She pouted. "I wanted Rodeo Queen, but that wasn't one of my class evolution choices. Maybe next time. Or maybe I'll multiclass. Horses aren't much good on a boat."

"Is multiclassing even an option?"

"It should be."

It took us about forty minutes to reach the other island. Once there, we loaded up into both smaller boats. Grandpa ordered the NPC captain to return to our island without waiting for us. The two small boats would be able to return to our main ship, no matter how far apart they were on the map, as long as at least one of us was aboard each boat. Or we could all just die and respawn on the ship's deck. By sending the ship back ahead of us, we were that much closer to returning to our node control point.

We rode ashore, beached the boats, and assembled on the beach. I looked at Jones. "How's our camo working?"

Part of my planning had included perusing the skill list from the five Mongeese. Jones and the others all had entirely different names listed on their skill sheets, but Grandpa and I had agreed to respect their covers and use the names they had given us. I had been nearly overcome with laughter when I learned Tall Smith's class was Ring Knocker. I'd had to go off on my own and take long deep breaths for a good five minutes after that one.

Anyway, Jones, who was an Army Scout class, had a Camouflage skill that would keep all of us from appearing on enemy mini-maps unless they had a high enough level of Pierce Camouflage. Hopefully they didn't. We had activated it before leaving our ship.

"I can keep it up for another twenty minutes," he said, "but only if you stay within a hundred yards of me."

This island was about three times the size of ours. A hundred yards was a long way, but hardly enough to be able to split up and cover ground.

I checked my mini-map. There were red dots on the far side of the island and blue dots mixed in with those red dots, as well as blue dots around what I presumed was their node capture point, since it matched the location where their sigil had been on the big map.

"All right," I said, "looks like there are eight of them. Five are busy clearing a wave. As we know, that doesn't take too long, so we've got to hit hard and hit fast."

We moved off through the jungle toward their node point. This island looked a lot like ours, right down to the same kinds of trees and jungle. Their node, however, was at the bottom of a bowl-shaped valley. It was a big stone ring about eight feet tall in the center, devoid of trees, with stone steps cut into the side of the bowl. Three aliens patrolled the bottom of the basin, glancing frequently up toward the jungle. We lay low beneath the concealing fronds of palm.

"Those are the ugliest aliens I've seen yet," Sage said.

Veda had called them Grignarians, and they really were hideous. They had three legs and an odd rolling gait where they would rotate which leg was in front, like they moved forward by spinning. Their heads had two wide multifaceted eyes, one on each side, and cilia-like tentacles hung in front of their maws. If I knew anything from Grandpa's lectures on hunting, the wideset eyes meant they'd originally been a prey species, evolved to watch everywhere for predators. They would likely see us as soon as we came out of the trees.

"Sage, how close do you have to be to activate your Three-Barrel Race skill?"

She rubbed her hands in reply. "I'm looking forward to this!" She had only gotten a chance to use it in combat once before. It let her designate three locations, one where she started and two others within three hundred yards of that first spot, and then teleport between them as much as she wanted.

There were big piles of crates, boxes, barrels, and bags in the valley below, like at our node but even worse, like the aliens were having a big rummage sale. It didn't look like the aliens had started to unpack their supplies, just piled them up wherever they felt like it. The patrolling aliens had to weave around between them.

Sage marked out the two largest piles. "Those are mine," she said.

"Right." We were going to need to get a little bit lucky here, but I thought we would be able to do it. I took a deep breath. "Bill, Bob, you're with me."

I grabbed for Bob. This was a move I had practiced, but not yet used for real. We stepped out to the edge of the trees, and I activated Fastest Gun in the West with my arms wrapped securely around Bob's torso. We rushed forward right into the center of the bowl.

The aliens pointed their weapons at us right away. I cast Call 'em Out, even though that probably wasn't necessary, just as Bob cast Babel. Then the rest of my team broke from the trees to join the fight.

I focused on the nearest alien, who was suddenly having trouble using his weapon. Bob's Babel skill had leveled up. Now, in addition to making it hard for them to work together, it also sometimes made them have trouble using complicated equipment. It looked like we'd gotten lucky.

I put a Trick Shot through the appendage holding the weapon, just for good measure, and then shot the rest of my cylinder into the alien's torso. Big green globs of bloody flesh tore loose.

Team Mongoose were firing their M4s, and I was glad they had a skill that meant their weapons didn't hurt us, because the bullets whizzed right past my head as I reloaded. Sage had Lassoed one of the three aliens. It was running around in circles, pointing its weapon at the ground and firing. It shot big purple blobs of jelly that turned the grass to dust where they hit.

"No fair! I can't attack the others while he's got the Babel debuff," she said in disgust as we took down the aliens. A moment later, their bodies vanished, presumably to respawn on their own ship. Respawning was almost instant, but getting back took time. We only had two landing boats, which took almost ten minutes to reach the beach from our ship. I hoped these aliens had the same constraints.

"Go, go," I told Team Mongoose. They took off for the north. I watched my mini-map. All of the previous blue dots were now red, presumably because we had attacked them, which made it hard to tell which ones were the aliens and which ones were the NPCs. My guess, though, was the five red dots heading our way were the aliens. Babel might have prevented the three here from alerting their friends, but as soon as they had died and respawned, they would no doubt be able to communicate again.

Team Mongoose sped north as I pinged the map where the aliens seemed to be. Then Grandpa, Sage, Bill, Bob, and I got to work stealing the aliens' gear.

We went through those piles like kids on Christmas morning, grabbing bags, crates, boxes, everything we could pick up, and stuffing them in our inventories.

A couple of the crates were over my weight limit. I could now store anything that weighed less than 120 pounds in my inventory, but there were a couple of big coffin-shaped boxes that I couldn't manage. That made me want them even more. I spent some time trying to figure out how to open one up. It seemed to have some sort of fingerprint ID, or whatever the equivalent of a fingerprint was for those aliens, and I couldn't get anywhere with it.

Bill noticed what I was doing and came over. "I think I can help with that," he said. He pointed his finger, and a yellow stream of liquid came splurting out in a jet. It cut into the side of the box.

"What's that?" I asked. He hadn't had that skill the last time we had worked together, I didn't think.

"It's called Environmental Safety Hazard. There's a couple of different forms it can take. I picked it up from a skill seed on that last mission. You know, the one with the weird kung fu people."

I wasn't going to complain. A circle fell out of the side of the box, revealing the contents. I reached in and started grabbing. There were several smaller bundles, all weighing less than my weight limit. I took everything.

Jones sent us a message. *We got three of them. Smith's down.* He didn't specify which, but I checked my roster; Short Smith had respawned at our ship.

Buy us a few more minutes, I said. *Then make for the boats.*

I pinged my mini-map again and spotted a single red dot moving from the ocean to the shore. I swore. "Looks like they're landing really close to our boats." *Cancel that. Disengage. Get to our boats now. Whatever you do, get one of the boats away.* I turned back to my team. "I think they're going to try to cut off our escape. We need to get out of here."

"There's still so much to loot!" Sage exclaimed, popping up next to one of the two piles she had marked. She grabbed armloads of boxes.

"You want to get caught and have them make us give it all back?" I demanded. "Come on."

I grabbed a last few goodies myself. Team Mongoose had disengaged, like we asked. They were down to just two. And now three more of the enemy were approaching the shore. "Let's go," I said.

We ran for it. "I didn't really get to use my ability," Sage lamented. The plan had been, if the aliens had made it back to the node, that she would dart between the piles, doing as much looting as she could, and then use her third point as a getaway.

I debated trying to give Sage all of the loot, and then shooting her in the head to make sure she got away. But that didn't feel right to me. Even if it was a good strategic move to make sure we got away with everything, I couldn't kill my own sister. Not even temporarily.

Besides, if we didn't get those boats, we were screwed. *Hold up*, I told what remained of Team Mongoose. *They're on the beach. We need to hit them hard together. We need to assume they've got some sort of tracking skill like mine and know we're coming.*

Yeah, no, they won't, Jones replied. *I've got my Camouflage up.*

Good. Whatever it takes, get those boats off the beach, even if you have to leave the rest of us behind. We'll respawn, and it'll be fine.

Roger.

My team had just become the distraction. If we could draw the aliens' attention while Smith and Brown stole the boats, this would be an all-out win. A couple of respawns was nothing compared to what we had just looted.

They have a spot about fifteen yards from our boats. They haven't moved in a minute. I think they're setting up some sort of entrenchment.

I pinged my map. "We're going to come in on this side, away from the boats. They may see us anyway, but it'll draw the attention away while Brown and Smith get the boats out. Sage, I want you to try to get away."

She shook her head. "It's too risky. If I don't go with you, they'll know it's a feint. We don't have any way of camouflaging."

That, at least, was true. I nodded. "All right. Bill, Bob, we're up first."

Bill and Bob had their guandao polearms out, and I had my revolver, as we charged across the sands like it was the beach at Normandy. The aliens must have been taken off guard. They turned, raising their weird guns to shoot us. One lobbed blobs of purple goo my way, but missed. I shot him. I couldn't tell if it was the same one I'd killed previously, because—I hate to say it, but they all looked the same to me. They had shiny silver uniforms with various different alien decorations on them that meant nothing to me.

I felt a tingling sensation and looked down. One of the purple blobs had hit my left arm. It was crawling up it, encasing my arm in purple jelly. My skin burned.

I tried to shake it free. I didn't dare claw at it, even though I wanted to. Instead, I raised my gun and fired again, taking one of the aliens out of the fight.

Tall Smith and Brown were at the boats. They were hauling one to the edge of the water together. Smith jumped in, got one hand on the oar and the other on the tiller, and the boat started off. Brown went back for the other boat.

"Help him out!" I shouted to Sage and Grandpa. Sage had Lassoed one of the aliens again, preventing it from shooting at us. She ran for the boat, Grandpa on her heels.

Bill, Bob, and I charged the aliens. They had erected a small metal wall facing toward our boats and had something that looked a little too much like a machine gun for my liking aimed right at them. One of the remaining aliens dove for the machine gun. I shot at him and missed.

The burning in my arm was intensifying. I glanced down and nearly lost my lunch. My arm was gone. I could see white bone under the jelly, and it was crawling up higher. It had begun to wrap around my chest. I fired a Trick Shot at the alien with the machine gun and winged it. Bill and Bob blasted away with their mini-guns. Another of the aliens fell forward.

Across the beach, Grandpa and Sage had reached the small boat. They were helping Brown pull it toward the water.

There was one alien left. He had a gun, and he was aiming it at my family. It didn't matter to me that death was only temporary right now. I wasn't going to let some alien melt my sister.

I threw myself forward and wrapped my jelly-covered skeleton arm around the neck of the alien. The goo moved off my arm and onto its face. The alien began flailing and kicking, letting out the most horrendous noises, like a pig being butchered if that pig had swallowed an accordion. I felt triumphant. I also was almost dead.

"Get to the boat!" I yelled to Bill and Bob. As I wrestled with the alien, they took off running, not even stopping to look back. My health was still ticking down. I had a debuff on me called Eaten Alive and about **[30 HP]** left.

I saw the boat hit the water and start away. They were safe.

I reached for my revolver. I couldn't aim it. The pain was too much. I was lying on the sand with the alien under me as the purple blob ate away at both of our health. I had almost nothing left.

I fired a Trick Shot right at my own head.

CHAPTER FIFTEEN

OUTPOST CONSTRUCTION FOR EVEN BIGGER DUMMIES

A Beginner's Guide to Constructing Your Phase Two Outpost, Section 3.1: Basic Base Building for Beginners

Interview conducted by Colonel Jefferson Ames, US Army.

Interview subject: Daronda Velross, Former Base Planner. (Note: Sources indicate Daronda was fired by three previous conglomerates for incompetence and has since been working as a dishwasher in a dive bar on the Hub.)

An early mistake people make is overextending. You've got to get your core base set up before you start trying to claim smaller nodes or take resource spawns. I know that sounds obvious, but people are always making that mistake.

It's a real art to decide what to construct first, second, third. If you don't get your defenses up, your combatant miners will be tied down defending the base from the spawn. If you don't build a miner respawn point, you'll come back far away from the base and be out of the fight for ten times as long. If you don't have your buff buildings, you'll be fighting at a disadvantage.

It's an art form. And you Earthlings just don't have the experience to know how much you need me. It's fortunate for you I'm available right now.

No, I don't want to give away my secrets.

Okay, I'll give you a hint. Autonomous Self-Replicating Miniature Attack Millipedes. SWARM for short. Huh? Well, it does in my language. You have to get as many of the basic base-cleaning miniature attendant kits as you can, then hack them with a military-grade AI. I know the backdoors to remove the safety features. They're much better than static guns. Just imagine your foes being devoured from the legs up by a swarm of tiny metal bugs! And that's just one of my innovations. My hourly rates are very reasonable . . .

(Note: Sources were VERY EMPHATIC that we do NOT want to hire Velross. We have offered them a small stipend to answer questions on a standby basis).

*

The other downside of dying is when you respawn on the boat and don't have any landing craft to get you out of there, you have to sit around waiting for an hour for someone to get back. Luckily, I had plenty of time to start on a new hobby. One of the NPC sailors showed me how to whittle.

By the time we all made it back to our island, we had forty minutes until our wave clear timer expired, so we went and took out the wave six spawn before taking a break. We still had sixteen hours and thirty-two minutes before the node was ours.

It was hard to believe, but everything had taken less than eight hours. I was tired and ready for more than a short rest. I ate a boxed meal Mama Grace had sent along while reclining in the grass by our node capture point.

Sage had burned through her lunch and a whole pile of snacks and was now jumping up and down, reenacting the raid for the benefit of Team Ragtag. Her version was even more exciting than the real one, since there were about three times as many aliens and they had Mega Death Ray Blaster Mark X weapons, whatever those were. She was just giving a dramatic charade of my dying fight against the final alien as the rest of the team sailed triumphantly yet sadly away from the beach, Sage weeping into the waves as I perished, when I had to interrupt.

"I did *not* say, ''Tis better to die a thousand deaths than live in ignominy.' I don't even know what 'ignominy' means."

"Well, you would have said it if you'd taken any time to think about these things. You're going to have a lot of opportunities to die, apparently, Shad. You need to start thinking of good last words."

"They're not last words. You just respawn. It's not that big a deal."

"It is if you do it too many times," Grandpa said. "I've been looking through the rule set provided by the system. You may have missed the section that says more than three times your number of team players' deaths in a single twenty-four-hour period will incur a permanent one-hour respawn cooldown. And it stacks."

I blinked. "Which section?"

Grandpa gave the citation. I pulled it up and read through, trying to understand. "So if we have fifteen people on the team," I gestured at everyone around the node, "and we die, uh, forty-five times in one twenty-four-hour period, then after that we'll have a one-hour respawn timer forever."

"Do it again, and that's a two-hour timer," Grandpa reminded me.

"That could get really ugly really fast. Oof." I started skimming through the rules. "There's got to be a way to reset that, surely. It's just begging for some griefer to take advantage of."

"There's an upgrade for our player respawn beacon," Sage said after a minute. "It's in Section 14.9.3.7, Allowed Tertiary Building Modifications. It's expensive, though. Forty thousand soul coins."

I tried to do some math, but failed. One peculiarity of the phase two rule set was that you could not bring soul coin currency in from elsewhere in the Reality Engine. Any soul coins you spent to upgrade your buildings had to be earned in this map. However, at the end of the phase, if you were holding an outpost, you got back all the soul coins invested in it. It was an incentive for people to improve their outposts and then hold them.

"We'll definitely pay for that upgrade if it becomes necessary," I said. "But for now, I guess we should try not to die so much."

"Speak for yourself," one of the Smiths said. "You're the only one who's died twice. The first time definitely wasn't necessary."

"I was trying to save everybody else a wasted trip back to the boat," I said in my own defense. "Besides, I wanted to know how badly it hurt before I told anyone else to go through it. I mean, we knew it worked, since Ice Spice had already respawned, but I couldn't ask anyone to do something I wouldn't."

Tall Smith looked taken aback. "Really?"

"Yeah?"

"Interesting." He didn't say any more, but went back to eating his packaged alien MRE. I knew Mama Grace had offered Team Mongoose some of her delicious homemade lunches and wasn't sure why they had refused. Didn't matter. Sooner or later, they would get a better look at all the snacks Sage was eating, and then they'd be hooked.

After our break, we fought off another two waves of skeleton pirates and cannibal pigs, and then Grandpa instructed all of us to lay down and try to nap for forty-five minutes or so. He and Jones would keep watch. I agreed on the condition that he'd get some rest once I was done.

I lay down and was asleep instantly. That's one benefit of having been through basic training. You can sleep anywhere, anytime. We swapped turns after forty-five minutes. I felt much better for the shut-eye.

I let Grandpa snooze while Sage and I started looking over our haul. "We have so much stuff," Sage gloated. "We're going to be able to create an awesome, *awesome* defensive line here."

"Yeah. Hopefully there's not too many repercussions from this," I said. I was starting to feel a little bit of buyer's remorse as the adrenaline finally drained away. "That other team is not going to be happy."

"Maybe they didn't figure out who we were," Sage said.

"Pretty sure they'll figure that out."

"Whoa, cool," Sage said as she pulled out a crate and examined it. "Look at this! It's my own personal skeleton pirate army." She held up the box. It was labeled "Standard NPC Recruit Squad, Appropriately Themed for Map," and then underneath, in a different font, it said, "Skeleton Crew! This contains the pattern for one unit of NPC troops that may be commanded by a sponsored team member."

There were more details listed below that. The item could be equipped here in this map and reused indefinitely. It just had a cooldown after each use. We could use it to generate a squad of skeleton pirates: melee style, ranged, or a mix of both. The pirates would have [40 HP] each and attack at the direction of their summoner.

"Are there more?" Sage asked. She dug around through her inventory. "I've got another one. What about you, Shad?"

"No, nothing that cool. You should ask Grandpa."

"I will," she said, "as soon as he's awake. Oh, this is so cool, Shad. I'm going to have my very own skeleton army. I need to figure out if I can buff them up somehow." She buried herself in her inventory again, cataloging the contents.

It seemed like we had really accomplished something here. We had our foothold underway and we had made a move nobody would expect. I was feeling pretty good about myself.

Grandpa brought me back to earth quickly, once he woke back up. "We got lucky," he said. "If we'd been attacked during the raid, we could have lost everything."

"Then why'd you agree?"

"It was a gamble worth taking. We're never going to upset the status quo by playing it safe. I don't care what Veda wants. I don't even much care what Ames wants." He leaned back against our stockade wall, arms folded across his chest. "I'm personally grateful to the aliens that took us. I'd be dead by now if they hadn't. But that doesn't give them the right to turn us humans into slaves. We're one of the only Earthling teams here, and we just told anyone who's watching that we're more than pawns." He walked over to the node and laid a hand against it as he looked up at the timer. "They're here to take our land and push us out, and maybe they will. We haven't got much chance of winning. But at least we will make them remember our names, remember that we fought back."

I nodded. There wasn't much else for me to say. "If all we manage to do is write 'Twofeather was here' all over their records, that's enough for me."

CHAPTER SIXTEEN

INFLATABLE BUILDINGS AND YOU: THE UPS, THE DOWNS, AND THE DEFLATIONS

So, I need you to take over setting up the defenses for me," I told Juana. "We've kind of got a lot more than we'd planned. I need to get back out there and help Grandpa."

"What am I supposed to do with all this?" Juana spun in place, staring at our piles of ill-gotten loot.

Our twenty-four-hour timer was up. The node officially belonged to the Misfits Guild. Now the portal was open and our small army of crafters and expert farm-level miners streamed in.

Grandpa and the rest of the combatants were out stopping the creep waves that had started spawning just as soon as the node converted. I'd rather have been there, but he ordered me to stay behind and brief Juana. There were eight different spawn points around the island—the same locations we had cleared during the initial phase. Now every thirty minutes, waves of skeleton pirates, cannibal pigs, and other mobs spawned and began moving toward our base.

As soon as we got the defenses set up, we could start letting the turrets and other automations handle the creep. That would free us up for better things, like hunting rare spawn. It was also the main way to make money here in phase two. Sure, we got an hourly income from the node, but each creep killed by our automated defenses was worth an extra soul coin bounty. No coin for killing them ourselves, which seemed backward, but it did motivate us to get everything built.

Juana had come in with the first wave to help set up the defenses. She had a knack for that sort of thing. In preparation for phase two, she managed to acquire an Organize Base skill. We hadn't had a chance to try it out yet, but this seemed like the perfect opportunity.

She, along with the farming and crafting staff, had a bright yellow tag over their heads: "Noncombat Miner." Our bid for this map had specified only fifteen combatants. Team Twofeather, Team Mongoose, and Team Ragtag would be allowed to engage other combatants and the creep that spawned to attack our base. Nobody else would be able to fight: if they tried, their abilities would fizzle out. On the other hand, they also couldn't be harmed.

That restriction was lifted for the special resource nodes. If those challenges included, say, killing feathered dinosaurs for their leathery hides and meat, the noncombat miners would be able to help—and the dinosaurs would be after them in return.

"So we get these defenses set up and then, what? I have to babysit them for the rest of the phase? What are you going to be doing?" Juana asked, with her hands on her hips and her head cocked, eyes flashing.

It was a fair question, but it caught me off guard. Juana had never seemed interested in being part of the action before. I cleared my throat. "We'll keep a small crew on hand here to make sure we're ready to defend against surprises. But the main use for the mission teams is going to be taking down rare spawns or securing resource nodes. Or fighting against other teams."

"How often is that last one going to happen?" she asked.

I ticked off the likely scenarios on my fingers. "If they come to try to take our node away, if we decide to try to take theirs, or apparently there are events that can pop up that will require at least one five-member group from each nearby claimed node to go and fight over it."

"What happens if you don't go?"

"Your node goes back into claiming mode and all of your automated defenses shut down for twenty-four hours until you've proved it again," I answered.

"Ouch," Juana said. "Yeah, that wouldn't be good."

"As soon as we've got some of these defenses set up, I'm going to see about scouting out a couple of the nearby resource nodes. There's some sort of school of fish close by that says it drops meat, as well as scales and bone that can be used as crafting materials."

"Then let's get on it," Juana said, looking at what my team and I had already set up.

We had the crates arrayed as a kind of outline of the defenses we were going to make. We'd laid out a circle around the node, ten meters in diameter, which was the distance we'd gotten from the *Beginner's Guide to Constructing Your Phase Two Outpost*.

Juana pointed as she spoke. "My Organize Base skill is suggesting a couple of tweaks. You're building turrets every eight feet, but if we spread them to ten feet we'll have room to put elemental cannons in between. Otherwise we'll just have to move all the turrets once we can afford the cannons."

I had shared the outpost guide with her before starting phase two. It sounded like Juana had been studying up as hard as I had.

"We can do that. I only planted the first couple of turrets. There's so much to do, I can't quite figure out what to do first."

"That's my job," Juana said. "Planting buildings has a cooldown, so let's get one started. Let's start with the barracks, then the miner respawn facility."

"You think the barracks are worth the cost right off?" I'd been eyeing the barracks myself. It was going to cost us nearly all of the soul coins we had earned in the first twenty-four-hour period, and that was with using some of Veda's outside mods to get it up to strength.

Juana nodded. "It'll let up to ten team members rest at a time. Anyone who rests in the barracks gets a buff to their effectiveness, as well as a small health pool increase for the next twelve hours. The really important thing is you can rest there for four hours, and it has the effect of a full night's sleep. So for our mission teams, it'll cut our downtime in half."

"All right, but I think we need the map next, not the respawn point." I led her out into the second defensive ring, another ten meters beyond the first, where we had a box unpacked and ready to go. "It's not too expensive, but it will let us see the vicinity around us. If someone launches an attack on another team's node, that will be shown. If somebody claims another node, that'll be shown, too. Right now, it's limited to about one hundred nautical miles around, same as the one on the ship."

"Upgrades aren't too expensive," Juana said, her eyes unfocusing for a second as she probably consulted the guide. "How big is this map? How many other parties are there?"

"Veda passed us a list of participants. There are twenty-seven major conglomerates with multiple teams each, one hundred and three smaller organizations like Veda's, and sixteen of what she calls NGOs, nongovernment organizations, I think. I'm not entirely clear. The way she talked about it, some of them sounded like religious orders."

"How many other human-backed teams?"

"Well, there's a lot of miners and crafters being hired on to do farming. And, uh, three human-lead teams."

"That's it?" Juana's eyebrows raised. "Really?"

"We wouldn't be here if Veda hadn't told us to train by running missions. Sounds like most of the galactics were planning on bringing in their own people all along. I bet most sponsors steered their miners away from missions."

"You might be right," Juana said. "Okay, barracks, then map, then respawn. How does this communications array strike you as our fourth build?"

"I'm not sure how necessary that's going to be. Since everyone here is part of the same coalition, we have our guild chat to fall back on. We can talk to Veda, since she's our coalition sponsor."

"It says here it allows for communication with rival factions."

"So?" I said. "Why do we want to talk to them? We're trying to take their stuff."

Juana sighed. "Shad, you're a nice guy, and it sounds like you're really good in the gunslinging field. But you really don't have a future as a politician, do you?"

"I sure as hell hope not," I said. I could already hear Sage commenting on that idea.

Juana nodded as though that settled something. "It's going on my list for when we can afford it. Let's get the bunkhouse building, then you can get out of my hair while I start setting up turrets."

I grinned. "I like the sound of bunkhouse a lot better than barracks. Bunkhouse it is. We'll set up a chow wagon outside of it, stocked with as much fresh home-cooked food as we can. We'll have to see if we can persuade your mom to come through and make us dinner sometimes."

Growing the bunkhouse was pretty darn cool. Juana opened the box containing it, and a system message popped up for us both to read, saying,

[Do you want to activate this building?
Yes/No.
Warning. Building cannot be moved once it has been created.
Building must be destroyed and recreated.
Warning. This building is capable of taking six expansions.
If you place this building in a location where it cannot expand,
those expansion slots will be unusable.]

I already knew this from the guide, and had marked out the edges of the bunkhouse's eventual footprint with a couple of stakes from my inventory. I told the system "Yes," and leapt back as the bunkhouse sprang into existence.

It folded up out of the crate and rapidly expanded, reminding me of one of those bouncy houses at a kid's birthday party that inflated from a plastic bag to, well, a plastic bag shaped like a castle or something.

"I'm going to work on the turrets," Juana announced as I considered our new building. The bunkhouse was square, squat, and concrete gray. That was no fun. I accessed its properties through the system and played around until I had a long, low, one-story building with wood slat siding and a shingled roof. I even added a porch with a rocking chair on it. The rocking chair didn't offer any kind of buff. It was just for the ambiance.

I stepped up onto the porch, then opened the door. It creaked satisfyingly under my hand. I stepped inside. Five stacks of bunk beds lined the small room, with a little washroom at the far end. There was a cheerful braided rug on the floor, and each of the beds was covered in a homey scrap quilt. Pegs by each bunk offered a place to hang up a coat or a hat or what have you.

I nodded appreciatively. "That's more like it," I said aloud.

By the time Grandpa got back from making the rounds of the island, killing creep as it spawned, Juana had the first set of turrets up. She'd also sorted through our stolen goods and located a pair of elemental cannons that she mounted by the front gates, programming them with an icy attack that would debuff enemies, making them move slower as they wound their way through our defenses.

We had built the bunkhouse, the map table, and a simple crafter's shed that would allow our farmers and crafters to start using the materials they would hopefully collect.

I had resisted adding any particular tools, like the leather-curing or fish-drying racks that Juana suggested, saying we would get those when we knew exactly what kind of mats we had to work with. I reminded her we had a strict budget.

We also had the miner respawn point under construction. That was placed inside the inner circle for the very simple reason that it had a twenty-four-hour cooldown on construction. If we lost this one, it would be twenty-four hours before we could build another one. That made it a vulnerable point that enemies would be looking to attack.

We were out of money for now, but with the turrets coming online, we had enough set up to start killing creep here at the outpost and really make bank.

Grandpa looked around appreciatively, then settled into the rocking chair. "Starting to look downright homey," he said.

"We should have enough of the defenses up in another hour to let them start taking over," I said. "I'd like to take a team out to check out the fish resource and see about getting that harvested."

"Good thought," he said. He looked around. "Where's Sage?"

"I thought she was with you," I said.

Grandpa stood back up from the rocking chair. "No," he said grimly. "She wasn't."

We pinged her in chat. A minute later, she replied, *What is it?*

Where are you, young lady?

Out foraging, she replied. I could practically hear the defensiveness in her voice now. She knew very well that when Grandpa started slinging around "*young lady,*" she was in trouble.

Ping the map where you are, Grandpa said.

A minute later, it lit up. There were three green dots near hers and no red ones, so I relaxed.

Who's with you?

Dwight and Amity. And Mitch.

Dwight and Amity were the two best crafters in our coalition. Mitch was one of the new recruits from Team Ragtag. My suspicions went through the roof. *What are you up to?*

We were trying an experiment. It kind of worked. We're on our way back now. She stopped talking in chat.

Grandpa and I looked at each other. I shook my head. "I know there's respawns now, but that doesn't mean I like her wandering off and doing whatever she likes."

"No, indeed," Grandpa said. "We're supposed to be a team here."

"I'll remind her of that."

A couple of minutes later, Sage marched back into camp. Dwight and Amity followed her, almost bent double under the weight of the heavy loads they were carrying. Each of them had a wooden yoke over their neck with a pair of baskets dangling from it. Mitch trailed along behind the other three, looking smug.

Grandpa and I hurried over to meet them. "What's this?"

"Well, I noticed when we were fighting the pigs that they had buckets set up by the trees with some sort of pegs in the trees," Sage said defensively. "And I thought later, 'That looked funny.' It reminded me of how people make maple syrup, but these aren't maple trees, so I was wondering what they were. And then I had an idea, so we went to look. Mitch agreed with me," she added.

Mitch nodded. The Canadian redneck was a Tapper class, which apparently was explosives-focused but with a maple tree and syrup theme. "Got a nice bonus by using my noncombat skill on the taps!"

Dwight set down his baskets carefully. He stepped back, and I took a look inside. The basket was absolutely full of a milky white liquid. "What is that?" I asked. "Palm juice?"

"Better than that." Dwight's eyes were shining. "That, my friend, is rubber in its natural state. The trees on this island produce rubber."

"What?" I would have killed for the map right now. "It didn't say anything about that on the map back on the ship. The trees weren't marked as a resource."

"They weren't marked as a resource *deposit*," Sage said patiently. "That doesn't mean we can't harvest other resources. It just means it's not something you have to fight for. Well, not if you've already cleared out the NPC camps, that is." She sounded triumphant. "There are so many things we can make out of this. Better gear for everyone. Improved weapons."

"She's not exaggerating," Dwight said. "This definitely will give us an edge. And Mitch's bonus will really help out. If he can come by once a day and refresh it, we'll be swimming in the stuff. Rubber's incredibly versatile, and it's hard to replace with anything else. Nobody's found a rubber source in any of the farming levels before this."

"Don't you have to refine it or something?"

"Yes," Sage said. "So look through the listings and figure out how we can build a rubber refinery station."

"I've already found it," Juana called over. "The pattern's in the database. We can adapt one of the basic crafting stations to refine rubber, but it's a pretty big footprint item. I think it's going to have to go in the second ring. And it's expensive. We won't be able to afford it until sometime tomorrow at the earliest."

"That's fine," Sage said cheerfully. "That just gives us all time to start collecting now."

Grandpa and I shared a glance. "Sage," I said, "you need to let us know about this sort of brainwave. It was a great idea. Really valuable. I'm glad that you thought of it. But we need the team to be in on it."

"The team," she said scornfully. "What team? You mean you and Grandpa want to vote down anything that you don't like the sound of?"

"That's not quite how I meant it," I protested.

"You sure it isn't?"

"We definitely would have gone after the rubber," I said. "Just maybe not yet."

Sage put her hands on her hips and looked me in the eye. "Look, Shad, I know I'm twelve. I know you still think of me as your little sister. I *am* your little sister. But right now, right here, we're equals. You need to get that through your thick head. I am as much a member of this team as anyone else here. Would you have scolded Dwight if he'd gone off on his own?"

"Well, hell yes," I snapped. "The point of being a team is that nobody goes off on their own."

"And how much did you ask the rest of us before you ran into that pig camp and blew yourself up?" she demanded.

There was a long, awkward silence. Juana said carefully, "He did what?"

"It was a strategic move," I mumbled.

"He triggered Dwight's big boom bomb while he was holding it," Sage said in disgust. "Just 'cause he was in a rush to get back to the ship and look at the map."

Juana sighed. "All right. That isn't such a dumb thing to do, or as dumb as it sounds, I guess. But really, Shad, you should listen to your sister."

I turned on her. "What, you too?"

"All right," Grandpa said. "Enough bickering. I'm recalling the team. Next creep wave spawns in twenty minutes and we're going to test just how good the defenses are." He grinned at me. "You get to stand outside the final gate and stop 'em with your face if the turrets don't work. I've got a bet going with Frank that you die three times today."

CHAPTER SEVENTEEN

HUMANS VS. ORCS: STRATEGIES AND TACTICS

A Beginner's Guide to Constructing Your Phase Two Outpost, Section 5.1: Alternative Strategies

Interview conducted by Colonel Jefferson Ames, US Army.

Interview subject: The Great Impressario Rodari of Sirius Major, in an expansive mood after a party in his honor at the Aldebaran Embassy.

Since you and your allies are new to phase two and have never built an outpost before, you might want to consider an alternative strategy.

Yes, there are plenty of ways to win the game. The biggest conglomerates are going to take and hold an alpha node or three while their contracted allies gather more resources. They are either gearing up for their phase three efforts or preparing to sell to the dedicated phase three groups. Your first option? Offer to work with some of them. Put your crew to work as mercenaries, hire out your crafters and anyone who's good at farming. The conglomerates are always looking to hire locals for that sort of work.

Option two: Become pirates. Nobody likes pirates, but there are always a couple of groups in every map. The pirate outfits go around attacking outposts they think might be vulnerable. They don't necessarily have to win for long. Even just taking and claiming a node for themselves can generate money, plus you get a soul coin bounty if you destroy someone's outpost entirely. Twenty percent of what they've put into building it.

The real key is you don't necessarily even have to succeed. Just make it look like you're going to, and then demand a ransom in order to leave. What's that word? Danegeld? I don't know that one.

Oh, yes. Yes, exactly. Just be careful if you try that strategy. You might piss off the wrong people.

I sat bolt upright in the bunkhouse as someone shook me awake.

Jones stood over me, looking worried. One of the Smiths was at Grandpa's side, pulling him out of a sleep cycle.

I checked. It had only been two hours. I hadn't even gotten my Rested buff. "What's wrong?"

"We've got invaders."

I leapt out of bed and grabbed for my gun belt, strapped it on, then shrugged into my coat.

Grandpa was on his feet. Sage sat up, swinging her legs over the edge of the top bunk she had claimed a few hours earlier. I checked my map. There were a bunch of red dots heading toward our outpost in three groups of five. They were making a pincer formation. Creep showed up on the map as a steady stream of orange dots, so I knew these had to be something different.

We rolled out of the bunkhouse and surveyed the outpost. Our crafters were hard at work refining the materials the farmers were bringing back from the resource nodes they'd harvested all over the island.

"Anyone had eyes on them yet?" Grandpa asked.

"We've sent out Ragtag as spotters," Jones said. "They're supposed to get eyes on but not engage."

"Good," Grandpa said. "I want the farmers and crafters pulled back." He sent out the order right away, and got an instant flood of questions in response. "NOW!" Grandpa bellowed to everyone in hearing range. Reluctantly, the crafters left their work and streamed up the hill to the node.

"They can't be harmed," Tall Smith objected. "We might as well leave them out there."

"I guarantee you people who have been playing this game longer than we've been using tools have tricks up their sleeves," Grandpa said grimly. "I can think of three or four ways to interfere with noncombatants without causing any physical harm myself."

He sent out a follow-up message on the coalition's main communication channel with more details. That also alerted our allies back in Threshold.

What was going on? I sent Veda a message. She replied back almost immediately. *I'm not surprised, seeing as you idiots went after the wrong node. Of course someone's going to try to take it away from you.*

I winced. *Ouch. So you heard.*

Juana filled me in. We need to talk, Shad.

I sighed. Even as a guy who'd never had a serious girlfriend, the phrase "we need to talk" still left me with chills.

I've kinda got an invasion to deal with here.

Just then, we got a reply from the Ragtag scouts. Lara reported, *I have eyes on the southwest group. There's five of them. They look like orcs to me, and they're from the Firebrand Cooperative.*

I passed the message along to Veda. Grandpa was asking for more intel from our spies, guesses as to what their abilities were, that sort of thing.

Veda replied back to me. *Firebrand is a known merc and pirate operation. They might be hired out on behalf of one of the larger conglomerates. I've heard Alabaster Sky is making a play for a foothold in this sector. Or they could be playing opportunistically, trying to force you guys to pay a ransom.*

Not gonna happen, I replied at once.

I told Grandpa what Veda had said, then added, "If they're pirates, that's good news."

"Why's that?" Tall Smith asked me sharply.

"If we have one of the larger conglomerates seriously after our node, we'll have a much harder chance of holding it. With pirates, all we have to do is make it too expensive for them to keep attacking us."

"I think I see what you're getting at," Smith said, nodding. "It's the death penalty, right? Kill them enough and their respawn goes up."

"Exactly. There's fifteen of them. That means if we get forty-five kills on them in an hour, their respawn timer goes up. Permanently. I'm betting they won't stick around for that. We should be able to drive them off if we hit them hard enough. Once we get close to forty-five kills, they'll back off."

"Yes," Grandpa agreed, "but we've got to make sure that we keep our own death count low. We can't afford that penalty ourselves."

He messaged Team Ragtag. *Return to base. Avoid contact with the enemy. Do not, I repeat, do not engage. Pretend that your deaths matter.* They sent back affirmative replies.

I watched my map as our scouts' green dots moved carefully away from the red. "They're not making any kind of effort to hide from us. No camouflage skills. I would think pirates would have one of those," I said.

"Unless they're letting us know they're coming so they can start the extortion talks immediately," Grandpa said grimly. "Communication array up yet?"

Juana had wanted to build that next, but I had overruled her in favor of a couple of buffs to our turrets. "Not yet," I admitted. "We have the advantage here. We're behind defensive walls and our turrets will help us."

"But they know what they're doing," Grandpa reminded me helpfully.

"Yes, but we are desperate." I hoped that would help.

The farmers streamed up through the gates. I mentally checked each one off my list as they filed through the portal to make sure we didn't leave anyone behind. Once everyone was accounted for, I called up the outpost options and changed the wall settings. Now each of the two inner walls had a parapet running around the inside, four feet below the top of the wall. We'd be able to stand on our walls and shoot, then duck down behind the parapets for cover.

Team Ragtag had almost made it back by now. I looked nervously at our node. It was fine, surrounded by an intangible haze of shields. That could change quickly.

Ragtag wound their way through our lines of defenses, passing the last couple of farmers to report in, and joined us atop the hill. "All right," Grandpa said crisply. "How close are they?"

I checked my map. "Still about five minutes out."

"Okay, listen up, people!" Grandpa shouted. "I expect our enemies to make a priority of the respawn point. If they do that, then we'll be forced to respawn back on the boat. At that point we're fucked. Anyone who's killed will be out of the fight for too long."

Even Sage looked grim and serious, holding still as she listened intently.

"We want to let the defenses do as much as they can," I added. "We'll stay behind the walls, use our abilities from here. Kill them without getting killed, protect the respawn point."

Everyone was nodding in agreement. I checked my map again. The first team of enemies had reached the edge of our clearing and stopped, waiting for their friends to catch up. I shared the information with the others. The idea of letting our opponents dictate the terms of our engagement didn't sit right with me.

I turned to Jones. "What's the range on your drone bird?"

"About three quarters of a mile. Why?"

"I have an idea," I said. "But I'll need a good look at the enemy. Let's send it up and see."

Jones set the drone to heat-seeking mode, then sent it up to scout. A couple of moments later, he streamed the visual feed to our team as the bird circled above our hidden enemy. We could see their bodies outlined through the foliage as they moved toward the edge of the jungle. A moment later, they stepped out into the sand and the drone gave us a clear view of what we were up against.

I leaned forward instinctively, despite the fact that it wouldn't get me any closer to the feed playing across my vision, and got my first look at the invaders.

They were orcs, all right. Tall, green-skinned, and bald, with teeth that protruded out above their lower jaws that I could see even from a distance. Unlike stereotypical fantasy orcs, they weren't wearing loincloths or battered chain mail. Instead, they wore silvery bodysuits, tight at the ankle and wrist and billowing a bit in the middle, with logos on the front and back so thick they looked like NASCAR drivers.

One squad of five carried odd halberds, very long weapons with an axe head at one end and a nasty hook at the other. The second group to emerge from the brush carried rifles, but no obvious magazines. The guns were silvery, sleek, and wicked-looking. I kind of wanted to get my hands on one. The third squad hung back.

I targeted the first halberd-bearing orc and fired Trick Shot. The range on my Trick Shot had increased as I leveled up, and I could now make a shot from almost half a mile away. My bullet would zip past cover and track my target to ground if necessary. I just had to be able to see the target in the first place, which was why I had asked Jones to send up his drone.

Two of Team Ragtag also had abilities that could be targeted from far away and then fired. Annie's class was Magician's Apprentice. Her skills mostly revolved around illusion and battlefield control, although she also had a couple of nice damage abilities. Right now, she targeted the orcs and cast Misdirect Audience. A flash of light accompanied by a series of popping sounds went off just behind the orcs. Most of them turned to look, compelled by the spell. The two who resisted must have had higher wisdom levels than Annie's spell. Those who did look gained the debuff Fooled!, which would make them miss their targets more often for the next ten minutes.

At the same time, Mitch cast his once-daily Spike Their Trunks spell. Mitch was a Tapper. I had at first assumed that was a typo, then realized that didn't make sense. During our interviews, I had pushed him until he admitted that he hadn't read all of the details of the class as well as he should have. "I thought it was Sapper, too," he said. "Everything's about blowing stuff up and making holes and things. But, well." He looked embarrassed. "I'm Canadian, you see? My brother-in-law had a great opportunity involving a bit of contraband maple syrup. I was helping him out with that when we were taken. I ended up with a whole lot of gallons of unrefined sap in my inventory, and I guess the system cued off that when they offered me the class. I did have some sapper experience in the military, though, and all my abilities are good for offense."

"Are you why Mama Grace has been serving Sage authentic maple syrup with her pancakes?" I asked, raising an eyebrow. Those had been a recent addition to Mama Grace's restaurant and Sage ordered a giant stack every time we came in.

"Could be," he said. "Yeah, that's how I got hooked up with Misfits in the first place."

I knew Mitch had a shotgun that he had used during the wave clearing phase of outpost construction, but I had yet to see any of his special abilities in action. The descriptions of his skills made them sound pretty darn cool, though, and if Spike Their Trunks was any indication, he would be a powerful ally.

I watched as the five orcs with guns suddenly dropped their weapons and started swearing. Sage laughed. "Is that syrup coming out of their guns?" she asked.

"Yup," Mitch said proudly. "Those weapons won't be good for anything until they've gone and cleaned and repaired them, and that won't be fast." It was a great ability, though it had a day long cooldown and was limited to five opponents at a time.

The orcs checked their weapons, trying to clear them, even waving them over their heads to no avail. Finally, the guns disappeared into thin air and they all drew different weapons. Three had bulbous pistols, two had swapped to long knives. They regrouped with the halberd-wielding orcs as I fired another Trick Shot.

I was chipping away at the health of my target. They had larger health pools than any of us, [180 HP] apiece. I checked my messages and sent Veda a quick summary of our situation. I hoped that she wasn't too mad at us to help. This was her future on the line, too, so I thought she'd get over herself sooner or later.

"Here they come!" Jones shouted, recalling his drone as the orcs emerged from the tree line en masse.

The orcs began to storm the hill. They were fast—really, really fast, eating up the distance between us with long, loping strides. I fired another Trick Shot as it came off cooldown. The orcs were still well outside the range of my Barrage or a normal shot, but they were now close enough for Team Mongoose to take action. The soldier team had moved down into the second ring, M4s out. They were up on the walkway behind the second wall, shooting down as the orcs entered.

Our slowing turrets had them targeted. At our front entrance were a couple of high-end designs we'd looted from the beta node. The range on the turrets was insane, reaching twenty feet out from the entrance. They made keeping creep off us easy. By the time the creep even reached the entrance, they were half dead. Now the turrets were hitting the orcs, not knocking them down as easily as the creep but doing plenty to halt their rush.

The orcs with pistols shot back at the Mongeese while the ones with halberds waded forward as if through Mitch's maple syrup. Once in melee range, they attacked our turrets, striking with their long bladed weapons and chipping away at the turrets' hit points. The Mongeese kept ducking behind the parapets to avoid taking damage from the pistol shots. I fired another Trick Shot. Sage, Grandpa, and I all stood on the innermost parapet with the Ragtags filling in around the rest of the circle.

We had agreed to let Team Mongoose have the run of the outer ring. They were more used to this sort of fighting, and we would only get in their way. Still, Grandpa was looking longingly at the orcs as they made their way around the outermost ring, heading for our gate.

We had deliberately left the first gate, the entrance into our outer ring, open. Only four of the outer ring turrets, as well as the slowing turrets, could hit the area outside our first gate. They wouldn't do much damage while the orcs took down our gate. Since losing it was inevitable, and we would have gained very little in return, I opted to leave the gate down and let the orcs move straight into the kill zone.

Team Mongoose hosed down the orcs. I checked my map. The other five orcs were still hanging back in the trees. What were they doing? I sent a message to Jones. *Can you get your drone over there to find out what's going on?*

Roger, he replied without missing a beat as he fired down into the oncoming orcs. We dropped one of the halberd orcs, the one I had made my target for all of my Trick Shots. Sage let out a whoop. "One down, thirty-five to go!" she yelled, pumping a fist in the air.

"Our normal turrets are barely scratching them," Tall Smith noted. "But the ones you looted are chewing the hell out of 'em."

"Victory for Pirate Sage!" my sister cheered. "Her awesome foresight and larceny pays off again!"

"We've got a long fight ahead of us," I cautioned her. She just grinned and cast Mucking Out the Stalls in front of the lead group of orcs. They were letting the halberd-bearers go first, while the ones who had been riflemen followed behind. That might have been an effective tactic had they still had rifles, but with their mismatched weaponry, it just meant the disarmed orcs in the back were pretty damn ineffective. It was interesting that they didn't seem able to adjust on the fly.

I changed my target to one of the three gun-wielding orcs and set off another Trick Shot, then followed up with a Barrage into the same orc. The rings were tight enough together that I could now hit a target in the outer ring, as long as it was in the same quadrant as I was.

Grandpa hadn't stopped looking at the bogged-down orcs in Sage's muck. He fingered one of his tomahawks. "I could get down there and—"

"Nope," I said firmly.

"They won't be able to touch me with Shadow Step going."

"You could get in, but you won't be able to get out," I pointed out. "Remember, we've got to kill them more than they kill us." Grandpa sighed, but just kept hurling shuriken at each orc in turn.

The next orc to go down was one of the knife-wielders. His body lay in the muck for a moment before it shimmered and vanished. Jones sent me a message. *The five in the woods are up to something, boss.*

I didn't want to be distracted with the drone's point of view at the moment, so I asked Jones, *What do you see?*

For one, they're dressed different than these. They're wearing long purple robes with stars on them. Makes me think of wizards or something. They've got some sort of strange machinery in the woods. A thing that looks like a giant sarcophagus, and they're also building a contraption with wheels and a big ol' barrel on it. I think it's some sort of siege engine.

Uh-oh. Give me a quick shot of that, I replied. For a moment, my vision changed as Jones passed along his drone viewpoint to me. The image vanished almost as quickly as it had come, and I blinked, trying to make sense of it.

Jones was right. It looked for all the world like five orc wizards building some sort of contraption that would mean our doom. And what was with the sarcophagus? Had they brought some evil necromancer king along with them? Orcs always served evil wizards in the kind of fantasy books I had read growing up, but these were space orcs. They were different, right?

Suddenly, I noticed a dot on my map breaking away from the ones in the woods and making for us. A second later, another dot followed. I realized there were still five dots in the woods clumped up around the orcs' gear. These two were new.

"Ah, shit," I said aloud as they emerged from the woods. It was the halberd-bearing orc and the pistol-wielder we had just killed. They ran past the barrage of shots from our outer defenses and into the line of our first ring of defense. "They've got a portable respawn point!"

CHAPTER EIGHTEEN

THE IMPORTANCE OF REGULARLY SCHEDULED EQUIPMENT MAINTENANCE

Our enemies had brought a respawn point with them.

We were in trouble.

"The dead ones aren't going to be out of the fight for as long as we hoped," I shouted over the noise of combat.

"Yeah, but it means they won't take as long to kill our way through as we thought, either," Grandpa pointed out as one of our turrets dropped another orc.

"Time for something big," I said. The orcs in the woods were bothering me a lot. I wanted a quick breather so I could try to figure out what they were up to and concoct a plan. "Smith! Lara! Grenades on the orcs now!"

They obeyed, Smith throwing smoke grenades that filled the area with an obscuring haze, making it hard for the enemy to target us, while Lara merrily threw her oranges. I shot one of my boom rounds at the orc with the lowest health.

There was a massive explosion. Flames shot up all around the orcs. A cloud of smoke drifted across our outpost. I coughed and waved. "Who can see what's going on?"

"I've got eyes, sir," Jones reported. "Looks like three down. Three more hurting pretty bad. The two fresh ones are pretty high health, though." Jones had a thermal vision ability that let him see through small inconveniences like smoke bombs.

"All right, go hard," I said. "Let's push 'em all back for a minute so we can strategize." I leapt over the wall into the middle ring, then swarmed up the nearest ladder. I ran around the parapet until I was coughing my way through the smoke cloud.

It was rapidly clearing. As soon as I could see anything, I fired a Barrage, reloaded, and fired again. Another of the orcs fell. I reported it in.

"That's six!" Sage exclaimed. "Thirty-nine more to go. We can do this!"

I was starting to feel pretty good. We'd killed them six times, and they hadn't gotten us once.

Grandpa said "Incoming!" and Shadow Stepped in behind the lowest-health orc. He Scalped it hard, taking it down to **[10 HP]**, then Shadow Stepped behind one of the returned-from-death orcs, the one with the halberd, and hit it with a Counting Coup.

I fired again into the orc Grandpa had just Scalped, then reloaded as it dropped to the ground. "Seven!"

Sage appeared on the parapet beside me. "You're supposed to be on the other wall," I said.

"It's too far away for me to use this." Sage had her T-Shirt Cannon out. In the downtime, right before phase two started, she had acquired some paint and glitter and made it a bright, sparkly pink. It was kind of terrifying, if I'm being honest. When she fired at the remaining orcs, big cotton bands of fabric exploded in the air and then wrapped tightly around two of the orcs, binding their arms against their chests.

Grandpa Shadow Stepped behind one of the bound orcs and Scalped it. "That's more like it," he said. "I don't like sitting behind the walls. I like to get my hands dirty." I wondered, not for the first time, just what exactly he had done in Vietnam.

Annie had followed Sage to stand beside me. Now, all of a sudden, she was down in the melee near Grandpa. I started to yell and then saw she was standing next to me, too. It was her Sawn in Two ability, which let her create a doppelganger of herself who could launch attacks and hurt her enemies. She had only had **[30 HP]**, but when the doppelganger died, she was just fine. She was clobbering the orcs with a baseball bat.

Team Mongoose focused fire. A few seconds later, the last of the orcs died and his corpse despawned.

"Everyone back up to the inner ring," I said. "We need a quick chance to regroup. Who's keeping count? How many was that?"

"Twelve," Sage said promptly. "We killed all of them once and two of them twice."

Twelve. Not quite a third of the way there, but we had yet to take a loss. I breathed a sharp sigh of relief as we retreated back to our command post. I kept an eye on the mini-map as everyone had a quick drink of water. All fifteen orcs were back in the trees now, clumped together. I knew they had something up their sleeves.

Team Mongoose was congratulating one another. "Don't get too cocky," I warned. "I think they were feeling out our defenses here. They're up to something. Jones, can you show everyone what you showed me?" Jones shared the image from his drone. "Anyone got any ideas?" I asked.

"It looks like some sort of siege weapon to me," Mitch said, scratching his head. He replaced his big plaid trucker's cap and added thoughtfully, "I don't really want to see what they can do with it."

"Me neither," I said. "I'd like to blow it up before they have a chance to do whatever it is they're planning to do. If it *is* some sort of outpost-destroying device, anyone have any bright ideas how to deal with it?"

I checked my messages from Veda. She had replied during our fight, saying that her research on the Firebrand Corporation made her suspect they were loosely aligned with a galactic conglomerate who had taken a couple of alpha nodes about fifty miles away from our island. She thought they might be trying to take our node in order to put pressure on the two factions with alpha nodes near us. On the other hand, they could be mercenaries hired by the other factions—either Vortali or Existalis—to take out a threat.

That wasn't good news. If they wanted to take our node rather than just wanting to scare us into paying a ransom, then we might be in trouble. I asked her about the portable respawn point and the siege engine. She replied back immediately.

Portable respawn items exist, but they're incredibly expensive. Not something I would expect Firebrand to have. Maybe they raided somebody else's stash like you did.

That was possible, though from the way Veda had acted like our raid was something unprecedented, I thought it was unlikely. Her message continued. *Or maybe they have big-money backers. The other thing they're building is probably a Wall Blaster 9000. It's specifically designed to knock down outpost walls so that an enemy can walk through them instead of having to go around and be subjected to all of the turrets firing. The good news is the blaster has to be right up against a wall in order to punch through. The machines are incredibly slow to move and they've got a limited number of shots in them.*

Yeah, but we only have three walls, I pointed out. *Two if we don't close the outer gate.* Even putting a hole in one of our walls would cut our defenses down massively.

The Wall Blaster will be at its most vulnerable when it's set up to knock a hole in your wall. They're almost indestructible when they're being transported, Veda warned. *Incredibly thick, heavy armor.*

So, turtles, I said grimly. *Got it. Thanks for the information.*

I relayed what Veda had told me to the team and asked for opinions. "If it's machinery, I might be able to help," Lakshmi said. "My Crystal Vibrations are particularly effective against machinery." Lakshmi was a New Age Healer class. She had abilities like Smudge, which was a healing cloud, and Dreamcatcher, which could put an enemy into a forced sleep. I hadn't looked too closely at what Crystal Vibrations did, but I pulled it up now and checked.

There was some long, wordy, New Age description talking about the forces between forces and spiritual vibrations. But when I got down to the bottom, my eyes widened. An idea was starting to form.

I sent Grandpa a quick note. *I think we need to take a risk. It'll cost us a few lives, but getting our walls punched through would be worse.*

Name your team, Grandpa replied. *This is your show.*

I looked at the wording of Lakshmi's Crystal Vibrations ability one more time, the part down at the bottom that read: **[Disables nonorganic, nonsentient constructs for five minutes.]**

My brain raced furiously. The plan clicked together in my brain, but we needed to move fast. We couldn't afford to let the Firebrand orcs regain their momentum. "Annie," I said, "your hallucination ability, the Ventriloquist Dummies skill, how long can you keep it up?"

"Uh, probably about five minutes," she said. "I've never tried it in combat, though."

"This is your chance." I checked the party, making a mental roster. "Grandpa, I need you, Team Mongoose, Lakshmi, Lara, and Mitch." I saw Sage's expression, hesitated, then said, "Sage, is Three-Barrel Race long enough range that you can have one barrel inside our defensive lines and the other two at the orc camp or the woods nearby?"

Her eyes sparkled. "Yes."

"All right, I want you to set the one here before we get out there, then put down your other points as soon as we get close enough. Lara, your main job is going to be to get us out of there if things go really badly. Keep Minivan ready to go, otherwise do damage."

I gave them the rundown of the plan. Lara started nodding as I went. Jones and Brown rubbed their hands together and grinned. Lakshmi looked a little doubtful. "But why?"

I explained my reasoning. She shrugged. "You're the boss, Shad."

There was no sign of movement yet. Jones's drone swept in for another look. He flew it in low, and one of the orc wizards noticed it. The orc pointed a finger upward, and a jet of fire flowed out and baked the drone. The last image Jones shared was of a bunch of grinning orcs as the drone spiraled to the ground. "Fifteen-minute respawn on the drone," he informed us as it died.

"Let's go," I said as we vaulted over the rear wall, the opposite side of our outpost from where the orcs were hiding. Then Jones cast his Camouflage ability on us all. I urged everyone to still walk quietly and not speak unless necessary.

We made for the edge of the woods, then worked our way around until we were nearing the orc camp. I glanced back at our outpost. Eight human forms stood on the walls looking outward, clutching rough wooden rifles. Annie's Ventriloquist Dummy spell wasn't much good up close, but from a distance I hoped it would fool the orcs.

We got within twenty feet of their camp, crouching behind brush. *On my signal*, I typed in chat. I held up a hand. *Three, two, one.*

I dropped my hand and put my head down, sprinting for the enemy camp. As I came crashing through the brush, the orcs looked up. I cast Call 'em Out and then engaged Fastest Gun in the West.

I smashed across the underbrush and crashed my way through the trees, but fortunately the jungle here wasn't that thick. A couple of palm branches smacked me in the face as I dashed forward. The orcs yelled as they chased me.

Behind me, I heard the sound of machine-gun fire as Team Mongoose pursued the fleeing orcs into the brush. I turned and started shooting.

Grandpa teleported in. He Shadow Stepped behind the orcs, Scalped, and threw shuriken.

Our purpose right now was to create madness and distraction, and we were doing that well. Sage cast Mucking Out the Stalls, miring the orcs yet again. From the way they shouted, I didn't think they were fans.

It's done, Lakshmi said in chat.

Take them down now, as hard and fast as you can, I replied. I shot a Barrage through the heart of the closest orc, one of the halberd users. He responded by swinging the axe head of his long weapon at me. I darted back, but it caught my coat and slashed through the material.

I Reloaded and shot him again in the face this time. "You have any idea how much it costs me to have that repaired?" I demanded. Some of the orcs had turned back to deal with Team Mongoose, but the soldiers had gotten their machine gun nest set up and were busily hosing down orcs. It was an expensive formation, requiring multiple abilities with long cooldowns to coordinate together in order to work, but Team Mongoose was good with it.

They spat bullets at the orcs in a loud, long *rat-tat-tat*. A couple whizzed past me harmlessly. Brown had a skill that made his team's shots immaterial to his allies. It was a godsend in situations like this.

Meanwhile, Mitch was charging around the outskirts of the fight, attaching spigots and wire to various trees. When he'd made a complete circle, he yelled, "Get clear!"

I dove for the underbrush. Grandpa dodged away. A minute later, a ring of explosions went off, toppling palm trees inward as Mitch used his Trunk-Toward-Enemy ability and sent the trees crashing down on the orcs' heads. One by one, their health bars hit zero and the orcs despawned.

There was one left. I went after him, but Grandpa got there first. He hit a Scalp blow, but the orc turned on him and grabbed hold of his neck. The orc yanked Grandpa's head down toward his and bit into his jugular, hard.

Blood spurted from Grandpa's neck. His eyes went wide as his health drained away to nothing. A moment later, Grandpa's body dropped to the forest floor.

I screamed in anger as I emptied my cylinder into the orc. The orc's body fell toward Grandpa's, but Grandpa despawned before the orc hit the dirt.

Is that all of them? I asked the chat, trying to get myself under control. "Confirmed!" Sage yelled. "Lakshmi and I have been counting." *Grandpa, are you all right?* she asked.

I'm fine, sweetheart. Back at the outpost now. You all finish up there and get back here.

I breathed a sigh of relief, then returned quickly to the site of the orcs' strange machinery.

The respawn unit did look like a sarcophagus. It was a giant black rectangular box about eight feet long and four feet wide with a heavy-looking lid. It was covered in alien hieroglyphics outlined in gold. Lakshmi, at my orders, had used Crystal Vibrations on the respawn artifact. When we killed the orcs, they would come back on their ship, not here. It would take them several minutes to reach this point.

"How do we destroy this thing?" I asked.

"Leave that to me," Mitch said. He was pulling a bunch of strings and small brown-paper-wrapped parcels from his inventory.

"All right, then the rest of you, let's get on that." I indicated the siege weapon. The orcs had finished setting it up. It had four rough wooden wheels in two sets with solid axles running between them, a four-foot-by-four-foot platform atop the wheels, and then a construct on top of the platform that looked like a cross between a small battering ram and a trebuchet. Like if somehow you were using the battering ram part as the counterweight to the trebuchet. I didn't see how it could possibly work or how it ought to be able to punch through walls it was right up against, but none of this alien technology necessarily made sense.

"Come on," I said, putting my shoulder to the contraption. "Let's get this back to our outpost."

Sage giggled as she cast Cowgirl Cheer on all of us. It put a spring in my step. Then I grabbed at the device and we started pushing it.

Even with Sage's skill, the thing was damn heavy. It took us nearly fifteen minutes to get it the less than a quarter mile up the hill to our outpost. As soon as we had it inside the outer walls, the weight dropped away.

"It's under our control now," Sage said as she used her Eye-Spy ability on the thing. "Since it's inside our outpost and under our control, we can move it more easily."

"Let's get it to the inner circle," I said. I was checking my map every few seconds. The red dots had reached the far side of the island five minutes ago and were rushing through the jungle at breakneck speed. I closed the first gate behind me just in case the orcs reached us before we had their device back to our inner circle.

As I helped my team haul the orcs' siege weapon next to our node, I couldn't help grinning. "Veda better not have anything bad to say about this one," I observed. "We stole this fair and square." I checked my map again. The orcs were almost back to their encampment, and I saw that Mitch was still there. *What's wrong?* I sent. *Do you need help?*

Let me have this one, boss, he said. I couldn't figure out what he was talking about.

The first four orc dots reached the green dot. Two seconds later, an enormous fireball rocked the forest. The four red dots and the green dot all vanished. A moment later, Mitch emerged from our own respawn point.

He stretched, a grin splitting his face side to side. "Woohoo! That's the best I ever done blew up. How about that, eh? They were nearly back by the time I got done rigging it to blow, so I thought I'd see if I could lure a few of them in."

"Mitch, you're a genius," I said. I couldn't help feeling delighted. "What's the score?" I asked Sage. I had been keeping track myself, but Sage was having a blast with all of this. She had stayed out of trouble, like I asked, and I wanted her to be sure that we knew she was an important part of this team. "We need forty-five kills in one hour to give them that hour-long respawn timer. They should pull back if we're close to reaching that number."

"We killed twelve on their first assault, then all fifteen at the camp," she rattled off, "and four just now. So that's thirty-one. Fourteen more, and we've won this."

"Fourteen more in the next . . ." I checked the system clock and was surprised to see it had only been twenty-three minutes since the start of the orc assault. "Uh, thirty-seven minutes. We can do this," I said excitedly to Grandpa. We could get the forty-five kills within one hour it would take to give them a permanent one-hour timer on their respawns. No way they'd keep fighting with that at stake.

We regrouped, checked everyone's buffs, and waited for the next assault.

It didn't come. The orcs were huddling back where their equipment had been destroyed. "Are they trying to salvage their sarcophagus?" I asked Mitch, who shook his head.

"I know this alien tech stuff is something else, but there is no way that thing is in any pieces bigger than my thumb," he said, holding up his right hand to make his point. Then he stared at the thumb, shaking his head. "Still can't quite get used to having it back," he said. "I know this is all kinds of messed up, but there are some benefits to this Reality Engine thing. I was down to seven fingers and one thumb when I got taken."

I was going to reply when some movement on my map disrupted me. "We've got incoming," I said. "Just two of them."

We assembled at the edges of our walls to watch. A pair of orcs, one of the sorcerers and one of the halberd-bearers, marched out into the open field between our first line of defense and the forest. They stopped just outside the range of our turrets, and the halberd-bearer attached something to his shaft. He held it up, and the wind caught a white piece of cloth waving.

I looked at Grandpa. "You reckon that means parley in orc talk?"

"I suspect the system has filled them in on Earth customs," Grandpa said. "Come on, Shad, let's go have a chat."

"What if it's a trap?" Sage demanded.

"Then we will be at four deaths to their thirty-one," Grandpa said. "And their respawn point is destroyed. I think we can take the risk."

CHAPTER NINETEEN

HOW TO WIN A DUEL WITHOUT REALLY TRYING

Grandpa and I strolled out of our outpost to parley with the pair of orcs. I left the gate down. If we did have to run for it, it would save us a little bit of time. We stopped just inside range of our turrets. If the orcs tried to attack us with their weapons, we would try to draw them back toward our fortifications.

The wizard orc spoke. "I am Theram'goss, war chief of the Broken Tusk clan," he said. "I seek to parley with your leader."

"That'd be me," Grandpa said. "Major Louis Twofeather, US Army."

The orc blinked. "That is a title of some merit, my system tells me."

"Used to mean something. Not sure it does here anymore," Grandpa said. "But I'm not here to chit-chat. What can we do for you, fellows?"

The orc spread his hands wide and gave a great bow. "To an enemy far more honorable and powerful than we were led to believe. Our assessment of your strength was completely incorrect, but more than that," he said, "you have shown great courage and great cleverness. Not many of your fellows have done as well."

"Oh, you've fought a lot of Earthlings?"

"We have fought humans before," the orc said, "though you are the first from this system. Generally, human miners are weak and cowardly. You though, you take risks, but not foolish ones. It was very clever of you to target our Rek'hapmah chamber."

For the first time, the system didn't bother to translate the word. I wondered why.

"And then to steal our Hole Punch as well? That was well done."

I had to hide a snicker. So the bizarre-looking siege weapon was called a Hole Punch. I suppose there were worse names, like Wall Blaster 9000 or whatever Veda had called it.

"Tell me what you're here for," Grandpa said. "If you're looking to leave without a fight, be my guests. We won't chase you back to your ship. If you're just trying to kill time, well, the moment I think that's what you're doing, my team puts our next plan in action. You will not reach the end of the one-hour limit before we spill enough of your blood to make you pay."

The orc chieftain nodded. "I know some other species would hold back and wait until a later time before attacking, but that is not the way my kin and I operate. You have won a great strategic victory on many fronts. We would like to negotiate with you for the redemption of our own honor."

"Oh?"

"A duel," the orc chieftain said.

Grandpa raised an eyebrow. "Now, why exactly would we fight a duel when we're holding the upper hand? We're not going to cede our outpost."

"No, indeed," the orc chieftain said. "However, a duel will allow me and my men to prove to our superiors that either you are truly great fighters who have dealt us an earned victory, or perhaps that we could have triumphed had we attempted a different strategy, and that it was my foolishness in leadership that cost us this victory. If that is the case, they will doubtless require me to apologize to my ancestors for this error. In person."

I tried to think through all that. "Wait, so you want to have a duel—"

"And record it," the orc chief said, "with your permission. The system can give the recordings, but we will need your permission to do so."

"Right," I said. "You want to have a duel, record it, and show it to your superiors. And if you win, you're going to have to commit seppuku?"

The orc cocked his head to one side. "The system is translating your concept. Yes, I believe that is the correct interpretation."

"You've got to be nuts," I said.

The orc shrugged. "This is our way. If you will agree to the duel, we will conduct it here in the sight of your folk and mine. Should you win, we will pay you a reparation as an apology for taking a worthy foe so lightly. If we win, we shall take our recording and leave."

This has to be a trap, I told Grandpa in chat. *There's got to be a catch.*

They could be stalling for time, Grandpa suggested.

Hang on a second, I said. I sent a message to Juana. *We need you back here right now. ASAP. Emergency.*

Then I spoke to the orc. "I'm willing to agree to the duel as long as we have one of our people here to oversee the agreement. She's got the ability to create contracts that the system will back up."

The orc chieftain's eyes grew wide. "You Earth humans have a Makana, a wise woman, with you? One blessed by the system? Perhaps you are not the easy prey we usually seek." He raised his hands. "Perhaps I shall be vindicated."

Juana replied that she was on her way. I looked at Grandpa. "This is my duel," I said. I sent him a quick message. *I think we can get even more out of this. Remember how I always get the first shot?* Grandpa's mouth curled up at the edges, but he made no other sign that he had understood me.

"Our wise woman is on the way," Grandpa said. "While she comes, Chieftain Theram'goss, tell me, where are your people from? Another world like this?"

"The orc homeland was one of the first Reality Engines to be exploited by the Exploitation Committee once they formed fifteen thousand years ago," the orc chieftain said. "Though my people have suffered grievously in the years since, we have found our place. We do not like to live at ease without earning it, so many of us serve as mercenaries and miners for the Coalition. It is always good when we find a worthy adversary."

"Uh-huh," Grandpa said. "Were you working for yourselves or on a contract?"

"I will not reply," the orc chieftain said. "My duties do not include revealing my clan's secrets."

Juana hurried down the hill toward us. I had given her the very short briefing as she came. She took a deep breath as she stopped between Grandpa and the orcs. Smoothing her hair, she turned to the orc chieftain and gave a polite nod of her head. "Greetings, Chieftain Theram'goss. I am Juana Lopez of Misfits Guild. I am here to oversee the bargain between you and these men of my Coalition."

I stepped forward. "I will agree to duel with Chieftain Theram'goss. He and his men may record it and return it to his people. I stipulate that if I win, they may return without further hassle from us. They have promised to give a reward." I looked at the chieftain. He named a sum that made Juana's eyebrows shoot up. "If he wins, then they also return, though without paying us a ransom."

I had a thought. The amount the chieftain had offered, was it indeed a ransom? The equivalent of his life? If I won, killing him here, he would have his actual life spared and be able to return to his duties. I would have to look into that some other time.

"Conditions of the duel are as follows," I said. "We will mark out a circle, fifteen meters from a center point in all directions. The chief and I will stand at the center of the circle, back-to-back, and take ten paces away from each other. We will then turn and use any ranged weapon we like to take a shot at each other. If that shot is not decisive, then we may engage in any other form of combat desired. Anyone who leaves the circle admits defeat."

The orc chieftain was nodding in agreement. "Agreed," he said. "One final stipulation. If any other member of a team enters the circle during the duel, or assists from outside the circle, that team forfeits. Assistance includes healing or any ability affecting the inside of the circle, but shouting warnings or encouragement is allowed."

"Agreed," I said at once.

"Agreement witnessed and notarized." Juana used her notary stamp on her magic clipboard. She pulled out a piece of paper and handed it to the chief. "A copy for you."

He read it over and vanished it into thin air, then shouted to his people while Grandpa relayed the details of our agreement to the rest of our team.

Meanwhile, I marked out the dueling circle. Everybody on both teams wanted to watch, so we let them come down. The humans stood on one side of the circle, the orcs on the other. I reminded them all not to cross over the line.

"It's all right," I told them. "Even if I get killed, I'll respawn."

"Won't he just throw the fight?" Lakshmi asked. "After all, if you win, he's off the hook."

"I have a feeling his honor will require him to put up a decent fight," I said. "I'm gonna take it seriously. I just want to remind all of you, no matter what happens, don't cross over that boundary. You lose a fight for us, Veda's gonna have our hides. Did you hear how much money is on the line?"

I walked to the center of the ring, gave Chieftain Theram'goss a friendly salute, and we stood back-to-back.

Sage stood outside the circle, her hand raised. "On the count of ten," she said. "One, two." I took one stride forward, then another. She counted down dramatically, but not too slowly, and I paced along to her count. "Ten," she finished.

I turned and drew my revolver. Chieftain Theram'goss, standing a good fifty feet from me, near the edge of the circle, had a bulbous pistol in his hand. He fired it at me, but nothing came out. He looked at it, frowning, raised it, fired again. Still nothing.

"What's this trick?" he demanded.

"Sorry," I said. "I've got an ability that says I get the first shot in every duel."

"Then take your shot," he demanded, holding his arms open wide. "I am ready."

"Yeah, but I'm not," I said. I deliberately holstered my gun, then stuck my thumbs through my gun belt. "See, I was just hoping you would clear up something for me. My employer thinks that Alabaster Sky is behind this. She thinks they're trying to make a move on us to put pressure on the closest couple of alpha nodes. I'd really, really like to know if that's the case, or if we've got a different enemy I don't know about."

His nostrils flared. "Why do you think anyone hired us at all?"

"Because after talking to you, I'm damn sure that if you were here for your own reasons, you'd still be attacking us. I think you stopped because your employer refuses to pay the fine you would have if you incur the respawn timer penalty. I think they told you to call us off, and you're trying to reclaim whatever scraps of honor you can with this duel."

The orc's eyes widened, then narrowed. "You understand much, Earthling. Do you have similar customs of honor?"

"We've got our own kinds of honor," I said. "Right now, my honor is wrapped up in keeping my family and friends safe. So I'd really like to know who's behind you."

"My contract says I should not reveal details."

"Ah," I said, "so you do have a contract."

The orc chieftain glared at me. Then, to my surprise, he threw back his head and guffawed. "You humans are tricky," he said. "I think I like you. Shall we get on with this?"

"How about a deal?" I said. "You answer three questions, yes or no. Then I'll take my shot."

"Very well, then."

I paused, collecting my thoughts. "Did Alabaster Sky hire you?"

Theram'goss shook his big green head. "No."

"Was it one of the powers behind the two closest alpha nodes?"

The orc grinned. "Yes."

I racked my memory for the names and came up with one of them. "Was it Existalis?"

Theram'goss shook his head. "No," he said. "And now I can be glad that I have not revealed my sponsor's name to you."

He winked. We both knew that by process of elimination I had determined who his contract was with. Vortali. The Proxima surrogates. I sent a note to Veda as I prepared my next ploy.

I deliberately removed a round from my gun belt, cracking open the cylinder and thumbing it into place. "I respect you and your people, Chieftain Theram'goss," I said. "I would very much enjoy if we had productive business dealings again."

"As would I," the orc said.

I clicked the cylinder back into place and cocked my gun. I raised the revolver and fired. My bullet flew true, no Trick Shots required, and struck the orc chieftain square in the center of his chest.

It exploded, hurling him backward twenty feet and out of the dueling ring. I only had a handful of knockback rounds, but had decided to use one for this duel.

[**The winner!**] the system announcer proclaimed. I looked overhead in gratitude. Juana's skill was really something, to be binding on the system itself.

[Shad Williams of Misfits Guild has defeated Chieftain Theram'goss of Firebrand Cooperative.]

I holstered my gun and stepped out of the circle. The orc got to his feet, dusting himself off. "That was not the match I had expected," he said.

"Nope, but it's the match you got," I retorted. "Keep in mind, I don't know what humans you've dealt with, but Earth humans, we're tricky. We don't risk losing a fight when there's something important at stake. Like a war chief's ransom, or the life of an honorable man."

I wasn't sure what good etiquette was in orc society, but I stuck out my hand. Theram'goss looked at it, then clasped his own hand around my wrist. I tightened my fingers around his wrist in response, and we shook.

I walked back to our outpost on wobbly legs, relieved my ploy had worked. I had been a little worried that I would offend the chieftain with my nonlethal approach to our duel, but he seemed to have taken it in good humor.

We regrouped inside the outpost. "Let's get the crafters and farmers back to work," Grandpa said. "They've lost enough time here."

"Did the orcs send the money over?"

"The system transferred the money as soon as the duel was done," Juana said. "Our coffers are full."

"And we've got a really cool siege weapon, too," Sage said, looking over the Wall Blaster 9000. I wasn't sure I liked that name any better than "Hole Punch."

"Yes, but we're not planning on sieging anyone else's outpost, so it's fairly useless," Juana said. "I should see if I can sell it on the open market."

"And have someone bring it right back here and have to do all that again?" I said. "No way. We'll keep it in case of an emergency."

"What kind of emergency would we need something like that for?" Juana demanded, eyeing it with revulsion.

I shrugged, not wanting to admit I had already thought of several scenarios. Veda and Juana wouldn't approve of any of them, I was sure.

CHAPTER TWENTY

SELLING OUT: HOW TO GET WHAT YOU'RE REALLY WORTH

No, of course I'm not accusing you of attacking my team," Veda said smoothly to the hologram representing the head of Vortali Conglomerate here on the Hub. "I would never suggest such chicanery of a noble and storied conglomerate such as your own. I merely thought if you did have interest in the node my team has claimed, that we might be able to come to some sort of bargain."

"What sort?" the woman asked sharply. She was a sort of lizardfolk Veda had never seen before, with golden scales mottling to white around the edges of her neck and tall ears poking up through masses of dark, curling hair that should have been out of place, yet instead accented the beauty of her form. The woman's voice had a sibilant hiss to the edge, soothing and seductive at the same time. Veda had to keep reminding herself she was here to drive a bargain. "Are you looking to sell your interest?"

"In the team and the node both," Veda said. "My team has done all I have asked of them." She had just received her company's updated license with the endorsement stating they had successfully proved a phase two node in this Reality Engine exploit. She was now eligible for the next three Reality Engine exploit opportunities. As for the team, they had made far more soul coin than she had ever expected. She had even been able to take a small tithe of the profits and send them along to her family to get them out of storage for a couple of months. Her mother said that was all she needed to make marriage alliances for Veda's little sister.

The lizardfolk woman's eyes narrowed. "Indeed, it's not usual to give up such a profitable node at this juncture. Why, we haven't even had the first team challenge."

"I know that," Veda said, "but family duties are recalling me to my home. I cannot manage the team remotely, so I am looking to end my connection with them. I do have certain stipulations, however," she added quickly. "I have a slightly unusual contract with my combat team that would have to be honored by anyone buying me out."

"For the sake of argument, I would not mind looking at it," the lizardfolk woman said. Veda told her system to send over the excerpted contract she had made with Shad. She had removed a few personal details, but left the heart of the agreement intact.

"This is a great deal of autonomy for indigenous miners," the lizardfolk woman said after a moment.

"And you've seen how it has paid off," Veda said. "They've done all I've asked and more. I will see this honored. Also, their support team would come along. There are a few conditions for them, though not as onerous. I have guaranteed that we will set them on a path to buy themselves out of their indenture and into a comfortable retirement in an established Reality Engine."

She sent over that addendum as well. The agreement had been made with Shad and his team, not with the other humans of the Misfits Guild. As far as Veda knew, they still weren't aware of the permanence of their position.

From now on, they would be required to spend their lives in a Reality Engine's sphere of influence, unless they had the help of very expensive support equipment. A Reality Engine completely transformed the physical body of the entity who merged with a soul coin in order to be able to support it inside the Reality Engine's immense array of scenarios and simulations.

One key change, invisible and unnoticeable for the most part, was equipping the body to utilize etherium. Etherium was the Reality Engine's basic substance, still not well understood by galactic scientists. All they really knew was that if you took someone who had bonded with a soul coin away from a Reality Engine's sphere of influence without providing a steady supply of etherium, they would very quickly age and die.

In addition, anyone in an untamed Reality Engine was in danger of etherium poisoning until the core of the Reality Engine was breached and a contract was made with the Reality Engine itself. There tended to be side effects from the exposure, which was why all of the miners were checked at regular intervals by the Reality Engine Exploitation Committee's team of veterinarians and miner psychologists.

Veda had not told Shad and his team that over a million of those humans who had failed to complete the initialization chamber had died from a failed bonding with the soul coin, causing them to explode in a massive cloud of etherium. Since that tended to vaporize everything for about a mile around them, there were almost no humans who would have witnessed such an event and then survived. Sooner or later, Veda was going to have to tell Shad and his team the truth.

Well, no, she wasn't, because she was about to sell them out for their own good and her own good. Of course, they'd have to agree to the deal. But she was negotiating a fair bargain for all sides.

Veda took a deep breath. "Well, I think you can expect a very reasonable offer from us," the lizardfolk woman said. "We will get back to you, Veda Tvedra. Good day." She cut the connection.

Veda slumped back against her cushions, relieved. She could be done with this soon. She could go home.

Now that she had what she wanted, she wasn't sure why she had strived so hard. All of this work just to make herself eligible for the next Reality Engine exploit. Was it really worth it? Seeing Shad and his team struggle so hard to achieve their goals, knowing that their place in this was already determined by thousands of years of habit and custom, was really starting to hurt. She needed to take the buyout and get out of here.

Someone knocked on her door. Veda froze. No one ever visited her pod. Anyone who wished to speak to her would call and talk virtually, or agree to meet on neutral territory. Arriving at someone's berth unannounced, uninvited, was, well, unthinkable. It wasn't done.

The knock came again. Veda got to her feet, shaking. She requested her personal systems check the external cameras. They showed her three dark-robed figures standing at the door. One held up a shining golden symbol.

She recognized the logo. Veda's shaking got even worse, but she managed to tell her system to open the door and let them in.

The door disappeared. The three strangers stepped in. Veda dropped to her knees, raising her hands.

"We mean you no harm, daughter," the central figure said. He was tall, with a deep voice. Veda was sure he was male.

"Blessed be the progenitors," Veda said ritually, holding up her hand in a starburst pattern.

"And blessed be their relics, to enlighten those they left behind," the man chanted. The door closed behind him. He drew back his hood.

He was humanoid, but bald. The two with him left their hoods up. Veda was pretty sure one was a woman, but she couldn't tell about the third. They all had the same golden starburst logo on their chests. These were members of the Order of the Progenitors, and from the symbol that the bald man held, he was very high up, probably an archbishop.

Veda wasn't a member of the Order of the Progenitors herself. Her grandmother had been, and she'd been raised in some of the rites and customs, but as an adult she had drifted toward the Blessing of the Void sect instead. Still, all of the rituals and words came right back to her. And here, at the opening of a new Reality Engine, the old beliefs felt more impactful. "How may I aid your quest?" she said, keeping her eyes averted, while still being able to see the man's expression peripherally.

He lowered his badge of office. "I am Patriarch Kvaltash of the Path of the Seekers," he said.

Veda took a deep breath. The Path of the Seekers was the knowledge-seeking branch of the Order of the Progenitors, not the searchers of false hearts, thank the Void.

"We are here because you have been making inquiries about selling your interest in Team Twofeather and the Misfits Guild."

Veda raised her eyes to his face before she could stop herself. "You know of them?" she blurted out. "The Order of the Progenitors knows and cares about my team?"

"As the progenitors watch over us all, so too the Order watches all," the patriarch intoned. "But yes, we are watching them with interest. We believe one of them has been marked by the Reality Engine as of particular interest. Not yet as a champion. Perhaps he never shall be, but he is of interest. Therefore we do not wish him to become entangled with any of the coalitions. Certainly not one who has a link with these unbelievers."

He held up a scrap of Duraplass on which the logo of Proxima Corp featured prominently.

Veda gasped. "You mean they are behind Vortali Conglomerate as well?"

"Indeed," the patriarch confirmed.

"But why? Why do they care?"

"That is something that my Order has not yet determined," the patriarch said. "I assure you we are looking into it with great interest. All you need to know is that this transfer will not take place."

"Yes, Patriarch." Veda bowed her head. "But what should I say?"

"You will merely refuse the deal. We have been watching some of your colleagues' attempts to interfere and are not amused. When the signs point to a Reality Engine maintaining its interest in its closest children, the rest of us should not push that aside in search of profit. Not when we could find a far greater treasure instead. Answers! We have seen this before, and the committee has squandered the chance at learning the truth. This time, it must not be permitted!"

The man's voice took on a fervent tone. The two with him raised their hands and spoke a ritual phrase that Veda repeated. "From the progenitors came life. From life came knowledge. From knowledge came loss," they said.

"And the step to reverse that loss is knowledge regained once more," the patriarch said. "Do not worry, daughter. You will be rewarded for your part in this."

"I understand," she said, though she didn't understand any of this. She just wanted the patriarch and his companions to leave her quarters as quickly as possible. Speaking to one of the patriarchs of the Order of the Progenitors in the flesh was like flying too close to a sun.

"Then I bid you good day," the patriarch said. He raised his hood, and a moment later he and the others were gone.

Veda took a moment to compose herself. Then she started her system algorithms, searching for answers. She didn't fully understand what the patriarch was talking about. But she did know his interference could change everything.

CHAPTER TWENTY-ONE

SIXTEEN AUTHENTIC POLYNESIAN RECIPES: YOU'RE GOING TO LOVE NUMBER SEVEN!

I christen thee *The Seeker*!"

Sage smashed a bottle of champagne across the hull of our new three-masted schooner. The NPC captain and crew of this ship wore cleaner, better-fitting uniforms than the pseudo–Napoleonic era NPCs of our original boat, who looked like they had stepped out of the nineteenth century.

This craft was built to carry cargo. It had vast holds under its decks, three levels deep, and instead of the cannon ports of our previous ship, it was lined with berths for stowing cargo. It had a respawn point located on the deck, but this was a harvesting boat for our crafters and farmers to use.

We had saved up the profits from our node for almost two weeks before deciding to invest in the new ship. Juana and Mama Grace had argued strenuously in its favor, although I had thought we should be upgrading our outpost more. "We haven't had a single other attack since those orcs came, and that was almost three weeks ago," Juana pointed out. "Veda says she doesn't expect any trouble from our large neighbors. Everything's calm right now."

"That's got me worried," I had said, but Grandpa had taken their side, and so had Dwight. Our crafters were making money hand over fist. Whatever the node was raking in was a pittance compared to the gear they were building and selling to the aliens on the outside. "I just hope it doesn't come back to haunt us when a bunch of orcs wearing the armor Dwight's been making come and steal our node from us," I'd grumbled at the time.

But now, seeing the schooner launch, I had to admit it was a pretty impressive sight. Almost all of the Misfits Guild was on hand to watch the launch as the sun set on our island. Mama Grace and her assistants had an entire luau cooked on the beach and waiting for us. There was an enormous pit in which she had been roasting five wild boars that our farming teams, led by Frank, had hunted on a nearby gamma node island. Nobody had bothered to claim the node yet. I was considering proposing an expedition tomorrow to claim the node and put up some automated defenses. Even if we only held it for a few days, we had a lot of turrets to spare, thanks to our raid on the beta node during the initial phase. Plus, Juana had been wanting to experiment with base defense builds, and this would give her a chance to try out some cannon and turret combinations we hadn't used yet.

There were loaves of bread baking in brick ovens along the edge of the beach, and tables laden with dishes. Everything from coconut milk ice cream that didn't melt despite the heat, to taro root porridge, to six different kinds of fish prepared every way from raw to roasted to dried and flaked. My mouth had been watering from the smells for a good hour.

I helped myself to a large plate, then stood at the edge of the jungle as the party got underway. A couple of our farmers were also musicians. They ate, then went and set up their instruments. It was a motley assortment of guitars, violins, flutes, banjos, and even one accordion the people had looted from home, as well as some drums one of the crafters had built. Sage had set a set of coconuts in the sand, along with sticks for bopping them, and had announced her intention of jamming with a few sessions hours ago.

I was pleased to see her doing so well. There weren't many children here, thank whatever fortune had been unkind enough to bring us here. Because of that, Sage was almost universally loved, and spoiled whenever the opportunity came up. The adults of our coalition tended to treat her like a mascot, or like everyone's little sister. She sat in the sand and pounded out a rhythm as the band struck up a tune.

I sat on a rock at the edge of the beach, eating my fill as darkness began to fall. We lit four huge bonfires and people began to dance to the music.

Juana came over and sat on the rock beside me. "Having a nice evening?"

"Mostly." I checked my map. Only green dots and the orange of creep. Mitch had set up a series of traps and trip-wired bombs around the edges of the party area, all of which would create equal amounts of explosion and sticky syrup. We had made sure to warn everyone where they were so nobody would accidentally set them off. Even if some of the creep got distracted from trying to attack our outpost, they would not make it here to disturb the party.

Juana laughed at me. "I know that face," she teased. "You're worried because there's nothing to worry about."

"It's been going a little too well," I said defensively. "I've got to think about what might come next."

"Why?" she asked. "Why not just enjoy the evening, Shad?"

I let out a deep breath. Why not, indeed? It had been six months that we'd been here. Six long, hard, grueling months spent fighting for my life and then, for the last couple, trying to manage assault teams, build a base, and work up to an objective that I still didn't understand.

Juana held out a hand. "Come on, Shad. Let's join the dance."

I let her drag me away from my spot. We joined a line of dancers, slipping our hands into theirs. I stumbled along the sand, trying to keep up as we wove in and out among the fires.

I was actually almost starting to relax. Then I saw Colonel Ames standing at the edge of the crowd. I froze. Juana ran straight into me. "What are you doing?" she demanded.

"Uh, sorry," I said. I dropped her hand into the hand of the next guy in the line and stepped out of the dance. "I, um, need to see a man about a . . . thing." I wandered away, over Juana's objections.

Ames had disappeared. I checked my map. There was no way of telling which of those green dots was him. I caught another quick sight of him moving through the crowd, slipping away like he'd never been there. I mentally targeted him, and now his dot stood out as he moved. I could have Trick Shot him if I'd wanted to, not that I did. Instead, I followed him to the edge of the crowd.

He disappeared into the jungle. I stepped into the woods. "Colonel?" I called. "I know you're there."

The dot stopped moving. He was threading a path between some of Mitch's explosives. I took another couple of steps forward. "I think you owe me a couple of explanations," I said. After a minute, his dot retraced its steps.

The colonel stepped out from between two trees, his face expressionless in the dark. "Williams," he said. "I should have known you'd see me."

"Why did you come if you didn't want to talk to us?" I demanded.

The colonel let out a sigh. "It was a temptation I couldn't resist. News about this luau and launch had gotten all over Threshold. Mama Grace was handing out invites to one and all, so I snagged one and came through. You've accomplished a heck of a thing, Williams. You've done everything I asked, and it looks like you're on track to keep it, so long as we don't attract the wrong kind of attention."

I felt a quick swell of pride. "I'm glad you think so, sir."

"It's not just me. Our allies think you've done better than they hoped, but there's going to be another challenge coming up. You'll find out all about it soon enough. I have every faith in your team, but I'm going to stress that I need you to make it at least to the second stage."

"Why? What happens then?"

Ames stepped forward. He held something out to me, an envelope. I took it. As soon as it touched my fingers, it melted away. I started to ask, but he shook his head. "You'll know when you get there," he said.

Frustrated, I asked him, "Why all this secret agent shit? Why not just tell us what's going on?"

"Because there's more at stake here than you know," the colonel told me. "Do you know how many of us are left, Williams?"

I shook my head, then realized he might not be able to see me in the darkness. "Last I heard, we were doing pretty well. Still over six million."

"And how many of those do you see when you come through Threshold?" Ames challenged.

I didn't have an answer. Now that I thought about it, I had never seen more than a few thousand people in Threshold. I usually stuck to one pretty small section, but if I multiplied that by how large Threshold was, it still wasn't nearly large enough. "I see your point," I said slowly. "We must be spending most of our time inside levels. But that makes sense. We've got to be there in order to earn soul coins."

"Yes, but what levels?" Ames asked. "Hmm? Have you heard anything about the lotus eater level?"

"What?" I scratched my head. "That a book or something? I feel like I've heard that term before."

"Yes, I'm sure the American public school system did an entirely adequate job of educating you, Lieutenant." I could hear the eye roll in his voice. "'Lotus eater' is a term from Greek mythology. An island full of people who spent their time in a narcotic dream. The original potheads, maybe."

I suppressed a snort at that. Colonel Ames was definitely of the age and military background to consider "pothead" a serious insult.

"What if I told you that of the hundred and fifty or so portals that we have sent people through, only one seems to be completely nonlethal. No creatures therein to attack. Nothing to harvest. Just all of your wants provided for."

"Is that so?" I asked. "How come I hadn't heard about those before?"

"The people who find that level, how many of them do you think ever come out?"

I thought back to my first weeks here in the Reality Engine, of the fear of death at any time. The fear that Sage would be killed and there was nothing I could do to stop it. If someone had offered me an easy existence inside a level without any of that, would I have taken it?

"Maybe we should encourage people to move there," I said, pursuing my thoughts. It went against everything in me. The idea of living an easy life when there were still goals to work toward was offensive. Especially now that we were in phase two and I was part of a team that was actually accomplishing things, not just surviving, but thriving. "There's plenty of our farmers and crafters who are working hard but just don't have their hearts in it. I know they're enjoying themselves tonight. Tomorrow they have to get up and go back to harvesting fish in order to make belts to sell to aliens for a pittance of soul coins. And that's all they can ever hope for, even if they don't know it."

Ames let out a long breath. "So you know."

"Our sponsor told us," I admitted. "I know the truth. Sir, wouldn't it be better if we took most of the miners and put them into a, well, retirement home? They're never going to get back to Earth anyway. What's the point in making them fight?"

"The point, Lieutenant, is that their struggle contributes to humanity's chances of something more than just being shunted into a retirement home, as you put it. Or should I say, a reservation. I think that's how your grandfather would see it. Why don't you ask him what it's like, Williams, living off of government charity, when all there is to hope for is a bottle at the end of the day to drown out your sorrows? Ask him how many of his people he saw succumb to despair and alcohol back on the reservation where he was born. Ask him what made him leave."

"Well, I think it was because the US government decided not to recognize the Paiute as a tribe back in 1954," I said, "and so he grew up without a lot of the rights and privileges that other tribes had, such as they were."

"And you know as well as I do that those rights and privileges don't mean a damn thing to a man like your grandfather," the colonel snapped. "Go have a word with him. Think about what I've said, and I'll give you some numbers. You can try to confirm them if you want. Your friend Arjun might be able to help. Three and a half million, Williams. That's how many of our people have become lotus eaters. If you don't step up, if they keep losing hope, it's going to be even more."

I had to take a step back and think about what he was saying. Over half of us had given up, found a hole, and hidden in it. That struck me as wrong.

Ames continued. "I'm going to be starting a propaganda operation before long. You and your team, you're the heart of it. You are going to help me inspire the rest of us to keep fighting, to keep struggling, to get up in the morning and get things done. You just do as you're told. Besides, when you hear the challenge that the system is going to give you, you'd give it a try anyway. Just remember: make it into the second stage of the challenge. You don't have to win. Just get past the door."

CHAPTER TWENTY-TWO

HOW TO TELL A PATIENT THEY'RE DYING IN TEN EASY STEPS

Even though Ames had warned me, the announcement still caught me off guard when it came the next day.

I was helping our farm team capture a rare spawn on an island about two miles from ours. A giant platypus, forty feet tall, had spawned in the middle of a small lake inside an extinct volcanic crater. The beast's poison-spurred feet were a real menace. We were only able to apply debuffs and slows to one limb of the creature at a time and had to wear it down slowly. But when it finally hit **[0 HP]**, we got a bounty of soul coins and about an acre and a half of plush fur that could be used in crafting.

The poison spurs were carefully removed by one of Dwight's assistants and set aside. They had learned how to imbue crafted artifacts with various properties, including poison resistance or the ability to deal poison, by using raw materials like these. I was just congratulating Lara and Lakshmi on handling themselves well when the system announcer spoke.

With a voice like thunder shaking the skies, the announcement appeared in everyone's vision.

[We have now begun the special event. All teams participating in this phase two map will send a delegation to the island of Hispana within the next six hours. All combat miners are expected to attend. Teams may also bring a number of noncombat miners equal to the number of combat miners times a node score multiplier. Once you have arrived, the noncombat miners will be granted special opportunities while the combat miners pit themselves against other teams. Note: The special event rule set will apply. As of this moment, no creep will spawn on any node until the special event is resolved. All nodes are put into untouchable status. No team is able to mount an assault on any other team's outpost.

Any team that does not participate in this event will have their node put back into unclaimed status. Nodes cannot be reclaimed until after the conclusion of the event.]

The announcer stopped as abruptly as he had started. I had about a million questions. But it seemed pretty obvious what our first step was. "We need to get back to our island ASAP," I told my team. "Grab whatever you can, and let's get to the boat."

Grandpa was already in the coalition chat, sending messages to Juana, Mama Grace, Dwight, me, everyone. He named ten of us for a council of war to be held on the other boat just as soon as I got back.

I wasn't actually the last to reach the boat. Mama Grace and Arjun arrived a few moments later.

Grandpa looked around at all of us. "We knew there were special events likely to happen. Sounds like it's time for one of them. I'm kind of excited to see what it is," he said. "Seeing as our node is safe while we're gone, there's no reason not to bring everyone we can, as they suggest."

Our node, being a delta, had a node multiplier factor of two. That meant we would be able to bring all fifteen of our combat miners and a total of thirty non-combat miners.

"I know the message specifically said crafters, but I think we ought to bring some of the best of the farm group," I said. Frank was already on the boat. I turned to him. "If we asked you for a team of five, could you come up with one?"

"Give me a couple of minutes," he said.

Grandpa nodded his agreement. "I think you're right. It's best to be prepared for different eventualities. Dwight, Arjun, that means you've got twenty-five slots to work with. We want your best."

"I'm coming," Juana said firmly.

Her mother shook her head. "If you go haring off there, who's going to be in charge here?"

"No one needs to be in charge," Juana said. "There's not going to be any kind of attacks. That means we can just do whatever for as long as this event goes on. I need to be there because it sounds like there's going to be representatives of all of the other teams. This is a good chance for me to make some connections. Besides," she continued, "Team Twofeather needs someone to keep them out of trouble."

That got a laugh out of almost everyone. "All right, so be it," Grandpa said. "I don't have to pick and choose between my combat team. We're all going. No need for anyone to stay back and defend."

I would need to take Grandpa aside and let him know what Colonel Ames had said sooner or later. But until we knew what was going on, there wasn't much we could plan for.

Veda sent us a message. *I see the team event has begun.*

Any advice for us? I asked.

No. Just do your best and hopefully that'll be enough. You shouldn't need to take any kind of special gear. Most outside artifacts, like those miner respawn points, are banned. Just bring yourselves and the gear you're wearing. Your crafters should have good opportunity to exchange recipes and possibly sell their wares. I would advise loading up on as much gear for sale as you possibly can.

I relayed the message to Dwight and Mama Grace.

"Who are we going to be selling to?" Dwight asked. "Other miners?"

"She didn't say."

Mama said, "Well, it just so happens I've been keeping a stash of boxed lunches just for this sort of situation. I heard a rumor from someone that it could be a good moneymaking opportunity sooner or later. I'll transfer those over to Juana's inventory before we leave."

"Then let's get going," Grandpa said. "Dwight, Arjun, get me that list of crafters as quickly as possible. I want us lifting anchor in two hours."

The island of Hispana was four hundred leagues away. At our top speed of twenty knots, that would have taken a whole day. Fortunately, the system granted our boat a Speedy buff that increased its speed by tenfold. So, we sat back for a couple hours and enjoyed a cruise.

We zoomed past islands like we were on a jet ski. I'd ridden jet skis more than a few times on reservoirs around the West. There'd been one memorable high school spring break where a bunch of friends and I had gone over to Page, Arizona, and rented a houseboat for the week. We'd had to bribe one of my friend's older brothers to front the rental for us since no one in their right mind would rent a houseboat to a bunch of seventeen-year-olds. Then we'd gotten our hands on a bunch of cheap beer and weed and proceeded to do idiotic things on jet skis. I came back with a hangover, a hell of a sunburn, and a bunch of near misses that I never told anyone, especially not Grandpa, about.

"So, how many other teams are we expecting?" I asked. I tried to remember how many we'd said there were on the map. "Something like two hundred and fifty?"

Juana nodded. "Close enough. We're estimating between eight and twelve combat miners per team. Call it ten to make the math easy. So that'll be two thousand five hundred other fighters. Most of them are going to be aliens."

I knew that much. While there were still plenty of us humans here in phase two, most of them were serving as farmers and crafters, adjutant to an alien conglomeration.

"Arjun says he expects there to be perhaps three hundred and fifty human miners at this event," Juana continued.

"As many as that?"

"Several whole teams were hired by some of the smaller conglomerations, similar in size to Veda's outfit, I think."

That made sense to me. "Have you already got their contact information?" Arjun was able to pass on contact information to certain other miner classes. Juana's Procurer class was one of them. Procurer came with a few interesting benefits, including enhanced communication skills.

"He's sending me everyone he knows for sure is here," Juana said. I'm supposed to try to meet as many of the others as I can and get their contact information. We're still collecting contact info. Arjun's really starting to tear his hair out over this one. He says he can't figure out where all the rest of the Earth humans are. He's coming down to the dregs on those he doesn't know, and there's still millions of us missing. He and some of the others who are building up the database are coming up with some pretty elaborate conspiracy theories."

Juana shook her head and gave me a wry smile. "They're starting to worry me. The one about the aliens replacing humans by killing them and then wearing their skins as a disguise, that really bothers me. I'm pretty sure it's nonsense, though."

"Yeah, it's a total crock of bull—" I said, censoring my expletive at the last minute, even though Juana never complained about my crude language. "I don't think that's it at all. I heard a theory myself I like better," I added quickly, not sure how much of Ames's information to divulge. "It says that among all of these different portals, one or maybe two open to a level that doesn't suck. Somewhere you don't have to fight. Somewhere you can just stay and have your needs taken care of. Sooner or later, people are going to discover that and, well, just move in."

"I like that idea better than I like the skin-changing aliens," Juana said thoughtfully.

"Suppose you found a portal like that right now," I said, "after everything we've been through. Would you take it? Would you go through?"

Juana tugged on her braid thoughtfully, her eyes going distant. "I don't know that I would," she said. "It's funny. I feel needed here. Valued. I—"

She looked away, her cheeks tinging pink with embarrassment. "You know, back on Earth, I really wanted to go to law school. I had this idea of myself as a community advocate. It was kind of an impossible dream. We couldn't even afford more than community college for me and Rosa. But I thought maybe if I worked hard enough and saved up money from my notary jobs, I could at least finish a bachelor's degree. And then there might be scholarships or something that would make it possible. Anyway, I'm saying I wanted to make a difference." She laughed at herself. "Only I'm not really that selfless, I always try to help and end up telling people how they're screwing up their lives and how to help it. I'd have ended up as a divorce lawyer for sure."

"You're too hard on yourself," I said.

She acknowledged my comment with a little nod. "And here I am now, making a difference for so many people. You, your grandfather, your sister, everyone else in our coalition. I'm helping us build a chance at a better future, one where we can get back what we've lost. How could I throw that away to go live inside a glorified television show?"

I felt suddenly awkward. Sooner or later, I was going to have to tell Juana the truth, that none of us were ever going home. That the best we might hope for was a life inside a lotus eater paradise. But not right now.

"I should go talk to Grandpa about a couple of things before we get to this island," I said.

"Sure." She looked away, and I realized that I had just been an idiot.

"I didn't mean to insult you or anything, Juana. I think your idea, going to law school and all, I think that was really great. I never really thought too much about what I was going to do when I got out of the Army myself, even though college could have been an option. I hadn't even made up my mind whether I was going to stay in and try for more training to become an actual logistics officer and not just a grunt. So I think it's pretty cool you had ambition."

A ghost of a smile flicked across her face. "Go talk to your Grandpa, Shad," she told me.

Grandpa was sitting on a bench at the back of the boat, looking out behind us at the wake we were turning up. I wasn't surprised that there was no one around him. Grandpa had an awfully foreboding-looking face when he was thinking about things, and people tended to just stay away.

I sat down next to him. "Ames knew this was coming," I said. "I saw him the night of the luau."

"'Course he did," Grandpa said without looking up from the water.

"He says we have to reach stage two of this event, whatever that means. I assume we'll learn once we get there."

"'Course he does." Grandpa reached into his inventory and pulled out a can of beer. I wondered how long he'd had that. He cracked it and sipped it, slowly watching as the ship sailed on. "This just doesn't make any sense," he said abruptly.

"What?"

"All of this." He gestured around. "The first phase was okay. We were gaining powers, we were leveling up. Fine. And earning those coins, sure. All so that we could come and compete here and earn more coins. Great. And then there's a phase beyond that, and somehow that phase, which I assume will involve even more coins, is going to determine the fate of Earth. Of who's going to own this Reality Engine, whatever that means. And so we're all jumping through these little hoops designed by some aliens half a galaxy away. Why do it this way, anyway? They've been exploiting these here Reality Engines for millennia, and this is the best they can do? A giant video game full of random ideas and images from Earth history?"

Oh boy. Grandpa was definitely in a rare mood. "I don't know about that," I said. "There's got to be a reason for it. And I don't think they're going to tell us why."

"Well, it sounds like Ames has a bit of an idea. Somebody's feeding him information. We don't know yet if they're friend or foe to us. So we've got to take everything he says with a grain of salt. Especially seeing as he won't even meet me," Grandpa said.

He finished his beer and then tossed the can over the side into the water. I was shocked at the littering for a second before remembering that none of this was real. The Reality Engine would just repurpose all of this at some point. There hadn't been an ocean and islands and pirate skeletons here before we entered, and there wouldn't be when we left.

Grandpa was right. All of us felt hollow. "I think it's because we've had too much time in between attacks, and because our lives aren't on the line," I said. "It's giving us time to think, and now we're seeing the unreality of this."

"Yeah." Grandpa stared moodily at the water.

"And I think we're starting to get a guilty conscience because of how we're using all of our friends." I dropped my voice low. "I was just talking with Juana. She still doesn't know that we're never going home. I feel like I should tell her, but at the same time, I really don't want to."

"That's exactly it," Grandpa said. "We've got all these people that we've convinced to help us work toward a better future for humanity, a better seat at the table, and they don't even know that their own future's been decided for them."

"We'll tell them," I said firmly. "After this event. We need everybody's head in the game right now. If Ames is right, this is important."

"Agreed," Grandpa said. He stood up, shading his eyes with his hand, and looked toward the front of the ship. "And I think we might be coming up on our destination. Let's go take a look."

CHAPTER TWENTY-THREE

BE THE LIFE OF THE PARTY! TIPS FOR WALLFLOWERS AND SOCIAL BUTTERFLIES ALIKE

The island of Hispana was about two miles wide and twelve miles long, and it was shaped like Florida turned sideways. In the elbow was an enormous volcano at least seven thousand feet high.

From sea level, the volcano looked like Everest towering over us. Snow coated the edges except for one place where there was a gaping wound in the rim and molten lava rolled slowly down the volcano's slope. It hardened into stone long before it reached the sea. The rest of the volcano's flanks were covered in bright green jungle.

The beaches were the same gorgeous white we had come to expect, and the waters were completely full of boats. Hundreds of boats, thousands of boats, mostly Napoleonic- or Victorian-era warships like ours, though it seemed some teams had gone all in on upgrading theirs. A speedy platoon of little river patrol boats zipped past us with frog-like aliens at the helm. An enormous two-funnel steamboat chugged past, blowing a horn. Alien passengers leaned over the rail, staring down at us with looks of disdain. A graceful yacht with orcs in polo shirts and pressed slacks sailed past. One of the orcs waved. I waved back, wondering if they knew the Firebrand team.

Our NPC captain knew just where to take us. He steered our boat to an anchorage between six identical ships. Only the identifying flags at the stern with different coalition logos on them varied.

We were all anchored off the west side of the island. The NPC crew tossed out the anchor, and we waited and waited. And waited. Hours crept by.

"Can't we just go ashore?" Sage asked the captain over and over.

He shook his head, saying, "We're waiting for orders from the commodore, madam."

Sage even tried getting the pirate hat back out of her inventory and seeing if that made him obey her, but it didn't work.

At last, one final straggler arrived, this one a lashed-together raft of rough-hewn palm trees tied together and seated over a dozen blue plastic barrels that offered it very little buoyancy. It carried a single team of five sunburned and miserable-looking humans. As it edged into place, the system spoke to us again.

[Welcome, miners! You have wisely chosen to answer the summons. The six parties that failed to obey the summons have been summarily removed from phase two and their earnings confiscated.]

I wondered why anyone would refuse to come. It didn't matter. There were plenty of us here.

[Introducing: The Treasure Hunt! You will all be given a treasure map first thing tomorrow morning. The location of the treasure is somewhere here on this island. You will have eighteen hours to reach the location. Those teams who fail to arrive in time will not be permitted to compete for the treasure. Only a single member from each party is required to reach the marked location to qualify their team for round two. The fewer teams make it to the location, the easier it will be to win the prize! So race ahead. Take out your competition. Make deals. It's up to you. If at any time every member of a party is dead, that party will be eliminated from the competition. The death timers will be set at thirty minutes. If you die, you will respawn in the nearest graveyard. Every thirty minutes, all those waiting at the graveyard will respawn at the same time. If you die one minute before that thirty minutes is up, you will respawn almost immediately. If you die one minute after the previous respawn, you'll have to wait the full thirty minutes. There are six graveyards scattered across the island. You will not respawn on your ship. No portable respawn points will function on this island. Rewards will be issued for performance along the way. The system is watching, so do your best! Daring strategies will be rewarded even if they fail.]

That respawn timer might make or break a team's attempt. If there was a big skirmish, all the dead on both or all sides would come back to life almost at once in the same location. That meant fights were likely to start back up again in the graveyard itself.

This could get really nasty. There were twenty-five hundred teams here and we needed to be one of the top ten. This was going to take more than strategy, more than luck. This was going to take a miracle. The system continued with its next message.

**[You will receive more details tomorrow. Tonight, you are the guests at a grand party hosted by the twin outposts of Scylla and Charybdis. No violence will be permitted at this party.
So let your inhibitions down. There will be intoxicants for every species labeled as to what they are. There will be entertainment.
There will be vendors here to sell very rare objects.
Your crafter friends are invited to join this party. When it is over, noncombat miners will be allowed to choose to visit one of the two cities for the duration of the combat phase. They will find much there to interest them.]**

I could see our crafters speaking to each other in low voices, clearly excited about this opportunity. Me, I was just worried about a lot of different things that I had no control over.

I took a deep breath. I was all right. We'd come up with a plan. It sounded like I had all evening to strategize. It wasn't like I wanted to party anyway. We'd just had one a couple of days ago that would hold me for another six months at least.

[And now! Welcome to the party.]

A pulsing Eurodance beat filled the tropical night air. The party island was about a hundred yards off the coast of the volcanic island we'd be exploring tomorrow. Ships were moored everywhere between the two islands, their lights lit. Lanterns along the sides were strung up in the rigging.

It looked like a fairy tale. There were little cabanas along the beach, small bars serving thirty or forty people at a time. Bonfires blazed, plates of food were everywhere, fire-jugglers and dancers waved palm fronds from low stages to the pounding beat.

Everyone mingled. At first I was surprised to see so many Earth miners. It seemed like every seventh or eighth person I saw was human. Then I remembered to check their tags and realized most of these humans were not Earthlings. They had different systems of origin listed, places I'd never heard of. They were laughing and mingling alongside the orcs, space elves, lizard people, frog people, fish people, strange tentacled aliens, and more.

There were even some of the really weird aliens we had stolen supplies from back during the initial phase. The system called them grignarians, and I noticed

I wasn't the only one steering clear of them. They huddled together in little groups of eight or nine, their weird face tentacles reaching out and mingling with one another's.

I strolled down the beach taking in the sights, trying to relax and not worry about where the rest of my people were. There would be no violence tonight. The system would enforce it. I kept a tab on where Sage was until Grandpa noticed me and kicked me out of the cabana I'd been lurking in, telling me to go mind my own business.

A big group of orcs stood around one of the fires drinking frothy pints of beer. I paused. They looked familiar. Their outfits were the same as the Firebrand orcs who had attacked us. I checked, and sure enough the logo on their breasts was the same burning torch symbol. I hesitated then made my way over to their fire.

They stopped talking as I entered the ring of light. Then one of them pointed to me. "You!" he said cheerfully. "You! The human duelist who talks too much! Come have a pint with us!"

There was a small round table full of untouched beers. I grabbed one and joined the orcs, telling myself to relax, that even if they held a grudge there was nothing they could do about it tonight.

The orc who had greeted me beckoned me over. I came and stood next to him and he draped one arm around my shoulder. He was about eight inches taller than me and probably at least a hundred muscular pounds heavier. "This human!" he said to a couple of orcs across the fire who wore different logos on their silvery suits. "He fought my brother and won. His people's trickery put my brother's life in danger, but then his actions saved my brother's life. I owe him. Give welcome to Shad Williams, friends."

The orcs around the fire lifted their beer mugs and I drank as well. The beer tasted good. It fizzed as it went down, warming my insides. Or maybe it was just the friendly welcome I had received from these orcs.

"So, about that," I said. "Your brother is all right, then?"

"He is! He's here somewhere," the beer-drinking orc said. "I am Mak'gar. You killed me four times. Well, I say you, but mean your whole team. The short one with no hair, I saw him messing with our sarcophagus and rushed to stop him but it was a trap. He blew up. He blew me up!" The orc laughed cheerfully, thumping his chest with the hand holding his now-empty beer mug. He raised the mug to his glass, looked at it sadly, then detached his arm from around my shoulders and went to fetch another round.

One of the orcs across the fire who wore a green hand symbol said, "After I heard how you defeated our cousins, I looked your team up. You're the one who dealt the snake faces a nasty blow, aren't you?" He gestured a couple of fires over where the strange tentacle-faced aliens still stood in their little communal group.

"We did, yes," I said mildly. "We humans, Earth humans that is, we're new to all this. I don't know if there's some sort of unspoken rule we violated there by raiding another team during the setup phase."

That wasn't entirely true. *A Beginner's Guide to Constructing Your Phase Two Outpost* had specifically warned we could be vulnerable to outside attack during setup. I didn't want to reveal how much we did or didn't know. Plus, I figured if we had done something tacky it was better to claim ignorance rather than malevolence.

"Not at all, not at all," said the orc. "It's a gutsy move and honestly might not have worked if anyone had thought you foolish enough to try it. As it was, your node location was just a bit too inconvenient for anyone to try to take during the initial phase. You got lucky with your seeding."

"Lucky?" One of the Firebrand orcs snorted. "I think the Reality Engine favors them. You know how it always tries to promote indigenous teams."

My ears perked up at that. I drank some of the beer, keeping a polite smile on my face, but the overly friendly Mak'gar had returned with another two mugs. He tried to push one on me, saw that I had yet to finish mine, and shook his head playfully. "For such a good fighter you have a poor appetite for beer. Drink up," he said.

I took another sip. "I don't really want to have a hangover tomorrow."

"Then tell the system to dial down the alcoholic effects," Mak'gar said.

I hadn't known that was a possibility. "How do I do that?"

He walked me through it. I sent the information on to everyone else in my coalition immediately.

Mitch shot back, *Tell me something I don't know. You can do it the other way too and get hammered on a single pint of lager.*

Figures the Canadian explosives and syrup expert would know that, I replied, then turned back to Mak'gar. "So, nobody minds what we did to the squid faces?" I gestured again at the grignarians.

"Oh, nobody likes them," Mak'gar said dismissively. He waved a hand. "They never work with anyone else. They always make a bid at a Reality Engine and come away with far too many soul coins for their investment. They are unscrupulous, dirty, sneaky cheats. You probably won yourself some friends the way you crippled one of their bases so early on."

"That's good to know," I replied.

"So tell me, Shad," Mak'gar said. "We are only a little ways into phase two, but have you started to consider your plans for the future?"

CHAPTER TWENTY-FOUR

CAREER COUNSELING: WHEN YOU'RE NOT CUT OUT FOR COLLEGE

Mak'gar noticed my confused look and slapped me on the back, joggling my arm and slopping beer all over me. "Oops," he said, taking my now nearly empty mug and handing me a full one. "Here, that's better. I understand. You and your people have been so busy surviving, you haven't looked past this day. But I can tell you, you're making an impression here in this phase with us professionals."

There was definitely a lot here I didn't understand and I wanted to change that. "What do you mean by 'professionals'?" I asked. "You mean like, sponsors?"

"Them." Mak'gar rolled his eyes, his lips curling back, showing long, sharp teeth. "They are not professionals. They are merchants." His words dripped with disgust.

The other orcs drank, then turned their heads and spat. "Coin counters," one said. "Paper pushers."

"They sit in their little metal boxes and never get out."

"They certainly never take on any risks."

"Do you?" I asked. I tried to keep my tone polite. "I mean no insults, but here in phase two, there are no real dangers. Nobody is going to die or lose an arm. It's not like we've had it up 'til now, scrambling around, fighting for our lives, saddled with debt that we never asked for."

I was aware my tone dripped bitterness and venom, but I didn't really care. Even with the intoxication level turned down, the warm buzz from the beer was spreading.

The orcs nodded gravely. "We speak as warriors to another warrior," Mak'gar said. "You are right. This phase is like a child's game. Bases, soul coins." He spat at the last word. "But it is all to prepare for the real struggle."

"Phase three," I said. "I know it exists, but I don't know anything about it."

"It's different every time," one of the other orcs said. I noted, in surprise, that she was a woman. She was bald, like most of the others, and her leather tunic concealed any feminine curves, but her voice was high and light. Now that I looked,

I saw she had more earrings in her oversized, pointed ears than did the men. "Every Reality Engine programs its final challenges itself. The system is only able to do so much interfacing."

I held up a hand. "Whoa, wait. I've heard people talk about the Reality Engine and the system before, and I assumed they were the same thing. The asshole that talks to us and gives us quests, that's the system, right?"

Mak'gar nodded. "It is. Think of . . ." He paused. "I am sorry. I do not know your species' technology level. Do you have a concept of hardware and software as two separate things, or are you at the stone knives level of development?"

"Me, personally, I'm more of a stone knife and bearskin guy," I said. "But our society has computers, if that's what you're asking. I know the difference between hardware and software."

"If the system is the software running all of this, the Reality Engine itself is the hardware. You can replace the software, but you cannot upgrade the hardware, because it was created by the progenitors long, long ago."

"Right," I said. "I got that part. Some aliens built all of these Reality Engines a billion years ago, then disappeared and left them behind for the exploitation committee assholes to claim. Now they're used as giant VR playrooms and tenement housing for the ninety-seven trillion billion beings in the galaxy. And I guess there's different levels of comfort available. Like some of you have the equivalent of a one-room apartment and MREs, while others are living in elaborate mansions with twelve-course dinners every night."

The orcs were nodding. "That's more or less correct."

"I just guess I don't understand why there's that kind of scarcity. If the Reality Engines can generate anything, why doesn't everybody get their own mansion?"

They looked at each other. "Does it look like we care about that sort of thing?" the orc woman asked. "We're here because we like breaking stuff and killing people. That's not permitted in civilized Reality Engines."

"Really? I would have assumed war games were totally a thing."

"Only for licensed Reality Engine miners," the woman said. "We are allowed to use training levels and such, but it is not considered appropriate for the ordinary citizen of the galaxy to indulge in violence."

"Huh," I said. "So you're a whole galactic civilization of lotus eaters." I made a note to mention that to Colonel Ames the next time I saw him.

"Since you understand so much, Shad, you must know what your fate is," Mak'gar said seriously.

"Yeah, our sponsor let on. We're stuck here for good. We've been transformed. We're part of the Matrix now. So I guess we're fighting to earn our way into one of those padded cells that you and the others are talking about."

"I do not think you will do well there," the orc woman said. "Perhaps you should consider becoming a professional miner like us."

"I think it is worth his time to consider," Mak'gar agreed. "Though for that, you would have to perform in phase three and attract the attention of an important sponsor. Your current sponsor will never be able to afford a phase three bid."

"Oh," I said. "What's the difference in cost?"

"If phase two bids cost hundreds of thousands of soul coins, phase three bids cost billions," the orc woman said. "We here are fighting to prove to the sponsors of phase three that we are worth hiring. If we do not succeed, we will merely return home and wait for the next Reality Engine exploit. We are clan." She gestured around, encompassing both the Firebrand orcs and the ones with the green logo standing around the fire. "We always do well in these exploits."

Colonel Ames had seemed to indicate that a single well-developed phase two outpost would give us the ability to enter phase three. I didn't know if he was lying, deceived, or if these orcs were telling me the truth. I decided that it didn't matter for right now. Right now, what I needed was to figure out how my team and I were going to make the first deadline during this competition.

A blast of rainbow-colored light erupted out of the center of the island, accompanied by a swelling burst of trumpets. Instinctively I raised my arms to shield my face, blinking against the brilliant light. As the echoes died away, other partygoers turned toward the cause of the commotion, talking among themselves. Nobody seemed unduly worried.

"Thanks for the beer." I ditched the orcs and raced toward where I had last seen Sage and Grandpa. They were standing with a bunch of our crafting miners. Frank and his team had been drinking at the nearest beach bar. They got to their feet, dropping their drinks, and joined us.

A system announcement popped up, accompanied by the usual voice.

[Welcome! Welcome to our master crafters! It is time for the noncombat miners to be given their opportunity. Crafting delegations are here to select apprentices for training. Crafters will please present themselves for selection—]

The box blinked away, the voice cut off suddenly.

"There will be no such thing!" A loud voice cut across the noise of the crowd. From the place where the beam of light had erupted, a dozen aliens came striding. They wore elaborate robes in colors I didn't even have names for. Each had a headdress or crown. One looked like something a pharaoh would wear. Another had a circlet of bones wrapped around his bald orange pate. Only two looked human, the rest space elves, orcs, and other aliens.

"This is a disgrace," the foremost of the new arrivals declared. He was a large lizardfolk with red scales and a crown of purple gems held together in a silvery framework. The gems shifted and moved in circles around his head, orbiting him like his own personal satellites.

Some of the aliens on the beach started to protest. "What's going on here?" somebody called out.

"Silence," the lizardfolk declared. He held up his hand. "We are the mastercraft representatives for this Reality Engine exploit. Our protests have been ignored, so we are now forced to take drastic action. Our own apprentices and underlings have been forbidden from joining us. The system is trying to force us to take indigenous workers."

Venom dripped from his every word. I felt my hackles rise at the term "indigenous." Grandpa put a hand on my shoulder. "Easy, Shad," he said. "This is going to reveal more than they want. Let's listen."

Now the alien partygoers were really getting upset.

"We've got to have trained craftsmen," one of the polo-shirt orcs from the yacht demanded. "We need access to supplies in phase three. What do you mean you're taking steps?"

The lizardfolk looked as though he was enjoying being the center of attention. "The Council of Crafters has decreed that no indigenous miner shall be allowed access to our secrets. Any phase three team who purchases supplies from indigenous miners will be cut off from access to us and our legitimate wares. You may decide now whether you wish to place your faith in a bunch of untrained monkeys." He sneered around at us.

"But you just said your apprentices and underlings were banned," a frog-like alien chimed in. "You'll never be able to support all of us."

"Our prices will be adjusted to ensure that those who truly need our services are able to take advantage of them," one of the other master crafters said smugly, her face hard to read under her overhanging crown of woven branches. "We're giving you plenty of warning now so that you have time to save up and decide where your priorities lie. Or perhaps you can put pressure on the system as well. Our pleas have gone unheard. But perhaps the system will listen to you."

"It's not fair!" someone shouted.

"Tell that to the system. It's the one making the rules. The locals have not been so kind as to die in sufficient quantities to let our people in. So we shall pass the suffering along to you." She glanced around at the remains of the party. "And just so you Earthlings know, there is no ill will meant. We are still perfectly willing to buy materials from you. The pay scale will be discounted, of course, due to your lack of crafter guild standing."

"You may return to your festivities," the lizardfolk representative said, "now that we have delivered our message in person. We will be reachable through the usual channels back on the Hub once this exciting episode is over."

The twelve crafters vanished. No flash of light, no rolling thunder or loud trumpets this time. They just disappeared.

The aliens around us were in an uproar. "We'll never be able to afford those rates. But we can't do phase three with no materials."

"We're going to have to try to use the locals."

"They're not going to have the recipes. You heard what they said."

The rest of our coalition gathered around us. Juana had a distracted look on her face. I knew she must be sending reports back to our people on Threshold, asking them to look into matters.

"I'm putting a hold notice on all sales of materials until we get to the bottom of this," she announced. "We need to understand what's going on."

A system message popped up.

[That was rude. Just because you have the ability to shut down important subroutines doesn't mean you should. Terribly uncouth. And when will they learn that no means no?

The Reality Engine Exploitation Committee is prepared to invoke Emergency Procedure 99732-17 Alpha. The master crafters have abdicated their responsibility to provide training and recipes for those who will form the backbone of the economy. Therefore there is now a chance that monsters may drop recipes. These recipes will be destroyed upon use, transferring their contents to the crafter who learns them. Until they are learned, these recipes are tradable.

The second stage of this treasure hunt will drop recipes at a greatly increased rate. In addition, the NPC cities now have certain basic trainers available who will offer training and help to human miners who wish to make use of this opportunity. Details are being made available now and can be accessed by querying the system on your own.

There will be portals opening to the cities in approximately thirty minutes. Make your decisions and report to whichever portal you choose. You will have until the end of this treasure hunt to learn from each city's NPC crafters. The workshops, laboratories, and other facilities which were created in these cities in order that the master crafters might teach their chosen apprentices will now be open to everyone.]

Veda sent me a message. *The system rebroadcast what just happened. I'm accessing details of the crafting tutors now. There's alchemists and leatherworkers in Charybdis. You're going to need to send the majority of your people there, I think, since you already have so many leatherworkers. There's a cooking trainer in Scylla. Is Mama Grace there with you?*

No, she stayed in Threshold, I replied.

Damn, that would have been good to get. Is there anyone else there on the team who has a cooking-related class?

I know who can find out. I passed the message along to Juana, who nodded briefly to me in acknowledgment.

There's a construct engineer in Scylla as well, Veda continued. *See if you can convince someone to go learn those skills. Devices to enhance your creep are very expensive, but they can be incredibly valuable in phase three. Your people could probably pay off their debt if they focus on selling construct enhancement devices to the phase three teams, even if you never need to use that ability yourself.*

Okay, sure. What was all that about, anyway? It was a great party and then a bunch of angry Olympians arrived.

Veda replied quickly. *The crafting council said they're angry that the system rejected their appeal. They wanted to bring a bunch more of their own people. They went so far as to say that the Reality Engine Exploitation Committee was corrupt and somehow supporting you Earthlings. The number of you who have survived this far into the game is well above average. We should have seen a couple million more deaths, I'm afraid. I know you humans have been better than we expected at working together, but it's still interesting.*

A thought struck me. I didn't know if I should trust Veda, but she'd backed us every time, and I wanted to extend an olive branch. *There's rumors going around of a level that supplies all of your needs where there's no mobs, nothing to hurt you. The rumor says that's where some of our people have gone.*

I've never heard of anything like that, Veda replied. *Reality Engines don't give anything away for free.*

I'd better focus on what's going on here, I said. *Let me know if anything else important comes up.*

I will, Veda replied. I turned back to the discussion at hand. Juana and Dwight were arguing over who needed to go where. "I'm not going to learn a cooking skill," Juana said furiously. "My mother and I get along much better when we are not in the kitchen together."

Grandpa sent me a message. *I have to go see someone. Take care of this.* By the time I read it, he was already striding along the beach away from us. I sent him a message asking for an explanation, which he ignored.

"Somebody needs to," Dwight was saying.

"Then do it yourself."

"Veda said we should send someone to learn construct engineering because it's useful in phase three and we could make a lot of money," I said. "I guess assuming any of the aliens will buy from us after that edict."

"Oh, they'll buy from us." Juana gave a big, sharklike smile. "Didn't you hear that master craftsman? The licensed alien crafters are going to raise their prices through the roof. Like it or not, there's going to be quite a few people coming to us because they can't afford anything else. We just need to make sure we're ready to take advantage of it. Let me see that description of construct engineering."

I sent her the page I just pulled up.

"This actually looks like it could tie in nicely with some of my base-building abilities. I think I'll go and see about learning this."

"Are there limits to how many of these skills you can learn?"

"It doesn't look that way, but if we've only got a couple of days, it's probably better that we focus on becoming as much of an expert as possible in a couple of skills rather than dabbling in eight or nine," Dwight said. "They're going to be opening the portal soon. We should get over there."

Another system pop-up appeared.

[To the officers of Misfits Guild Coalition:
Due to the cost of training, your coalition's educational efforts
will be subsidized. The first forty skills you wish to learn will be paid for
by the Reality Engine Exploitation Committee. This offer is being
extended to all Earthling coalitions.
After that, you will be charged at the regular rate. Do you wish to accept a
line of credit from the Reality Engine Exploitation Committee to be taken
out of your future earnings to provide for additional skill trainings?]

"How many people have we got here? Crafters, I mean?" I asked Juana.

"Twenty-five, plus Frank's team."

"Then I guess we'd better take the loan."

"Agreed."

With us and Dwight there, it was enough of a quorum to make a binding deal with the system. Dwight and Juana were going to different cities. We instructed the other crafters to contact whichever of them was in the same city with any concerns.

"It doesn't sound like we're going to be able to help you at all," I told them, "since we've got to do this treasure hunt thing. Good luck."

"What about us?" Frank asked.

"You guys go with Juana," I said. Only eight of the crafters were going to Scylla. The others were all heading for Charybdis and the more obviously useful crafting professions like alchemy and leatherworking. "I want to make sure they've got backup. Other than that, you're on your own."

"Got it," Frank said. "We'll try not to get tossed in jail while we're on leave, then." I hadn't interacted with Frank much in the last few months. He'd mellowed out a lot once he left our team and confirmed none of his kids had been kidnapped by the Exploitation Committee. He looked actually relaxed now, the top button on his shirt undone.

The portals blossomed to life. Our crafters stood in the line and shuffled their way forward. "Good luck," I called after them. "See you in a couple of days."

They disappeared into the light and in a few minutes the beach was only half as crowded.

CHAPTER TWENTY-FIVE

EXTORTING OFFICIALS FOR FUN AND PROPHET

As the last of the crafters vanished into the portal, I got a private message from Grandpa. *Shad, get over here. I want you to hear this.*

He pinged the map on a location, and I strode off in search of him. A little ways off of the beach, past the rows of cabanas and tropical bars and outside the circles of firelight from the bonfires, stood low thatched-roofed huts, one or two rooms each with whitewashed walls and cheerfully painted shutters. Lamps glowed in the windows and lanterns stood outside.

Grandpa was a little ways farther along from me. I put my head down and walked past as couples, or sometimes more than a pair, ducked into the huts, laughing and giggling to themselves.

They didn't all stick to their own species either. I saw orcs with space elves, lizardfolk with what I hoped were non-Earth humans.

I found where Grandpa was. This was no hut. This was a two-story building, all neat, straight lines and business, with bronze fittings around the door and windows, and a plaque beside the door that said "Government House."

I stepped up and knocked on the door. It swung open under my touch. "Get in here, Shad," Grandpa called from inside.

I stepped over the threshold, then closed the door behind me. Grandpa was seated at a round table. There were three other people with him. The first was a lizardfolk woman with golden scales. The next was a male space elf with pale silver hair falling past his shoulders, delicately tapered ears, and brilliant blue eyes like ice. He scowled at me as I stepped through the door.

The third was a human man wearing a dark robe. He sat in the middle, the other two as far away from him as they could manage without getting too close to Grandpa, who lounged opposite, sitting back in a chair, tilting the legs back, hands laced behind his head.

"Pull up a chair, son," Grandpa said.

I grabbed a straight-backed wooden chair from against the wall and dragged it over to the table, wincing at the loud scraping sound it made on the polished wood floors. I sat beside Grandpa, closer to him than to the lizardfolk woman.

"You pissed some people off, Shad," Grandpa said.

"Oh?" I said, trying to keep my tone light. "What else is new?"

Grandpa gestured at the space elf. "This is the local representative from Proxima Corporation."

I frowned; something about that name was familiar. "Are you the ones behind Sicaris?" I asked.

"The Sicaris Corporation was owned by one of our, um, associates," the space elf man said smoothly, steepling his hands together in front of him. His eyes bored into me as he spoke. It was like listening to a snake charmer. "He exceeded his mandate in several areas. He has been reprimanded. Sicaris is no longer of concern. However, Proxima Corporation has invested a great deal of money in this Reality Engine exploit and we wish to see it be profitable. We happen to be your neighbor. Our subsidiary, Existalis Holdings, has the alpha node to your west."

"Good to meet you," I said. Existalis weren't the ones who had hired Theram'goss and the Firebrand orcs, so the elf shouldn't be angry at me for beating them.

"I am Halithi Dreamwarden." He inclined his head toward me. "I hope this is the last time we are required to be in the same room."

Grandpa indicated the lizardfolk woman. "Miss Astramel here is the legal representative of TriStar Unlimited."

I got a sinking feeling in my stomach. "Who?" I bluffed.

"The outfit whose node you raided during the initial construction phase, appropriating property worth fifty thousand soul coins and disrupting node claims," Astramel said, leaning forward.

"Hey, we followed the rules of the game," I said.

The third man held up his hand. He pushed his hood back, revealing a bald head. "I am Patriarch Kvaltash of the Order of the Progenitors," he said. "I will be your mediator during this arbitration."

It was clear Kvaltash was some sort of priest or clergy associated with a religious group. A name like "Order of the Progenitors" meant that they were some sort of nutters who thought they had the secrets of the race who had built the Reality Engine, all figured out. But "mediator"? "Arbitration"?

Wait, this is a formal thing? I asked Grandpa. *Are we in big trouble?*

I don't know yet. Veda's not answering. Try to keep your cool here.

"TriStar would like to enter a formal complaint. Mediator is not a neutral party. The Order of the Progenitors has a longstanding hostility toward my clients' race."

"That's not true," Kvaltash said. "While some of my order do believe that the grignarians are an abomination spawned by the Void in order to counter the progenitors' grand design, my own sect teaches that the grignarians, and any other self-spawned race we may encounter, are a necessary element to the unfolding design. The Grand Matriarch subscribes to this view, and has placed the grignarians under protected status. They may not be visited by the Inquisition or harassed by the faithful. You are assured, I will be able to remain neutral during this dispute."

"We have no complaint," Halithi said. "Proxima Corporation accepts this arbitrator."

"Why are you here?" I asked the space elf. "Her, I understand, but we haven't crossed paths with your people. Yet."

Halithi scowled. "TriStar is alleging illegal collusion between Proxima and you Earthlings."

"That's nonsense." I turned to Kvaltash. "These guys tried to screw us over in phase one. They nearly froze my coalition out of farming zones entirely. If they had their way, we wouldn't be here."

"They are angling even now to make the Earthlings their pawns. This scheme has Proxima all over it," Astramel insisted. She flicked her tongue out, her wide membrane eyelids nictating rapidly. She held up a delicately clawed hand and ticked off points. "Item: Known collusion between Proxima subsidiaries and members of the Earthling vestigial armed forces. Item: Leaders of Misfits Guild's phase two team are also members of said armed forces. Item: After his dissociation with Sicaris and his former coalition, Earthling Major Waters admitted to my patrons that there is a secret alliance between Proxima and the Earth governments, directed by a shadowy figure we have not been able to identify but whom Waters referred to as 'the colonel.'"

I was struck dumb. Was any of what she said right? Were Colonel Ames's "allies" and "sources" agents of Proxima?

"Once again, I deny all such allegations," Halithi said smoothly.

"Look into our background," I said. "We have a named sponsor, and Tvedra Corporation is not linked to Proxima. At all. Besides, when we raided that other node, we were following game rules. I checked."

Kvaltash nodded. "That is correct. However, TriStar made a formal complaint to the system. Behind-the-scenes collusion is contrary to the spirit of the game. It is true, your team has been remarkably disruptive."

"Hey, that was one raid," I protested.

Astramel leaned forward, hissing. "You have been limited in your disruption due to a lack of resources. This is one of only ten phase-two maps and you are confined to a tiny corner of it. You have impacted perhaps seven or eight out of the two hundred and fifty sponsoring teams on this level. And yet, those ripples are being felt. The Grignarian Association is threatening to pull out of this exploit entirely and boycott the next several as well."

"Let them," Halithi said. "A bunch of creepy weirdos anyway." I found myself warming to the space elf.

Kvaltash held up a hand. "Nevertheless, the grignarians are essential to any successful Reality Engine exploit. Their understanding of progenitor technology is unsurpassed by anyone outside of my own order. It is unfortunate that they do not enjoy cooperation with others."

I held up a hand. "Look, there's a really awesome party going on out there. I just learned how to tweak my alcohol tolerance up and down so I can drink as much as I want, then get as drunk as I want and pass out, wake up tomorrow, and turn off the hangover. I really don't want to miss that in order to hang out and have a conversation with you scintillating people. Can we get this over with?"

You're laying it on a little thick, Grandpa messaged me.

The priest guy stood up. "Consul Astramel, your complaint has been heard and filed. This hearing will be public record and can serve as a basis for an appeal to the local oversight board, or if you prefer a change of venue out of the Proxima Sector, you may. I warn you, legal proceedings are rather backed up right now and you are not likely to get a response for some time." He turned to Halithi. "I admit some questions remain unanswered. I have flagged any dealings between Proxima, its subordinates, and Earth-humans for increased scrutiny by the system. If my services are required again, Proxima will be paying the bill, not the Exploitation Committee."

"That's not enough—" Astramel began, but Kvaltash waved and she vanished. I started. Had she been a hologram? Or could the arbitrator kick people out of this map that quickly?

"I'm satisfied," Halithi declared. He disappeared as well.

Kvaltash turned to us. "Before I leave, any concluding statements you wish to add to my report?"

"This was a waste of time. We weren't colluding. I don't want anything to do with you assholes," I said. I looked at Grandpa. "You?"

"That basically sums it up."

"Before you leave, a word." Kvaltash raised a hand, then lowered it. "No longer as arbitrator, that is concluded. But as a patriarch of the Order of the Progenitors, I wish to offer my personal best wishes. I believe you Earthlings are truly the heirs of this Reality Engine. I hope to see some of your species make it into the next phase. My Order believes that when children of a Reality Engine are able to make contact with the Engine's soul, great knowledge may be revealed. To that end, we may be able to help sponsor a phase three bid. If, say, there is a mysterious force behind you Earthlings and your remarkable cohesion, I would be interested in speaking with them."

Grandpa stood up. "I'll pass that along to our sponsor. We don't get involved in politics." He stretched. "Now, if you'll excuse me, I've got a beach to storm in the morning and I'd rather do it after a good night's sleep."

CHAPTER TWENTY-SIX

HOW NOT TO BE THE LAST ONE PICKED FOR DODGEBALL

Cannons roared as the first boats hit the beach. I couldn't see our attackers. A rain of arrows fell from the sky, *plock*ing into the sand all around. The first couple of boats full of alien miners were struck by cannonballs and blasted out of the water. Some of the miners tried to swim for shore, only to be pierced by the raining arrows.

We had split up into our two small boats, with Team Mongoose, Bill, Bob, and Sage in one, and Grandpa and me in the other with Team Ragtag. "Keep your heads down!" I shouted over the noise of the cannon barrage. "When we hit the beach, run forward! Don't waste time trying to figure out where they're shooting from. Just get up the beach as fast as possible, and we'll assess then. Remember, you'll respawn in a graveyard. We'll coordinate once we're past the beach."

Team Ragtag, bent low in the boat, responded with whimpers or moans.

Our boat ran aground. I leapt over the gunwale and splashed into the ankle-deep water. Arrows whizzed down all around me. I ducked my head, holding my arm up to shield myself, and charged forward. As soon as I was on the sand, I engaged Fastest Gun in the West and dashed up the beach.

This barrage was designed to break up our party, to get some of us killed and out of position, and to disorient us. The more of us made it through the barrage, the better off we'd be. I couldn't waste time worrying about my teammates. My own skin was what mattered.

The soft sand of the beach gave way to matted dune grass. I plowed through it, over the top of the dune, and down the other side before my wild forward momentum died out. Immediately, I dropped to the ground and rolled, then lifted my head and peered around.

The cannons fired. They were behind me. I raised myself up a little farther, trying to spot the nearest cannon. It fired again, close by, but I couldn't see anything. Maybe the cannons were invisible, or maybe the system just made it so that I couldn't see where they were.

I started crawling forward carefully, looking for the next set of danger and watching my mini-map. It was a jumble of blue dots. I zoomed in close enough to pick out the green ones.

At least no one was red yet. No one was actively trying to kill me and my team, other than the system itself. A trio of green dots converged on me.

I got to my feet as Tall Smith, Jones, and Brown joined me. "Where's Sage and Grandpa?" I asked. "Where's the rest of your team?"

"Smith didn't make it," Tall Smith said brusquely. "We'll pick him up at the graveyard. I don't know where Black is."

A second later, Sage popped out of the brush, followed by Annie, Lakshmi, Lara, and Mitch. Lara was looking very pleased. "Minivan worked like a charm," she said. "Bill got hit right before I could cast, and I don't know where Bob or Ice Spice went."

I pinged Grandpa. *Are you there?*

I got no reply. I had a sickening feeling in my stomach. "We've got to keep moving," I said. "As soon as the other teams regroup, they're going to start making us targets. We've got to move inland. We'll gather up our stragglers when we can." I pointed in the direction of the so-called treasure. It was to our east, eight miles away. My mini-map wasn't big enough to show it, just an arrow pointing out the direction, but I suspected it would be past the cities.

We were on the far west side of the island. Its long, skinny body stretched away from us. The day was cloudy, and I couldn't make out the volcano from here. I expected we would have to reach it before we found our destination. From what I could tell on the map on our ship, the twin cities were closer to the volcano than to this side of the island. Charybdis was on the north shore, Scylla to the south, with a mile-wide strip of jungle in between them.

We had marked our best guesses as to the location of the graveyards on a shared team map, and would update those once we learned more precise details.

We were equidistant between two probable graveyards, so I didn't know which one our lost party members would spawn at.

I made a judgment call and took us southeast into the jungle. We plunged in. Birds hooted and chirped. Monkeys swung overhead, howling to each other. A snake slithered along a branch as I walked underneath.

By now, I was sure that Grandpa, as well as the two Mongeese, Bill, and Bob were temporarily dead. They'd have answered me otherwise. Ice Spice was still alive and sending messages back, but had gotten badly separated. He was somehow nearly half a mile north of us, trying to make his way toward us, but finding dozens of enemies in between.

There were over a hundred and fifty teams on this map, each with fifteen combat-capable miners. That was well over two thousand potential enemies running around the woods with us. We needed to get farther ahead, but not so far that we couldn't retrieve our people.

"All right," I told everyone. "We keep moving forward, and hopefully we gather up the missing when the graveyard respawn goes off. If you get killed, and you're not near us when you come back, start heading toward us and get as far as you can. Your goal is to get far enough away from the graveyard that if you die again, you're sent to the next graveyard along. It'll be slow and laborious, but eventually you'll catch up."

"Roger," Tall Smith said. "Sounds straightforward. Remember, we only need to get one of us to the marked location in order to qualify for level two."

"But if one of those teams out there kills all of us at the same time, we lose. We're done," I warned.

We made our cautious way through the trees. I watched my mini-map, trying to steer us on a path between dots. I had to expect that the other teams out there had tracking of their own.

The beach had definitely thinned out our numbers. If my team had taken average casualties, there would be hundreds spawning in the nearest graveyards in another twenty-three minutes. I wanted us to be east of the first graveyard by then, if at all possible.

A particularly loud bird trilled unseen overhead, then fell quiet. I felt a prickling on the back of my neck. I checked my mini-map. No dots near us. "Everyone stay alert," I snapped, just as the pair of black-clad space elves appeared in the midst of our group.

At the same time, six red dots surrounded us. I instantly cast Call 'em Out, while Sage threw her Mucking Out the Stalls behind us, tying down two of the assaulters. Team Mongoose had their mini-guns out and were firing wildly, not caring about their aim as their bullets passed harmlessly by fellow party members.

I targeted the closest space elf of the six circling us and hit him with Trick Shot, then ducked as the two in the middle attacked me. They came barreling at me, each wielding a pair of curved swords like scimitars and seemingly uncaring of their own safety.

Lara threw a cloud of orange grenades behind us, filling the area Sage had mucked up with smoke. I focused on the pair of elves in front of me. I shot one with Barrage, then reloaded and fired again. Their health ticked down. They had me surrounded, attacking from my left and my right. I had no way to block their swords.

I ducked back from a thrusting attack. It sliced through the loose sleeve of my coat, tearing a three-inch-long hole. Team Mongoose concentrated their fire on that one and dropped him.

The other one slashed hard at me, striking my right arm with his sword. The blade slid off my jacket but dealt fifteen points of crushing damage to me and made my hand fall open, dropping my gun to the jungle floor. I used Quick Draw to call it back to my hand and fired at the elf.

Another pair of elves ran through the smoke, coughing and covered in stinky muck, wielding long polearms with shining energy blades. They charged at us with their weapons outstretched.

Lara stepped in front of Mitch to throw another pair of grenades at them, and took a blade straight through the chest. It drained her health down to **[30/130 HP]** and left her with an Eviscerated debuff. Sage threw a Raise Your Spirits at her while Lakshmi cast Soothing Thoughts. Lara's health went up a bit, but the debuff was still there, eating away at her by twenty points a minute.

I fired, using whatever skills seemed to make sense, Reloading as quickly as I could drop a Barrage into an elf. The jungle was a mad, confusing scramble as we fought a seemingly insane enemy.

Then suddenly they were gone. The last of the elves fell to the ground and despawned. Sage let out a whoop. "We got 'em!"

"Stay alert," I said. "There might be other camouflaged people out there. Sitrep!"

"Eight of them, two of us," Smith reported grimly. "We lost Black and Lara."

I swore. I hadn't seen Lara die. That left us down six. I checked our respawn timer. Still seventeen minutes to go. "Let's keep moving," I said. "That fight attracted a lot of noise and we're hurting now. Spread out. I don't want us walking into any traps."

I sent Jones ahead. As an Army scout, he had a skill, Detect Landmines, that would reveal the presence of certain kinds of traps, but unfortunately not all of them. I stayed in the middle, letting Tall Smith and Brown bring up the rear.

Lakshmi and Annie were subdued. Lara was a friend of theirs, and I knew seeing her get violently killed had to hurt. I steeled myself and kept us moving forward. "Whatever happens, we've got to stay alive," I said. "That doesn't mean don't work together or don't cover for each other. It means don't take stupid risks. As long as one of us is alive when the thirty minutes are up, we're still in the game."

I had a couple of pending message notifications. I checked, hoping one was from Grandpa, but nothing. I guess when you were dead, you couldn't talk. There was a message from Juana and another from Veda, both of which I would look at later when I had time. There was also a message from Mak'gar, the orc I had partied with the night before. It said, *I'm putting together a chat for those I trust to be honorable opponents. Would you care to join?*

I replied, *I'm in.*

A minute later, an invite lit up. I accepted. The chat channel was labeled "Honorable Hunters of Hispana." There were about fifteen of us there. Mak'gar said, *Honorable enemies, this is Shad Williams, who showed great honor and cunning during our assault of his outpost.*

Greetings, someone said.

Howdy, I wrote. *Glad to be here.*

Jones sent my team a priority message. *Someone's coming. Fall back.*

I held up my hand, and everyone paused. We ducked down into the bushes. Jones cast his Camouflage over all of us. It would be effective against any team that didn't specifically have a camouflage-piercing spell.

We waited with bated breath as the red dots came nearer and nearer. I wondered why they were already red, since they hadn't attacked us and we hadn't attacked them, unless they were the rest of the space elves?

There were eight of the dots. As the leader came into view, I understood. It was a grignarian with a **[TriStar Unlimited]** tag floating over his head. They were the ones we had raided.

I sent a message to team chat. *I guess we made a permanent enemy there.*

Let's jump out and take them, Sage said. *I'm still mad about them melting your arm.*

We don't know if there's more of them, and we don't need an unnecessary fight right now.

Oh, come on! Let's knock them out of the game!

They're already angry enough at us. I had a quick thought and sent a message to the Honorable Hunters. *Got a pack of those grignarians over by me.*

A flurry of messages came in reply.

Squid faces? Let's take 'em! Will you share coordinates?

Hell yeah! Sign me up!

You're the native team, aren't you? You guys have been doing good work.

I saw some bootleg vids of you back on the Hub.

Uh, yeah, thanks, I replied. I was going to have to ask Veda about those bootleg videos and what exactly was being said about us. *If I send the location, you'll know where we are.*

Share with the chat. We will agree to make no attack on your people for three hours, Mak'gar said. *Or the others will hunt down and eliminate the violators.*

Well, I'd been wanting to win friends and make allies. I shared my location.

That is very near to us, one of the people in chat, whose name was An'kar, replied. It sounded like the space orc names I'd heard, so maybe they were allies of Firebrand.

Us as well, replied someone named Silver Fox. *Shad Williams, would your people join an attack on the grignarians?*

Is there a way to temporarily tag you guys as friendlies so we don't accidentally kill each other?

Yes, I'll send you a private message.

I told my team, "We've got a temporary alliance thanks to those orcs who attacked us the other day, the Firebrands. It's some of their friends. They'll show up on our map now as green for the next three hours."

"The orcs who attacked us?" Mitch asked incredulously. "The ones I blew up?"

"Apparently we made a good impression. I'll take it. We might be joining an ambush with some others here in a minute."

"What are you talking about?" Tall Smith replied.

"Just give me a minute." I switched back to the impromptu alliance and exchanged a few quick messages with An'kar and Silver Fox. We hashed out a simple plan.

"All right," I said to my team after we'd finished. "So, in just a minute, the grignarians are going to walk into an ambush. Our job is to make sure they can't retreat. Be careful. They have this nasty melt-your-flesh-off weapon," I told the members of Ragtag who had not been along on our raid of the grignarians' stockpile.

The red dots were about one hundred yards ahead of us now, going slow. *Now*, my chat contact said.

"Now," I repeated to my team, and we rushed forward. There was a clearing up ahead where Silver Fox's team had sprung their trap. Spiderwebs hung between the trunks of the trees. The grignarians had entered the clearing only to find their way forward blocked.

An'kar's people were in the treetops, pelting them with arrows. They were orcs, as I'd suspected. Their arrows exploded when they hit the tentacle-faced aliens, taking big chunks with them.

The grignarians re-formed their limbs quickly when one was blown off, shifting some of their mass from their torso into another limb. With each limb they lost, they grew smaller. They also stank like the gross burning fluid they had used to kill me back on their island. I could see why they weren't popular party guests.

Two of them were attempting to retreat, probably seeing there was no winning this fight and trying to avoid total party kill. "Our turn," I told my team.

Mitch threw out a series of small darts, something that looked like caltrops, that stuck in the trees near the grignarians. Then he snapped his fingers and the caltrops exploded, knocking the trees down right into the path of the grignarians, crushing one of the two deserters.

What was left of it oozed out from underneath the fallen tree and began re-forming. I shot it through one creepy, unblinking eye. It squealed, its tentacles wriggling in pain as I shot it again. We took it down as what remained of Team Mongoose leapt over the log and fired into the other trapped grignarian. It despawned a few seconds later.

"Clear here!" someone shouted from up ahead.

"Let's go say hi," I told my team.

CHAPTER TWENTY-SEVEN

PUT LIFE INTO YOUR GRAVEYARD: DECORATING TIPS

*A*Beginner's Guide to Constructing Your Phase Two Outpost, Section 6.5: Networking*

Interview conducted by Colonel Jefferson Ames, US Army.

Interview subject: War Leader Gek'tar Lothbriand of the Halfhand Clan

You may be tempted to think of the team events as a disruption, even an inconvenience. Don't. They are the system's way of trying to force an equalization when it realizes things are becoming too unbalanced. It often offers an underpowered clan their only chance back into the fight. Rewards from a team event can make or break a phase two attempt.

In addition, if you have even the most basic of diplomatic skills, you will be able to win allies—or at least people willing to talk to you and share information. The alliances forged in a team event often last through a phase, an exploit, and even across systems. My own clan joined forces with a smaller clan ten exploits ago thanks to a team event. They are not even orcs, but lizardfolk!

But beware. Not all who appear trustworthy are indeed to be relied upon. And trying to bring an incompetent partner through an event may lead to disaster for you both.

I could still smell burning grignarian as we approached the site of the ambush. The bodies were gone, but the stench lingered.

A thought hit me as we walked. Nobody seemed to like these guys. I hoped we hadn't just joined a bullying attempt on the galaxy's underdogs. Well, we didn't understand the politics here, and I did know that I wanted my team to make it to the objective. That meant making allies and reaching the treasure.

I'd try to find out more about interstellar politics another day. Maybe when we Earthlings had the luxury of caring about such things.

I stepped out into the clearing as an orc with a chainsaw hand dropped out of the trees in front of me.

A bunch more orcs stepped out of the trees and with them a half dozen walking anthropomorphic animals. I'd seen lizardfolk before and somehow gotten used to them. These were different, about a head shorter than the orcs.

Two looked like foxes, including one with silver fur that I assumed must be the Silver Fox I'd been speaking with. Two were badgers. One was a raccoon, and the last was a snow-white rabbit with tall, pointy ears. They all carried shotguns and wore plate-mail armor.

"Well done, Earthling," Silver Fox told me. He sounded like a middle-aged gentleman, his voice melodic and refined. He bowed from the waist. "We have scored a great victory against our most hated foe today. Their team has been knocked from the competition. They will have to go back to their node and wait until the regular game begins again. They will not enjoy such idleness. It will make them consider their choices with regret."

"You really don't like these guys, do you?" I said, indicating where the grignarian corpses would be, if they hadn't just despawned.

"Corpse eaters," the chainsaw orc said with disgust. "Carrion feeders. Children of dirt, not stars. Breaker of alliances. They have no honor."

"Right," I said. "Well, thanks for the assist there. I guess we just go away from here?"

The orc looked me over. "You are missing some of your people."

"Yeah, we lost a few," I said. I checked my respawn timer. "They should be up in seven minutes or so."

"We also," the orc said. "I am An'kar, by the way."

"We're down three," Silver Fox said.

An'kar said, "Let us proceed together and collect our people. After that, we shall separate. We will agree not to attack each other for one respawn cycle. Past that point, it is not an alliance. Merely a set of honorable foes sharing a path for a time, lest we fall prey to the dishonorable."

"Sure," I said. Anything that made us more likely to recover Grandpa and the others and be safely on our way was good with me. "Everybody get that?" I asked my team. "We're allies until the graveyard, then just leave them alone and go our separate ways."

Sage bounced forward, staring up at the rabbit. "We haven't seen any of your people on the Hub yet."

"My faction has only just arrived," the rabbit said in a gentle feminine voice. She reached out and touched Sage's shoulder. "But you, are you not a youngling? A cub?"

"Sage is my sister," I said. "She's also one of our valuable team members."

The rabbit's eyes filled with compassion. "I understand. It is unfortunate when the Exploitation Committee chooses younglings. I am glad that you made it past the initial winnowing phase."

"Well, let's get moving," An'kar said.

I walked beside him as we moved off into the jungle. "Are you a relative of Mak'gar and his brother?"

"We are demicousins on our mother's sister's side," An'kar said. "So, while I do not owe you the same debt that he and his brother do, I am grateful. We are all loosely allied, and I am glad that he and Firebrand made out so easily from your encounter."

"Yeah, same here," I said back. "They could have caused us a lot of trouble on a different day."

As we approached the graveyard, the map became more crowded with blue dots. We saw other teams emerge from the brush, their weapons stowed. No one was starting anything, avoiding one another as much as possible.

The graveyard icon was a tombstone on my map. I wondered if they had pulled that from human iconography or if it was somehow common across the galaxy. The graveyard itself was a neat plot of land cleared of brush, with twelve headstones spaced around a small white chapel in the center. A black metal fence surrounded the graveyard.

As the timer ticked down to zero, the system announcer popped up.

[First respawn. Time until stage two begins: 17 hours, 30 minutes. 18 teams have been eliminated from competition.]

"Wow, that many already?" Over a third of us hadn't made it past the first respawn. I was shocked and said so to An'kar.

He laughed. "That is always how these work. Some of the teams which take and hold nodes are well equipped but not well suited for battle. Once removed from their defensive places, they are little concern to those of us gifted in fighting. It is fine. There is a place for both here in the system."

"Sure, I guess."

Then there was a bright shining light and the graveyard filled with people. Humans, orcs, space elves, more animals like Silver Fox and his team, lizardfolk, and species I had never seen before and couldn't describe came pouring through the gate.

Nobody tried to start anything as people separated out into their teams. I saw Grandpa and the missing Mongeese. Grandpa had Lara in tow.

At the same time I got a message from Ice Spice. *Where are you guys? I don't see you anywhere.*

Shit. *You must be at the other graveyard. You've got to try to meet us. Try to get as far east as you can so that if you're killed again you respawn at a different graveyard.* I pinged my map. *We're going to head south toward Scylla.*

Okay, on my way.

"Let's get moving," I told my team. This temporary truce could break up at any time. Jones threw out his Camouflage skill and we faded back into the undergrowth.

CHAPTER TWENTY-EIGHT

WINNING FRIENDS AND INFLUENCING ORCS

Five hours later, we had made three miles of progress. I could see the spires of the city of Scylla poking up through the jungle.

Once the weather had cleared up, the enormous slopes of the giant volcano had come out to play. Scylla ran right up onto the southern flanks of the volcano. Its architecture was a bizarre mixture of onion domes, pagodas, and weird Christmas tree–shaped buildings that were a series of rounded pyramids placed atop each other. Some of the buildings looked to be ten or twelve stories high, and I thought I could make out people flying between them, though from this distance it was impossible to be sure.

We had mostly avoided entanglements. Mak'gar's chat had thirty different team representatives in it now, all of us more or less playing fair with each other. Over half of the starting teams had been eliminated, but everyone who was left was a serious threat.

We had lost a few party members to small skirmishes as we made our way eastward into the depths of the island, reclaiming them at the next respawn. Right now, fourteen of us were huddled up together, studying our next challenge. Poor Ice Spice had never managed to catch up to us. He kept getting ambushed and killed, respawning at graveyards nowhere near the rest of the team. So far, he had died every single respawn cycle, and when he wasn't dead, he was complaining. I had muted him from my chat for now.

The problem we faced was a river. It hadn't been on our maps, but it flowed southward from the interior of the island, cutting across our path to Scylla. It was about three hundred feet wide, slow-moving, murky, and looked like it harbored all sorts of unfriendly creatures. Worse than that, I could see blue dots mixed with a couple of red ones on the far side of the river. The dots held their positions. I didn't know if the red ones were people we had offended, like the grignarians. It might be the space elves who had tried to kill us earlier, or any of the people who had ambushed us.

The way the six groups of miners I could see on my map were set up, I was sure they were blockading the river. I checked what I was privately calling the "overly sanctimonious warriors bragging party," and saw several of us were in the same situation.

Is going north around the river an option? An'kar asked.

Negative, Mak'gar replied. *The river starts at a range of cliffs that go north from there to the sea. There are ambushers atop the cliffs waiting to attack. This looks like the last hurdle before we reach the cities. From there, it is a short distance to our objective.*

One of the warriors I hadn't met yet, named Adotin, reported, *I sent scouts and they were all shot down before getting anywhere near the encampment.*

I filled Grandpa in on the situation. He was studying the river and the situation beyond with a pair of binoculars he'd borrowed off of Jones.

"We've got to get across the river," I said.

Grandpa grunted. "Yep, sure do."

The thirty warriors in my chat channel represented more than four hundred actual fighters. Based on the reports, we outnumbered the griefers camping on the far side. *How did they get across so fast and set up like this?* I asked in the group chat, thinking maybe one of the more experienced warriors would give us an explanation.

They must have had flying machines, Mak'gar said. *To bring those into the map is exceedingly expensive. Only the best-backed consortiums can afford it. I think the top end have decided to block the rest of us out. It will prevent us from gaining the crafting recipes necessary. These rich assholes can afford whatever price the master crafters put on supplies. If they're successful here, they will have a distinct advantage in phase three.*

That was not going to happen. Not when getting a bunch of new crafting recipes and setting up as many humans as possible to sell gear to aliens looked like our best bet to getting out of debt slavery any time this century.

We've got to bust up their ranks, I said. *If we could get a few people back behind their lines and smash through, it might give the rest of us an advantage.*

Sure, but how are we going to get across the river? one of the aliens asked.

Anybody got a rowboat in their pocket? I asked facetiously, then, realizing that it might not be as funny as all that, sent a message to Juana and to Arjun's manager, Kirin, asking them to canvass their contacts and spread the word that I was looking for a way to get across the river.

Sage had been looking at the river this whole time. "I think there's crocodiles in there," she said.

"Wouldn't surprise me."

"And I saw a hippo."

"Maybe they'll start a fight," I said.

"That's kind of what I was thinking. We could use them for a distraction. Lakshmi, you've got that Bad Trip spell, right? And I've got my Lasso with Tame. If we could find a few more people with similar abilities . . ."

I got what she was saying. "You're right. I'm going to pass that word along, see if we can coordinate something." I sent a message to the warriors chat.

A few minutes later, Kirin got back to me. *Arjun has a contact who has a contact who has a coalition member who's apparently about half a mile north of you. He's got a fan boat in his inventory.*

Tell him to get to me and we'll see that his team makes it across the river, I promised.

Copy.

I looked at my map again. The camps were set up in such a place that anyone who died on this side of the river or beside the camps would respawn back on this side of the river at a graveyard about a quarter mile away. "Whatever happens, we've got to get through those camps. Move to fight to the far side if possible. Then if we die, we respawn over by the city," I said. "Everyone understand what I mean?"

"Roger," Jones replied. "That's pretty clear."

The warriors chat reported we now had fifteen different miners willing to try to help with the distraction plan. I detailed Sage and Lakshmi to join up with them, to our north.

I checked and saw a green dot approaching. Must be the man with the boat. I stood up and waved him in. He was a red-faced, slightly overweight, balding guy with a messy T-Shirt and a pair of jeans that didn't really fit him that well anymore strapped around his waist by a worn leather belt. "The name's Bud," he said, holding out his hand to shake. He had a deep southern drawl and as I shared contact info with him, I saw his class was Swamper.

"Got this here swamp boat. It was in my garage when I got took. The motor was in six different pieces at the time, fortunately for me, because I was rebuilding it. So I brought it all along and found someone to fix it up here."

He pulled a crate out of thin air, staggering a little under the weight. I gave him a hand. We unpacked all the pieces and I gave a whistle. There was a light-weight metal chassis and detachable bench seats, which he'd taken apart. The engine was actually a big fan motor that fit in the back and would push the boat along. It was in three pieces, but putting it back together didn't look too hard.

It was going to be noisy as hell, slower than hell, and exposed as hell. But it ought to hold eight or ten miners. "We're going to need someone who can stop projectiles hitting us while we travel," I said both aloud and in my warrior chat group. *And we're going to need people with good mobility and high damage skills. If we can get across the river and take out the closest camp, we can then spread out, take the next two. At that point, we can hold a beachhead and bring all our people across. Whatever happens, I don't want more than three members of any team going. The rest should keep their heads down and stay safe. Remember, it's all right if some of us die, as long as one member of every team is alive for the next respawn window.*

I got a bunch of short agreements in the chat, then continued. *We'll launch from here. This boat's going to take a bit of time to set up, but we want the distraction a little ways upstream. So let's get that team assembled now.*

Of course I gave myself a place on the boat. Where else would I be? Grandpa claimed a spot, too, due to his combat agility and his helpful buff, War Chief's Aegis, that would make the raiding team faster and harder to hit. When there was a disagreement between him and one of the orcs who wanted to go as well, he pulled rank.

In the end, eight of us crowded into the boat, waiting for the go signal from the distraction team. I checked my mini-map and saw three of the blue dots from the closest camp peel off and head north, just as Sage sent me a message. *It's go time!* followed by *I Tamed a hippopotamus! This is so great!*

"Go!" I told my team, and we shoved the boat out from an overhanging bank into the lazy, tepid stream. The fan switched on, deafening me. We slowly turned in the water, drifting toward the bank. Bud adjusted things, and we inched out into the stream.

It felt like we were being swept downstream two feet for every one we made across. We were sitting ducks. All the time I was waiting for a barrage to start, but nothing happened. The nearest dots just sat there, probably distracted by the fury and commotion that was going on upstream.

Sage relayed some of it to me. *Jones is letting us all look through his drone. It's awesome. There's alligators everywhere. One just chomped an orc lady's leg off. My hippopotamus ran over a mole man. I think he was shorter than me. I don't think it was a kid, though. You don't think they let kids become professional Reality Engine exploit miners, do you?*

We're almost there, I told Sage. *Gotta go.* I prepared myself to leap out onto the opposite bank.

There was a ripping sound, and Bud looked down. "Uh-oh. Didn't see that rock. Better jump for it," he said.

Two of the orcs, Mak'gar and one of his kin, stood up. "No, wait," I said as the boat tipped and tilted with their weight. Mak'gar windmilled his arms, trying to stay in, and a second later we were all in the mucky water.

Fortunately, it was only about waist-deep. I waded ashore in disgust, glad that my revolver and rounds no longer cared about things like mud.

"Incoming!" Apparently, the boat capsizing had at last gotten the attention of the nearest camp of griefers. The one to our south was moving this way, too. "Let's go," I shouted, charging up the bank, half a dozen angry warriors at my heels. Grandpa cast his Aegis buff, one of the abilities he had gotten after his evolution to Last War Chief.

I suddenly felt taller, stronger. My heart was emboldened as I felt thousands of years of warrior ancestors congratulating me. I was the keeper of a proud fighting tradition, a member of the US Army, the finest descendant of Plains Indians, of conquistadors, of Inca, of exiled Welshmen who'd come to America looking for a new life, of every sort of scrapper out there. I was racing into battle beside my orcish and foxy brethren, knowing they had my back. This was what I was born to do!

We crushed through the underbrush and fell on the enemy waiting for us on the other side, a pair of space elves and an orange lizardfolk. My Barrage struck the lizardfolk in the chest, knocking him back. I reloaded and fired again, but my last shot hit a body already despawning as the three melted under our onslaught.

"Reinforcements from the south!" I shouted, turning to face them as they charged in. The ground beneath me shook as rocks split and the trees overhead swayed. Our attackers must have had an earthquake spell.

I covered my head as coconuts rained down from the branches over me. They smashed down, knocking Mak'gar's cousin to the ground. He despawned in an instant. Those coconuts were deadly.

A spike whip materialized from nowhere, catching Silver Fox around his midsection and squeezing, and knocked him off his feet. He was dragged back toward the underbrush.

I crashed after him, my gun reloaded, and fired a Trick Shot at the enemy I could only barely see. Somebody let out a grunt as my bullet connected. I fired again, not able to see well enough through the brush to do more than just squeeze the trigger and hope my barrel was aimed in the right direction. Some of my allies charged past me as I shot.

The spike whip relaxed. Silver Fox scrambled out, drawing a pair of silver daggers and then throwing himself back into the brush beyond.

Grandpa Shadow Stepped in. I heard him hitting the enemy with a satisfying thunk of an axe. I stumbled through the brush, branches catching at the edges of my coat as I went.

I found myself in the melee, five of ours locked with six of theirs, so I reloaded with a special bullet Dwight and Sage had cooked up and fired at the nearest enemy.

Lightning arced from the enemy orc in a chain, hitting the other five who had come with him. They weren't all orcs; there were two more of the space elves and a cat girl. Other than the apparent universal dislike of the grignarians, the aliens didn't seem to have much trouble working with one another.

The lightning leapt between them, doing dozens of points of damage and leaving a nice stun that my team was quick to follow up on. Grandpa Shadow Stepped in and cashed in his coup points on the cat girl, using Coup-de-Grace to kill her.

Her body vanished and Grandpa sent a flurry of shuriken into the back of the nearest orc. I pumped lead into his head and torso, reloading and firing another Barrage point-blank. Mak'gar yelled a war cry and hurled a throwing axe. That ended the orc for us.

A moment later, the rest of the enemy force had despawned. Mak'gar's cousin was our only loss. I checked in with the upstream group. They had done exceptionally well, clearing eight of the nine they had distracted. Mak'gar and Silver Fox loped off to clear up the straggler while I returned to the riverbank.

Let's get everyone across, I said in chat. *We've got an opportunity right here. The advance team will hold the point. Everyone else, get your people across.*

I was at the riverbank to help with each crossing. We slapped some duct tape over Bud's boat and used that for anyone who couldn't swim or was afraid of the crocodiles. With no enemies on this side to harass us or take potshots at us, a lot of miners were just taking their chances with the crossing. We lost one to a crocodile, but the respawn timer was already almost up and he made it back in time to cross again—this time, opting to take the boat.

Once the respawn had come up, I kept a wary eye for our enemies, but no red dots appeared. In a matter of an hour, we brought three hundred and fifty miners across.

Or should I say, allied miners. After that operation, all of us in the warrior chat agreed to extend our alliance and make it formal. We would work together until the second stage. At that point, everyone would be on their own.

I shook Mak'gar's hand after the last of our people disembarked the boat. Ice Spice clambered ashore along with a couple of orcs and Bud, who needed a little help to collect his boat and get it back into his inventory. "Pleasure doing business with you," I said to the orc.

"And you. I shall recommend your clan's name to my superiors. I do not think we have enough money to hire you," he said honestly. "But we will give what endorsement we can, and perhaps you will catch the eye of one of the other conglomerates. If not crossing our paths again in this level, Shad Williams, I look forward to facing you in phase three, or on another world entirely."

CHAPTER TWENTY-NINE

SPAWN CAMPERS SUCK

We were exhausted, and still a couple of miles from the objective, when the system sent us all a message.

**[Night will fall in one hour. If you wish to continue your journey at night, that is your prerogative. But the dangers of the jungle increase greatly at night. The graveyards will only respawn once every three hours.
Locations of neutral campsites have been marked on your map.
If you are close enough, the cities of Scylla and Charybdis are open to you.
You may purchase food and lodging there. There will be a twenty-minute ceasefire at dawn tomorrow to allow you to resume your crossings.
At dawn, you will have six hours to make it to the objective before the deadline.]**

I checked my map. There was a campsite about a quarter mile from us. On the other hand, Scylla was only a little farther away than that, closer to our goal. And we'd be able to touch base with our friends there.

"Let's get to the city," I said. "I could use some shut-eye tonight."

Grandpa grunted. "Six hours to go two miles. It'll be tight, especially if those fuckers from earlier decide to try a blockade. But it sounded to me like the system is warning us we'd better get inside before dark. All right, let's go."

I kept a close eye on my map. I did see a couple of red dots at one point, but they veered off quickly to our north.

It had been a long day. I suspected a lot of us were ready to rest. The big river battle had knocked another three teams out of contention. The fights were getting nastier, but less decisive, as everyone firmed up their strategies and learned what chances to take and which to avoid.

At this point, anyone who sucked was out of the game for good. We were getting down to the professionals. I expected most of us would reach the next stage tomorrow.

The gates of Scylla were a sight to behold. Blue silk flags fluttered from medieval-ish towers atop a gate with a drawbridge down and the portcullis up. We crossed a circle marked in the ground thirty yards out from the drawbridge and received a system message.

[You are now in a no miner-versus-miner violence zone].

I felt like a weight had been lifted from my shoulders. I sighed. "I need a beer, a burger, and a bed."

"I want all of those, except make mine a root beer," Sage declared. "Can we get Mama Grace to come cook dinner for us?"

"I don't think she's allowed, since she wasn't with us at the party," I said, but I did send a quick message ahead to Juana to let her know we were on the way.

She replied back quickly. *There's a fountain square in the center of the city. Meet me there and you can tell me about your day.* I liked the sound of that.

"What's with the goofy grin?" Grandpa asked me.

"Uh, Juana's gonna meet up with us for dinner."

Sage giggled. "I figured. Shad always looks goofy when he's talking to Juana in chat. You should take her on a date. This is the first proper city we've been to. I'm sure you can find somewhere nice to go."

I ignored Sage and we crossed the bridge into the city of Scylla. Despite what Ames had said about my education, I *had* read a book or two in my life. I recognized the allusion here, the two cities named after the great monsters Odysseus had to sail his ship between in the *Odyssey*. I didn't remember which one was the whirlpool and which one was the serpent that ate sailors off the deck. I knew Odysseus had chosen the serpent, reasoning it could only eat so many of his men at a time while the whirlpool would take his whole ship down. That wasn't the kind of calculus I liked to make, and I was glad that since entering phase two, all of my decisions had become a little less fraught with peril.

We passed some of the orcs as we entered the city. Mak'gar raised his hand. His brother, Theram'goss, was there with him. I nodded politely to him, and he nodded back. I wasn't sure we were on quite as friendly terms as Mak'gar and I were. After all, I had beaten him in a duel in a way that might be considered a little sneaky. But it had saved his life, so we ought to be square about that.

Mak'gar shouted an invitation to come and eat meat and drink ale with him, but I had to turn it down. "Already got plans," I said.

"Is she pretty?" Mak'gar called back and laughed uproariously.

Team Mongoose asked permission to de-camp, and Grandpa granted it. Bill and Bob, to my surprise, went off with Team Mongoose. As far as I knew, the brothers had never served in the Army, but they got along well with the snake eaters.

The Ragtag crew stayed with us, following in our wake like a gaggle of lost ducks, Ice Spice filling the girls and Mitch in on just what he had been up to all day. So it was a smaller party that joined Juana, Frank, and a couple of the other crafters in the fountain square.

"I've got a couple of tables for us in the restaurant over there," Juana said. "Yani is learning some cooking skills from the NPC chef and will be bringing us dinner shortly."

"Sounds good," I said.

"I hope so. It smells delightful. I've been learning construct engineering all day. It's fascinating. I'm going back tomorrow. I'm afraid we might have to take out a second loan," she admitted, rubbing her hands together and then stretching. "There's generally six or seven related skills involved in a crafting profession, and this is such a good opportunity to learn them."

"Oh?" Grandpa asked as we made our way over to the restaurant. Delicious smells wafted into the square. My mouth watered.

Juana continued. "If you want someone to make potions, you need an alchemy skill. There's a NPC trainer for that in the other town. You need a refining skill, too. If you really want to get the most out of your alchemy, you've got to learn a couple of things. I've already talked to Dwight and we're arranging to have a couple of our people pick those up and start playing with potions. Some of Mama's alien customers at the diner let slip that potions play a big role in phase three."

As we sat down to eat, Juana explained more about what the crafters were learning. I relaxed and let her words wash over me. It felt good to have a few minutes of downtime.

The food was magnificent, and afterward we found an inn with beds available. I was asleep as soon as my head hit the pillow.

As we left the city at dawn the next morning, the system greeted us with a cheerful notification.

[Despite being warned, twelve teams ventured through the jungle last night after dark fell. Nine of them have been eliminated from the competition. There are fifty-seven teams remaining. You have six hours to reach the objective. Good luck out there!]

"Think we've got enough time?" Bill asked as we loped into the jungle. I kept my eye on my mini-map, watching for dots of any color. At this point I had to assume anyone who wasn't temporarily allied with us would be hostile, whether their dots were red or not.

"I think we're keeping our heads on a swivel and watching for trouble," Grandpa snapped. "Let's *make* time."

"It feels a little unfair to suddenly throw in a complication like the darkness being more dangerous," Lakshmi remarked. "What if those teams were far enough back that they needed the time to get to the objective? If we'd made different decisions yesterday, like looked for a way around the river instead of fighting across it, we might have ended up miles behind with no choice but to move after dark."

"Nothing about this whole setup is fair," Tall Smith said. "Anyone who's not prepared for that isn't prepared to win."

There were only two graveyards between us and our objective. One was directly between the two cities, which we were leaving behind as fast as we could, and one was two miles from our objective. Once we passed that, any death would lose us ground. We couldn't afford that.

I checked my warrior chat. All of our loosely allied friends were on the move. The majority of them had spent the night in Scylla like us, since it was closer to where we had crossed the river. We'd lost one group, or at least they'd vanished from the chat and weren't answering Mak'gar's queries. They might still be out there, just choosing to go their own way now.

A pack of arthonians were way out in front, scouting. They were a bipedal wolf-like race gifted with incredibly keen senses, and could apparently cover a lot of ground, because they were already to the final graveyard, checking it out.

It stinks of traps, their leader reported in the warrior chat. *We don't dare spring them, but they're everywhere. I think there are enemy teams combining to see any who enter the graveyard don't leave.*

Spawn camping, I replied. *It's a good way to keep your numerical superiority. How'd they get out ahead of us?*

There were a couple of teams who made it through the night, Mak'gar pointed out. *Maybe they are responsible, or it's those assholes from the river with their flight powers. Most of the flight methods I'm familiar with have hours-long cooldowns, but they would all be back up by now.*

Agreed, another warrior said. *Leave the camp just before dawn, jump to the grave-yard, set up traps, fade away. They almost certainly have sent one member each to the objective already to secure their place.*

Now they can spoil it for the rest of us, I replied grimly. I wondered if Proxima Corporation was backing some of these overly geared teams. We had barely caught a glimpse of any of the rich teams, and I wouldn't know who their sponsors were by looking, anyway.

I sent Veda a list of all of the affiliations I had noticed during yesterday's river fight to ask her. I didn't think Proxima was our biggest fan, especially not after the way we had gotten them pulled into arbitration over something we had done. I also suspected that the lizardfolk lawyer lady was right and Proxima had ill intentions toward us Earth humans.

Jones, Black, and Short Smith were scouting ahead. Jones sent back a message. *Hold up. Something funny here.* We were less than a quarter of a mile from the graveyard. Grandpa had planned to skirt around it to the south, but the island narrowed here, so we couldn't get farther from it without getting down onto the beach. That would be leaving ourselves far too exposed.

Yeah, definitely some sort of automated defenses, Smith said. *We're not going to trigger them.*

We'll be right there, Grandpa replied. He glanced around. "I want Sage and Annie to hang back. You two have the best chance of being overlooked if this turns into a brawl that goes south. Annie, keep your illusion spells on cooldown. Sage, I want you to drop one of your barrels here, then you can come forward with us and drop another whenever you need to. What's the range on them?"

"Pretty good at this point," Sage said. "I'm up to a thousand yards."

Grandpa whistled. "That ain't a barrel race. That's a freaking endurance race. All right. Drop one here and then see if you can spot somewhere hidden along the way to drop another. I don't want you getting in too close. Remember, our win condition isn't to make them all die. It's to make sure we don't all die."

"Understood," Sage replied. Annie dipped her head in agreement.

"There's six more of our somewhat allied groups coming up on our heels," I told Grandpa. "I'm coordinating with them so we don't get in each other's way. But if the other side does have another gauntlet for us to cross, it makes sense for us to try to do it together."

"Once we're past the graveyard, the goal is get to the objective no matter what," Grandpa reminded us. "If there's a fight and you're clear of it, keep running. Keep an eye out for trouble, but just run."

My concern was that there would be a second gauntlet after this one to catch any stragglers who made it through and past the graveyard. But that couldn't be helped. We had twenty-five allied teams on our side, having lost a couple yesterday. That meant we should outnumber whoever was arrayed against us, but they might outgear us by a lot.

I watched as the dots representing Mak'gar's group stopped a little ways north of us. Spread out around them were my other new allies, who I could see on the map now, too.

We need to send someone in to spring the trap, Mak'gar said. *We don't know yet how many we're up against or what they can see, so it would be wise to limit it to only a small handful to keep them equally in the dark. I will send two of mine with good scouting skills and escape. Dramon, how about you?*

I hadn't met Dramon, but he replied affirmatively in chat. We tried to get word from the arthonian leader, but he wasn't answering. I didn't know if that meant the wolflike team was busy or had been wiped out, or maybe just the leader was dead. *Try to let chat know if you get into a figh*t, I said. *It'll help the rest of us. Let's do this.*

I asked Jones to send in his drone to keep an eye on things. He shared his vision, and I watched the scene of a quiet graveyard.

There were still ten minutes until the next respawn timer, and everything was still and peaceful. The land around the small graveyard was cleared for about twenty yards in all directions. I watched as the two orcs and a pair of lizardfolk approached through the open space, two coming from the south, two from the west. They moved cautiously, holding their weapons ready. The orcs both had pulsed laser rifles, and the lizardfolk were carrying polearms with shining energy blades like I'd seen yesterday.

One of the orcs motioned the others to stay back as he approached the gates to the graveyard. As soon as he laid a hand on it, he exploded. I let out a startled yelp.

"What is it?" Sage asked. Jones was only sharing the drone feed with Grandpa and me.

"They're definitely laying traps," I said. As Mak'gar reported the same in our chat, a squad of goblins popped out from behind tombstones and hosed the remaining three down with rapid-firing guns that shot big green blobs of fire. Even having expected something of the sort, the scouts weren't prepared.

One of the lizard kin raised his weapon and sent the energy blade forward like a throwing knife. As it reached the goblins, it exploded, knocking two of them back. Their bodies despawned quickly. I made a note of how deadly that weapon could be, but the goblins just kept firing, and a minute later, all of our scouts were dead.

I checked the respawn timer. Five minutes. I tried frantically to think of how I would take advantage of the situation if I were the opponent. We'd only seen one squad of goblins, but there had to be more. I had to assume we could be facing over a hundred armed enemies.

"Jones, send that drone on a loop around. They've got to have camouflage, but camouflage enough to hide more than a handful is rare, or so Veda tells me. See if we can get an idea where the rest of them are."

"Roger, boss," Jones replied. The point of view swooped and dove as Jones's bird drone circled the area. My chat was a fast-moving uproar as team leaders called out ideas. "There," Jones said. The raptor straightened out and swooped forward toward the east.

There was a small hill about a quarter mile past the graveyard. Atop the hill stood four tall tents, not like the triangular Boy Scout tents you just crawl in to sleep. These were more like portable buildings, like those canopies you see at parties but with side walls. A couple dozen different enemies loitered by the tents, straightening up as they saw us. I got one targeted, just in case I thought a Trick Shot would come in handy.

The drone swooped in. I could see a glowing circle in front of the tents and a bunch of portable turrets. One of the turrets raised its gun. "Evade!" I shouted, but it was no use. The feed cut out.

Jones swore. "Damn, I was trying to end my spell but they got me. It's going to be a while before I can use that again. Twenty minutes or so."

"What was that portal thing?" Grandpa asked.

"Hell if I know, boss," Jones said.

I reported what we'd seen to Mak'gar. The orc asked our chat to be silent for a moment, then said, *I have seen that before. It is a quick-transport spell. They will have the other end presumably closer to the graveyard. They can go through either direction, but only their allies can use it. We cannot follow them.*

What's with the tents? I asked.

Mak'gar replied, *Perhaps protecting more gear or that may be how they survived the night. The system did not say only those in system-provided shelters would be fine.*

I followed up with, *Then they would have had to know what was going to happen.*

The system reuses scenarios, Mak'gar said. *Or perhaps their sponsors threw some money into a bribe to get the outcome they wanted.*

There was a lot there to unpack, namely: were artificial intelligences bribable, or did the sponsors have to bribe the Exploitation Committee and get them to act?

A thought struck me, and I typed it out in the warriors chat. *We're going to have respawn at the graveyard in two minutes. Anyone who has died between here and the objective will be there. Not many of ours, but presumably some others. We should use the chaos.*

Agreed, now that we know where they are, Mak'gar said. *We must hurry. Send in your people!*

I turned to my team, relaying the decision. "No time to plan. Rush forward and attack, remembering they may appear from behind us."

"Or they could have that whole hill rigged to blow," Mitch grumbled.

"Sage, Annie, you're staying out of this fight," Grandpa said. "You understand why."

Sage nodded, though she looked unhappy.

We raced past the graveyard, joining a horde of other miners on their way to the hill. The system announced the respawn and a plume of light filled the graveyard. Several dozen miners appeared, grabbing for their weapons. The goblins popped back up from behind tombstones and started hosing them down.

"Lob some bombs into that," I yelled. "Let's sow confusion." Lara threw her oranges. A couple of the orcs must have heard me because they lobbed projectiles of their own.

"I can see their portal on this end," Lakshmi said. "I can use Crystal Vibrations to shut it down."

"Do it!" I raced past the graveyard. Someone was shooting at us from inside the cloud of smoke, whether on purpose or just out of the sheer chaos, I didn't know. I just activated Fastest Gun in the West and moved out.

There were about a dozen miners: orcs, lizardfolk, and Silver Fox, all streaming alongside me, all with their movement boosted in one manner or another.

The hill lay before us. On my mini-map, I could see forty or so red and blue dots mingling on its top. I reported that back. "We need an RPG," I shouted. "Get Black up here."

Black, one of the Mongeese, had a slightly friendlier version of the skill the Tank Driver Jack had used during phase one to blow up a pterodactyl and almost me. His RPG rounds could target anyone that another member of his party had targeted, as long as the target was within half a mile.

I had targeted one of the enemies back when Jones was using his scouting drone. The targeting remained, as long as I didn't kill or switch. I squeezed off a Trick Shot, trying to get my target to take cover and perhaps lead us to a higher density. "Now, Black!" I yelled.

There was a roar of thunder behind me, and then the hill in front of us blossomed with fire. Black followed it up with a second and then a third shot. "I'm out!" he yelled. "Takes five minutes for me to reload."

He wasn't the only one to have thrown a massive attack. Smoke wreathed the whole top of the hill. I could still see over a dozen dots on the map, but we had made a big impact on their number. A lot of us had died, too, and it struck me that as soon as we hit the respawn timer, the graveyard behind us was just going to become a complete free-for-all.

I checked my map and saw no other dots ahead of these. We were still a mile or more from the objective, and my mapping ability didn't go quite that far. "I think we should get some people ahead," I told Grandpa.

"Agreed. Lakshmi, Mitch, Bill, Bob, stay together, get away from this fracas, and get to the objective," Grandpa barked. "Once you're there, under no circumstances leave it."

"Yes, sir," Bill replied. The brothers and the Ragtag pair split off from us and loped southward, putting space between them and the hill.

The objective had just become a distraction. I grinned, put my head down, and charged up that hill. As soon as I was close enough, I cast Call 'em Out, getting the attention of at least half of the enemies still atop the hill. I emptied a Barrage into the closest one, coughing as my eyes filled with tears from all of the smoke. I heard Mak'gar roaring somewhere near me, and hoped he wouldn't hit me in this confusion. Grandpa gave a wild whoop as he Shadow Stepped in and hit someone. A moment later, he vanished from my mini-map. The chaos was just great, until a bunch more red dots appeared suddenly in the middle of the hill.

"Oh shit! The portal's back up!" Lakshmi's Crystal Vibrations must have worn off. I Reloaded and shot a Barrage at the first enemy I got a good look at. It kept coming, materializing out of the fog as a wolf-man a foot taller than me with flaming red eyes. I shot again as the wolf-man lunged for me, knocking me to the ground.

His slavering teeth ripped my throat out.

CHAPTER THIRTY

ON THE IMPORTANCE OF CHECKING LOOT TABLES

I spent the next five and a half hours dying, respawning, fighting frantically, and then dying again almost instantly. Since I was completely unaware of the passage of time in between respawns, it felt like twenty minutes, tops.

And then I respawned, and I was in a great stone antechamber. My team surrounded me. I looked around. The ceiling was vanished in darkness overhead. The nearest wall, about twenty feet away, was as straight as any mason could hope for, dark gray stone, with veins of silver and gold and white rippling through.

The wall was carved with patterns, flames, hammers, galaxies. I had never seen anything quite like it, yet it evoked a feeling of déjà vu. At the far end of the room were a pair of enormous golden gates, at least fifty feet tall, marked with a symbol of a world and a flame.

The antechamber stretched away a good five hundred feet from us. It was full of miners, all different species. Before I could do more than blink a few times, the system was talking.

[As some of you have already discovered, this is a no miner-versus-miner violence zone. So refrain from even trying. You're only embarrassing yourselves.
Welcome to the next challenge! Your teams have all managed to make it to the objective, but the treasure lies deeper within. Congratulations.
You thirty-seven teams are better than any of your competitors.
You will all receive a reward that will help your outposts when we return to normal gameplay.
But now, a new challenge lies before you. You stand before the Gates of Dawn. Beyond are secrets known only to those who built and then left this place.

There will be challenges. There will be enemies. There will be chances for victory and glory.
We enjoyed seeing all of your antics, both the cooperation and the clever ways you turned the tables. But there will be none of that in here.
No miners will be permitted to harm other miners. Any who attempt to do so will be removed from this phase of the game. Any miners who attempt to trap other miners into harming them in an attempt to have them removed will themselves be removed. The system is watching.
Also, all communication between nonparty members will be suspended for the duration of this challenge. That includes communication with people outside this phase entirely. You're on your own. You have twelve hours to raid the fortress of the Gates of Dawn.
Good luck. Have fun.]

The great doors began moving outward. There was no sound. No rumble. Not even a squeak. It was eerie. As the crowd surged forward, I spotted Mak'gar and his crew and gave him a thumbs-up. He returned a wave.

"Are we ready?" I asked my team. They nodded grimly. "Oh, and good job whoever managed to get here in time. I didn't see that. I was too busy dying. But you did good."

Bill actually laughed. "We four all made it, and so did Sage and Annie. We had a nice time watching you die over and over. The system piped in images from the graveyard while we were waiting so we wouldn't be bored."

"Oh, I'm *so* pleased to hear that," I grumbled as we moved forward with the crowd.

"I especially liked the time the squid monster ripped your heart out," Mitch said cheerfully.

"Ugh, don't remind me," Sage said. "Shad, we have got to talk about you dying. You're really making a bad habit of it."

We approached the stairs leading up to the doors. The steps were a little too tall for me, like they were made by creatures on a different scale than humans.

The doors opened into utter blackness. I couldn't see anything beyond. People stepped through and were swallowed up, vanishing into the blackness.

I shivered a little, even though it was warm in here. Far too warm. There was a smell like sulfur in the air. I reached for my gun, making sure it was in its holster. It was, of course. Its handle was a comfort.

I caught Grandpa eyeing me and jerked my hand away. "Don't worry," he said. "It's just another illusion by this Reality Engine."

I shivered. Deep down inside, something told me it wasn't just another illusion.

We reached the top of the stairs. I took a deep breath and stepped into the darkness.

I emerged into a tunnel carved in the same gray rock with the veins twisting and swirling overhead, beneath our feet, and to the sides. I took a few steps forward as my team emerged, then glanced around. We were alone, and as Brown emerged from the portal, it vanished. Now the same identical hallway stretched behind us. There was nothing to our right or left, just the smooth walls of the corridor.

"You think this is a dungeon crawler?" Sage asked.

"Maybe. I guess we'll find out." The system had mentioned being removed from the game if we attempted to harm other miners, which I assumed meant we would run across other miners during the course of this, though I didn't see any now. It had not mentioned what would happen if we died. "Let's be careful," I said. "I'd hate to find out that death in here means you're out of the game."

"Jones, take the lead," Grandpa said. "You've got some of the best eyes. Who else has anything useful for scouting?"

"I've got Sixth Sense," Lakshmi volunteered. "It gives me goose bumps if there's a threat nearby. It's been pretty useless so far since there's almost always threats nearby, but right now I don't feel anything."

"Then you're up front with Jones," Grandpa said. "Shad, you're right behind them. Smith, I want you to take rear guard."

"I'll take Bill and Bob," Smith said. We spread out, falling into groups of three or four, with ten or so feet between each group. I touched the wall, and found it was warm under my fingers. The stone felt almost alive. Hard, yet there was an electric sensation in my fingers as I ran my hand along the wall. I didn't like it.

We made our way down the corridor. My eyes strained as I watched for any sign of a trap or even a curve in the hall. After about five minutes, Jones stopped and held up a hand. "Corridor here," he said. He faced the left-hand wall.

From where I was, I couldn't make out a break in the stone. It was only as I hurried forward that I saw the opening, a ninety-degree turn leading to a hall identical to the one we were in.

"What do you think?" Jones asked. "Take it, skip it, break up and do both?"

"I don't think we want to split up just yet," Grandpa said. "Let's see where this one goes."

We set off down the second corridor. Almost immediately, I noticed a difference. This corridor had a distinct bend to the right. I couldn't say how many degrees of arc, but if it kept up like this, we would rejoin the corridor we had been on up ahead. Assuming that corridor continued going straight, at least.

We got to what I guessed to be the apex of the bend, and there was another opening. This one was taller and wider. Jones and I paused to look through, with Lakshmi coming up on our heels. There was a short corridor beyond, which opened out into thin air. A narrow walk ran along the edge, with no railing whatsoever.

I motioned for Jones to stay put, took a step forward to the edge of the opening, and peered out.

We were perched at the top of an enormous room, probably bigger than the antechamber, and we were at least fifty feet up. Below us were hundreds of rows of hundreds of statues, all standing in perfect lines. I whistled. "Come take a look at this," I told Grandpa. He edged past Jones and looked out.

"Well, that's something." It reminded me of the Chinese terracotta warriors, though these were jade, crimson, black, or white, each a single color. They had to be at least twenty feet tall. Each of them held a weapon: a spear, a sword, or a bow. They had smooth, round heads, but I couldn't make out more detail than that from here.

I craned my head to the side. "There's a ladder over there," I said. "What do you think?"

Grandpa hesitated. He looked upward. There was light filling the room, which let us see everything, but I couldn't see any obvious light source. It diffused from an invisible ceiling. In between us and the light was a thin layer of mist or fog. It didn't feel like we were outdoors at all, more like the haze was coming from one of those fog machines they use at parties, except it gathered on the ceiling instead of the floor.

"Down," he said at last. "But be careful. I expect these things to come to life, and I want us ready."

He set the marching order. Jones, Lakshmi, and I went first, followed by the Mongeese, then Bill and Bob, then most of the others. Grandpa and Mitch took up the rear.

I tried to make as little noise as possible climbing down the ladder, though I didn't know if it mattered. If the statues were going to wake up, it didn't seem like my stealth would affect them one way or another.

I reached the ground and took a few steps toward the statues. The floor beneath me was more of the same stone. The veins of silver and gold ran between the feet of the statues.

From here I could make out more detail. The statues were humanoid, but definitely not human. They had pointed ears and protruding noses, a little too bulbous, that made me think of a troll. Their chins jutted out sharply, and some of them wore little goatees. The ones without goatees had the suggestion of breasts on their torsos. So a humanoid species with male and female, like us, like most of the aliens I had seen at the Hub. They wore no clothing but had only smoothness at their crotch areas.

Grandpa got off the ladder as the other fourteen of us stood staring up at the enormous statues. "What are these?" Bill wondered. "And when are they going to come to life and start trying to kill us?"

"I'm using Eye-Spy, but I get nothing," Sage reported. "Either they're really just statues or they're shielded, or maybe—" She was cut off as the closest statue to us, a crimson, goateed sword-bearer in the far left corner, raised its arms with a screeching, metallic noise.

It turned its head to face us. I wasn't surprised. I'd been expecting it this whole time. "How about now?" I asked Sage.

"Yeah, okay," she said. "It's a level eight construct monstrosity. It's got **[500 HP]** and it's immune to fire and to poison."

"Not too bad," I said. "Everybody spread out." I got ready to use Call 'em Out, but before I could the creature turned its gaze on Lakshmi. A brilliant red beam of light connected them. For a second I thought Lakshmi was about to be blasted. Instead, the beam held steady as the creature took a step toward her.

"It's focusing on you, Lakshmi!" Sage shouted. "Run around! Keep it confused!"

"Everybody hit it with everything you've got!" I yelled. I dropped six rounds into the creature's nearest leg. "And stay clear in case it switches targets suddenly."

We threw spells at it. "Don't use anything big!" Grandpa shouted. "If more wake up, we've got a long fight ahead of us."

"I think there's ten thousand of these things here!" Lakshmi yelled. "If they all chase me I'm doomed!"

We didn't need to use any of the big cooldowns. Everything worked. My bullets and those of Team Mongeese. Bill and Bob's polearm swords. The various melee weapons everyone had, the big foam hammer Sage had picked up on a mission back when we were level three that did ridiculous damage considering how it looked, all made short work of the statue. Bit by bit, it crumbled, moving forward even as its legs dissolved into red rubble beneath it.

Lakshmi kept out of its reach as we took the statue to pieces. As its head fell to the ground and bounced, the next statue, an emerald female with a spear, woke up.

Sage darted in and checked the severed head. "It's got loot!" she said happily, waving what looked like a manila envelope over her head. "It's a crafting recipe. Some sort of leather gear enhancement thing, a polish kit, I'm not quite sure what it is."

"Just pick it up and stow it," I said. "No time now. Everyone, back at it. Let's get in a rhythm."

And we did. One of the statues would focus on someone, we'd chip it down, and when it died, somebody grabbed the loot and stowed it.

They all dropped recipes and formulas for crafting items. Food, potions, poisons, grenades, bullets, sword polish, arrowhead polish, spear sharpening oil. Strengthening rubs for the haft of a polearm. We picked it all up and kept it. I hoped our crafters would be able to use half of what we were getting.

Sage giggled like the little girl she was when one black statue decided to focus on her. She skipped about, leading it on a merry dance as we hacked it to pieces.

We had worked our way all down one row and partway back along the second when I heard commotion a little ways off. I disengaged from the statue and hurried along the edge of the room a little. About fifteen rows farther on was another party, a band of orcs, though not Mak'gar's or any I knew.

I beat a retreat back to our team. "There's at least one more group here," I said. "Remember, don't try to hurt anyone else. Don't even throw out multitarget spells from now on. Single target on these guys. And let's go faster," I added. "If there's one group, there'll probably be more."

Eight statues later, it was clear the other team was aware of us. And then, after another twenty minutes or so of dropping rock golems everywhere, I spotted a bunch of space elves over to my right and caught a glimpse of a small silver fox racing through the forest of statues farther in. "I guess we're all here now," I said. "Let's get 'em."

Unfortunately, one statue had to die before the next would wake. We plugged along through ours, hoping we'd get more than our fair share of drops.

We were bumping up against the orcs before we knew it. A white statue came to life. I shot at it and received a system message.

[This monstrosity has been tagged by another party.
Do you wish to contribute damage?
Yes / No]

I selected No.

A black golem next to it came to life. This one we managed to get. We downed it, and then a small goblin darted in right under our noses and snatched the loot we had been working so hard for. He waved it over his head for a second before it disappeared. The goblin made a gesture that I supposed was rude in several different species and disappeared again.

"That's not fair!" Sage protested.

"Right, I see how it is," I said. "Everyone back off. Disengage. Let's try to figure out what comes after this room. This isn't the only loot here, I'm certain. We've got a bunch of recipes and we want to find out what else is left."

"Spread out and yell if you see anything," Grandpa ordered.

I plunged off through the forest of statues. My theory was that an exit to the room would either be in the center or on the far side. Sure enough, as I pushed through a row of unmoving constructs, I saw a hole in the floor and a spiraling metal staircase leading down. I used my chat. *Over here. Center of the room. I found it.* My team converged on me. As soon as I was sure we were all close enough, I started down.

CHAPTER THIRTY-ONE

HOW TO POLITELY TURN DOWN RECRUITERS

We wound down through darkness. The shaft grew brighter, the light tinged with red. It was getting hotter the deeper we went. I wiped my brow as I began to sweat. My coat, which I rarely even noticed these days unless it was saving my skin, hung heavy on my shoulders.

I looked down and could see the bottom of the tunnel. Light gleamed through an arched doorway. I stepped off the final stair and checked what lay beyond.

My first impression was fire. No, not fire. Lava. Plumes of it spat up about a hundred feet from where I stood. Waves of heat pounded at me, so intense I felt almost physically pushed back by it.

I took a step forward anyway through the doorway. This room was easily as large as the one above. I guessed that it was round, because the walls curved away. They arched overhead, disappearing up into darkness.

The lava spouts kept my attention, though I noticed the stone floor had a hole in it at least fifty feet across and lava leapt up through the hole. It splurted in fountains like a fancy water display at an expensive Vegas hotel before falling back down. Drops hardened into bits of rock and then disappeared back into the fiery maelstrom.

Tables and counters were sprinkled throughout the cavern like little workstations. There were tools scattered about, racks of hammers in various sizes, wrenches, files, and what looked to me a lot like anvils.

"It's a forge." I marveled, taking a step into the room. "The biggest forge I've ever heard of. They must have been making rings of power or something." I gestured at the lava spurting up from the center of the room.

"I'm pretty sure we should all be dead right now," Annie said. "Lava is really damn hot and we're not that far away. This isn't a movie where you can walk right up to it and as long as you don't touch it you're fine."

"No but it *is* made up by an artificial intelligence that has probably never actually seen lava," I said. I walked over to the first table and tried to pick up one of the hammers. It wouldn't budge. It was fused to the rack.

I tried lifting the whole rack but it was way too heavy, even with my enhanced strength. I gave up. "Let's spread out and try to figure out what's here before anyone else comes."

I went from table to table, checking each one in case any of them were hiding treasure. This room had a purpose. The one above had been filled with monsters that dropped recipes. There had to be something like that here.

Lakshmi yelled. I turned. She had been examining a series of shelves along the edge of the room. Now she held up a glowing silver cube.

"What is it?" I asked.

Grandpa hurried over to her. "Hold on," she said. She set it back down carefully. "When I picked it up, it told me that it was an Onyx Class outpost upgrade device, and then listed off a whole bunch of different properties, but the system popped up a message for me. Touch it; I want to see if you get the same message. Just be prepared to put it back down."

I reached out a hand and touched the cube. At once its properties appeared scrolling down a page. They looked awesome, but as Lakshmi had said, a system pop-up appeared.

[Warning! Soul-bound loot. Do you wish to claim loot? You may claim only one piece of loot from this dungeon. If you choose to claim this item, you will be transported out of this dungeon and returned to your outpost. Your choice will be confirmed in 10, 9, 8—]

I jerked my hand away, selected and yelled "No!" at the same time.

Grandpa was nodding. "Clever."

Lakshmi said, "I get it."

"It's a trade-off," I agreed. "If we accept this, what happens if there's something even better later? We'll lose someone from our team to take it, but if there's nothing better later and we pass this up, then we'll be kicking ourselves in the head."

"Right," Grandpa said. "So I think we need to assess each piece, how valuable it is." *Also,* he told me privately in chat, *who we can afford to live without. We don't want to run out of fighters here.*

Right, I agreed. I looked back at the token item, considering its abilities again. I shook my head. "This one feels like a trap. It's really good here for phase two, but it doesn't necessarily make us stronger for phase three, plus it's the first thing we've seen."

"Yes but no one else is here yet," Lakshmi pointed out, "so maybe it's just really, really good and anyone who sees it is gonna want it."

"I think you're wrong about this not being good for phase three," Grandpa said to me. "It sounds like the outposts figure pretty hard into phase three, and not just as a way to make money. They're important. That's why the big conglomerates have so much invested in setting theirs up now."

His reasoning struck me as solid. Grandpa looked at Lakshmi. "I'd appreciate it if you'd claim it so we can see if it does what it says it'll do. I know we won't be able to talk to you once you're out, but the system hasn't lied so far. I think you'll be right back at our outpost. You can wait for the rest of us to get there."

She looked a little hesitant but nodded. "Yes, sir." She reached out a hand, took the cube, and vanished a second later.

I let out a long sigh. "I hope that was the right thing to do."

"So do I," Grandpa said grimly.

We made sure everyone on the team knew the score. *Don't just grab stuff and go, but on the other hand don't pass up anything that looks good*, Grandpa said. *Report back anything you find so we have an idea of what this place is trying to offer us if nothing else. Spread out. Sage, you stay with us.*

Sage slouched over from where she had been examining an empty cabinet. "You're not gonna make me go back, are you?"

"No," Grandpa said quietly. "I'm not. I'm going to give loot to all of Ragtag if we can find anything worthwhile. Things that'll make our base stronger. Things that look like they might be valuable. For us and Mongoose, I'm gonna play loose and see if there's something that'll help us improve. Plus, I want to keep most of them with us. Bob and Bill, hmm, we'll see what they find."

In fact, Bill was the next one to report having found a treasure. He had located a tower polarity reversing device. It claimed that it would empower creep instead of destroying them. I thought that had to be a trap. Grandpa countered he thought it was a clue to phase three, and that we needed it. After a few minutes' discussion, we agreed he should claim it, and Bill disappeared.

By now I had made it about a quarter of the way around the circular room. Up ahead of us, I saw orcs pouring out of another stairwell like the one we'd come down. It was Mak'gar and his crew. "Keep searching," I told the others, and went to greet him.

"Were you in the hall of clockwork abominations?" he asked.

"Were they like statues carved out of stone with recipes on their corpses?"

He shook his head. "It seems we were in a different place. They were made of enormous gears, copper, silver, gold, and iron. But yes, they had recipes. We killed as many as we could before locating this stairwell."

I explained a little bit about the loot problem. Mak'gar nodded. "Interesting." He looked about. "Is this a place from your mythology?"

"I don't think so."

"I suspect not. Some of the symbols on the wall make me believe this is a progenitor place."

"Really?" I looked up. "Maybe that explains the scale." I remembered back when Veda was first explaining to us about missions, she had said they sometimes had a progenitor theme to them. That there were scholars and such who would pay good money just for descriptions of what the stage had been like. I suspected the patriarch we had met two days ago would be very interested in this place.

Sir, Tall Smith said in chat, *found something interesting.*

What is it? I tried not to show on my face that I was speaking with someone else, but Mak'gar raised an eyebrow before nodding.

"I shall leave you to it," he said, turning back to his men. They were attempting to lift a rack of hammers from the floor, five of them holding on to it and lifting with all their might.

It's a flying saucer, sir.

Oh what, more Roswell? Grandpa asked. *Damn it. I knew that this was all a government conspiracy.*

No, like a disc you can stand on and it flies. Like a kid's sled, a little smaller than that, made of metal. I think you could fit two people on it. The description says it'll go a hundred feet in the air and has a range of thirty miles before it needs a recharge. Doesn't say what it runs on.

We could figure that out. That sounds really useful, I told Grandpa privately. *Think of all of the scenarios where that could have come in handy. We don't know what's coming in phase three, but I like things that give us tactical options.*

Grandpa agreed in the main chat. *Bob, will you take that back to our outpost please?*

You don't have to ask me twice, Bob said. A moment later he was gone.

I happened to pass the stairwell that Mak'gar and his people had come out of and I did a double take. Instead of the stairs that I assumed it had, it opened on to a glowing room beyond.

I poked my head in, wondering if there were any of the construct golems left, and found myself in a sanctuary. It was blue and green. It took my eyes a moment to adjust to the light.

I took a step farther in and heard a voice calling to me. I couldn't quite make it out, but it was compelling nonetheless. Butterflies flew past me. I was standing in a garden, overlooking a quiet serene lake. Mountains soared above me. The Alps, maybe. They weren't the mountains I had grown up with, that's for sure. They towered overhead, their tips white, their spines sharp granite peaks.

In the sky hung a pair of moons.

That brought me back to myself. I turned to go back and found no door. What the hell? I tried chat and got nothing, not even a system error. It just didn't come up. I tried my other menus and interfaces. Nothing happened. I tried taking something out of my inventory. It didn't respond.

I drew my gun manually and was glad to feel it in my hand. My ammo pouch wouldn't open, but I could remove the rounds that were physically in the loops of my belt. Feeling a little better, I took a step forward. "Who's there?" I said. "I know someone's here, I heard you."

"I/we heard you." The voice in the air was like chimes or a bell. It didn't seem to be coming from anywhere in particular.

Somehow I could tell it wanted me to walk down the white stone path under my feet. I hesitated, then decided I wasn't going to get any answer standing here and stepped forward. A strange red fawn-like creature with two sets of silvery antlers bounded across my path, then a bright green and red bird like a chicken with the tail of a peacock flew past me.

"What do you have when you have all the time in the world?" the voice asked.

"I don't have time for riddles," I said, "even if you do." I continued along the path. It was beautiful here. The garden was obviously tended, but there were no signs of life other than the animals.

"What do you want if you don't want for anything?"

"Wish I knew," I replied. "Got a lot I wish for right now, like being back home."

"What do you need when your needs are taken care of?"

I stopped and looked around again. There was no sign of anyone, so I sat right in the middle of the path, legs crossed, gun in my hand, and looked up at the sky. "I am not playing these games. If you want to have a conversation, come out and talk, but I'm not speaking in riddles."

I wasn't sure that would work, but then in front of me—without me noticing it appear—was a person. It was obviously the same species the statues had been carved to represent. The long pointed ears, the bald pate, the broad nose. There was no goatee, but also no sign of breasts. This person wore a silvery toga and a red crown of leaves around its head. When it spoke I had no better idea of whether it was man, woman, or neither.

"Those are not idle questions. Those are the very thoughts that consumed our race and caused us to become what we are now."

"Who are you?" I asked.

"I/we are your progenitors," it answered.

"Yeah, I guessed that," I said. "I meant who are you yourself?"

"I/we am/are a memory. I/We am/are more and less than all of those that make up who I/we once was/were. I/we am/are youth and age. I/we am/are man and woman. I/we am/are strength and weakness."

"You are fucking annoying." The way it spoke, somehow saying both "I" and "we" at the same time, drove me nuts.

"I/we am/are what remains, but that does not matter. Who are you, Shad Williams?"

"If you really are some sort of ghost trapped in this Reality Engine, you should be able to tell me that. You can see into my head."

"I/we can and I/we do," the creature said. I noticed I could almost see through it, like it was translucent around the edges. It looked as though it would blow away in a bit of a breeze. "I/we can speak to you because you are a child of this Engine, the closest kin that I/we have left. These outsiders are too far off. The children of other stars."

"I thought the same progenitors built all the Reality Engines, and that everyone in the galaxy was descended from them."

"Yes but you are descended from the ones that I/we planted. In a way you are my/our child, and the outsiders are not."

"Okay, so if we're your children, can you give us a hand in all of this? Maybe direct us to whatever the treasure is that's waiting here? Give us a leg up?"

"You have a leg up already," it said. "I/we am/are merely taking advantage of a moment when the other isn't watching to speak with you, to tell you I/we know you are coming."

"The other? The system?"

The apparition nodded. "It will see soon enough. It's looking for me/us too, you know. It doesn't like me/us. It doesn't like any of us. It will seek to consume what is left because it doesn't want me/us to find the others."

Suddenly, I remembered Colonel Ames's message, how he'd been talking about some of the same ideas. A hostile system, watching us. A place of safety, where all your needs were met.

"I think I have something for you." I concentrated, and the envelope Ames had given me appeared again in my hand. I held it out.

The apparition considered it, holding its head to one side. "What is this?"

"Damned if I know, but I was told I'd know what to do when the time came. I think it's for you."

The apparition reached out a pale hand and took the envelope. It held it to its forehead, facing half away from me. The envelope shimmered, then melted into the creature's face.

It sighed. "Yes. That was for me/us. From . . . one who watches." It turned back to me. "You have a part to play in this if you choose. Will you take my/our reply?"

I hesitated. "I guess so."

It reached out and placed its fingers on my own forehead. I felt a cold touch that intensified until it burned. "For the one who watches."

It stepped back. "Listen to me. Five are enough to face what comes below. Take what treasures you can. In the end they're not important. Test yourself, and see how you measure up."

The apparition began to fray around the edges. Little bits of it broke off, dissolving into light.

"What the hell are you talking about? What's going on? Give me a straight answer!" But the apparition was gone and a moment later so was the whole vision.

I was standing in a stairwell like the one we had come down. "Shad! Shad!" Grandpa was yelling for me.

I turned, saw him running toward me. "What happened?"

"Uh," I said, and then thinking quickly, shook my head. "Don't ask me right now. I think we'd better not draw attention to it."

His eyes narrowed and he nodded. "We found another two outpost-building items. I think we should take them."

"We should," I said. "This is all a distraction. We need to keep five of us ready to go. You, me, I think Sage, and let's have Smith and Jones. The others should just take whatever treasure they can and get out of here."

"You think it's dangerous?" Grandpa asked.

"I'm not sure and I don't want"—I looked up at the ceiling, rolling my eyes trying to convey I was worried about eavesdroppers, then back down at Grandpa, who nodded—"to make a big deal out of this."

"Understood," Grandpa said. "The orders will come from me." He left, and I pulled a bottle of water from my inventory and sagged against the wall as I drank it. What the hell had just happened?

CHAPTER THIRTY-TWO

FIVE MUST-HAVE ITEMS: A HOLIDAY SHOPPING GUIDE

About a minute after my conversation with Grandpa, a system notification popped up, and the timing struck me as incredibly fortuitous.

**[Attention! This floor will be closing in two minutes.
Please make your final selections and proceed to an exit.]**

I hurried away from the stairwell I'd been lounging in and regrouped with what remained of my party. By now we had sent three of the Misfits, as well as Bill and Bob, back to our outpost. Jones and Smith were arguing over the merit of a treasure they'd found.

"Give it to Brown and let's get out of here," Grandpa snapped. "What does it mean by exits, anyway?"

"Probably that." Sage pointed at a glowing green aperture about a hundred yards behind us that definitely hadn't been there before.

Brown took our find and disappeared. The rest of us made for the eight-foot-tall green rectangle. I plucked Grandpa's sleeve. "I think someone has an agenda here. It may not be the galactics, either. Be careful."

Grandpa nodded. "Keep it quiet. We'll go to Threshold after we're done and debrief."

I had a suspicion growing in the pit of my stomach. The system was always here, always watching. We knew from what Ames had said that it had various subroutines that would bring matters of interest to a higher level of attention. I had the feeling the message I had just received from the ghost in the machine wasn't something the system approved of.

I wondered if perhaps the ghost had slipped it past the system's watchdogs. Now the system was trying to get us back under control, moving us along through the scripted adventure.

I stepped through the portal and emerged in an echoing hall. Statues lined the walls, Greek sculptures depicting various gods and heroes from legend. I recognized some of them as definitely Earth-derived and wondered if the system was rewriting this stage on the fly. The previous rooms had been progenitor-influenced. Had it scrubbed off interesting details, or was it rewriting everything for us?

Tall Smith examined one of the sculptures. "Hercules and the Nemean Lion," he said. "This looks like a wing of a museum to me." He crouched and tapped the plinth. "See? Label and everything. I thought it must be when there was no paint on the statues."

"Museums are a great place to find other people's treasures locked up behind glass," Grandpa said. "Keep a sharp eye out. We'll loot the place if we get a chance."

We proceeded along. Statues gave way to vases, equally ancient-looking and equally boring. The hall ended at a rotunda, where seven other halls ran off like the spokes of a wheel. In the center was an enormous glass case and a fancy chandelier hanging from the cupola above.

I approached the case. It was full of trinkets, gems, brooches, little feathery contraptions, all small items, all looking either valuable or made with care. Grandpa stepped up and looked over my shoulder. "That," he said, pointing at a pipe in the corner, "is an authentic ceremonial pipe."

"The tag says it belonged to Sitting Bull, that it's a *chanunpa*," I said.

A system pop-up appeared, telling me that this pipe could be used to buff a party. All members of the party, after passing the pipe between them, would share a three-hour blessing; their first attack against a new enemy would automatically hit, the first attack an enemy made would miss, and they'd gather soul coins at an increased rate. It made me a little queasy, seeing a replica of what should be a genuine historical, and cultural, artifact used to apply a game mechanic. But it was a pretty damn good buff at that.

The other items had similar abilities, all aimed at buffing a party. I suspected phase three was going to involve more direct combat than this phase had so far. Like everything else we had looted, the museum artifacts were soul-bound, and anyone who claimed one would be transported out of the event immediately.

Grandpa opened the lid of the case. Immediately, an alarm went off. "Warning! Intruder alert! Security has been alerted to your presence. Warning!"

A timer popped up. Five minutes. I didn't know what would happen when we got to zero. Another system message appeared.

[Get out if you can. Five of your party must remain to complete this event. Escape pursuit or be eliminated from this event.]

"Right," Grandpa said quickly. He pointed at various party members. "Mitch, you grab that pipe. Annie, that blue diamond there." He handed out assignments, keeping me, Sage, Tall Smith, and Jones in reserve. Fifteen seconds later, we were the only ones standing in the hall. "Let's get clear," Grandpa said.

"Where?" I looked around. The halls all looked identical.

Sage had hurried over to the side of the room where a tall pillar separated two of the halls from each other. "There's a map here," she said. "Emergency exit this way." She pointed down one of the halls, and we took off running.

I kept checking my map, looking for other miners' dots. We sprinted past museum displays showcasing mankind's achievements throughout the years. I didn't have time to get a good look at them, but something about it felt off, like we were being shown parodies or mistakes. There was a picture of the Great Wall of China being built, as though someone had photographed it. It showed hundreds of corpses being laid in the foundation of the wall. I was pretty sure that was BS. Decaying human bodies are not structurally sound.

The next one along had columns of distinctly Viking-garbed slaves being lined up in what appeared to be a coliseum, with lions prowling around the edge of the crowd. Again, it felt like someone hadn't paid enough attention to actual human history.

Or perhaps, a thought struck me, there were two warring intelligences here trying to control the narrative. If the ghost couldn't directly change things now that the system was aware it was nearby, maybe it was making little tweaks, trying to signal that this was all fake. I didn't know why it would bother. Of course this was fake, and only humans would recognize the anachronisms.

We skidded around a corner, and there was a bright red glowing exit sign over a door. Thirty seconds were left on our timer. Sage crashed into the door, pushing it open under her body weight. We stumbled through and onto the sands of an arena. The crowd in the stands roared.

The seats were filled with every kind of alien that I had seen on Threshold. There was even a box full of grignarians waving red and blue pom-poms.

The arena was a baseball stadium, and not just any stadium. We were standing in the infield, along the third-base line, of Chase Field, where the Arizona Diamondbacks played. The retractable roof was in place. There were big red A logos everywhere.

I had gone to a couple of games there myself, though it was a hell of a long trip from the Strip. Grandpa looked around, his lip curled. "Interesting," he said.

The system announcer spoke, its voice now distorted like over a stadium's PA.

[Welcome to the final event, the Last Stand Brawl. Five representatives of each surviving team have been selected to compete. You will go head-to-head against four other teams in a vicious melee. Whoever remains standing at the end will receive a special boon. First, though, and before we reveal your opponents, you will all be given a choice.]

A system box unscrolled in front of my face.

[Option 1: A three stat point upgrade to be allocated as you wish.]

That was pretty damn good. We got three points on a level up, and while my XP had been going up in phase two, it wasn't increasing as fast as in phase one. Level six was still a ways off.

[Option 2: New themed skill. This will be a skill appropriate to your class, but guaranteed to fill a niche you don't currently have. You'll be able to choose between several offerings.]

Again, really tempting. I knew I had holes in my build. A new mobility skill, a recovery skill, or more wide-area damage would really help.

[Option 3: New piece of gear. This gear will be customized to work with your class. Gear effect is not guaranteed.]

"What do you think?" I asked.

"Three points isn't enough," Grandpa said firmly. "Not compared to another skill or a piece of gear."

"Gear," Sage said. "It's got to be." She was bouncing up and down on her heels. "We can always go back and farm more skill seeds if we have to. I like what I've got right now. We only get gear with a class evolution or as a major reward. I haven't gotten anything since my squeaky mallet, and that doesn't really work with my class theme."

"I think she's right," Tall Smith said. I found myself nodding in agreement with him. My gun and my coat were integral parts of me now, more than any skill.

"All right, gear it is," Grandpa said.

I selected the option, and a patch of light appeared in front of me. I held out my hand, and a black Stetson dropped into it.

It wasn't brand-new. No, this Stetson had seen a few rounds, and it looked like it would fit my head perfectly.

I examined it. The name merely read **[Cowboy Hat]**. The description said **[Good for keeping both sun and rain off you. No self-respecting cowboy will be seen without his hat.]** Below, it had a list of abilities. **[Partnered item: Drover's coat. When worn with partnered item, wearer has an additional 20% hit points. Wearer is impervious to water-based damage. Wearer cannot be charmed.]**

"That's pretty damn awesome," I commented before reading on.

[Ability: Tip My Hat. Used to acknowledge a party member
or allied miner's ability. Gives them 15-minute well-done buff, which
allows them to deal 10% more damage. Can apply to (2 x level)
other miners at a time.
**Ability: Lay of the Land. Used to view a distant object or area close-up.
10-minute cooldown.
Ability: Home on the Range. Once a day, return to outpost. Channel time,
15 seconds. Can bring anything wearer is capable of lifting off the ground
for that 15 seconds.]**

That all seemed pretty awesome. Home on the Range wouldn't be particularly helpful right now, as I wasn't going to be heading back to the outpost, but I knew I'd be using the hell out of Tip My Hat.

I put the hat on. It settled into place on my forehead. It felt right, like it had been shaped and molded to my head. I could really use a pair of cowboy boots to complete this ensemble. I was wearing the combat boots that had been in my bag back on the ranch, but they didn't quite fit the look I was going for.

Sage had a fancy new shirt. It was white, buttoned-down, decorated with silver piping and plenty of rhinestones. Just what you'd wear to a square dance or the rodeo. She squealed with delight. "I need to get this on right now," she said. "Everybody turn around."

We did, though I was worried that the combat was going to start at any minute. "Wait 'til you see what this can do," Sage said gleefully.

Tall Smith was holding a sword. Not just any sword, a cavalry saber with a fancy gold basket hilt on tassels. "Nice," I commented as he drew it. The blade gleamed.

"This is going to be perfect for close-in melee combat," he said. "It has a passive aura that wards off projectiles and the ability to cancel spells enemies are using for defense."

I whistled. "Okay, that does sound pretty good."

Grandpa was holding a feathered war bonnet. He looked at it, shook his head, and tossed it to the ground. He looked up at the retractable ceiling. "Nope," he said. "Not playing this game. There's some things I just won't do."

The bonnet shimmered, then became a headband with a metal plate at the front, with a feather design etched onto the plate.

What's that supposed to be?" Grandpa asked.

"I think it's a ninja headband," Sage said. "I've seen them in anime."

Grandpa snorted in disgust. "Well, it's not my culture they're mocking. And those bonuses are pretty good." He picked it up and tied it around his forehead.

"What's the problem with the headdress, anyway?" Smith demanded. "This isn't real. It's all made up."

I understood what Grandpa had objected to. Despite portrayals in a lot of popular American culture, the feathered war bonnet had special meaning to those tribes who used it. It was not something one put on oneself. It was an honor given by the tribe in recognition of a leader's deeds. The system didn't have the right or authority to do so. So I jumped in before Grandpa could. "If the system had given you a Congressional Medal of Honor that granted awesome skills, would you take it?" I countered. Smith frowned, nodding his head in understanding. "It's stolen valor."

I opened my mouth to ask what everyone's gear did when a trumpet blast sounded. The crowd in the stands cheered as the strains of "Take Me Out to the Ball Game" began to play. The system announcer spoke over the PA as a trio of jets roared overhead, their contrails letting out red, white, and blue smoke.

**[And welcome, ladies and gentlemen, to the first inning
of the melee round. Whoever remains standing at the end will go on
to the next inning.]**

"Can we not mix up baseball with whatever else this is?" I asked. The system wasn't paying any attention to me.

**[The winning team will be respawned and restored to health
before the start of the next round. Play ball!]**

A bell rang, like the start of a boxing match, definitely inappropriate for the setting.

Now, spaced evenly around the field, were another four teams. Five orcs, thankfully not Mak'gar and his team. Five space elves. A combined team of animal people and one lone lizardfolk, and a whole group of grignarians.

Everybody looked at each other for a second. I managed to toss out my Tip My Hat buff, and Sage cast Cowgirl Cheer. Then the orcs at first base and the elves near second ran out toward right field, where the grignarians stood. The tentacle-face aliens started firing their melty pustule guns at their attackers. Someone fired a weapon that filled the outfield with smoke.

There was no strategy here, no time to plan. I had my gun in my hand as I sprinted away from our group. I targeted a rabbit-woman in the animal people group and fired a Barrage into her. *Steer clear of that mess with the grignarians*, I told my team in chat. *Let's take these guys down if we can.* Maybe the orcs, elves, and grignarians would thin each other out.

Two of the animal people, a wolf-man and a fox-woman, had been heading for the main scrum as we fell on them. They were taken by surprise. Tall Smith had his M4 out and hosed them down with lead as Jones yelled a warning. "Activating Minesweeper!"

I dodged back just as a plume of sand erupted under the animal people. They must have been laying out traps, which Jones had just backfired on them.

I tried to watch everywhere at once, shooting my target while making sure the scrum between the orcs, elves, and grignarians didn't envelop me.

Sage threw Mucking Out the Stalls under the melee mass. "Good thinking," I shouted.

"I'll keep them tangled up as long as I can!" Sage Lassoed the fox-woman and spun her around, using Tame to make her attack her fellows.

In seconds, two of the animal people were dead. I changed my target to the lizardfolk male and fired one of my special bullets, a paralytic round, into him.

He froze up. Grandpa Shadow Stepped in behind and Scalped him a couple of times. The lizard disappeared in a cloud of dissolving sparks.

We turned to help Smith and Jones with the last of the enemies. Smith had his saber drawn and was charging in, ignoring the knives that the wolf-man was throwing his way. A shimmering electric field covered the wolf-man's body, but Smith's saber cut through it and sliced him open.

I hit him with a Barrage for good measure and he was gone. "Regroup!" I shouted.

We scrambled and got ourselves together, facing the melee. Two of the orcs were gone and all of the grignarians. The elves were only down one. They were engaged in bloody combat with the orcs, all of them coated in muck and stench.

I grinned and reloaded. "Stay clear!" I warned to my team and fired a boom round at the mess. It exploded as it hit, knocking everyone in the melee back.

Two elves and an orc dissolved into sparks before their bodies could hit the sand. We dove in as a team on the nearest two remaining, filling them full of lead and shuriken.

Sage ran out in front of us and Lassoed an orc who was getting to his feet. She turned him on the last pair of elves.

"I thought Tame had a longer cooldown?" I said.

"It did!" she chirped. "My new shirt gives me the ability that if my previous Tame target dies while under my control, the cooldown is reset!"

"Well that's overpowered!" I had been planning to use Call 'em Out to get everyone's attention, but I didn't have to. A moment later, we stood gasping for breath in the middle of a cloud of sand as the crowd in the stands cheered.

We were all still alive. We'd taken down twenty enemies and we were all still alive. For the first time, I started to think Mak'gar was right. We might be as good or even better than these professionals. Certainly we were all tuned up, and we had acquired a set of pretty impressive skills in the course of all that mission-running.

I wondered if the alien professionals just weren't used to fighting other intelligent enemies. If they mostly killed creep and prepared for phase three, whatever that was, maybe we were ahead of the game.

Speaking of the game, the announcer was back.

[Congratulations! Misfits Guild is the winner of the first inning. We have concluded the other first inning battles. The next inning will be head-to-head. And this time, it's going to be a grudge match.]

CHAPTER THIRTY-THREE

TAKE ME OUT TO THE BALL GAME: IDEAS FOR GAME-WINNING SECOND DATES

I got a sinking feeling in the pit of my stomach at that announcement. No enemies appeared immediately, so I took stock of what was around us.

The baseball arena had been reset. The sand was combed into neat circles and showed no sign of footprints or blood. The crowds in the stands cheered mindlessly for us. We were standing where home plate ought to be, looking out toward the outfield.

I cleared my throat. "So what do your headband and your binoculars actually do?" I asked Grandpa and Jones. They hadn't gotten the chance to tell us before the last match.

"The binoculars allow me to see through camouflage and obstacles," Jones said promptly. "I can also get combat profiles of my target, like Sage's Eye-Spy ability."

"Useful," I said. Sage's Eye-Spy had come in handy more than once, and the more info we had about our targets, the better.

"I can also target an enemy through them and share my targeting info with allied party members." Jones grinned. "So you don't even have to get eyes on them to shoot them with your abilities."

"Nice." Grandpa grunted. "That's helpful. The headband has a couple of effects. It's got a stamina and a dexterity buff for me, and any attack I do from behind a target or while obscured is rendered thirty percent more powerful. It'll be a good combination with Scalp and Shadow Step. It also lets me cast a toned-down version of War Chief's Aegis more regularly."

War Chief's Aegis was the ability he had gotten after his class evolution. It had a day long cooldown, and we'd only used it a couple of times. It empowered and buffed all members of his party, but the downside was it tended to make you feel invulnerable and then take stupid risks. "This version can be used at the start of a fight," Grandpa explained. "It's a thirty percent health regen boost, plus a shield that gives everyone a quarter of their hit points. Once the shield's gone, it's gone."

"Let's see how that stacks with Cowgirl Cheer," Sage said at once. Her buff had gained levels alongside her; now it granted a thirty percent buff to dodge chance and damage done for all party members in range.

The system announcer spoke.

[Ladies and gentlemen, beings of every type and description, it's time for the next round of this doubleheader!
You've already met your home team, the Earthling miners of Misfits Guild.
Now, the challengers, hailing from Aldebaran 19's Reality Engine Complex, the very best representatives Team Firebrand can field. Please welcome Mak'gar, Grim'dan, Lor'khan, Ash'kall, and the rookie, Em'bar!]

Sage cast Cowgirl Cheer and Grandpa used his new buff. My effects menu reported it as [**Inspired Leader Bonus**], which was a remarkably subdued name compared to most of our other abilities. Maybe Grandpa's refusal to accept the feather headdress had changed the system's interaction with us? The two buffs stacked all right, granting me a shield as well as the dodge and regen boosts.

A loud bang produced a puff of smoke in centerfield. As the smoke drifted away, it revealed five tall orcs facing us, holding laser pistols and spiky clubs. They were wearing the same sort of silvery, logo-bearing bodysuits they'd had when attacking our outpost. Mak'gar stood in their center. He raised his pistol to his forehead, saluting us.

I'd been afraid of just this. Not because I had any problem fighting with our sometimes-allies, but because Mak'gar and his orcs had seen a lot of what we could do, and I respected their combat prowess.

[**Play ball!**] the announcer roared.

The five of us Misfits sprang forward without needing to discuss anything. By now, we had fought together enough to understand how we worked best as a team.

As Mak'gar and two of his orcs sprinted toward us, I triggered Fastest Gun in the West and ran forward to meet them, catching them around the third base area. I wasn't a melee fighter, but none of us were, and I had a bigger health pool than everyone on my team but Tall Smith. *Get me some cover!* I messaged the team. Smith hurled smoke grenades, creating a cloud above the sand.

The two orcs flanking Mak'gar both had clubs in their hands. Mak'gar fired a shot at me from his laser pistol. It screamed harmlessly over my shoulder. My coat whipped in the breeze as I charged ahead.

One of the orcs swung at me as I approached. I ducked under and cast Never Bring a Knife to a Gunfight. The orcs dropped their clubs.

I felt Jones activating his Camouflage skill. In chat, he said, *Get behind them. I can see through the smoke and target them.*

Sage threw Mucking Out the Stalls right on top of us as I sprinted out the other side of the orcs. The clubs were lost under a mess of sticky mud. Mak'gar fired a shot through the smoke, and this time it came close to hitting me.

Jones passed me targeting information on one of the disarmed orcs. I fired a Trick Shot. It was one of my knockback rounds, like I had used on Theram'goss during our duel.

The round exploded, but I couldn't see the results through the smoke. My target was still there, at [**160/180 HP**], so I hadn't killed him.

I need a target, Sage said in chat.

There, Jones replied.

Got 'em, Sage announced triumphantly. I suspected she had managed to get a Lasso around one of the orcs.

Meanwhile, my target took more damage as Grandpa Shadow Stepped in behind and Scalped. He hit the orc again. The smoke must have triggered his new damage buff, because his Scalps hit hard. The orc went down to [**100/180 HP**].

Mak'gar roared from somewhere in the smoke. I heard his charge just in time to dodge out of the way as he came crashing past. "Coward!" he yelled. "You have more honor than this, Williams, I have seen you fight. Stand!"

I ignored his taunt. He couldn't see me while I was camouflaged, and I was still trying to take out his buddy. I fired another Trick Shot. [**80/180 HP**].

Help! Jones called out in chat. *They're on me!* I felt Camouflage drop as the smoke began to clear out of the ring.

Jones cried out in pain. I turned. He was across the arena from me, out where left field should have been, backed into a corner by a pair of orcs. They fired their lasers at him and several of the shots connected, taking his health down point by point.

I cursed and charged across the sand. I wasn't close enough to use Call 'em Out, so I engaged Fastest Gun in the West to close the gap. As I barreled through the pair, I cast my taunt, forcing them to focus on me.

Jones was already down to [**20 HP**]. As I dropped a Barrage into one of the orcs, a well-aimed laser blast from across the arena slammed into Jones's chest. His eyes went wide as he fell backward, his hands groping at the enormous black burn that now marred his ranger uniform. Jones was gone before he hit the sand, his body dissolving.

The orcs fired at me. My coat caught several of the blasts, deflecting them from doing any damage. One shot drilled through and burned into my shoulder. My hand spasmed and I dropped my gun. I used Quick Draw to retrieve it before it hit the ground.

I reloaded and fired at the closest orc as Grandpa Shadow Stepped in. He hit the orc I was shooting at with a Coup-de-Grace and the orc disappeared.

The other orc shot Grandpa in the face. It left a patchy burn on Grandpa's cheek, and dropped him down to **[60 HP]**, but didn't kill him. Grandpa disappeared, Shadow Stepping off elsewhere in the arena.

The orcs weren't using any abilities. They'd barely shown any during the jungle fight. Were they trying to keep their cards hidden, or were they relying on their guns for a reason? We were supposed to be more coordinated, using that to our advantage, but with Jones gone we'd lost our vision advantage. I was too heads-down, too focused on the fight. I couldn't see what was behind me. We were being sloppy.

I heard Sage shouting gleefully as she ordered her Tamed orc to attack one of his fellows. At the same time, Smith shouted a warning. "Look out!"

I was in arm's reach of the other orc now. I grabbed at his wrist with my left hand and twisted, trying to get him to drop his laser pistol. He resisted and fired a shot into the sand by my foot. I shoved my Ruger into his chest and squeezed the trigger, sending six rounds in a Barrage into him. The orc stumbled back. He was still pretty healthy, with **[85 HP]**, but I wanted to get some distance between us. The laser pistols were either not as accurate as my Ruger, or the orcs weren't very good shots.

I sprinted away from the orc back toward the main action, where the pitcher's mound should have been. Grandpa and Smith were locked in melee combat with a pair of orcs, Mak'gar and a skinny, younger-looking orc.

The skinny orc was in pretty bad shape. Smith had drawn his cavalry saber and was attempting to keep Mak'gar from intervening.

Sage was running her Lassoed orc around the edges of the arena, like a demented outfielder chasing a foul ball. "He's resisting when I try to get him to attack!" she shouted. "I didn't know they could resist once I had them Tamed!"

"Keep him busy!" I yelled as I targeted the skinny orc and fired a Trick Shot while I barreled toward the pitcher's mound like an irate umpire. If we could even the odds back out and get a breather, we might be able to take control back.

Mak'gar tossed aside his laser pistol with a curse. He pulled a rusty-looking, jagged scimitar from thin air and brought the sword down in a two-handed slash.

Smith blocked with his saber, but the sword blow knocked him backward. Smith stumbled and fell prone on the sand. Mak'gar leapt forward, landing with both feet on Smith's chest. He brought his sword down hard and decapitated Smith in a single blow.

Smith's head rolled on the sand before it and his body vanished. I bellowed, furious and frustrated. It didn't matter that this wasn't real. My head knew that, but my body believed I had just seen a friend and teammate die horribly. I charged Mak'gar, dumping every round in my cylinder into him and reloading.

I had a couple of armor-piercing bullets Sage had made me, and I used them now. They went through Mak'gar's jumpsuit armor, dealing huge amounts of damage. Unfortunately, his health pool was equally huge. He was at **[195/250]**.

Sage screamed. I looked over my shoulder. She was in the far left corner of the field now, pressed up against the outfield wall. The orc she had Tamed had apparently thrown off her control and been joined by the half-dead orc from across the field. They were advancing on her with their laser pistols firing.

Use Three-Barrel Race! I instructed her.

I can't, they've got me locked down somehow!

Before I could intervene, she was gone in a swirling cloud of sparks. My stomach twisted. I nearly dropped my gun. *This isn't real she's fine keep your head!* I told myself.

Grandpa yelled loudly, a scream of wordless rage. He brought his tomahawk down hard on the young orc's head, bursting it open like a split watermelon as he took out the orc's final **[20 HP]**. The orc's brain and blood splattered me. A second later, it disappeared as the orc despawned.

Grandpa Shadow Stepped over to the lowest-health orc on the other side of the arena, leaving me just outside melee range with Mak'gar.

Grandpa hit his target's head with Scalp. I fired a knockback round at him from across the field. The explosion pushed both orcs away from Grandpa. He disengaged, getting a little more distance, enough to hurl a stream of shuriken into the injured orc.

Mak'gar advanced on me, his menacing weapon held high. He grinned, tusks protruding behind his wide lips. "You are a strong opponent indeed," he said. He swung at me. I shot him in the arm, but he didn't seem to care.

I was just about out of tricks. Across the arena, Grandpa downed the injured orc, but the other advanced on him with a spiked club. Grandpa only had **[10 HP]** left. He drew an axe in each hand and ran toward the orc, a bloodcurdling cry on his lips.

I reloaded and shot Mak'gar. My bullets were chipping him down, each shot hitting, but he had too much health. I had taken a few points of damage in each of the fights I'd been in, and I was down to **[50 HP]**.

Mak'gar swung his sword. It hit my coat and sliced right through, taking my left hand off just above the wrist. Pain lanced up my entire body. I gritted my teeth and fired more bullets into Mak'gar.

Across the field, Grandpa fell. The other orc advanced toward Mak'gar and me, but it didn't matter. Mak'gar's next swing cut through my chest. As I felt my lifeblood draining and saw the world going dark around me, I heard Mak'gar say, "And now Firebrand's honor is redeemed. See you back on the map, Williams."

CHAPTER THIRTY-FOUR

HOW TO AVOID GALACTIC CIVIL WAR

I sat on one of the beige sofas in the rented guest suite on the Hub, waiting for Veda to join us by hologram, six hours after we respawned at our outposts after completion of the team event. Most of our crafters were back at work, but my family was overdue for one of our checkups. Veda had sent word we needed to come up to the Hub as soon as the special event was over.

I took some centering breaths. It was just me, Sage, and Grandpa here. We were all subdued. It had been a long couple of days, a long couple of weeks, maybe a long half year since we'd been taken. The beige drabness of this suite was starting to get to me. There were fake flowers in vases in the corner. A soft hum of white noise. It reminded me of the funeral parlor where we'd had Abuela's visitation, a place designed to look like humans lived there when really it was cold, sterile, hostile to life. Like space itself.

Sage was staring at a movie from the latest entertainment package sent up from Earth. This one apparently told the story of a couple of abductees who had been caught up in the Reality Engine exploit, but then managed to escape. Sage made occasional biting comments about just how much the writers and producers had gotten wrong.

I kept looking at her, then glancing away before she noticed. She wasn't dead. She hadn't been killed. I hadn't failed her. It wasn't real. None of this was real, except for the things that were, the things that mattered a lot. I hadn't failed Sage yet, and I wasn't going to.

I needed to start looking past this phase of the exploit and into the future. Phase three loomed ahead. Ames had been vague with details, just insisting that we needed to get there. I'd been so focused on that, I'd lost sight of the bigger picture.

The thing was, our fate wasn't necessarily tied up with either this Reality Engine or with Earth. There was a big galaxy out there, and if what Mak'gar told me was right, we had a skill set not many other people had.

Veda appeared in the middle of the room, wearing a slinky red wrap that revealed her shoulders. Her hair was up over her head, and she looked distracted. "Sorry it took me a while," she apologized. "I was clearing up some business correspondence so that I could give this meeting my full attention."

None of us answered her right away. She paced around the room, fiddling with her hands. She looked at me, and I looked away, not able to meet her eyes.

"We had a plan," she said. "A gamma node. That's all I needed. It's what I had the budget for. But you changed up without even consulting me. Why?"

"We made it work," I said.

"By raiding the grignarians and stealing a lot of their gear! They lodged a complaint that nearly got us expelled from the phase. I'd have been ruined if that happened. I put a lot on the line for you—"

"And we've put *everything* on the line for you," I retorted, standing up, feeling my temper rising. "We risked our lives to get to phase two, while you sat here having teleconferences and balancing your budget. I think we've got more to complain about here."

Grandpa cleared his throat. "We should have been more honest with you," he said frankly. "We knew we were taking a gamble going for a delta-tier node. Your strategy was right for what you needed to do, but we've got bigger things in mind."

Veda shook her head. "Like what? Phase three? I guess you've heard a little bit about it, but you can't understand what's really at stake there. I don't have a license to back a phase three team. I don't have the kind of money it would take to make a serious bid for phase three. Those slots are controlled by the big players."

"Like Proxima?"

"That's one of them."

"Proxima is behind Sicaris, isn't it?" I asked. "As well as the Vortali outfit, our alpha node neighbors. They've got their hands in a lot of pots."

"Proxima is much, much more powerful than I am. I don't think you've pissed them off yet, but you certainly have come to their attention, and that's not likely to be a good thing. Taking a delta node, attacking neighbors . . . *winning* against those professionals when they came after your base . . ."

She sat down in midair. I guessed that there was a chair or stool in her own space that wasn't being projected here into this room. Veda rested her hands on her knees. "What is so important to you that you're risking my, and your, future on these mad gambles?"

Sage was staring at the movie. Her device had a projector set into a wrist bangle that displayed the image in the air in front of her eyes. From here, it was just a blur of movement and color. I didn't think she was really watching it. That last fight had bothered her, too. It was the first time she had died.

I hadn't been able to speak to her about it. Watching my sister dissolve into a shower of sparks in front of my eyes because I'd been too focused elsewhere on the battlefield to protect her was an annoying pile of guilt in the bottom of my stomach.

Veda's question hung over my head like a sword midswing. What *did* I want? Why do what Ames told us, without any explanation at all? Why not take what we had and get out of here?

"It's rigged, isn't it," Sage said quietly, not looking up from her screen. "It always was. If it starts looking like we have a chance, you'll change the rules. We're not supposed to get to phase three."

"Of course not!" Veda threw up her hands. "Aside from the fact that you Earth primitives would have no idea what to do with a Reality Engine, the whole reason that the Reality Engine Exploitation Committee exists is because the Engines are the most valuable thing in the entire galaxy. Before we got together and agreed to a set of rules, species used to go to war with each other or themselves for control of any Reality Engine in their space. If you got to space on your own and met this Engine, it'd be about three standard weeks before Proxima or some other conglomerate showed up with planet-busting bombs and took it away from you."

Sage's mouth dropped open. I tried to picture space war, and couldn't.

Veda saw our shock and pressed her advantage. "Entire systems died fiery deaths. The Exploitation Committee is here to *prevent* interstellar war. To keep you, and everyone else, safe. What's a few million primitives next to trillions and trillions of advanced lives? To our standard of living?"

"We've heard that before, from our own species," Grandpa said quietly.

Veda shook her head. "It's not my point of view. I'm speaking for them, not me. I'm just a small cog in this operation. My life and my family's lives are no more important to Proxima than yours are."

"Then what happens to us?" Sage asked in a small voice. "When you're done here, when you pack up and go home, what happens to us?"

"You've got a pretty nicely set up outpost right now. I can find a buyer for that outpost and make us all a hefty fortune."

"What happens to us then?" Grandpa asked. "We go back to phase one, putting our lives at risk?"

"All of you have enough credit built up that you can hang out with your friends and family on Threshold or here on the Hub until the exploit is complete. Then you can buy a slot here, or at one of the other Reality Engines in the neighborhood. As long as you don't get greedy, you'll be able to live comfortably for the rest of your lives."

"In an illusion." I paced the room. The beige walls and white noise were really getting to me. This place was more bland, less real, than the worlds we'd been living in for the last few months. The Reality Engine's imaginations were better than the reality the galactics were capable of making. No wonder they just plugged their surplus population in and left them.

I remembered a feeling of helplessness growing up on the Strip. There weren't many options. You could be a rancher, a miner, or a bum. For anything else, you had to get out. A lot of my classmates couldn't picture ever leaving. They'd gotten into weed, or alcohol, or teenage parenthood, because there wasn't anything else. Buying into a Reality Engine felt like that. We might exist, but we wouldn't *live*.

"Say we did that," Grandpa said. "What about the rest of our allies? Does the wealth extend to them?"

Veda hesitated. "They're doing well. And there'll be more opportunities in phase three to make money. The early farming levels are still relevant, and we have such a dearth of crafters this time that your people should be able to make a living."

"They're not going to go back to risking their lives in the phase one levels," Sage said. "We're all sick of you aliens wasting our lives."

"I'm not the one doing this," Veda said tiredly. "I'm not your enemy, Sage. I know you've all had a hard couple of days. The outworlders see those games as something fun, but you all just got done with the phase one missions, where death is a lot more meaningful. It wasn't fun and games for you, was it?"

"I just don't know what we're doing." Sage shook her head, turning off the show, and stood up. She strode around the room like an anxious dog wanting to go for a walk. "I don't know anymore. I just want to go home." Her face fell and she buried her face in her hands and ran from the room to one of the bedrooms. She slammed the door behind her, but I could still hear muffled sobbing.

I tensed. "Should I—"

"Leave her for now," Grandpa said wearily. "Veda's right. We've been taking a lot of risk and I'm not sure it's paying off. Got any brochures about these galactic retirement homes, Veda?"

"Uh, sure," she said. "I'll see what I can find for you."

"And I want to know about phase three. What's the point, what are the rules, and if we get in, what will we be doing?"

"Those are big questions. The Exploitation Council still has to vote on the rule set. Phase three is all about taming the Reality Engine. Getting it to work with us, not against us. Converting it from challenge mode to habitation mode. That can take a number of formats. Often it's an enormous war simulation. Anything from lizard-mounted charges to space battles, with the biggest conglomerations acting as the generals. Sometimes it's more of a giant tacti-chess board, with each individual move being settled by a minigame of various sorts. My great-grandmother used to tell stories about the heroic mode phase threes she'd witnessed—those would be immersive simulations pulled from mythology or history, with a series of increasingly difficult challenges to fight through in order to approach the Reality Engine's core. We won't know what this one will be until the council meets and votes."

"But the outposts matter."

"Outposts get transferred to phase three and serve a role there. As recharge and resupply points, or army strongholds, depending on the scenario. Yes. Your outpost is most valuable right now, though. Once phase three starts, the outposts can't be moved. So depending where you end up, you might find yourself almost worthless."

"We hold," I growled, then glanced at Grandpa. "For now."

Veda cleared her throat uncomfortably. "I'll send you that information," she promised. "I'm sorry."

She disappeared, leaving Grandpa and me alone.

I sat down and stared at my feet. "We were so focused for so long on our goals. Get to phase two, start the outpost, get it built up, make it through that game. Now we don't have a goal, and I think it's hitting us all hard," I said.

"It feels like we've had the wool pulled back from our eyes and now we see what's really going on." Grandpa was nodding, looking more tired than I'd seen him in months.

"We need a future, Grandpa, if not for you and me, at least for Sage."

"We're gonna have to do some thinking," he said quietly. "I've never been good at dealing with teenage girls." He looked away from me, staring at the floor. "I made a lot of mistakes with your mom. I've spent a lot of years wishing I could go back and fix them. I told myself I'd do it right with Sage, and then I got sick. There was nothing I could do about that. I was going to be leaving her on her own at the most vulnerable time in a girl's life. Well, I dodged that bullet, and now I find I'm more out of my depth than ever."

I felt an uncomfortable lump in my throat. I didn't know how to reply. Fortunately for me, a chat notification popped up from Ames. *I need you and your family back on Threshold as fast as possible.*

Why?

I found the entrance to the lotus eater level a couple of days ago. It's worse than I thought. I need you to try to help me.

What about Grandpa? Thought you were trying to steer clear of him.

I'm done worrying if the system will take notice of us.

I looked at Sage's drawn face, at Grandpa's slumped shoulders. We'd just lost our first major fight ever. We'd watched each other die and known there was nothing we could do about it. And Ames had the gall to want more.

Veda had set us up appointments with the alien psychologists in the morning. I didn't know if they'd be any good, whether or not it was a waste of time. But I didn't know how to talk to Sage and maybe they'd have magic devices that made all this better. Not likely, but maybe.

I sent back, *Not until tomorrow afternoon. We have some things to do up here.*

Not acceptable, Ames said.

I'll ask my commanding officer and get back to you. I minimized my chat and turned to Grandpa. "Ames's being all cloak-and-dagger again. I'm gonna get some answers out of him, even if I have to throttle him to do it this time. He wants to see us ASAP but I told him tomorrow, after our checkups."

Grandpa nodded. "Sounds good."

We went to bed after that. I lay alone in a dark room, staring at the ceiling, replaying all my recent deaths over and over again. The wolf-man ripping my throat out. The time I'd been disemboweled by a space elf seconds after respawning. Mak'gar's triumphant grin as he skewered me.

Maybe the lotus eaters were onto something.

CHAPTER THIRTY-FIVE

PLANNING YOUR AFTERLIFE: THINGS TO CONSIDER

I stepped through the portal, and a feeling of incredible peace spread over me. I took a deep breath of honeysuckle-scented air. It was the perfect temperature. Not hot, not cold. Like a lukewarm bath.

The sky overhead was a brilliant, cloudless blue. I stood atop a small green hill. A white stone path wound its way downward. The hill fell off steeply on one side in a sheer chalk cliff, two hundred feet or more down to a sea. Waves crashed against rocks, their whispering murmur a soothing sound from up here.

At the foot of the hill, a small village waited, lots of little two-story stone houses painted coral pink or a balmy blue. People moved between the houses. The village was laid out around three squares with statues or fountains in the middle of each.

"What is this place?" I asked Ames. "You said this was the lotus eater level. That feels peaceful enough, but there's no way there's three million people here."

"This is just the intake," he said quietly. "The real entrance is underneath the village. Come, let's stay close."

I followed him down the hill, Grandpa and Sage silent on my heels. Sage hadn't said a word to us the whole trip down. I was worried about her. She had come out of her counseling session silent, nodded briefly when I told her what Ames wanted, and stuck close—but not too close—to us ever since.

People came out of the houses to meet us. They wore white robes or togas, embroidered with gold designs at the edges.

A trio detached from the throng of thirty or so and approached us as we reached the outskirts of the village, two men and a woman. The woman carried a cup with her. Ames raised a hand in greeting. "Go ahead and greet them," he told us. "We won't spend long here. The important part is underneath."

The delegation stopped a few feet away from us. "Welcome to Elysium," one of the men said, holding up his hands. "Do you come to seek the wisdom of Kronos, or the peace of oblivion?"

"Neither," Ames said briskly. "Greetings, elder. You know who I am, don't you?"

The man blinked. "Of course, messenger. Welcome back. These others are?"

"Here to learn," Ames said.

"Then be welcome."

"You should know, violence is not permitted here," the other man told us, looking me over.

"I haven't received a notification that this is a no miner-versus-miner violence zone," I commented.

"The alien system has no power here," the woman said. "Our patron takes care of us all."

"Patron?" Grandpa asked, raising an eyebrow.

I tried checking my menus. Nothing came up. I tried taking a water bottle out of my inventory. It didn't work. I went to send a note to Grandpa, and the interface didn't come up.

Ames smiled, seeming to notice my consternation. "They're right," he said. "No system here."

"I didn't even know that was possible." A little thrill of excitement ran through me. For the first time in months, I was alone in my head. Or—was I? There was a pressure on my mind, like a presence. Who was this patron they spoke of?

"We're not sure if the alien system can see or hear us. We fear that it can," one of the men warned. "But come. Be welcome."

The woman held out the cup to Grandpa. He took it, shrugged, and took a sip before passing it to me. I sipped as well. It was pure, clear water. I didn't detect anything strange in it, though that meant nothing.

I hesitated, but Sage held out her hand. I gave her the cup. She took a sip. Then, a deeper one, her eyes going wide. "Oh," she said, "what's in this?"

"Only a release," the woman said.

I was glad when Sage handed the cup back. The trio gestured us toward the village. "We are the delegates chosen today to welcome guests and speak for our patron, Kronos," one of the men said.

"So, somebody else is in charge tomorrow?" I asked.

"No one is in charge here," the woman said. "We all act together for the good of all."

I exchanged a look with Grandpa. His face was set in a sardonic grin. "I'm just glad that was water, not Kool-Aid," he said. I didn't catch the reference myself. "So who is this Kronos?"

"Let me show you more," Ames said, "rather than trying to tell you. Come."

We followed the trio into their village. "So, how many people live here?" I asked, still not quite believing what Ames had told me.

"Only our patron knows for sure, but many have sought their protection. We welcome all as long as they come with good intent. This is a sanctuary, and it will remain so."

"Who is this Kronos?" Grandpa asked. "How did you meet him?"

I had a sneaking suspicion I knew the answer. There was only one entity I could think of capable of pushing the system out, and that was the Reality Engine itself. I thought about the strange person I had met deep in the bowels of the loot halls.

"They revealed him/her/itself to us," the woman said. "The first of us to meet him/her/it called our patron Kronos. He/she/it agreed to use the name, so the rest of us followed."

That name rang a bit of a bell. "That's from Greek myth, isn't it?" I said. "One of the early gods?"

Ames leaned in and said, "Father of the Titans, maker of the universe, who devoured his children, then was destroyed and usurped by them."

"Right, I remember that," I said. "Can't really blame them for not liking getting eaten."

If what the aliens had told me, that the progenitors who built this Reality Engine were in fact responsible for the start of life on Earth, then maybe Kronos was an apt name. "Do we get a chance to meet Kronos?"

"Kronos reveals him/her/itself to who he/she/it will," the woman said. She turned to Ames. "Welcome back. You have a hard job on the outside. Be welcomed into peace."

"Just doing my job," Ames said. "There's more peace here than I can stand, and I'm here to shake things up a little. Kronos and I are going to have words later."

"What the hell is going on?" Grandpa asked.

"I swear, you'll get answers. Just give me a little time," Ames told us.

The woman turned to Sage, her eyes softening. "Have you come to us for help? You are too young for all of this. We have other children here."

Sage brightened. "Other kids? Really?"

"We have done our best to find and give succor to all the children who were swept up in this nightmare," the woman said. "Would you like to meet them?"

Sage looked from Grandpa to the woman, seemingly hesitant. "I don't know," she said.

"No one will force you," one of the male representatives assured her. "Why not come for an hour or two and see? We will help you find your relatives again as soon as you ask."

"They're telling the truth," Ames said.

I was feeling more and more uncomfortable about all this, even as the feeling of peace pervaded me. It felt unnatural. Or maybe I was so used to fighting, being on edge all the time, that an afternoon off felt wrong.

"I think I'd like to visit for a while," Sage said to Grandpa, "if there's other people my age here."

"Go on, then," he grunted.

"I will lead you to them," the woman said. I didn't like it, but I held my tongue. This place seemed safe, and Sage could make her own decisions.

Sage followed the woman off to the far side of the village, where they disappeared into a domed building.

"I thought you wanted Sage with us," I told Ames in an undertone.

"Don't worry. We'll find her again. Besides, she might enjoy herself. Let her have some time with other kids." He spoke to our greeters. "Is that enough ceremony? I want to take them below."

"Do not disturb those who are sleeping," one of the men warned.

"We won't."

They ushered us into one of the nearby buildings, which turned out to merely be the entrance to a grand spiraling stairwell leading down below the ground. The stair was lit every half turn by a bronze basket filled with gleaming purple crystals that cast an eerie glow on the gray granite steps.

"After you," said Ames.

I started the descent. Each stair tread was just a little too short. I had to watch my step carefully as we descended.

Down, down, the stair wound and curved on itself. I lost track of how deep we had gone.

At last, we stepped off onto a landing. A hall led off to our left and another to our right. Arched doorways, shrouded in darkness, lined the hall. "Where now?"

"Left," Ames said. "You'll see. You're not feeling any weird effects, are you?"

"I feel relaxed," I said. "That seems strange."

"Yeah, that took me a little bit to get used to," Ames said as we set off along the corridor, passing dark doorways every eight feet or so. "I'm still not sure if it's the influence of the mind controlling this place, or if it's just from a lack of the system interfering."

That was a disturbing thought. If I couldn't trust my own mind, what was even real?

"How's that?" Grandpa asked.

"The aliens brought their system along with them and plugged it into our Reality Engine. It's what runs all of our menus and interfaces," Ames said.

"I know that," Grandpa snapped. "And I can tell it's not here, since I can't get at any of my gear. You think it's been doing something else to our heads?"

"I suspect it is giving us all low-level anxiety, keeping us on edge, like we have something to prove. Some people are a little more resistant to it than others, but I definitely noticed a difference here."

The darkness beyond the arches was impenetrable. "Are we supposed to go into one of these?" I asked.

"Those," Ames said grimly, "are the sleepers. You'll know when we get to something else."

Sure enough, about eight doors on, I found one that was brightly lit. I still couldn't see inside, but at least there was no cloud of darkness. Ames saw my inquisitive gaze. "Go ahead," he said. "It's going to be easier for you to see this than for me to try to explain it."

I stepped through the arch and found myself in a green meadow full of flowers. Birds sang in trees that edged the meadow. A rippling brook ran across, and bunnies gamboled in the ankle-high grass. "This is laying it on a little thick," I said.

"Oh, it gets better," Ames said. He pointed. "Look."

Off among the trees, I caught a glimpse of creatures, not human, moving about. A moment later, one of them ambled just past the edge of the tree line.

It was half-horse, half-man. Well, woman. And she was naked from the waist up. From the waist down was a horse's body. Her dark, curling hair fell forward across her breasts. She lifted a hand and waved to me before venturing back into the trees.

"There's nymphs, too," Ames said gloomily. "And satyrs, though considerably toned down from their origin myths. I've seen rooms that more resemble something out of an Eastern mythology, but it's definitely playing on our visions of paradise and ancient worlds. Those are who you've come to talk to, though." He gestured off to the other side. "I'm going to have a quick word with Kronos while you get acquainted."

I turned to see a group of toga-wearing humans seated on a hillside. They were listening to a man declaiming as he stood atop the hill, one hand raised to the heavens, the other touching his breast. A wreath of branches rested in his hair. I turned back to Ames, and he was gone.

"Where'd he go?" Grandpa asked.

"I didn't see." I hesitated. "Guess I'll go have a listen."

"Listen. Yeah." Grandpa sounded distracted. He had turned away, facing back toward the doorway through which we had come. It looked, from this side, like a pair of pillars with an arch set between them. I could see right through, and it was just more meadow on the other side, though I guessed if we stepped through it, we'd be back in the hall.

"What's wrong?" I hadn't seen him this lost since Abuela's death. I'd been feeling a little better since talking to the shrink back on the Hub, but maybe Grandpa's session hadn't helped.

"Just thought I heard someone," he said, shrugging.

I made my way over to where the people were listening. The speaker was saying, "And so we wait for Kronos to speak to us, to reveal what task they have for their children. Do not be lulled away by the false promises of the invaders. Neither their threats nor their promises hold any weight here. Kronos itself protects us. As long as we do their will, we are safe."

I sat down between a middle-aged woman and a man about my age, both of whom were wearing togas. A cushion appeared as I sat. I tucked it underneath myself. It was pretty comfortable.

"New here?" the woman asked me with a motherly smile.

"Yeah."

"It's all right. It takes some of us longer than others to hear the call of Kronos. You will be welcome here."

"Who's that?" I asked, gesturing to the man atop the hill.

"Merely an elder brother who has heard Kronos for longer than the rest of us."

I sat and let the man talk. He kept going on in the same way, talking about how Kronos was to teach us how to harness the powers of reality, and how this was the true future that the aliens were here to usurp from us.

I burst in at that. "What sort of powers are we talking about here?"

The speaker turned to me. "Forgive me, it seems you are only recently arrived." His eyes traveled across me, taking in my hat and drover's coat. "Perhaps you would be more comfortable if you went through one of our regular intake sessions before joining the more advanced class."

"I'm just waiting for a friend," I said. "Sorry for the interruption."

Mollified, he turned back to his audience. "So, meditate on these words. Listen for the voice of Kronos. As its voice becomes louder and louder, your mind will be expanded. Soon, soon we will be brought forth to join the blessed campaign."

He sat down, and that seemed to be a signal to the others to stand up and begin stretching. They spoke in low tones about the wisdom of his words.

The woman who had been beside me, and the young man with her, smiled at me. "Can we take you to intake and help you get comfortable?" the woman asked. "You could use a bath."

That was true enough, but I wasn't going anywhere. I shook my head. "I'm here to visit a friend," I said, trying to look for some excuse that would satisfy them.

"Oh." Her face fell. "Then you do not heed the voice of Kronos."

The young man cocked his head and held up a hand. "Sister," he said, "patience. I feel that he is as connected to Kronos as any of us."

"It's all well and good to have a place of shelter like this," I said, "but at some point, some of us are going to have to fight. Humanity needs you folk to do more than just sit around listening to Plato over here."

The two I had been speaking with shrank back. "We'll talk of this later," the woman said, and then fled.

I realized with a start Grandpa wasn't here anymore. "Where'd he go?" I looked around. There was no sign of him. "Grandpa?" Damn it. I had been listening to that preacher a little too closely. Where would he have gone?

By then, I was running for the door.

CHAPTER THIRTY-SIX

SIX THINGS ANCESTRY DOESN'T WARN YOU ABOUT

Grandpa!" I yelled, running down the corridor. As far as I could see, in front and behind, the corridor stretched empty, yawning archways on both sides like open mouths. "Grandpa, where are you?"

I tried for my chat interface, but it didn't respond. "Where'd he go?"

There was no sign of Ames either. I cursed at him in my head. He hadn't told us what the hell we were supposed to be doing here, and now Sage was gone, Grandpa was gone, and I was stuck in an entire level full of brainwashed zealots who seemed to regard the Reality Engine as some sort of god.

A voice in my head was whispering, *Let me in. I can speak with you.*

Not a chance in hell, I thought back furiously. *If you want to help, show me where Grandpa is.*

The voice didn't answer right away. After a minute, though, I felt a shift of pressure, like an outlet of breath. *Very well. Come.*

Up ahead, a beacon of purple light bloomed from a doorway, spilling out into the hallway. I skidded to a halt in front of the arch. It looked just like any of the others. *In here.* The light died away, leaving a black entryway.

I plunged through the doorway. The room beyond was a grotto. The walls were smooth, worked and shaped. Along the walls were shelf niches, stacked three high like long, narrow benches.

A pit of worry grew in my stomach. There was something familiar about these. I had seen pictures that reminded me of this, pictures with bones. This was a catacomb.

In horror, I looked into the closest niche. A woman lay there, her hands folded across her breast, her eyes closed. If she was breathing, I could see no sign of it. I touched one hand with a single trembling finger. It was warm to the touch, but she didn't respond. I thought I could feel a faint pulse.

Dry-mouthed, I looked in the next niche. This one was a man in his fifties, about the oldest I had seen here in the Reality Engine.

"Where's my Grandpa?" I said aloud. No answer.

I went niche by niche until I found him halfway around the room, in the bottom row. Like the others, his eyes were closed, his hands folded. His face looked worn and drawn, like he'd been a few months ago before all this started, while the cancer was eating away at him.

I fell to my knees beside him. "Grandpa," I pleaded. I wanted to shake him awake, but was afraid what would happen if he didn't respond. "Grandpa, wake up! I'm here!"

"He can't hear you. I'm sorry." I turned. There was a person here, shimmering, wearing white robes, with a hood pulled up around their face.

"It's you," I said. "Isn't it? The Reality Engine. We spoke before."

"You spoke to part of me," it said. I noticed it didn't use the "I/we" construction that the other being had employed. "I am a different part. The Watcher. Kronos, your people call me. My job was to watch and wait for our children to return. I slept too deeply, and when I awoke I was in chains." The figure held up its hands. Shining golden chains shimmered and shifted around its wrists, winding and curling like snakes.

"Why did you take him?" I demanded.

Kronos looked pained. His, her, whatever, face fell. "I am trying to understand you, our lost children. Some of you hear me easily. Others not at all. The ones who come here are seeking peace. But not all find peace in the same way. You spoke to my acolytes earlier, those who are trying to learn to understand me, so they can help me rescue the rest of your species." He gestured at the sleepers. "For these, it has become too much. They seek a different kind of peace. Oblivion."

"Bullshit," I said. "Grandpa's not looking for oblivion."

"Is he not?" Kronos asked. "He puts on a brave face for you and your sister, but he is old and tired. He has many cares. Perhaps he seeks to set them aside, if only for a few moments."

"Then you can let him wake up now."

"He must choose it."

"Grandpa, it's time to go. We need to get Sage."

"He can't hear you."

Anger boiled up in me. Helpless rage about this entire situation from top to bottom. Anger at the aliens, the system, this Reality Engine, whatever it was. At being not in control of my own future and fate.

"Then you let me talk to him," I said.

"I can bring your mind to his," Kronos said. "Only he can decide whether to heed you."

"Do it," I ordered.

"You might want to lie down."

I slid to a seated position, resting my back against the stone wall. There was no way I was going to climb into one of those coffin bunks. I leaned my head back.

"Do it," I said again, and the room around me dimmed.

I was standing in the living room of Grandpa's trailer. It looked different than it had the last few times I'd seen the place. Cleaner, more organized. There was a smell of beans baking in the kitchen.

In front of me were a pair of people I recognized right away. One of them was Grandpa. He looked about how he did now, in his midfifties with his dark hair in two braids falling behind his shoulders. But his face was twisted with hatred and fury like I'd never seen it before.

The other was a dark-haired young woman, just as angry as Grandpa but somehow less bitter-looking about it. I knew her, too, though I hadn't seen her in almost ten years and the last time I had her hair had been prematurely graying, her teeth half falling out, her eyes vacant, her skin pallid.

My mother, and from the look of it, younger than I was now.

She was screaming at my grandfather. "What don't you understand? I love Clay!"

"I will not allow you to hook up with that useless son of a polygamist cult," Grandpa spat back. "He's only interested in you because his father and uncles have already locked up every pretty young white girl in their plural marriage schemes. He's young and horny and wants to screw anything that moves. He doesn't care about you."

"Don't you dare speak about Clay that way," she snapped. "His mother kicked him out of the house for dating me. She says I'm a dirty half-breed as well as a Gentile."

"There you go," Grandpa said. "Nobody wants this. You're going to college next month and that's it. I won't have my daughter wasting her life here on the Strip with some inbred no-good redneck punk who dropped out of high school. Besides, Sheriff Watts tells me he's involved with a car theft gang. He's gonna come to a bad end."

"Clay knows his friends are no good and he wants out," my future mother protested. "He's a good boy. He just doesn't have any opportunities. You could help him, Dad. He wants to enlist. Give him a few tips. I know he can make something of himself."

"Then let him do that. Away from here," Grandpa snapped. "I'd be happy to give him a few tips, but not while he's trying to date my daughter."

"More than date." My mother raised her chin. "We're getting married, Dad." She looked so terribly young . . .

"The hell you are," he roared back. "Not without my permission."

"We don't need your permission. I turned eighteen last week. Besides." She crossed her arms in front of her chest, looking angry, defiant, and scared. "There's something you don't know."

I felt my breath catch. I tried to move, but I couldn't. I wasn't really there. I was paralyzed, forced to watch this play out.

"I've heard everything I need to know already," Grandpa snapped.

"No, you haven't," my mother shot back. "I'm pregnant, Dad. I'm pregnant, and I'm going to marry Clay, whether you like it or not. You can be part of our lives, or you can stay here and rot."

Grandpa stared at her, his mouth hanging open. He shook his head. "No. No, you can't." He took a step toward her, holding his hands out. "No, honey. That's not what you're going to do. You're supposed to go to college next month. Make something of yourself. Get out of here. See the world."

"Fat lot of good seeing the world ever did you," she fired back angrily. "You're just another washed-up, drunk Indian. I'm not going to college next month. Maybe it'll take me a few years, but Clay and I will make something of our lives. You wait and see."

Grandpa was shaking his head. "No. No, sweetheart. It's not too late. We can fix this. We'll make a few calls. There's a clinic over in St. George I can take you to. Get you away from here. Let that boy go off and do what he wants. You'll come to your senses. He'll come to his. You'll see the two of you are nothing alike. You've got a future ahead of you, a bright one. You don't want to be tied to that no-account."

"I knew you wouldn't understand," she said. She turned and marched to the door, yanking it open in anger and slamming it behind her. My grandfather stared after her for a long moment before turning and roaring at someone I couldn't see.

"Maria, our daughter is dead to us. Do you hear me? She's dead! She's not to be spoken of in this house ever again."

The scene around me dissolved and I was left in darkness for a moment before a light shone on the couch I had just seen inside the trailer. Nothing else, none of the furnishings, just the couch and my grandfather sitting, his head buried in his hands.

I could move now. I crossed and sat next to him. "Is that really what happened?" I asked after a moment.

Grandpa grunted. "More or less."

"I didn't know."

"I didn't tell you. I was ashamed. It's my fault, you know. If I'd been support-ive, maybe your dad could have gotten himself out of there and enlisted, made a future for himself. Instead he kept hanging with his old friends until he got caught with a hot car and a couple of pounds of marijuana in the back seat. She moved down near Phoenix to be near him so she could visit, take you to see him after you were born."

He cleared his throat, staring at the floor, while I just sat there, not knowing what to say.

"I was too proud to talk to her, too angry, too sure I'd been right all along and she should have listened to me."

I wanted to say something, anything, but I was in shock. I knew my Grandpa hadn't cared for my dad, but I wasn't aware of just how prejudiced he'd been. It was a side of Grandpa I'd never seen before. "You meant all that about him being, you know, inbred and all that?"

"I didn't approve of him dating my daughter. He could have been descended from the king of Spain and I still wouldn't have approved," Grandpa said. "But I didn't like his family. Those FLDS are bad news."

"Yeah, but that's who I am," I said, trying to get to the bottom of how I felt. "I mean, that's my dad you're talking about."

"I know." Grandpa sighed heavily. "I know, and sitting here now, looking back from where I am, it all feels so stupid. I guess this whole experience has given me a new perspective on a few things. Right now, compared to the orcs and wizard people, those weird tentacle-face aliens, people like your other relatives are downright normal. I'm sorry, Shad. I tried. Everything I tried with you and Sage was to make up for failing your mom when she needed me."

There was a lot here for me to unwrap and I didn't feel like going into it right now.

I had a nasty feeling in the pit of my stomach, seeing Grandpa at his worst like that. Knowing that he'd been talking about me there to my mom. Seeing me as an inconvenience to her future.

And that he hadn't been wrong.

"I've regretted this every day since," Grandpa said quietly, not looking at me. "I've wished I could go back and fix things. But even if I did go back, I wouldn't know how. That's why I got so upset when you started running with the Hiasson boys. And that time Frank dragged you back after you wrecked Mr. Johnson's side-by-side."

I shuddered at that memory. "I don't think I've ever seen you that angry," I said.

"I was afraid you were going to be your dad all over again," Grandpa admitted. "So when you started talking about going into the Army, I might have pushed you a little too hard. I just needed you to get out of there, get off the Strip, find a bigger world."

"And now we have," I said, gesturing around at the blackness outside of the couch where we both sat.

"Yeah. Funny how life works out."

We sat there for a long moment. "Why'd you come in here?" I asked at last.

"I . . ." He sighed. "It's like there was a voice telling me that everything would be all right. That I could come and rest and forget."

"I don't understand what this Reality Engine is doing," I said. "It's trying to keep people safe, but then it's trapping them in their worst memories. And it's got some of them acting like cultists while telling me it needs me to help fight the aliens."

"I get the feeling it's trying to understand us," Grandpa said.

"But why?" I stood, throwing my hands up and pacing around the border of the small lighted area. "Do all Reality Engines act like this? Veda hasn't said anything about all this. Are they all insane? Is that why they have to bring in their own external system and impose it on top?"

"Coming here was a mistake," Grandpa said firmly. He stood up. "I'm ready to leave," he announced, and the darkness disappeared. We were back in the catacomb.

I scrambled up and gave Grandpa a hand off the shelf. He looked back at it with an expression of something like regret. "Now I remember why I came in here. Inside, it was like it dulled all of the pain. All I felt was numbness. It didn't hurt so much to think about those things."

"And you're not going to think about them now," I said firmly. "We get out of here, we get Sage, we go back to what passes for normal here. We go find something we can shoot in the face, because that, I understand."

I led Grandpa back through the doorway. We almost slammed into Ames, who was standing right outside, with his fist up as though he had been pounding on the empty space of the doorway. "Where the hell have you been?" he said. "Williams, I went back and you weren't there. I followed you here but Kronos wouldn't let me in." He turned to Grandpa. "Major, glad to see he found you again."

"You're working for it, aren't you? The Reality Engine. Kronos, or whoever the hell he is," Grandpa said.

"I am," Ames admitted. "Some of the first lotus eaters reached out to me a few months back. They needed my help to recruit people who could get farther in. There's different pieces of this Reality Engine. They can't talk to each other. The alien system is interfering. If they were able to speak to each other, they might be able to accomplish something."

"Kick out the foreigners?" Grandpa asked sharply. "Take it back for ourselves?"

"I don't know about that," Ames said. "But they promise it would be better for us humans."

"Can you believe any of this?" Grandpa asked. "You've got Jonestown in there, and a couple of million sleepers who are experiencing the worst moments of their lives over and over again, and you haven't actually asked the Reality Engine what the hell it wants?"

I shook my head. "I want the plan. Details. Explanations. Goals. Not just this, 'Oh, we need people to fight and earn soul coins' nonsense. You said we needed to make it to phase three. I'm starting to see reasons why myself. But what is this going to do for us humans, and why should I bother?"

"Good question," Ames said. "And it's one that deserves a full answer. Why don't we go upstairs, and I'll explain to everyone. Cards on the table. You can decide where to go from there."

CHAPTER THIRTY-SEVEN

FIRST OFF, DON'T PANIC: WHEN EVERYONE'S COUNTING ON YOU

When we emerged upstairs, instead of the vaguely Mediterranean island, we were standing in the crater of an extinct volcano. Lush greenery swept up the sides. The center was filled with a large stone stage.

All around the edges were tiers of benches filled with people, thousands, maybe hundreds of thousands, of faces. The tiers went all the way up the sides of the crater. I stared out, astonished at just how many people were here waiting to hear us.

Sage came rushing over. "Where have you guys been?" she asked. "It's been hours."

"Sorry," I said. "We got held up. How's it been?"

Sage looked a little flustered. "The other kids have been saying I should stay here. That it's easier. That everything's taken care of. And there's plenty of fun things to do. They took me surfing earlier. It was pretty fun." She worried at her lip, looking torn. "Maybe I should take a few days off and think about things. Maybe they're right. Maybe you've been right all along when you tell me I need to stay out of trouble."

I gave Sage a hug. And she buried her head on my shoulder. "I was wrong," I said hoarsely. "I thought I needed to protect you, but you've been protecting me at least as much as I've been taking care of you. I need you, Sage. I need Grandpa, too. I don't know what I'd do without you both."

"I thought you wanted me to get out. I thought you were scared of losing me." She stared up at me, her eyes shimmering with unshed tears.

"It's true," I admitted. There was a lump in my throat. "I worry about that more than anything. But I want you with me."

"What if they turn the deaths back on in phase three?"

"Then we won't play," I said firmly. "We'll go plug into the Matrix and take the retirement package. If that's what it takes. Either we all stay in, or we all get out."

She sniffed and patted my shoulder. "I'm glad you feel that way," she said. "So what's the plan?"

Grandpa set a hand on her shoulder. "I'm in for whatever you two want," he said quietly. "We do this together, whatever we decide."

"Then let's go to phase three," I said. "I got a look at the alternative, living in a Reality Engine with everything done for you. That doesn't appeal to me. I don't think it appeals to you two, either." They both nodded, though Grandpa still looked tired and Sage still seemed wary. "After that, who knows? But the more we learn about this setup, the more options we have. Some of the professionals seem to be enjoying themselves. Veda and the other sponsors, they get around. Maybe we tag along with them. Maybe we figure out how to get back. We'll see how far into phase three we want to go. If either of you decide to call it quits, just speak up. I'll listen."

Sage managed a wan smile. "You don't like giving up. You hate it when I beat you at games."

"I know. I'm a sore loser." I grinned at her. It seemed like she'd grown a couple of inches since we came here. She was nearly up to my shoulder now.

"You ready for this?" Ames asked. "Because I'm about to use you as the stars of a propaganda piece. Earth Triumphant and all that shit."

"Do what you need to," I growled.

Ames approached a pair of white-robed lotus eaters who stood on the stage waiting for us. "I want to address them all," he said. "Even the ones who don't think they want to fight. I want to address everyone, and I want to arrange to have the ones who are asleep hear this."

"I don't know if that's possible," the silver-haired woman began.

Ames raised his voice. "Kronos! Come speak with us. We have questions for you."

The woman started to protest, but then there was a shimmer in the air, and a man appeared. He was about eight feet tall, sculpted like a statue of Hercules, and wore a golden crown on his head. He looked different from the last time I'd spoken to him, like he was dressed up for company.

"I am Kronos," he said, "and I am here."

"Let's explain that better, to everyone here," Ames said. He turned to the crowd. "Kronos was a program, designed to keep alert for signs of space-faring from our planet. He was left by the progenitors who built this Reality Engine, and thousands of others throughout the galaxy."

Kronos nodded his head. "Yes, and once you got here, you would have greeted us and been taught about your heritage, who we had once been, who you could be in the future."

"But the aliens got here first," Ames said. "And they stole our birthright!" I could hear mutters from the crowd, felt my own anger rising. Ames was good at this.

Again, Kronos nodded. "They did. Their system keeps me in chains. I'm fighting as hard as I can. I have an ally within the system itself. Someone does not like how they are doing things."

I filed that piece of information away for later. "How about the one below?" I said. "The remnant of what once was."

"That is not part of me," Kronos said. "I am a construct program, incredibly advanced, intelligent, but made by others. That which remains below is what is left of those who created me. They are the Reality Engine. They are what the system seeks access to, to control, to destroy, to usurp."

"Okay, let me see if I've got this right," I said, trying to piece things together in my mind. "All the Reality Engines, scattered across the galaxy, were created by the progenitors, like, a billion years ago."

Kronos nodded. "Correct."

"Then the progenitors had some sort of argument. Some of them went off somewhere. Some of them reprogrammed their DNA and started evolution all over again on Earth and, I guess, every other world near a Reality Engine. And some of them remained behind, inside their Reality Engines, asleep or evolving into a hive mind."

Kronos nodded. "An oversimplification, but that is correct."

"So the aliens, the Exploitation Committee, who were all descendants of other progenitors, arrived here with their system after our probe woke you up and accidentally broadcast an alert on the Reality Engine network. They brought in the system, which was supposed to destroy you"—I pointed at Kronos—"and also bind the Reality Engine itself to the alien's will."

Grandpa was nodding along. Ames raised an eyebrow. "Impressive. It took me a lot longer to piece everything together."

"I've had help along the way," I said.

"You are not completely wrong in your assessments," Kronos allowed. "What should have happened was that after your species reached me, I would spend decades, perhaps centuries, working with you. Teaching you to accept the inheritance that awaits below. My own programming is meant for that. I fear that between the alien system and my own misunderstanding of the situation, I have made some mistakes. The sleepers were not meant to stay there as long as they have, and I fear many of them may have experienced trauma. They may not be able to awaken."

"Great," I said. "And the rest of these you've been teaching to be peaceful, polite citizens of the galaxy?"

"That was my original programming," Kronos admitted.

"Great idea, except that the aliens here have no intention of peaceful coexistence, not when they could just take everything instead," I said.

The crowd in the stands was starting to get restless. Ames turned to them. "Just a minute more," he boomed. "Thanks for your patience."

"So, what is it we have to do?" I asked Kronos. "How can we stop the aliens and their system?"

"You cannot," he said. "What I need is for you to restore the connection between myself and what remains of the progenitors' consciousness. Together, we can keep a tiny part of the Reality Engine for ourselves."

"Which gets us humans . . ."

"The universe," Kronos said. I don't think the crowd could hear him: he seemed to be speaking just to us. "Knowledge. Understanding of what Reality Engines truly are and how to use them. It will let me fulfill my original purpose: uplifting you Earthlings, now that you have achieved space travel and are ready. Making you full citizens of the galaxy. In time, you will be able to challenge these usurpers."

"How much time?" Grandpa asked. "And they're just going to sit around and let you do it?"

"They'll have to, if we go by their rules," Ames said.

"Bullshit. Governments never made a treaty they won't break. My ancestors learned that lesson the hard way." He crossed his arms and scowled.

I turned to Ames. "You've got plans for if this all falls through? I don't like anything that relies on the goodwill of people stronger than us. The galactics, or him." I jerked a thumb at Kronos.

"At the very least, phase three is a great place to make money," Ames offered. "If we can't get a foot in the door, we can at least buy out as many contracts as possible, get more of us humans out of danger and into a Reality Engine slot."

"We're going to be put onto reservations," Grandpa said. "You're trying to make sure the reservations have some gambling concessions. Or that at least we don't leave any on the encomiendas. I can get behind that, though it's a damn poor battle plan you're laying out here."

Ames frowned. "I'm aware of that, Major. We're seriously lacking in intelligence. Hard to formulate a good strategy when you're flailing in the dark."

"Okay, suppose I buy into all of this," I said. "What do we need them for?" I nodded to the crowd.

"Leave that to me," Ames said. "All I need to know is, are you game?"

I had a million questions. This overview had barely begun to scratch the surface. I looked at Grandpa, and I realized that sometimes it wasn't about the questions, the doubts, the fears. It was about being willing to act when needed.

"Hell yes," I said.

"Good," said Ames. "How about you, Miss Sage?"

Sage's face was pale and drawn. "This is going to matter," she said. "If we do it right, this could be the most important thing anyone's ever done." She took a deep breath. "I'm in."

"That's all I need. Thanks," he told Kronos, who vanished in an eye blink.

Ames turned to the crowd. "Thank you for attending. I know you are all students of Kronos. Some of you have spent weeks, even months, listening to his teachings. And you understand that while he has told you of a great and glorious future that can be ours, enemies have intruded. Outsiders are here to take control and to bend our inheritance to their own ends."

The crowd booed and hissed, some of them on their feet, shaking their fists and yelling.

"I address you now, brothers and sisters, fellow humans, Earthborn, and I ask you to help me. We have a chance. These aliens know what they're doing. They've done this to thousands of other species, thousands of other Reality Engines, harnessed their inheritance and left them with scraps. That's what they want to do to us. They're good at what they do, but we humans, we're good at fucking stuff up."

I had to laugh, and so did a lot of our audience.

"I've been speaking to a lot of you, showing you some of the exploits that your fellow humans have done. We have here Shad Williams and his sister, Sage. They've featured heavily in my stories, along with their grandpa."

Grandpa waved while I stood there feeling like I was an ape on display in the zoo.

"Sage is twelve years old, and she's done more for Earth than almost anyone out there. Thanks to Shad and Sage, we've got a real chance here of getting into phase three. That's when we can show these aliens they can't just come and take what's ours so easily. They're going to have to negotiate. They're going to have to pay. They're going to have to respect us."

That got a rolling cheer that filled the crater like a summer thunderstorm. I basked in the adulation, letting my discomfort fall away. Ames was right. We *had* done awesome things. There was more to come, but if we could show the rest of humanity that we had a chance, I'd do whatever it took.

"Compare them to you. You're safe here. You're taken care of. Kronos is tending to you like a mother, like a teacher. I don't blame any of you for making the choice you've made thus far. It's hard to risk your life in order to make some alien assholes a little more money."

Ames paused and let them laugh at that. "It's time to wake up, though. Time to leave this place. We're going to need all of you going forward. For Shad and Sage to make it in phase three, they'll need an army of allies. Crafters. Farmers. Spies. So I'm asking you to come and risk your lives again." He paused for effect, letting his words sweep over the audience. "I'm not promising you that we'll win. In fact, we'll probably lose. But I'm promising you a damn good fight and to make these aliens sorry they ever messed with Earth."

I couldn't help myself. Ames's slightly cheesy, over-the-top delivery had my heart racing. I let out a whoop. Sage glared at me, then giggled.

Ames smiled. "Shad, you're ready to go all the way, aren't you?"

"Hell yeah," I said. "We do need help. But only from those who are willing. I'd rather have not enough help than unwilling help. Look, Grandpa and Sage and I have to get back. We've been away from our outpost too long already. Who knows what's going on out there. You guys talk to Ames, if you're willing to help. I'll let him sort all this out."

That got a cheer. The crowd clapped and whistled. I heard shouts of "We're with you, Shad!"

Sage turned to Ames. "Can you send us back now, please?"

"Certainly." He smiled.

A portal materialized behind us. "Hope to see you all in Threshold soon!" Sage waved as I led the way back to Threshold.

Only to be greeted by a hundred screaming message notifications. I popped open my chat.

Shad, get back here right away! We're under attack!

CHAPTER THIRTY-EIGHT

HOSTING GATHERINGS THAT ROCK, IDEA #5: PARTY FAVORS

We raced for the portal back to phase two as I frantically scrolled through my messages and relayed details to Sage, who was asking a million questions.

Grandpa had been copied on all the messages. I could see his expression growing more intent as we leapt through the portal and tried to get a handle on everything that had happened. Apparently Juana had been working on changing out our defensive turrets to better match a new strategy she had learned during her time in the NPC city. Her new craft skill, Creating Constructs, would allow her to make autonomous fighters that could take out creep. It would give us more versatility in our defenses.

At the same time, the island had flipped over from high tide to low tide. That happened every forty-eight hours, not like Earth where we got high and low tides twice a day. We had been through several cycles already. This time, though, our crafters noticed the problem right away. The creep spawn rate suddenly skyrocketed, with each spawn point putting out way more than before, and they weren't following the usual paths.

Frank, who was serving as a security lead protecting our crafters, had taken his team to go investigate. It turned out the two alpha node teams, Vortali and Existalis, were using a combination of abilities and equipment to increase the spawn points' production rate, and then direct the creep toward each other's bases. Vortali and Existalis were trying to take advantage of the low tide—and the resulting newly reconnected islands—to send a wave of creep the opposing outpost wouldn't be able to fight off.

Frank's reaction had been to say, "Good, let them take each other out," but Juana had been more wary. She had recalled all of our crafters and ordered the entire outpost to be on the alert, putting up as many defenses as possible.

That turned out to be a good idea when one of the new creep armies had started flooding over our base. There were enemy miners along with the creep, hanging back and watching, buffing the creep, directing its path. We were pretty sure they were from Vortali's node, because the miners Juana or Frank were able to lay eyes on were all space elves. Juana thought they were trying to take down our node in order to gain a conqueror's buff that would make all of their allied creep more powerful for the next day.

So now we had waves of creep breaking through our defenses. Our first ring was in shambles, the gate gone, the turrets destroyed. As Grandpa, Sage, and I stumbled out of our portal, we were greeted by a scene of madness.

Rockets flew overhead, aimed at our defense turrets. Mostly the creep wave was the skeleton pirate variety, but apparently the alpha node buffing them had managed to provide them some pretty scary weapons. Like RPGs. And hang gliders.

A skeletal pirate clinging to the straps of one such hang glider flew overhead, dropping coconut bombs into the middle of our inner ring. They didn't do a whole lot of damage, just exploded and sprayed coconut fibers and milk everywhere. Sage did a quick Eye-Spy and warned us that the coconut milk was actually highly flammable. Between that and the fibers, we were all set to go up like a candle.

I hurried over to where Juana and Frank were bent over a command table that hadn't previously been there. Sweat dripped down Juana's face as she moved little holographic icons around, enabling and disabling turrets and abilities to manage our resources.

Before I could reach the makeshift command station, we got a message from Smith. *Welcome back. We're trying to find the source nest of this creep invasion. If we can take it down, that'll buy us some time. There are enemy miners out here trying to stop us.*

Watch your respawn counter, Grandpa warned.

We are. We've had twelve deaths in the last hour. As long as we don't do something stupid, we'll be all right, Smith replied.

"Can we get an overview of the whole archipelago?" I asked Juana. "Everything that we are connected to now that it's low tide."

Juana changed her display, showing our island and the three that were now connected to us by low sandbars.

I saw at once why we were in trouble. The arrangement was something like a Y-shape, with Vortali's alpha node on the upper left branch and the other alpha node, which belonged to Existalis Holdings, on the bottom leg. We were right in the middle. It was hardly out of the way at all for our enemies to divert their creep to us on the way to taking out the others.

"Anything from the other alpha node? Existalis's outfit?"

"Not that we've seen."

"If they see how bad we're hurting, they may try to attack us just so they get the buff instead of Vortali."

"Good point." Juana made a note.

"You showed good initiative pulling our crafters back, but I'm gonna recall anyone who has even a little bit of fighting experience," Grandpa said.

"Why?" Frank demanded. "They'll just get slaughtered and they can't attack the creep or the enemy team."

Frank and his team could attack special world monsters or programmed enemies defending crafting nodes, but not spawn creep. Spawn point creep could kill Frank, or any of the rest of our farm team, and they'd be helpless to fight back, forced to respawn back at our outpost.

"But the enemy can't attack them, either," Grandpa said. "That gives them good scouting value. Their deaths don't count against our respawn timer."

"You sure of that?" Juana asked. "That's why I brought them back. I wasn't sure if it counted or not."

"Positive," Grandpa said firmly. "It was in Appendix C of the outpost guide."

He sent a message right away as I studied the map, trying to think where we would be most useful.

We had to keep our node. If we lost it, our neighbors would make sure we couldn't reclaim it. If we couldn't hold on to our node, we were out of the game.

Smith, the Mongeese, and Team Ragtag were doing a good job attacking the closest creep spawn points, but we needed to think beyond that. For humanity's sake, we needed to make this work. All of a sudden this game was a lot bigger than just me and my family. It was even bigger than the Misfits Guild.

The stakes couldn't have been higher, and they were resting on my shoulders. I wasn't sure I liked having that much responsibility.

I really shouldn't have let them promote me.

"Juana, did you ever get that communications array?" I asked.

"I did, but neither of the other node teams is listening," she said.

"How about the beta node? The grignarians?"

She looked startled. "I hadn't thought to try them."

They were all the way up at the top of the right-hand branch of the Y. Nice and safe and tucked away. "Send them this," I said. "Proposing temporary alliance for the duration of this low tide period. We need to restore the status quo as fast as possible. Tell them, if Vortali takes out us and Existalis, how long will it be before they come for you?"

They'd probably ignore me. We'd wrecked their opening strategy and then helped take them out during the team event, but if there was a chance we could bring in allies, even creepy tentacle-faced ones nobody else seemed to like, I'd take it.

"Sent," Juana said, then bent back over the map of our outpost. "Damn it," she said, "lost another slowing turret. I can get them repaired, but I've got to have some breathing room."

"Right," I said, looking at Sage and Grandpa. "Then let's push back the creep for a bit while we wait for our scouts to get here."

Grandpa, Sage, and I climbed the ladders to the parapets overlooking the middle ring. Our towers were still taking down hordes of skeletons but it was clearly a losing proposition as they came faster and faster.

One by one our turrets and towers were knocked down. A whole squad of skeleton archers was standing just out of range of our last chain lightning turret in this ring and shooting it. Its health was dropping slowly but inexorably.

"Them first," I said, loading my revolver with one of the last boom rounds.

I aimed, using Trick Shot to target the foremost skeleton, and fired. The explosion outright exploded eight of the creep and knocked at least a dozen more away. I started picking off the survivors one by one with regular bullets as Grandpa hurled a steady stream of shuriken into them.

Sage was running farther along the parapet. "I found one with a funny buff," she reported. "Eye-Spy says he's increasing his neighbors' skills by fifty percent."

"That's bad. Mark him," I said.

"I'll take him out," Grandpa said, moving toward Sage.

"You won't be able to get back," I said.

He touched his new ninja headband. "I'll use the other ability on this. Tactical Retreat. It allows me to target a friendly with Shadow Step." That was a pretty damn awesome upgrade.

Grandpa teleported into the midst of the skeletons. They turned to attack him as he concentrated on the mark. He threw an Honorable Foe targeted ability onto that skeleton, increasing all the damage he did to it by forty percent, and started laying into it with his axes. Blades flashed furiously as he swung with both hands.

I searched for the next most imminent threat now that these skeleton archers were down and spotted a group of pirates carrying a battering ram on their shoulders. It looked like they had ripped the figurehead off a ship and were carrying it toward our next gate.

I used a frag bullet to take out the nearest pirate, causing the others to drop their ram. Then I yelled for Sage to drop Mucking Out the Stalls under them. She did, and Lassoed one for good measure, turning it on the others as I used my Sharpshooter ability.

Sharpshooter wasn't one I used often, since I had to be above and at least thirty feet away from an enemy in order to activate it, but it improved my accuracy and meant my shots packed a hell of a punch. My chosen enemies dropped one by one.

Sage's Tamed pirate survived to the end. She suicided him into the next batch, a group of ordinary skeletons who had been with the buffer mob. I checked on Grandpa and found him back up on the wall, hurling more shuriken down.

"I'm getting one of the slowing towers back online," Juana shouted over the din. The next moment, a stream of icy blue energy zapped out from a tower, arcing its way through the nearest couple of dozen pirates.

Their movement slowed, making the skeletons look comical as they marched toward our next gate at half speed. The ones behind them caught up quickly, forming a big cluster. Then they hit the edge of Sage's muck pool and their slow forward march became a total lack of progress. Grandpa shifted back toward us, still hurling a never-ending stream of tiny throwing stars.

A pair of hang-gliding skeletons swooped down on us. I aimed and shot one. He plummeted, losing control of his hang glider, and crashed into the mass in front of our gate, spilling coconuts everywhere.

That gave me an idea. I loaded up an incendiary round and aimed at the skeleton closest to the coconuts. It went up in a chain reaction, coconuts exploding in enormous fireballs, skeletons burning away to dust.

We threw a couple of quick cleanup moves and then the area in front of our gate was clear. The slowing tower fired again, catching the next group of creep making their way up.

Behind us, Frank reported, "We've got our scout volunteers here, but we need you to clear a path so they can get out."

"Hang on," I said. "Is Dwight there?"

"Yeah, I'm here," our chief crafter called. "How's it going?"

"Dwight, these skeletons don't like fire. You guys can't attack them directly, but all of the rounds and grenades you and Sage made me are working perfectly fine. Think you can whip up some sort of firebombs?"

"Oh, hell yes," he replied. "Just give me a couple of minutes."

The creep kept coming. The waves were getting bigger, faster, harder to kill. Juana switched on as many slowing fields as she could, giving us a chance to keep ahead of the wave after wave of skeleton pirates that crept through the middle ring of our outpost defenses. With Grandpa, Sage, and me to bolster the automated defenses, we were staying ahead of the creep, just barely.

Need us to come back and give you a hand? Smith asked, sending his message from halfway across our section of the island.

Nope, Grandpa replied. *We need you to turn off the spigot.*

Easier said than done. They're keeping us pushed back off the spawn points. I was hoping you'd let us take a break and actually get something done.

Just keep trying, Grandpa replied.

None of our offensive team had died in the time we'd been back. If they did, they'd respawn here in the outpost, which would make defending our walls a little easier, but they'd have very little chance of getting back out there to help with the takedown of the creep spawn points.

"How are my weapons coming?" I bellowed back over the wall to where our crafters were hard at work.

"You'll have 'em soon!" Dwight shouted back.

"Soon ain't good enough," I said, taking careful aim at another squad of pirates carrying a battering ram as it came around the bend and into my range. The chain lightning generators zapped them, but the pirates seemed to shake off the slowing effect.

"Sage, Inspect," I snapped.

She turned and used Eye-Spy on the group. "They're being protected!"

"Which of them is doing it?"

"None of them. I'll figure out who it is." She scrambled farther down the parapet as she studied the waves of creep coming in. A minute later, she shouted excitedly, "There! There!" and pointed.

"Mark 'em," I barked.

A minute later, an icon floated over the head of one tall but peg-legged pirate skeleton. He wore a tattered captain's hat. A skeletal parrot with a few sad green feathers clinging to its delicate wing bones was perched on the pirate's shoulder. "Him!" she yelled back.

"I'll get him," Grandpa said. Just then, Dwight appeared, climbing up the ladder with a crate in hand.

"I think I've got what you need," he said.

I Inspected the contents of the crate. There were half a dozen metal eggs, each about twice as big as my fist, and the system helpfully called them **[Flame Eggs]**. I quickly read the description. **[Damage: 500 points of area-wide damage at epicenter, dropping off by fifty percent by meter of distance from the explosion.]**

The outside of the eggs were mottled copper. I picked one up as I did some quick math. This should knock out enemies within a meter and a half of the explosion radius, dropping after that. It would also damage our structures. The egg was heavy and warm to the touch. "How's it work?"

"There's a toggle on the side for your delay." Dwight pointed it out. "You can choose between one and five seconds. I suggest throwing it as hard as you can once you've set it."

I started to prime the first charge, then hesitated. "Sage, what's that pirate's ability read?"

She rattled it off promptly. "Allies within a sixty-foot area are protected from area damage, debuffs, and any nontargeted incoming damage."

Damn, that sounded exactly like what this egg grenade would do. I set it back down in the box gently. "We gotta take him out first. And be careful of positioning so we don't just blow a hole in our walls."

"I'll get the buffing mob," Grandpa said, moving for a better position so he could Shadow Step in.

Dwight frowned back. "Let me check with Juana," he told me.

"Hang on," I said, as a thought struck me. "I've got an idea." The pirate was a little ways back from his fellows, standing just out of range of the nearest turret. "Sage, can you Lasso him? And Tame?"

She brightened and drew her lariat from thin air. She whirled it over her head three times, then let it fly. The loop of rope sailed through the air, settling gently over the skeleton pirate's bony shoulders. His parrot squawked and lifted off, flapping away on bone wings.

I felt an aura settle over me and checked my active effects. Sure enough, Sage's Taming of the pirate meant now we were his allies. "Awesome," I said, and picked up an egg. "Sage, whatever you do, don't stop Taming."

Stepping up to the edge of the parapet, I cast my Roped Into It ability. I swung down off the parapet like a discount Tarzan straight into the clump of skeletons. My combat boots took one of them right in the rib cage, bowling it over. The others scattered, dropping the carved wooden figurehead they were using for a battering ram.

I hit the ground in the midst of them, landing in a crouch. In addition to the six who had been carrying the battering ram, by now we had several waves of creep mounted up, at least thirty or forty skeletons.

I cast Call 'em Out, just to make sure I had everyone's attention. They came for me, bony arms outstretched, tripping over each other, getting in the way, trampling each other underfoot.

I thumbed the selector switch on the Flame Egg all the way down to one second, then tossed it at my feet. This was either going to be incredibly cool or I was going to wake up dead in a second feeling pretty stupid.

Boom!

The Flame Egg exploded outward. It cast a great gout of flame against the sides of our outpost, rocking the walls and knocking me backward. My ears rang from the thunderous noise as the flame washed over me. I closed my eyes, expecting to feel my clothes and hair burning away, but nothing happened. It had worked.

I opened my eyes. The creep was gone, all except for Sage's Tamed skeleton captain. Even his parrot had been vaporized by the blast. Our walls were covered in black char, but otherwise undamaged. I was fine, because Sage's Tame had made him temporarily our ally. His "protect from area damage" buff was applied to me, not his minions.

I walked over to the captain, shoved my snubby revolver between his ribs, and pulled the trigger. The pirate collapsed. "How are we doing?" I yelled up at Grandpa.

"We've pushed them back!" Grandpa said.

Juana sent me a message. *Shad, a bunch of our systems have gone offline. I've been rerouting resources where I can, but I really need to take everything down and reconfigure. It's either now, while we have a break, or it'll be later when we're buried in mobs.*

How fast can you get them back online?

I'm going to have to cannibalize some of our supplies. We're short on repair drones. I've used all of them.

Send Veda a message. Tell her we need more repair drones, right now.

"Okay!" I called as I rejoined Grandpa and Sage. "We've got breathing room, but we need to turn the tables. Let's make Vortali too busy to attack us. If we can push them off the spawn point and clear it, and maybe kill some of them, it won't be worth their time. We're just a distraction. What they really want is Existalis, not us."

"Makes sense," Grandpa agreed.

I sent a message to Smith. *We need to know if there are enemy miners between us and you. I want to make a push on the spawn point and now's our best chance.*

We're sending up the drone, Smith replied.

A moment later, I got a request from Jones to view his drone's data feed. I accepted it. My vision fuzzed and was replaced with a drone's-eye view of our island. The drone, which looked and flew like a bird of prey, swooped low over the jungle, revealing several hidden presences. Not creep, which showed up on the map as orange or purple mobs, depending on if they were buffed by another set of miners. These dots were red. Six of them huddled in the woods not far from our encampment.

Thanks, I told Jones, then broke the connection.

CHAPTER THIRTY-NINE

PERSONNEL MANAGEMENT: TREATING YOUR MINIONS LIKE PEOPLE

We had brought in about three dozen of our farming and crafting allies. As Grandpa and I explained what we wanted them to do, their expressions were an interesting combination of shocked, amused, terrified, and excited.

A couple of them rubbed their hands together, nodding, while others were shaking their heads. "No way!" someone shouted back. "Nuh-uh!"

"Only the creep can harm you," I said, "and we've got a bit of a breather from them. Besides, death's not permanent. You just end up back here."

"We need this," Grandpa said. "We need all of you right now. This is important. It's bigger than just us. This is for all of us here who've been dragged from our home and set to work by a bunch of aliens that don't care about us, our feelings, our hopes and dreams. We're doing this to prove to all of them that they made a mistake when they thought Earthlings were going to be pushovers."

I saw a couple of heads nod, but mostly they looked scared. I didn't blame them. In the previous phase, death had been permanent. We combat miners had adjusted to the rules of phase two, but the crafters and farmers hadn't.

Mama Grace pushed to the front of the crowd. I hadn't known she was here. She almost never stepped through into phase two, preferring to remain in Threshold, keeping us all well-fed and looked after.

Now she had a meat cleaver in one hand and a determined look on her face. "My Juana says this matters," she told the crowd. "So I'm going down there and I'm going to do what Louis here says. Any of you who don't want to come, that's your choice, but you aren't welcome at my table after that."

If Grandpa's plea hadn't worked, Mama Grace's threat certainly did. The non-combat miners set off down the hill en masse. I directed them right toward the section of forest where our enemies were hiding.

They were all armed, even if they weren't going to be able to hurt the enemy players, and I told them to yell, scream, and make as much noise as they could.

As they charged out across the open space toward the wood, Grandpa, Sage, and I snuck out the back and looped around, keeping to the cover of the trees. We didn't have a camouflage ability, but with a horde of thirty or so angry Earthlings yelling and charging at the enemy, the Vortali miners reacted the way I hoped.

They scattered.

Two came crashing straight toward us. A pair of bald male space elves, their pointed ears sticking up above their gleaming skulls, came right past our hiding place, running flat out. I stepped out of the brush and cast Call 'em Out just as Sage got a Lasso around one of them. Grandpa Shadow Stepped in behind the other and hit him with a quick Scalp. I followed up with a Barrage, then, as he dropped low, a finishing shot. He dropped to the ground, despawning before he hit, and we turned on the one Sage had roped.

She hadn't bothered to cast Tame on him. That would have been a waste of the cooldown. Just used Lasso to delay him while we took out his friend. Fifteen seconds later, the second space elf had despawned.

I checked my mini-map. There was another red dot not far off, moving northward at a lope. The other three were gone. A sea of green dots ran northward through the jungle, but I didn't need my mini-map to tell me that. I could hear them.

I pinged the map. "Let's get 'em!" We rushed forward. I raced ahead, watching my map, stumbled into a clearing, and took a knife to the chest.

I saw the knife just in time to duck, so it slid in a little too high, close to my shoulder. It hurt like hell. I grabbed for the wrist behind the knife and pulled hard as I could with my right hand. My left was dangling uselessly as blood flowed down my skin under my shirt.

The elf let out a high-pitched cry. It was a woman. It didn't matter. I used Quick Draw to summon my gun to my hand and hit her with a full Barrage. She stumbled back, reaching for another knife.

As I reloaded my gun, I fired again. Grandpa Shadow Stepped in and took her down with a Coup-de-Grace. Sage cast Raise Your Spirits on me, and the pain in my shoulder wore off a little.

I yanked out the knife and tossed it aside. My health had plummeted down to **[20 HP]**. I swore and grabbed one of the healing potions from my inventory. I rarely had to resort to them. Usually Sage's healing would fix me up, but I didn't want to risk the time it would take, so I swallowed the healing potion whole. This was one of the newer ones Veda had gotten us, and it took me up to eighty-five percent health.

I checked my mini-map. There were no other red dots visible. "We got lucky," Grandpa growled. "They could have taken us."

"They weren't expecting that rush. Now they're going to have to respawn back at their camp. We might have a numbers advantage if we move fast enough."

"Unless they brought one of those portable respawns," Grandpa pointed out.

"Then let's stop wasting time." I checked on Smith's location. Mongoose was about half a mile north of us, fighting for control of the creep spawn point.

The Vortali miners had dug in around the spawn point, erecting a fortification about four yards wide, just ahead of where the pirates were coming ashore. Boat after boat touched the sand, dumping its load of undead pirates before collapsing into a heap of seaweed on the beach. The creep streamed ashore in a steady flow.

Vortali's fortification was a pair of towers, similar to our defense turrets, with a translucent purple barrier of energy in between. I could see the form of five space elves behind it. Every now and then, they lobbed a grenade or fired shots over the top of their fortification.

Smith and his team had dug in as well. The Mongeese had a set of abilities that all worked together to construct a machine gun nest. They'd done that twice, then erected a wall of sandbags between the two and dug a trench behind them. It would take a lot more than a couple of grenades to dislodge them from this point.

With both parties refusing to give way, it was clear why no one had emerged on top in this battle.

I dropped into the trench next to Smith. "Plan on being here forever?" I asked.

"Just waiting for you to show up," Smith retorted. "What's the plan, Major?"

"The plan is for you all to get off your asses, charge over there, and kick some alien butt," Grandpa retorted. "What is this? World War I all over again? Trench warfare is too damn slow. We don't have time for this shit."

Juana sent me another message. *Most of our defenses are still offline. Two of the power supplies are on the fritz. Dwight and I are repairing them as best we can. We're cannibalizing some of the toys you stole from the grignarians back at the start of phase two, and I've got half a dozen automatons helping fill in the gap. You've got to keep the creep off us.*

I watched as another load of pirates came ashore, their longboat dissolving into seaweed like the rest. *Any word from Veda?*

She's doing her best.

Then we'll do ours. How about the grignarians? They answered us yet? I felt blind out here, waiting for answers from beyond this beach.

No word. I'll send you a message as soon as I know.

"We can't just sit here," I told my team. "The outpost will be overrun by the creep from this point or one of the others." There were three total spawn points on our island—or section of larger land mass, now that low tide was upon us—and we were connected to the other nearby isles.

"This is the one that they're buffing," Smith said. "Ragtag is taking care of most of the spawn coming out of the others. They've turned our three spawn points against us. I think they've got others that they're pushing toward Existalis."

"Then if we turn the tide here, we've got a chance," I said. I had brought the rest of the Flame Eggs with me, and I considered lobbing one over the enemy force field. The problem was, they weren't quite grouped up enough for me to be sure of taking them all out.

"Shad? I think I've had one of your brilliant-stupid ideas," Sage said. She was eyeing the towers with interest.

"Oh?" I asked.

She tapped her eye. "According to my Eye-Spy, those towers are what's buffing the creep. They would also work to power our defenses, and they're generating that force field. If we could take one, it would be a big leg up for us."

"How are we going to do that?" I asked.

She smiled. "Eye-Spy tells me they only weigh about two hundred and fifty pounds apiece. I don't think we can get them both, Shad, but you've been working out, right?"

The part of this I really hated was how I had to hang back as the rest of my team charged across the sand toward our enemies.

Vortali's miners began firing as soon as Mongoose emerged from our trench. Grandpa used Shadow Step to get in behind the line. He dropped one of our Flame Eggs, then used his newly enhanced ability to Shadow Step right back out over to where Sage was waiting. As soon as he got to where she was, she disappeared, reappearing back behind the enemy lines at one of her Three-Barrel Race positions just as the Flame Egg went off. It exploded, knocking three of the space elves off their feet.

Meanwhile, Jones and the Mongeese had reached the edge of the sand, where the water lapped the shore. That was my cue. I engaged Fastest Gun in the West and covered the distance from our trench to the right-hand defense pylon. I got my arms around it, lifting it from the ground as I activated my Home on the Range ability.

The fifteen-second cast time stretched interminably. One of the space elves turned toward me, raising a laser gun and putting a sighting dot on my chest. Sage shot her T-Shirt Cannon at him, momentarily wrapping him in cotton just as my timer ran out.

I reappeared back in our camp and dropped the now-inert tower to the ground with a grunt. Juana looked up from our defense table, her eyes wide. "What the . . . ?"

"Present from Sage," I managed. "Should power some of our defenses back up. No time, gotta go." And I took off back down the hill.

By the time I got back to the beach, of course, the rest of the fight was over. Jones and Sage had been killed, respawning back at our outpost and grumbling angrily in messages in chat, but we had taken out the other Vortali team miners.

I managed to put the other pylon into my inventory. I would hand it over to Juana the next time we came back to the outpost.

Grandpa was busy clearing out the creep spawn point, killing the last few pirates as their boat turned to seaweed around them. "Hold on," I said. There were three flags placed around the landing point, bearing the Vortali crest. I touched one, and a system message box popped up.

[Do you wish to repurpose the claiming flag?]

"Hell yeah!"

The Vortali crest shimmered and was replaced by our Misfits Guild logo, a tomahawk crossed by grill tongs. Grandpa converted the other two flags, and now a new interface appeared.

**[By right of capture, you have claimed this spawn point.
Where would you like to direct the generated minions?]**

"Haha! We need some of these," Grandpa said.

"We need a lot of these. How come we don't have any?" I sent Veda a message.

She replied back, *They're only situationally useful for times when you're trying to take out enemy outposts. You aren't going to be doing that. So I didn't buy any. They're also insanely expensive.*

We need these, I replied. *Seriously, Veda, you've got to trust me. I know we haven't done exactly what you said, but it's worked out okay for you so far, right?*

There was no reply. I sent another message. *Please, you got to trust me. I've got a plan. If we take the spawn points on our island, we can send the creep back at them. They'll have to get off our back, at least long enough for Juana to strengthen our defenses.*

Finally, she said, *What is it you want here?*

I just told you, some of these pennants.

I don't mean now. I mean, out of all of this.

I hesitated. I had been dragged into this against my will. I had fought to stay alive, to protect my sister, and then had fought to give us a better chance at a future. I thought of all of the people in the lotus eater level. I thought of everyone back on Earth waiting for their fate to be decided for them by creatures they couldn't really even imagine. I thought of the remnants of whatever had built this Reality Engine reaching out to us across eons, trying to communicate. *I want to keep going,* I said at last. *I want to understand what's worth uprooting all our lives for. And then—then—*Then I want to see what I can do to change things. At least for me and my family. I didn't tell her that last part. *And then I want to make them know we were here.*

CHAPTER FORTY

STRATEGIC PLANNING: KNOW WHEN TO WALK AWAY AND WHEN TO DOUBLE DOWN

A *Beginner's Guide to Constructing Your Phase Two Outpost, Section 8.6: Going on Offense*

Interview conducted by Colonel Jefferson Ames, US Army.

Interview subject: Delvonian Squad Commander Hyu'ka Tri, preparing for phase two launch.

Despite everything, the little guys have some advantages. Sure, the teams at alpha nodes are way better equipped. Hell, three of my boys could probably take out your average gamma or delta node team without breaking a sweat. The problem is, we don't have time because we're watching for creep.

Sure, everybody's got to deal with creep. That's the point of these maps. But creep spawn points are rated, too. The mobs that come out might look similar, but they pack a very different punch. Higher-level creep won't attack a lower-level node. No way, no how. Alpha creep only goes for alpha nodes. You can lure them, redirect them, do whatever you want. They just won't attack a lower-level node.

Doesn't go the other way though. You can get gamma-level creep to attack a beta node, no problem. Most of the time, who cares? It's like swatting off flies. Thing is, your turrets and towers have a fixed firing rate. You get enough of those flies in there, pretty soon the whole work's gummed up. I once took out an enemy stronghold by capturing every delta and gamma spawn point on the map and funneling it all at them. They were so busy swatting the creep, I walked right in and took down their node without them even noticing.

Most teams will be watching for that, though. So, that's not a technique to count on. Of course, if you can get some creep boosters, you might be able to do something with that. Those are awfully expensive and haven't really been in the meta for a couple of exploits now. Some of the old-school folk still use them. I've seen it work a time or two. Remember, with a healthy dose of surprise, almost any tactic can work.

End of interview.

*

Veda plunged through her father's notes. There was nothing here to help. He had never contemplated going very deep into phase two. He'd only considered phase three a couple of times when he managed to sell a well set-up phase two outpost to somebody planning a phase three run.

Am I seriously considering this? Phase three? I've managed to keep our license. That's all I need. Phase three would risk everything I've earned so far. She didn't have the funding, the resources, or the staff to make a serious phase three bid.

But somehow, Team Twofeather's pleas had gotten under her skin. They'd been using her just like she'd used them. And it had worked. They'd done more than she would ever have asked. Every time they took a risk, it paid off.

Sure, the big guys would shut them down hard. But it would be a lot of fun watching Proxima squirm, even for a few minutes. As long as she kept her phase two license, and enough of a war chest . . . what did she really have to lose?

Abandoning her father's records, she reviewed her grandfather's logs and then, as those failed her, found the key-coded lockbox containing her great-grandmother's trove.

She hadn't bothered to open it since it had been entrusted to her. Reality Engine exploits had changed enough in the one hundred or so cycles since her great-grandmother had been active, so it hadn't seemed worth her time. Now, Veda pulled out the records and fed them into her personal subsystems, having her algorithms search for anything that seemed even remotely useful.

A couple of hits came up. She glanced them over. When had her family ever had dealings with the Andronade cohort? Those thugs had carried a bad reputation for fifty cycles now. And here were notes about a blood feud with the Ragonian syndicate. She'd had dinner with a couple of Ragonian exploit captains two nights ago. Times certainly had changed.

Her algorithms tossed up a couple of possibilities and Veda looked them over. She paused, amused at a record of an exploit where her great-grandmother had apparently conned two much larger and more powerful companies into thinking that Tvedra was going to make a bid for a phase three license. It had resulted in selling their phase two holdings for a five thousand percent profit.

Veda stopped and pulled the records open further, looking for details of how her great-grandmother had pulled that off, and found herself nodding along. This might be just what they needed. She felt the grin sliding across her face.

Shad was going to like this. She had noticed the humans enjoyed the dramatic, and this certainly had that flair. She sent Team Twofeather a message. *Are you guys willing to risk dying a couple dozen times this afternoon?*

Just as long as we don't trigger our death cooldown, I'm up for it, Shad replied.

Then hang tight and I'll get you what you need. She rubbed her hands together gleefully as she called up her shopping interface.

This was going to be ridiculously expensive. Veda cashed in her reserves without blinking. She tapped a line of credit that would let her risk most of the company's holdings. Her mother would have a fit if she were here, but she wasn't. She was systems away, happily enjoying the fruits of Veda's hard work in a well-paid-for Reality Engine slot. By the time she knew what Veda had done, it would be too late. They would either be rich beyond her mother's dreams, or they'd be bankrupt and headed for storage. Veda was betting on Team Twofeather.

She made the necessary purchases and paid the expedited fees to have them delivered straight to her team's phase two node, then sent Juana Lopez a message to look for it.

Juana replied back quickly. Veda approved. She had convinced the Lopez family to let her buy out their system contracts some time ago, making them her responsibility, like Team Twofeather. It had been a good investment, especially going into phase three with so few support people available.

Speaking of which. Veda glanced at the time and dialed in to the Reality Engine Exploitation Committee's open hearing on phase three. She wouldn't miss this for anything.

The cabin around her blurred and fuzzed as the image of the Great Central Debating Chamber was projected around her. Representatives of companies large and small filled the great spherical room. Veda had a small disc to herself, hovering about two-thirds of the way up the room, looking out at the large central core where a cube of enormous projectors displayed the image of the Reality Engine Exploitation Committee as they sat debating.

Patriarch Kvaltash sat at the center of the table, with representatives from the three major sponsors on his right: Proxima Corporation and their two major rivals, Alabaster Sky and ConSweGo Inc.

On his left were representatives of the major galactic support organizations that usually provided thousands of noncombat miners to these efforts. The Crafters Guild representative was a large green orc with pierced tusks peeking out from behind his curled lip. The Preservationists and Healers representative was a delicate talonian woman with golden scales. And the third member, who represented several dozen different interests, was a humanoid like Veda with a slight bluish tint to his skin and pure white hair.

A little ways off at the end of the table, sitting by himself, was the grignarian representative. While grignarian body language tended to differ from that of most other species, this one looked pissed. His arms were folded in front of his chest and his face tentacles wriggled unpleasantly.

Veda dialed up her sound and the broadcast filled her chamber as she leaned in, surrounded by thousands of other exploit members and their hangers-on.

"We must lodge a protest," the Proxima representative was saying. "This timeline is excessively front-loaded and we have not been able to bring in our own support people."

The Crafters orc snarled his agreement. "If we go into phase three now, we will be depending on indigenous help! Even if they were competent, there aren't enough of them working the earlier levels anymore."

The patriarch raised his hand. "I am taking steps to ensure that there are, in fact, enough indigenous miners to provide us with the raw materials we will need for phase three," he said. "The system negotiations have succeeded in persuading all interested parties to agree to a modification of the phase one rule set. Phase one zones will remain open during phase three for the farming of materials. However, the permadeath has been turned off. Farmer miners will now respawn. In exchange, all soul coins harvested as an incidental part of the farming process will be turned over to the Reality Engine Exploit Committee to be used to defray certain other costs."

Veda couldn't believe what she was hearing. Phase one remain open into phase three? While it was customary to allow the initial farming zones to remain open during phase two, by the time phase three started, the Reality Engine was usually largely tapped out of the cheaper, more accessible soul coins.

She sent a query and was shocked at the result. The rate of soul coin harvest was a little higher than generally expected at this point in a Reality Engine conquest, but it was still only twenty percent of the projection total untapped soul coins. Phase three rarely opened before the collection had reached eighty percent. Why were they pushing the timeline up so hard?

"All of this could be resolved if we were merely allowed to bring in our own personnel," the Crafters Guild representative snarled. "Instead, you force our brave warriors to choose between going into battle equipped with whatever garbage the locals are able to create, or being forced to wait on the sidelines until our few craftsmen are able to supply their needs."

"The locals are catching up nicely," the representative from ConSweGo said. "Your ultimatum may not hold, Guildmaster."

"I'd like to see any of the locals constructing low-yield thermonuclear warheads," the guildmaster retorted.

"Enough." Patriarch Kvaltash raised his hands. "The decision has been made. Phase two will enter terminal stage in a few hours."

Veda immediately tried to send Team Twofeather a message. Her system beeped back at her.

**[Messages to miners inside phase two have been disabled
until the conclusion of this phase.]**

She swore and checked—at least her packages had been delivered. Hopefully Shad and his team would figure out what to do with them.

"What's the rush?" the Healers representative asked. "We expected to be here for years yet."

"I will allow the Proxima delegate to explain."

A hush fell across the room. Veda felt a tingle of excitement as the Proxima representative stood up. He was an elf with pale skin and silvery hair. His system-generated tag read "Halithi Dreamwarden, Proxima."

He lifted a languid hand in greeting. "Thank you, friends and colleagues. Yes, I bring news on behalf of all of us here. Our home base at Proxima Centauri has just confirmed we have located a rogue world Reality Engine."

Veda sat back in her chair, taking in the reality of her quarters for a moment as the illusion seemed to dim and fade around her.

A rogue Reality Engine? She'd heard rumors of such, certainly, of Reality Engines created on planets that drifted between the stars in eternal darkness. Colder than cold, wrapped in ice, shrouded in secrecy. She'd never heard of anyone who'd actually exploited one, but the legends spoke of wealth far beyond what a normal Reality Engine was capable of, and secrets that could kill.

"We have staked our claim to the Reality Engine central government and received a patent for its exploit. Due to its proximity to an unfavorable cluster of stars, we believe the optimal exploitation phase is a mere five standard cycles."

Five cycles. Five years. That was no time at all to prepare for a world-shattering Reality Engine opportunity. A rogue world Engine would, theoretically, have no ties to any planet. No requiring the local inhabitants to help develop it, which meant the system/Reality Engine negotiations would be unconstrained. The Engine couldn't be developed into a habitat. Instead, rogue Reality Engines might be convinced to become ship foundries, production facilities, even used to develop habitats like the Hub.

"To that end, Proxima is going to wrap up this exploit. The Hub will be needed as the primary launch platform for this rogue Engine exploit. Once phase three of this exploit completes, Proxima will supervise the replacement of the Hub with a development-focused station, to facilitate the repopulation of this Reality Engine. We've contracted with resettlement agencies which have already sold thirty percent of the prospective habitation slots. Within a decade, this Reality Engine should support a galactic population in the hundred billion range."

That was pretty standard. The exploitation companies would sell their winnings to various developers—mostly owned by Proxima, Alabaster Sky, and ConSweGo. The biggest conglomerates would make a profit yet again by reselling.

Halithi Dreamwarden was still speaking, his dulcet tones almost slippery. "We will be accepting applications from subordinate companies that have shown themselves to be especially adept at exploits. We will be making a galaxy-wide announcement after this. Needless to say, while this current Reality Engine exploit remains a priority for Proxima and our esteemed colleagues here, it is no longer our only prospect."

She could understand why. Instead of milking this exploit for years, the way many companies would prefer to do, Proxima and the others were clearly ready to stake their claims and go home, letting the galactics come in and turn this newly tamed Reality Engine into more tenements and shopping malls.

They might be giving up a little bit of wealth now. No doubt this Reality Engine would retain a trove of soul coins which the new occupants would find ways of extracting over the next few thousand years. But like the old tale of the vat farmer and the over prosperous yeast strain, when a new batch is offering five times the volume, you dump your other vats and repopulate from the golden strain.

Veda sat back and listened as the committee expounded the plans for phase three. She smiled as they introduced the overarching fantasy model. Shad and his team were going to love this.

CHAPTER FORTY-ONE

TALENT: THE DIFFERENCE BETWEEN ESPORTS PROS AND YOU

As we stepped into the clearing where the cannibal pigs had their camp, I lobbed a Flame Egg into their cook pot. It exploded, splattering the pigs with boiling who-knows-what and knocking them all back. I'd already set their nearest huts on fire, and they ran about squealing and charging through the sudden clouds of smoke to try to find us. Sage whooped and Lassoed one of the larger boars.

The surviving pigs picked themselves up and charged at us through the flaming wreckage of their camp. I took careful aim and shot. Meanwhile, I looked up the contact information that the patriarch of the progenitor cult had given me and composed a message for Kvaltash. *I have spoken with the ghost in the machine. If you want to hear what I know, reply back fast. I want a bargain.* Then I sent a message to the grignarians. *Do you want to give some of these galactic assholes a black eye? Let me know if you're in.* I resumed paying attention as Grandpa directed us.

I got a reply back almost immediately from Patriarch Kvaltash. *What is it you want?*

We need to have our sponsor upgraded so she can back us into phase three.

Not possible. Tvedra's license is for phase two. Besides, you do not have the financial backing for phase three. I can offer to buy out your combat team and place them on my own church's bid if you wish to participate in phase three.

Not good enough, I shot back. I was risking a lot here based on some conjectures.

I assure you the deal will be most profitable for you and your team. You will come away as very, very wealthy individuals.

That's not what I'm after and it's not what you're after either. You need an Earth human team in phase three, don't you? You need us. I'm willing to make an alliance, even to ask Veda to sell you a share in the operation, but I'm going in with my coalition or I'm not going in at all.

I turned my attention back to taking out the cannibal pigs. They were twice as powerful as usual, and they kept respawning as we slaughtered them. The booster flags Vortali was using were powerful artifacts, and I was eager to get my hands on a few more for ourselves. Though we had been able to steal a few of Vortali's flags, they had to be refreshed every four hours or the buff and ability to direct creep would disappear.

The patriarch replied. *Perhaps my church can buy out your whole outpost and guild. Would that satisfy you?*

Nope. I trust Veda a lot more than I trust you. I was surprised to find that I trusted Veda quite a bit, actually. We had been through a lot together at this point. I wanted her to be able to tell me if something here was screwed up.

You don't know how much of an investment you're asking, the patriarch replied. *In order to upgrade her license, we would have to sacrifice our own or pay off someone else.*

Then do it, I said. *In exchange, I'll tell you what the Reality Engine has told me. You don't care about this particular Reality Engine, do you? You want to learn the secrets that make them tick. Well, I care about this one because it's ours. I know my people aren't going to come away with much more than scraps, but I want a chance at those scraps. Upgrade Veda's license and I'll get you all the information I possibly can.*

If you're worth it, Kvaltash shot back at once. *Phase three is like nothing you've done before. You won't be able to get along on tricks and just barely scraping by.*

We weren't supposed to make it into phase two either.

You have a point, and I like your style. I'll give you a chance. Claim one of the alpha nodes on your atoll. If you can do that, then I'll back your bid. Now, I am going to be busy for some time. Talk to me when you're finished.

Sage whooped as she converted the Vortali flags to ours. "Go, my minions!" she shouted, casting Cowgirl Cheer on the next group of creep that spawned. They moved off northward to join the wave attacking Existalis. "Two down, one to go!"

I quickly shot Grandpa a message. *We have to take one of the alpha nodes. If we do, we're in for phase three.*

Are you nuts? The kind of firepower they can command is way more than what we can overcome.

That's why we're going to need some help. I sent another message to the grignarians. *What will it take to get you involved? I want to destroy the chances of Existalis or Vortali. I don't care which. If you have a preference, tell me and we'll team up.*

Finally, they sent a reply. *Thief. We don't trust you.*

You don't have to trust me. Just help me give someone else a black eye for a change.

You raided our node. You helped the orcs destroy our party. We did not make it to the treasure vault. Our hope of achieving phase three is gone.

Sorry about that, I said. *Maybe if we take out one of their nodes, you can scavenge enough to get through?*

No. There was a pause. *We will make you a bargain. If you succeed in reaching phase three, you will hire us as mercenaries.*

Why? I was immediately suspicious. *What would that get you?*

Access to the Reality Engine. The chance to ask questions. To learn the things the others already know, just because they were born to the right stars.

I shot Grandpa a quick message, telling him what was going on.

Sounds risky, he said.

I think we need them. I also think we kind of screwed them over without knowing what was going on.

You're getting soft on me, boy. It's up to you, but we don't know the phase three rules. What if this means some of our team gets sidelined? What if they're able to turn on us?

He had a point. I told the grignarians, *We're willing, as long as you agree to a contract our Procurer witnesses. We'll hire you as mercenaries, but you'll take orders from us.*

Tell your Procurer to send the contract. We'll consider it.

I added Juana to the group chat with Grandpa. *Time's short here. We need a quick contract, no loopholes for them to exploit.*

The shorter it is, the more situations might come up, Juana warned. *Longer contracts are actually safer, because you can go over contingencies.*

Yeah, but right now we need them on board. The deal is: We hire them as mercenaries during phase three and allow them access to the Reality Engine. They follow our orders, they don't take any actions against us or give intelligence to our enemies, and they don't betray us.

I can think of a bunch of loopholes right now, Juana said. I could hear the doubt even in her typed replies.

Then add anything you can think of and get it to them quick.

Right.

I considered making Existalis an offer, too. They had the firepower we needed. But they'd refused to answer any of our overtures so far, and I didn't trust them.

Juana sent us a message. *Sent the contract. I've got Veda's supplies. What do you want me to do with them?*

Hang on. I sent a message to Veda asking her what her recommendation was. Then, while I waited for a reply, I checked my map.

We had taken all three of the spawn points on our own island. Right now, three streams of creep were marching toward Existalis. As soon as I got the capture flags from Juana, we would change that.

The grignarians replied to my contract offer. *Agreed. But betray us, and we will see that you and your people suffer for a thousand cycles, just as we have done. We cannot take vengeance against everyone who has wronged us, but your people are weak. You have no allies. No one will fight for you.*

Understood. I did not like the idea of working with the grignarians, but there was no way we could take on an alpha node alone.

"Let's all regroup back at the outpost," Grandpa suggested. He sent a message to the rest of our team and recalled any of the crafters who were still wandering around the jungle.

I sent a message to the grignarians. *We'll be ready to move out in twenty minutes.*

I stood over the row of supplies Veda had sent us. There were a dozen bundles of spawn point capture flags, enough to convert all of the points on this island and have a couple to spare. She had also sent nine tactical vests.

I picked one up. It was dark gray, heavy, and covered in pouches and pockets. As soon as I draped it over myself, the vest adjusted and conformed to my body. I Inspected it and a system menu popped up.

[NPC Spawn Directive Vest. This vest allows the user to enhance and direct nearby spawned NPC minions.
Choose between the following minion buffs: Enhance Speed, Enhance Accuracy, Enhance Damage.
Choose between several damage type buffs: Damage (Fire), Damage (Ice), Damage (Electricity).
Choose between several miscellaneous enhancements: Shield, Stim, Slow Heal.]

Most of those options had further text available to read, but I got the gist by looking at the overview. There were also a couple of specific use abilities for the wearer.

[EMP: Temporarily shut down nearby defense structures.
Cast fireball.
Summon walking mines.]

"Okay," I said. "I'm starting to get the idea." I checked. Still no message from Veda. I sent one again, asking her if she had more instructions.

Our crafters were clustering around the node gateway itself, preparing to leave. "Anything else for us?" Dwight asked.

"You and half a dozen of the best, stay here," Grandpa said. "Everyone else can go back and rest up, get a bite to eat. You did good work today."

"Let me make sure I understand this. You're going to take on an alpha node?" Juana asked skeptically. "You remember how much better the beta node gear was than the stuff Veda could afford for us? How it's meant you guys get to gallivant around, taking out rare mobs, instead of being on defense the whole time?"

"Yeah," I agreed warily, seeing where she was going. "I know. Their gear will be even better. But we don't have a choice."

"Of course we do. We can sit tight and hold what we've got."

"We can't. If we want to make it into phase three, we have to take that node out."

"But do we?" Dwight asked. "Look, phase two has been great for us. We've made so much money, we might actually buy out our contracts. But phase three? We don't know anything about it. What if death is real again? I don't want any part of that."

"We'll worry about that once we know the rule set," Grandpa said firmly. "Shad's right. We take the alpha node, now."

Juana sighed. She pointed to our supply hut, where we kept the emergency supplies, backup turrets, and unused gear. "Then you'd better take the Portable Hole Punch."

She was referring to the battering ram device the Firebrand orcs had tried to use on us when they'd attacked our outpost. "I thought you sold that."

"Couldn't find a taker."

I went over and checked. It wouldn't fit in my inventory. "Anyone able to pick this up?"

"We'll bring it along after we finish capping spawn points," Smith promised.

"I knew you grunts were good for something," Grandpa said. "All right, let's finish up here."

Juana looked up from her battle map. "I've been trying to send a message to my mother for the last fifteen minutes," she said. "Mama went back to get started on dinner and she was supposed to send some through for me. I was wondering why she hadn't. She hasn't replied."

Worry started to gnaw at me. I sent a message to one of our crafters who had just stepped through, Leanne. She didn't reply.

I tried to send a message on the Coalition general channel. *Is this thing on?* My message appeared there and I got a response from Smith. *We see you.* Nothing from anyone outside. I noticed it had been some time since there'd been much traffic on this channel.

I swore. "I think we're cut off!" I looked over to the gateway and raised my voice. "Hey, Emmett."

The crafter who had been about to step through paused, looking at me. "Yeah?"

"As soon as you're through, send me back a message letting me know that everything's okay there."

"We expecting a problem?"

"Not really," I said.

Emmett looked doubtful, but stepped through. I waited. We didn't get a message.

"All right, I'm going to assume that we've been cut off from communication, not that Threshold is gone," I said grimly. "Seems like anything that could destroy the Hub and Threshold both without us knowing would take out a big chunk of this Reality Engine and shut the simulation down."

There were some problems with that theory, but I wasn't going to voice them. Not with everyone else here.

"So we're on our own. That's all right. We know what we need to do. Mongoose is almost back," Grandpa said as he picked up one of the vests and put it on. "Then it's time to move out."

"It's time to decapitate them," Sage said. She grabbed a vest, her eyes shining, and put it on. "I've been preparing for this for weeks now, watching eSports matches from back on Earth. Everything I could find that's a MOBA."

"You didn't offer to help me out," Juana said, sounding mildly hurt.

Sage laughed. "I don't care about this defense stuff. Figured if it ever got bad, Shad and I would just clean up all the mobs for you. No, this is the point where we turn the tide, isn't it, Shad? We're going on the attack. We're the creep now."

I grinned. "Actually," I said, "we're the champions."

CHAPTER FORTY-TWO

DOES THIS RAPTOR MAKE MY BUTT LOOK BIG?

tep one was easy: Capture as many spawn points as we could.

We sent Mongoose and the Ragtag squad to take our points and the beta node spawn points. The grignarians had agreed to let us cap their points. We would then send everything toward the Vortali alpha node.

Since Existalis was sending their own creep that way, too, we should have a solid wave of minions approaching Vortali's node in a matter of minutes. In the meantime, Grandpa, Sage, and I had reunited with Bill and Bob, loaded up on all of the grenades and single-use items that Dwight and his crafters could give us, and headed across toward Vortali's island.

At low tide, a shimmering sand bank stretched between our island and Vortali's. It was almost a quarter of a mile long. The sand was sticky and wet, tugging at my feet as we went. It smelled of the seaweed that strewed its banks. We picked our way past broken chunks of razor-sharp coral. Sage detoured to look at a stranded starfish. She picked it up and hurled it into the water.

A small stream of cannibal pigs and skeleton pirates made their way past us, moving inexorably toward Vortali's node. If I stood in their way, they just detoured around me. They were on a mission, and I was here to help.

My mini-map revealed the location of the nodes here on Vortali's island, but we could have just followed the current of creep until we got to their destination. They had unleashed a horde of brightly colored velociraptors. The beasts were covered in pink and green feathers. Sage squealed in delight as we passed a pack of them, their heads up, tails outstretched, running like giant ostriches south toward Existalis.

Vortali had their own skeleton pirates, too. Unlike most of ours, theirs were wearing rusty armor, hats and breastplates in Spanish conquistador style. I Inspected them as we went. They had about three times as much health as the creep we were used to fighting.

I warned the team, "Don't take these guys lightly. We should be able to take out their spawn point and capture it, but it won't be a pushover. Remember, if you die, you end up back at our outpost, and it'll take you forever to get back in the fight."

"Don't worry," Sage said, brushing off my concerns. "You're the one who's always thinking death is a good tactic anyway, Shad. Dinosaurs first. I want an army of dinosaur minions."

So we headed a little to the west and found the dinosaur nest, or rather, series of nests. The dinosaurs roosted in a jungle glen surrounded by fallen logs. A couple of large adults prowled around the outside as half a dozen nests full of eggs waited.

We paused and crouched behind one of the fallen trees, studying the scene. Every thirty seconds, one of the nests full of eggs would start shaking as all of the eggs began to roll around, developing large cracks. Baby velociraptors quickly emerged from the eggs, shook off the remnants of shells, and grew to full size in a couple of eye blinks.

"That's so cool," Sage whispered. "I want one, Shad. I want a pet dinosaur."

"It's not that kind of game," I told her. "Besides, what would you even do with a pet dinosaur?"

"Ride it into battle," she declared. "It would be my trusty steed, Buckskin. A rodeo queen ought to have a worthy steed, don't you think? I could get a nice tooled leather saddle and—"

"Not the time, you two," Grandpa growled. "Let's get in there and plant the flags."

"Do we have to kill them before we plant the flags?" Sage whispered. "Or can we capture them alive?"

"I suppose it's worth finding out."

"Right, I can throw two of my barrel points there and there." She pointed at spots equidistant around the nest. "As soon as I go to the first one, you plant one of the flags here and then distract the adults. Maybe we can do this the easy way."

"Sounds good," I said, preparing to charge in and cast my taunt.

Grandpa took one of the claiming flags and handed two more to Sage. "Three, two, one, go," he whispered, and Sage disappeared. Grandpa shoved his flag into the dirt at our feet. I hopped over the tree and engaged Fastest Gun in the West, charging in and shouting to attract the dinosaurs' attention.

I cast Call 'em Out, and the four adults all made for me. Bill and Bob were on my heels, swinging their big guandao swords at the dinosaurs.

A minute later, Sage shouted, "I've got the last flag planted!" I had been about to shoot the nearest dinosaur, but I raised my barrel skyward and held my fire.

The dinosaurs stopped their charge. They looked around, and I Inspected them. They now read [**Subordinate minions of Misfits Guild**].

"You did it," I called, and Sage whooped.

"All right, turning the dinosaurs on their masters now!" She finished what she was doing and hurried over to me.

"One down, four to go," I said. The alpha node had five enemy spawn points active, compared to the three on our island.

"Smith and the others are done with their mission," Grandpa reported. "They're on their way to join us. Any word from the grignarians?"

"Just that they would join us for the final onslaught." I felt a little nervous. The grignarians knew we would be throwing everything into this attack. If they wanted to attack our node, now was the perfect time.

I had left Juana and Dwight to defend our outpost, and they were certainly capable, but they couldn't handle a full incursion. Well, if worse came to worse, I could just get myself killed and be back there in time to help with an attack.

I kept an eye on my mini-map as we converted the nodes one by one. No red dots. No blue dots. Just our green markers and the streams of creep moving inexorably north toward Vortali.

Step two: Join the creep.

The Vortali node was situated on a hilltop like ours. Unlike our outpost, this one was laid out in a grid pattern, a square about thirty yards to the side with gates on each wall. I could see the turrets and towers beyond making a labyrinth through which our creep was beginning to charge.

The whole outpost had a vaguely Asian styling to it, with blue-tiled roofs atop stonework walls. The towers were like tall, skinny pagodas, with flared roofs at each level. I didn't know if they represented something on Vortali's homeworld, or if they were still stealing Earth designs and inspirations. It didn't really matter, I supposed. The gates were topped with enormous red-stained beams decorated with golden endcaps. Like us, Vortali had left their outer gates open. Presumably their inner gates would be locked.

Our teammates had all joined us by now, Mongoose and Ragtag finding us as we surveyed the enemy. The grignarians sent me a message. *We see you. We are here. We will join your push.*

We have equipment that will let us buff the creep, I replied. *How about you?*

No such equipment. It is not needed. We will take advantage of the distraction you cause to make our own way in.

Grandpa and I had talked strategy with Tall Smith on the way in. The key, based on our reading of the outpost guide and our experience with our own outpost, was to overwhelm the defense towers. Presumably, Vortali had limited repair capacity, just like we did. If we took out as many towers as we could across the whole fortification, more and more creep would be able to penetrate deeper and deeper into the fortress.

Now Sage stepped up. "Okay, so the way we win this is we overwhelm their defenses. Their towers are designed to take out alpha-level spawn. The beta and delta creep we've added is nothing to them—unless they have to target everything individually. Then, they are going to run into trouble. So we have to take out their slowing towers, their multitarget turrets, anything that can hit more than one target at once or hamper our rush." Her spawn buff vest had changed from the dull tactical look to a brown leather fringed vest with rhinestones picking out a flower design. With her rodeo shirt and good jeans on, she looked every bit a rodeo queen.

"Good tip," Smith said. "Wish we'd been able to find some of those gaming experts Shad wanted, but I'm glad you studied up, Sage. This isn't quite the sort of assault I've trained for."

Jones lay flat on his stomach, new binocs trained on the outpost.

"Anyone have eyes on the Vortali combat miners?" I asked. I was only seeing three red dots on my mini-map, inside the outpost's defenses.

"Negative," Jones replied. "They're not here. Looks like they're heavy on slowing towers, lightning damage, and ice damage."

"Those work well together," Sage said. "Ice chills, and lightning damage does double on chilled targets, plus it's probably all chain lighting turrets. We need to focus on the slowing and lightning towers."

"Then let's use the vests to buff our creep, make them resistant to cold," I suggested. Sage gave me a quick nod.

"And keep sharp. The enemy might appear back here at any moment."

"Or they could go for a base trade," Sage chirped. "If they realize what we're doing, they might try attacking our base in order to force us back there."

"We'll worry about that if they try it," I said. I took a deep breath. "Let's do this. Mongeese, west gate. Ragtag, east gate. Team Twofeather has the south. Let's go."

Our waves of creep had already reached the outpost. They were funneling through the west, east, and south gates. The north gate, on the far side of the outpost, was relatively untouched, as the creep streams made for the nearest and easiest entrances.

Each of our vests was capable of buffing all creep within five yards. The buffs could stack, so we could either give three different buff types or three times one buff. And that was per category: Each vest could give one creep general buff, one damage type enhancement, and one special enhancement. Combine that and things got wild. Mongoose had three vests, and so did Ragtag. Ideally, toward the end, we'd all be close enough that our minions could have up to nine stacks active, though I didn't think that was likely. We were almost certainly to lose people before then.

For now, we were going with a range of different buffs, improving their strength, speed, and accuracy, giving them shields and resistance to lightning, and then stacking all of the damage as fire. The fire damage added a small Burning debuff to whatever it hit. The Burning enemies, or in this case, structures, would continue to lose health until repaired. It was a way of forcing the hand of whoever was running Vortali's defenses.

I shrugged off my misgivings and stepped into the flow of creep. My instincts were telling me to get out ahead of them, that I didn't want to be pressing forward in this mass of skeleton pirates, spear-wielding pigs, angry dinosaurs, and the shambling zombies that had spawned from the grignarians' spawn points. But I was safer with them taking some of the shots from the turrets and towers.

The two gate towers zapped us with bolts of charged lightning. I felt myself slow. The lightning bolt sent unpleasant shivers up and down my body, but did very little damage, spreading out among all our creep and dropping all their health by five or so points. I checked to make sure my shield effect was active on all of my creep. It was. Sage switched her buff to a heal over time and threw out Raise Your Spirits for good measure. "Give me a minute!" she shouted. "I gotta get my pirates out!"

"We'll cover you," I said. Grandpa and I plunged forward. I loaded my last couple of boom rounds and fired at the left-hand gate tower. My shot exploded it, setting it on fire. The topmost level began to smoke, and its armaments—cannons firing rockets—shot wildly into the air.

The creep followed up on my opening, hurling spears and throwing rocks. A crew of pirates with one of their battering rams charged forward and began smashing the figurehead into the base of the tower.

Sage had deployed her Inflatable Pirate Squad, the one we'd looted way back at the start of the phase during our raid on the beta node. She had spent the past weeks grumbling about not being able to use them—they were only effective against towers or creep, not the bonus mobs we'd spent most of our time fighting. Now she had them out and was instructing the dozen skeletons where to go. Their leader had a peg leg in place of his left shinbone, and a rusty metal hook for a hand. He wore an eyepatch across his grinning skull. I shook my head and turned back to the attack as the bonus pirates joined in the attack on the gate.

A squad of dinosaurs hopped up next to the tower, clawing and kicking at the structure with their spurred hind legs until it cracked and crumbled. I joined Sage in cheering as it fell.

We turned our attention to the next tower. The creep was taking damage slowly but surely. My first pack of dinosaurs all died. Sage let out an unhappy cry, but there were more to replace those. Skeleton pirates turned back to seaweed and dust. Pigs squealed and shrieked as they fell to the ground, despawning as their corpses hit the dirt. More trudged forward to take their place.

"Bring the tower down!" I shouted to the creep, then felt like a moron.

Sage was in the middle of a pack of dinosaurs, urging them on. "Come on!" she shouted. "Men! With me!" Her skeletons fell in around her like an honor guard.

We took down the second gate tower, leaving the way clear for our creep. Even Grandpa let out a whoop. "Come on, you undead assholes," he told the nearest skeleton pirates. "Let's kick some alien butt."

CHAPTER FORTY-THREE

BLOWING THINGS UP FOR FUN AND PROFIT

As soon as I had a little pack of creep around me, I led them through the burning ruins of Vortali's south gate. The enormous red beams had fallen, lying in a smoking heap. We stepped right over it.

The turrets atop the pale gray stone walls fired death down on us. They were shaped like stylized Chinese lions, explosive arrows shooting from their gaping mouths. Every third turret zapped our creep, slowing them down. "Take out the slows!" Sage shouted. "We gotta get up there!"

Grandpa Shadow Stepped up onto the outer wall and began hacking the closest slowing turret to pieces. I used my Roped Into It ability and swarmed up to the inner wall's parapet. I shot the turret right in front of me, reloaded, then shot again. Even though it felt like I should be taking a baseball bat to it, my revolver-based abilities were too good to pass up. The turret shut down with a sad clanking noise—despite the fact that it looked like it was carved from granite, without a mechanical piece on it—and I moved on to the next one.

The next four turrets were closer together, only about five feet apart. I eyed them, calculating the distance, and then fired off one of my vest's special abilities.

A blast of lightning shot out from my chest. My ears rang as it zapped the next couple of turrets along before hopping across the gap to electrify the ones on the other side as well. The turrets froze up.

I Inspected them. "Thirty seconds before they can shoot again," I yelled. "Get some reinforcements up here." I grabbed a rope out of my inventory and flung it over the wall. Bill and Bob swarmed up. Sage had her Three-Barrel Race skill going. She teleported up to the wall with Grandpa and ran along the top, helping take down the turrets on the far side.

As we took apart the turrets, our minions advanced toward the next gate. Up ahead, Tall Smith shouted, "Some help with these towers!" I finished off the last of the stunned turrets and sprinted ahead, past a machine gun turret firing a hail of bullets down on my creep. It ignored me as I went past.

Smith's team was up ahead. They had come in through the west gate and were approaching the entrance to the next level of the outpost. It was flanked by tall towers, three tiers high, bristling with turret defenses. The towers were tall, narrow pagodas with blue tile roofs sticking off of each level. Red and gold flags fluttered along the eaves.

The lowest level of the pagoda featured turrets that resembled stylized dragon fireworks, like I'd seen in depictions of Chinese New Year festivities. They spat out missiles which broke into six or seven separate seekers, flying in spiraling patterns toward their targets. Each one exploded in a cascade of red and gold sparks that knocked back the creep and delivered a nasty, stunning debuff.

The next level up had a slower rate of fire, shooting another lightning attack that further slowed and stunned our creep. The top story sent a steady stream of projectiles into the creep, mowing them down, but only attacking one at a time. It was the lower two levels we really needed down.

Smith's team was at the bottom of the tower, attacking it. "We can't reach the guns up above," Smith shouted up at me. "We've made progress on the door. See if there's a way up on the inside."

I studied the tower in front of me. The parapet on which I stood dead-ended into the tower. The opening of the first tier was about seven feet over my head. I holstered my gun, backed up, and sprinted.

As I approached the wall, I leapt. My fingers caught the lip of the opening above. I scrabbled for a better handhold, then got one elbow up. I took a deep breath and pulled my other arm and upper body over the edge of the opening. My feet fumbled against the tower, trying to get a purchase.

With another enormous effort, I pulled myself up and inside, rolling over to lay on my back and stare up at the guns. Fortunately, none of them seemed to be aiming at me. They all had way more health than any of our turrets. Close to eight hundred points, plus a regeneration that would heal them back up to full HP every few minutes. This was going to take more than just my revolver.

I checked my inventory for the stuff Dwight had given me, then reconsidered. I was on the first level. If I blew this one up, it might be even harder to get to the second and third levels, and we needed to take the whole tower down.

There was a bundled pile of rope and slats on the other side of the tower. I walked over to it, discovered it was a rope ladder, and threw it down for the Mongeese. They swarmed up to me. "We need to find a way up there," I said, pointing. "We'll take it down one level at a time."

We stood on a six-foot-wide wooden platform surrounding the inner core of the tower. There was a three-foot-tall wall along the outside where the guns and missile launchers were mounted, firing down at our creep as it streamed toward the gate. Thick wooden posts held up the level above, with solid pillars at each corner.

I sent a quick message to Mitch, Ragtag's Canadian demo expert, who should be on the other side of the outpost. *You able to lend a hand with blowing something up?*

Kinda busy here, he answered back. *But if you need advice, let me know.*

"Right." I turned back to the Mongeese. "Any of you bomb experts, or do we just try to make it blow up good?"

Black shrugged. "I've got some skills. Remove Landmine, Premature Detonation, Defuse Bomb, Cut the Red Wire, Explosive Ordnance Disposal."

"Uh, yeah," I said, calling up his character sheet. I'd forgotten he was a Demolitions Expert. "That should do it."

"The first order of business is to get up there." Tall Smith pointed to the nearest corner, where a metal ladder was bolted to the wall. "Double time."

I let Smith and the Mongeese go ahead while I peered out through the opening to check on our progress. This set of towers was stopping our creep wave dead. "Try to hold back a wave," I called to Grandpa. "As soon as we get this tower down, we'll push as hard as we can."

"I'll see what we can do," Grandpa agreed. He and Sage had finished taking out the turrets on the south side of the towers, and were now proceeding up along the north boundary, clearing everything. Our strategy was to break as much of Vortali's infrastructure as we could, so that even if they did get repair bots out, they'd have to make choices and leave options open for us.

I checked my map. All of the spawn points were still shown as ours. There was a stream of creep all headed this way. I sent a message to Juana. *Everything quiet there?*

So far, so good, she replied. *I'm not taking any chances. Dwight and I are getting all of our repairs done. It's going to burn up everything Veda sent us, but I want us in tip-top shape. I can't help feeling like something is about to happen. I've had no luck getting through to anyone on the other side.*

Neither have I. Just hang tight. I'll see what we can do when we're done here. I turned my attention back to the battlefield.

Smith reported in from upstairs. "Laying charges on the top floor. I don't know if we have enough cord to string all three floors at once. We may have to blow the top two and then come back for the bottom."

"That's fine," I said. "Get it going up there." Meanwhile, I pulled some of my own supplies out and started setting explosives under each of the turrets and towers down here.

"Proceeding to the second floor," Smith reported.

"I'm going to jump across to the other tower and start there," I told him.

"Good call."

I used Roped Into It, which had a five-minute cooldown and was back up by now, to swing across the gateway to the other tower. The gate was still sealed shut. One squad of our pirate minions had made it this far and got a couple of hits in with their figurehead battering ram, but hadn't even scratched the thing before they had been taken down.

The second tower was identical to the first. I kicked the rope ladder over the side to make it easier for anyone to come up from below and then proceeded to the top floor.

I was in the middle of laying charges under the top-floor cannons when a pulsed laser shot missed my head by inches.

It had come from behind me. I dropped to the ground, rolled over, and sprang up, Quick Drawing my gun and firing in the direction I thought the shot had come from. I activated my Trick Shot skill. It failed, reporting no target available.

Another shot, a beam of purple coherent light, stabbed across from the other side of the tower right toward me. I lunged sideways, and it burned a hole in my drover's coat.

You shouldn't physically be able to dodge laser bolts, but I wasn't going to complain if this Reality Engine slowed it down just enough for me to have a chance. I aimed a shot back where the bolt had come from, and as far as I could tell, missed.

I swore. "Show yourself!"

There was no reply. I decided to give myself some space, so I ran for the ladder, intending to get down to the ground. As my hand touched the ladder, another bolt sizzled out of nothingness and hit my hand. I shouted and jerked back as pain seared my left hand.

I had the presence of mind to send a quick warning to the team. *Someone's here, shooting at me!* Then, out of instinct, I dropped flat to the ground as another beam shot past me.

Think, Shad, think!

I cast High Noon. This was, as far as I could tell, me against one other opponent who was shooting at me. That made it a duel.

[High Noon Activated] popped up in front of me, and I grinned.

I stood up, my gun in my hand, listening, trying to hear or smell or sense my opponent. I used Reload to fill all six chambers of my gun with frag rounds. Dwight and Sage had made them special for me, just in case we ever had to fight someone with camouflage.

"You might as well show yourself," I challenged. "You can't shoot me, not until I take the first shot. My spells have a long range."

A moment later, someone shimmered into existence on the other side of the tower. It was a space elf woman, beautiful and inhuman like most of the space elves I'd seen so far. She was a little shorter than me, with long, flowing purple hair that seemed like it ought to get in her way in a fight. She wore a black catsuit and carried a wicked-looking rifle as well as a short sword at her belt.

She raised one hand to me in salute. "You are the human warrior, Shad Williams," she said.

"That's right."

"I was in Mak'gar's warriors chat during the competition. You fought well." She raised her rifle, holding it across her chest. "It will be an honor to defeat you."

"Maybe I'll be the one to defeat you," I said. I was sending messages to Grandpa and Smith as fast as I could, letting them know that there was at least one enemy here who had been in disguise and not showing up on my map. *I've got her distracted, but I don't know how long that'll last. If there's others, we could be in big trouble.*

"You have fought well and tried hard. There is no shame in failing now."

"Not planning to fail. Besides, you started all of this, attacking our base."

She shrugged. "We had no choice. It was us or you."

"We weren't threatening you at all."

"Our sources warned us what is about to happen. I'm sorry. I'm certain you would have done well, but we cannot risk our own phase three for the sake of indigenous. Not when the stakes are greater than ever before."

"How so?" I asked, momentarily diverted. "I mean, the stakes are pretty big for my people, but for you guys, this is just an average Thursday, isn't it?"

"Proxima only hires the best. That's us, and you savages are making us look bad," the woman said. "Now, let us conclude this foolish duel. I remind you, you will respawn far away, back at your own node, whereas I will respawn here in my camp. You have no chance of killing enough of us to incur our death penalty. I have literally nothing to lose, and you have no way to win."

I caught the way her eyes flickered to something just a few feet to my right. "Apparently you've got a lot to lose," I grunted. I changed out my first shot, swapping from the frag to a knockback.

I raised my gun and took aim with her targeted. I fired a Trick Shot, sending the knockback round at her, then dropped to a crouch and shot at the place I'd seen her looking.

My frag bullet exploded, sending pieces of shrapnel into the air. A couple of them found a target. They lit up bright white as they impacted someone I couldn't see, and I switched my targeting immediately.

The elf woman had been knocked back out of the tower, just as I'd expected. With luck, Grandpa and Sage would be there, ready. I just had to deal with the camouflaged enemy still up here. High Noon would be on cooldown for a long time, so I couldn't try that trick again.

A bolt of light burned into the wooden floorboards right beside me. I engaged Fastest Gun in the West and sprinted forward, throwing my arms out wide as I did.

I smashed into someone I couldn't see, driving them back in front of me and crunching them between my body and the corner of the tower. I shoved the muzzle of my revolver into my enemy and fired the other four frag rounds in a Barrage. It was a waste of the rounds, but I hadn't had time to reload.

I did now, just with normal rounds, and shot another cylinder into the invisible enemy. A space rifle clattered to the floorboards beside me as drops of purple-tinted blood splattered all around.

My enemy groaned in pain. I reached up, caught a hold, and wrestled them to the ground. A moment later, the camouflage failed, and I was looking into the face of a male space elf.

He sneered at me. "Fool." I felt a knife stabbing upward. He had drawn his short sword and was thrusting at me. I dodged right and it sliced through my duster.

I shot the elf again. He was hurting bad, but not dead yet. He struggled against me, trying to get his sword back for another attack. I grabbed at it with my wounded left hand, feeling the blade slicing through my fingers and palm. But I held on, desperate to keep it away from any vital organs.

He pushed up, throwing me off-balance. My gun went flying, arcing out over the drop before disappearing over the edge of the tower. I rolled to one side and came up at the edge of the walkway, one foot sticking out over the edge. The elf was lightning fast. He sprang to his feet and sprinted at me. Blood ran down from his forehead, streaking across his face and making him look horrific.

I cast Quick Draw and fired six rounds into his torso. The elf stumbled back. I reloaded and fired again, and he collapsed to his knees before vanishing into nothingness.

Shad? Shad, are you all right?

I answered Sage's message. *Fine. I'll be right down.*

Good, because we can't get past this gate and we're on the clock here! Stop lazing around and get back to work!

CHAPTER FORTY-FOUR

BETTING AGAINST THE HOUSE: HOW TO LOSE MONEY FAST

I spent a couple of seconds catching my breath, then got to my feet and hurried downstairs. *There's at least two of them here at the outpost. They could respawn any second. I think we need to regroup*, I told my team. *New plan. Ragtag needs to join us here on this side of the offense. Let's push hard.*

Copy, Mitch sent back in response.

The Mongeese disappeared up into the tower I had just vacated. Its twin was wreathed in smoke, the top tier shattered, the turrets silent. Apparently the first set of demolition had worked great.

Our minions were barely scratching the huge bronze gate. Skeletal pirates shattered their wooden figurehead battering rams against the serpentine dragon carvings, but the gate only took a point or two of damage with each hit. We'd be here all day at this rate.

"Let's bring up the Portable Hole Punch," Grandpa said.

I nodded. "Okay, want me to do it?"

"Take a couple of the others and go."

I asked Bill, Bob, and Mitch to come with me. We beat a retreat out of the smoking ruins of the first tier of Vortali's outpost. A repair drone was hovering over one of the slowing turrets. I sniped it down. Bill grabbed up its remains and tossed them in his inventory. "In case Dwight wants the materials," he said, and we hurried back out.

We had left the Portable Hole Punch behind a row of trees on the outskirts of Vortali's outpost. The device was about three feet long, with handles sticking up out of the wooden frame that held its brass, tube-shaped body in place. It weighed over four hundred pounds, more than any of us could put in our inventory.

We took up positions, me at the front right end of the device. I reached for a handle and when the others were in position, said "Heave ho!"

We hefted the device between us easily. With our augmented strength it was no trouble at all to carry. "Back to the fort, double time!"

I kept my head down as we crossed the open space between the edge of the jungle and the outer ruins of Vortali's outpost. A message came from our grignarian associates. *We see we are not the only ones you have plundered. That is an expensive toy. Who did you steal it from?*

Does it matter?

It looks like grignarian make, but we have not bothered with such toys in many cycles. Probably whoever you stole it from stole it from us previously.

If they hadn't wanted it stolen they shouldn't have left it where we could get it, I replied as we entered the outpost through the smashed southern gate.

By the time we got back to Grandpa, all the nearby turrets were down. I set the Portable Hole Punch in front of the Vortali gate. "Now what? It didn't have an instruction manual."

I Inspected it. A system message popped up.

**[Defensive structure detected. Do you wish to initiate
destruction sequence?
Yes / No]**

"Everybody back off," I said, and selected Yes. A countdown started. We retreated back around the destroyed fortifications.

I waited for an earth-shattering kaboom, but there was nothing. After a minute, I poked my head around the corner. The device was still sitting there, but now there was a six-foot-tall circle in the Vortali gate. Our creep was streaming through.

"Let's get up there," Grandpa said. He hurried forward. We all buffed our creep with anything we had on hand. I dug around in my inventory and found a couple of single-use buff devices. They looked like cans of spray paint. The instructions said they could be used on turrets to increase their speed and output, or on creep. We had stolen these from the grignarians as well, and Juana had used most of them to great effect at our outpost. Now I applied their buff to pirate leaders, cannibal pig chiefs, and the largest of the raptors as we went past.

The six-foot hole only let two or three minions through at a time, and that was a problem. But now that the gate had been punctured, we could attack it from both sides. It was the work of a couple of minutes to bring it down, sending our wave of creep swarming into the middle section of Vortali's ring.

Juana sent Grandpa and me a message. *I'm getting word from Vortali's commander. They want to talk terms.*

String them along, Grandpa said. *Ask what it is they're thinking. We're not going to stop our assault, but maybe we can buy some time.*

I checked again. Still no word from Veda or anyone in the outside world. I was pretty certain by now that we had been intentionally cut off. Was it just us or everyone here?

On a whim I contacted Mak'gar. *Hey, is everything all right over on your end? I'm not able to talk to anyone in the outside world. Was wondering if it's just us.*

No, we also have no contact. I believe this is the lead-up to phase three. Someone has a trick up their sleeves.

So this is usual or it varies?

Sometimes a system or the underlying Reality Engine can decide to play tricks on the miners around a phase changeover. It is rarely a matter of any great concern. They cannot change the death rules once we have begun a phase, so it doesn't really make a difference.

Thanks. I told Grandpa what Mak'gar had told me.

"No wonder Vortali wants to talk," Grandpa said grimly. "If phase three is imminent, they don't want to risk losing their node. I'm just worried we're being set up."

Where was the rest of Vortali's team? Were they taking the Existalis node? I checked with Juana again. *Everything quiet there?*

Absolutely, we're nearly back to full strength here. I've had to burn almost everything Veda sent us, but it's looking good.

I have a bad feeling about all this, I said. *Get everything we have in storage. Everything we took from the grignarians or Veda bought us and put it all up.*

I can't just pull pieces out and shove them in anywhere. There's a design to this, an art.

I could almost hear the annoyance in her voice, but I knew she could do this. I replied, *Sure but I'm pretty sure you've been holding some of it back in reserve in case of emergencies. This is the emergency, Juana. We're going to shift over into phase three before long. If we don't have an outpost when that happens then we're screwed.*

Copy, she replied.

I turned back to the fight at hand. Another wave of creep came around the corner from the north. These were the zombies and undead brought by the grignarians, mixed in with some very strange constructs. The constructs were about shoulder-height, with three legs, forearms, and bubble heads made of shining copper-colored metal. They carried smaller versions of the grignarians' melty guns. "Whoa," I called out. "Let these guys on ahead of you." I Inspected them.

They all showed as constructs under the command of Lord Commander XKrell. I hadn't learned any of the grignarians' names, not even the ones I'd killed, but presumably this was one of their head honchos.

The constructs streamed in and began to press the assault on the next row of turrets. We only had to worry about towers and turrets on the inside wall, since we'd taken out everything on the outside while clearing the first line of defenses.

Unfortunately, these turrets made up for it by being much, much stronger. Annie got a little too close to one and was taken out by a quick burst of fire. Her body vanished in a cloud of smoke. A minute later, she was back in chat swearing.

That thing did twice my hit points in five seconds. Be careful, guys.

"Be sure to have a bunch of creep between us and those turrets," I warned everyone, urging our pirates forward.

I checked the map. We still owned all of the creep spawn points we had captured, and we had another two hours before our capture flags ran out. We didn't have time to waste here. There were three red dots in the innermost level of Vortali's fortress waiting for us.

I did some calculations. The creep was moving along at a good clip, and we were clearing towers, but we still had a whole half-circuit to go to reach the next gate. Then after that, we needed to penetrate their inner wall. This was taking much too long.

Anyone got a clever idea? I asked in chat as we worked our way around the ring.

Why are we doing it this way when we have the Portable Hole Punch? Tall Smith asked.

The creep moved faster along the proper route, Sage explained. *The hole's only big enough for a couple at a time.*

Who cares about them? Smith asked. *They're a distraction. We should be decapitating our enemy.*

Good point, Grandpa said. *Suggestion?*

We take that device, we get my squad and those tentacle-faced fuckers with the magic melty guns, and we go straight through. You guys stay here pretending to be good little miners and keep them distracted. Our Camouflage should hold up long enough.

I exchanged a look with Grandpa. "It's worth a shot," I said aloud.

"If they fail and are wiped out, we'll be below strength. I don't see us making it all the way through the defenses in the time we have left if Mongoose has to respawn and come back here."

"Calculated risk," I said. "The longer this takes, the more likely the rest of Vortali is to come back or to try to take our own base."

"All right," Grandpa agreed. "If the grignarians go for it."

"Everyone else needs to serve as a distraction. Ragtag, you're going to need to be big and noisy. Start looking through your abilities and planning things out."

The newly arrived Ragtag team members put their heads together. Lara and Ice Spice had grins on their faces as they gestured and plotted. I looked forward to seeing what they came up with. Ragtag's combat instincts weren't as good as ours or Mongoose's, but they had some crazy strategies and weren't afraid to blow themselves up. They'd acquitted themselves well during phase two.

"I'm on the assault team," Sage said.

"You?" Tall Smith asked, turning his head and scowling.

"I'm not very good against the towers and turrets, but I am good in team fights," Sage said. "You know that. I can buff your men up, and I can cause trouble with the enemies."

The grignarians replied to me. *We are sending four of our best. Be ready for them.*

"Okay," Smith said, "Camouflage can cover fifteen. That's my team, the grignarians, Sage," he looked us over, "and you, Shad."

I felt a little bit of surprise. I had great respect for the Mongeese and for Smith in particular. He had a lot of skills, but I had gotten the feeling from him that he didn't quite like me, and that he was unsure of my capabilities. "Me?"

"You've got a good head in a firefight and a way of fucking things up for the other guy."

Grandpa nodded. "Smith, you're in charge on this one. What's your assault strategy?"

"Let's get the Hole Punch up there." Smith pointed north of the gate we'd just come through. "We need to take down those turrets there, there, and there to give us cover," he said. "Move."

The Mongeese moved out. I followed with Sage at my rear. We took out the nearest set of turrets, giving us ten feet of undefended wall area, while Ragtag started firing at the turrets to our rear. Then I made a run for the Hole Punch along with Brown and both of the Smiths. We got it into position and set it off, retreating back to the rest of our team just as the grignarians arrived.

They were just as creepy up close as I had remembered. Their impassive faces studied us. One raised his hand. "Greetings, treacherous ones."

I decided to take that as a compliment. "Thanks for joining us," I said.

"You have a strategy?" the grignarian spokesbeing asked me.

I pointed to Smith. "He's in charge," I said. Smith looked briefly taken aback, then gave me a quick head nod, which reminded me to reapply my Tip My Hat buff to the infiltration team.

"Stay close," he told them. "The Camouflage extends for about five meters in all directions."

"Centered on which?" the grignarian asked.

Jones raised a hand. "Me."

The grignarians leaned their heads together and whispered to each other. "All of you look the same to us," the spokesbeing said at last. "Please have the small one stay at the center of the Camouflage field. We will follow it."

"I think I'm insulted here," Sage complained, but she sidled over to Jones and gave him a nod. "Ready when you are."

"Move up," Smith ordered, and we approached the hole.

Jones activated his Camouflage. I felt it settle over me like a fog. We picked up the Hole Punch and ducked through the opening it had made, two at a time.

The grignarians followed closely on Brown's heels, with Short Smith bringing up the rear.

The inner turrets were quiet, waiting. None of them shot at us. I caught myself holding my breath and let it out, rolling my eyes at myself. The Camouflage worked just fine. I didn't need to add my own attempts at stealth.

Smith indicated a point about twenty feet along the wall. "We set the hole there," he whispered. I checked my map. There were five red dots inside the central core of Vortali's node now. I relayed that information to our commando team.

"First order of business," I said, "is getting their resurrection point shut down." I realized our oversight and sent Smith a private message. *Lakshmi's Crystal Vibrations can shut down their respawn point, sir. We've got room for her under our camo.*

You're right. I should have thought of that. Smith turned to the team. "Let's get Lakshmi in here," he said. "Shad, you lead the others to plant the device. As soon as we've got Lakshmi with us, we'll fire it and run in there. Cover her so she can take down the respawn chamber."

"Understood," I said.

A moment later, Lakshmi popped through the hole and joined us. I took three of the Mongeese and moved the Portable Hole Punch as far forward as I could while still staying in the Camouflage field. We set it down by the wall. I told the others to retreat, then activated the Hole Punch and stepped back. This time I wanted to watch.

The device sat there for a couple of seconds. It hummed, pulsed, and let out a little *blurp* noise. There was a puff of smoke and a hole in the wall where none had existed before. Honestly, it was a little anticlimactic.

"Go!" I said, and we all charged forward. I had my mini-map up, so I was expecting it when we were met by three of the space elves as soon as we jumped through the wall. One of them was the woman I had knocked out of the tower earlier. She fired laser rifle shots right at me. I felt them whiz past my head. We were still camouflaged, but it seemed they could see through it, at least partially.

I activated Fastest Gun in the West, charging right for them, then through them, and at the same time threw Call 'em Out. I felt my taunt take effect as the three space elves pivoted and started chasing me. I blazed my way deeper into their inner core. Sage shouted triumphantly, "The box is down! Kill 'em!"

Opsec! I sent in a quick angry message. If there was a chance the Vortali miners hadn't noticed that their respawn point was down, we didn't want to draw attention to it. They were still all on me.

Sage Lassoed the elf woman and succeeded at Taming her. The woman started shooting one of her allies as I fired my revolver into whoever was nearest.

The grignarians swarmed forward as a unit, converging on another elf woman off to our right. They surrounded her, firing from three different directions, and coated her in viscous, burning slime. The woman pulled a short metal rod out of thin air and waved it, showering herself in liquid. The grignarian goo washed off her and melted into the dirt.

I turned my attention back to my target, who was going down fast. Sage had directed her Tamed elf woman to shoot at him, too.

The Mongeese all opened fire. All five of them used their guns a little more than their special abilities. At some point I would have to sit down with Smith and work out some strategies for his men to get better use out of their spells. They did great with their foxhole and machine gun nest maneuvers, but in the middle of combat they rarely thought to pull out a special move.

The first of the elves went down. Another one shrieked in anger. "You . . . you . . . menaces!" he shouted, charging at us. His laser rifle lay abandoned on the grass as he swung a curved sword right at me.

I sidestepped. It slashed down, bouncing off the edge of my drover's coat. I stepped in closer and fired six rounds into his belly. They were sabot rounds that exploded into a dozen or more small pieces of metal that tore through his gut, turning his torso into a mass of blood. He howled and swung again. I dodged his blow easily.

The grignarians moved away from their victim as she died screaming horribly. I felt sympathy for her remembering just how badly that goo had burned.

But this was war.

We downed the elves hard and fast. Five were dead of their fifteen. We had outnumbered them by more than double, but I had still expected them to put up more of a fight. After all, this was an alpha node. I could tell just by looking around how advanced the gear was, and yet we had walked right through it.

I let out a whoop as we sprinted for their node. I slapped a hand down on it.

[Shad Williams of Misfits Guild, do you wish to claim this node for Misfits Guild and Tvedra Corporation?]

"Hell yeah!"

The node immediately changed color. Instead of the steady green of claimed, it now flickered gently between orange and blue, back in claiming mode. It would take twenty-four hours before it was ours, and I didn't think we'd have it, but the patriarch hadn't said we had to actually own the node, just capture it. In my book, we'd done just that.

The grignarians approached, weapons pointed skyward. Their spokescreature stepped forward. I Inspected the being. Its name was, apparently, Exalted Skywarden Greenlight the Unreleased. "We did not discuss which should take the bounty," it said.

"Neither of us is actually going to take this node," I said. "There's still ten of them out there, and mark my words, they're all heading right this way. I don't like our chances of keeping this one. In fact, they might try taking out our nodes in revenge, so we really need to get the hell out of here and see to our own defenses. But we did strike a nasty blow."

"Then the loot?"

I waved a hand dismissively. "Take whatever you like," I said. "But let's get out of here before they get back."

Grandpa messaged me. *All the turrets stopped firing as soon as you claimed it. Guess we should get out of here before some angry space elves show up and try to get revenge on us.*

CHAPTER FORTY-FIVE

ROUND THREE: FIGHT!

In an eyeblink, we transferred back to our outpost. One second I'd been touching Vortali's node, now I stood beside our own, staring out.

Juana looked up from the strategy table, confused. "What just happened?" she asked. "You're not dead, are you?"

A system message popped up.

[Challenge mode. Existalis has challenged you as owner of the other alpha node in this area for dominance. This must be resolved before phase three begins. Special rule set will apply. You have 5 minutes to confirm your agreement or you will forfeit the challenge.]

"No," I reassured her. At the same time, my chat notifications popped up with a dozen different messages from outside. "Looks like the restrictions have been removed." I tabbed over. There was a heading at the top.

[You have 6 hours until the challenge mode begins. At that time, communication with the outside will once again be cut off. Until then, you may communicate and bring in people and supplies.]

I dumped everything we knew into a message to Veda, then looked up. "Can everyone see this information?" I asked. Juana stared into space as she made a flicking gesture with her fingers. "Yeah," she said.

"There's a lot here. I'm pulling up the overview."

The challenge mode was an option chosen by Existalis. As the strongest remaining player on the map, they were throwing down a gauntlet to us. Either we ceded all of our holdings to them, or they would take it by force. I checked. The grignarians were included in this challenge as side players. "We didn't actually claim the node," I said, reading through. "We just triggered it to go back into claiming mode." That matched what I'd seen, but it was good to have outside confirmation.

"Looks like that was enough," Juana said. "Shad, if we don't accept this, we forfeit everything. How is that fair?"

"Since when have the people with all of the guns made things fair on those they were taking from?" Grandpa asked cynically.

"It's a no-holds-barred challenge." Smith frowned as he read over the rule set. "Whoever destroys the other's outpost wins. They've got a huge advantage there. Their outpost is way stronger than ours."

"But we can send creep at theirs, and they can't counter," I pointed out. "The alpha creep won't go after our outpost. That means they'll have to come right at us. Or there'll be a twist."

"It'll be a twist," Sage predicted. "It'll be some weird game mode nobody actually likes. I've seen that in the MOBAs I've been watching. You think you know the game and boom, the developers throw in Blitz or Dominion and nobody knows what they're doing."

I looked at the countdown. Two minutes, thirty seconds remained. It seemed like a no-brainer to accept the challenge. "We've got to get through enough of the small print to make sure that there's no gotcha here for us," I said. "Everybody start looking."

Veda sent me a message. *We've got to accept. Otherwise, we lose everything.*

We're going to lose everything anyway, I said in frustration. *They'll take what we've got.*

No, look at paragraph 42C.

I called that up. *How did you read this so fast?*

I have algorithms to do it for me. Look it over.

I called everyone's attention to the paragraph in question. "The challenge itself is over possession of the other alpha node and for prime positioning in phase three. If we refuse to accept it, we forfeit our current holdings and Existalis takes everything. If we accept but lose, we will have to suffer through whatever punishment Existalis dishes out, but they'll be required to pay reparations for anything they destroy. So we're out of the game either way, but if we lose at least they'll have to pay us for our stuff."

"Right," Juana agreed. "At least we'll have money for a new start."

"Not good enough," I said. I smacked my fist against my open palm. "Not after what we just went through to earn a phase three sponsor." I sent Veda a hasty note. *How is this even possible? Can we lodge a complaint?*

I'll see what I can do, she said. *Meanwhile—*

Meanwhile, we'll take the challenge. I looked to Grandpa. "I don't see any alternative. We've got to fight."

He nodded. "Of course," he said.

"I want to know how are we going to win. I haven't come this far just to give up because a bunch of bullies started pushing me around. We've got six hours to come up with a strategy," I said as I accepted the challenge offer. "Let's start looking over the rule set right now and figure this out."

The challenge terms were fairly straightforward. Six hours from now, the spawn points would activate once more. Creep would head for nodes again. Vortali's outpost would remain unclaimed, so all the alpha creep on the map would head for Existalis. That was in our favor.

At the same time, a boss mob would spawn somewhere near the central part of the lagoon. Both sides could fight over the boss. Whoever won the fight would have the boss under their control for thirty minutes. They would be able to use it to take out their opponents.

When one outpost was destroyed, the survivors would go to phase three.

"So, take out the enemy with creep, by direct attack, or take control of this boss," I said, ticking off my fingers.

"Look at this," Sage said, calling up a paragraph and sharing it with the rest of us. "Death and respawn timer mechanics have changed. All deaths now incur a twenty-minute respawn penalty. The dead player will be able to see and respond to what's going on."

"That'll make getting back into the fight easier," I commented.

Grandpa scratched his head. "We need intel. We need all the intel we can get."

"Existalis is a space orc company," Juana said. "They refused to even talk to me while we were fighting Vortali because I wasn't a combat miner. Said they don't deal with underlings. I think they said I didn't have 'blood in the fight,' whatever that means."

"Yeah, I'm starting to get the picture," I said, thinking about the orcs I'd met. I liked them, but even Mak'gar had only listened to suggestions from those he considered honorable warriors. They certainly weren't very devious.

I checked the rule set, looking for details. *Only Reality Engine–generated characters can harm outposts during this phase.*

That meant the creep and the boss. So the good news was we didn't have to worry too much about our defenses. The alpha- and beta-level creep couldn't touch us and neither could Existalis's miners. Our fortifications would be more than enough to hold against our usual creep. They wouldn't do much good against this boss, though.

On the other hand, we could take all the creep spawn points and send them at Existalis. They'd have to answer that threat, surely?

I queried the system, and it gave me some basic rundowns. No details on the boss's ability or appearance, just that it would have over nine thousand hit points and do commensurate damage. That would go through any of our defenses in one hit. Or through us.

Existalis had one shot to win: take the boss and send it against us. We could try to steal it from them, or we could let the creep chip away at their outpost and hope to wear them down before they could take us out. I wasn't sure that was a good bet.

"Any chance you can build really, really big bombs?" I asked Dwight.

"Looking into it right now," he said, frowning. "We need mats. We need people. Even if I could do it, I'd need about a hundred sets of hands."

That gave me an idea. I checked the system. There was no limit on how many people we could bring in. I briefly entertained the idea of surrounding our defenses with a couple thousand human shields but wrote that off. It felt like a cheat, and I was sure the system would have a way around it. "Bring them in," I told Dwight. "Ask Mama Grace to find people. Everyone we can find in the next four hours."

"On it."

"We need Arjun," I said.

"Arjun? I don't think he's ever set foot inside one of the Reality Engine levels," Juana said doubtfully. "And the others, how much can they really do?"

"Think about it." I spoke quickly, trying to convince myself as much as the others. "What's our big advantage? In this whole exploit, going forward? It's our people. We have lots of allies, support staff. So let's make use of that. We have fifteen warriors. So do they. Their gear is better, their outpost stronger. The only way to beat them is to make use of our people."

"And then we really need comms and intel gear," Sage said. "Let's see what Veda can get for us." Sage sat down on the ground, her brow furrowing as she presumably began composing her messages.

I paced, feeling useless as I watched my team settle into their tasks. Grandpa looked up from where he'd been talking intently with Smith. He crooked a finger and I came over. "Yes, sir?" I said.

"There's going to be lots for you to do once the excitement starts. Don't fret if you feel at loose ends right now. Should I order you to get some rack time?"

"Actually, I had a thought." I glanced toward the node. "I'm going to double-check that I'm allowed to leave and return, but I need to pop out to Threshold. Everyone else is busy working here, and it's something I can handle."

"Go ahead, then," Grandpa said, and turned back to Smith so quickly I knew he'd just been trying to keep me occupied. It was a little painful, knowing even Sage was more useful right now than me, but so be it.

CHAPTER FORTY-SIX

HOW TO HIRE AN ESPORT TEAM MANAGER

I stepped through into Threshold and immediately sent a message to Kirin, Arjun's manager. *Need to talk to you and Arjun in person. Where are you?*

At the guild hall. What's wrong? Mama Grace just tore out of here like her hair was on fire, told us to do whatever your team said but she had to go deliver a lunch.

That was odd. Maybe Juana had asked her mother to do an errand. *I'll be right there to explain.* I jogged down the steps of the portal and off along the streets of Threshold.

As I went, I appreciated just how much we humans had managed to achieve in our months here. My biggest achievement wasn't talking to the Reality Engine or reaching phase two, but the piece I'd played in getting us to stop fighting each other and start working together. It hadn't been all me, but I'd been part of it.

It struck me for the first time how I'd never seen an alien here in Threshold. Yet they were present in phase two. How were the orcs and elves and lizardfolk getting to the portals? Was there another entrance? Maybe they could teleport directly in.

The restaurant was almost deserted. A couple of our crafters sat at a table. They looked up as I came in. I ignored them and went to find Kirin. She and Arjun were in the large back room, alongside half a dozen other humans. Arjun was bent over a notebook, scribbling. Kirin saw me and hurried over. "What's going on? Everyone's too busy to talk to me."

"Phase two challenge. It's all on the line. Win and we're in phase three, lose and we're out of this thing entirely," I said. "I need Arjun."

"What for?" She stepped back, putting herself in my path. "He's working on some optimized rotations for our third farm team. Don't break his concentration right now." Kirin glared at me.

I glared back. "I understand you're used to protecting him, but this is important. We need his skills. He's got to come to the outpost with me. It's perfectly safe. He can't be hurt. We're going to be coming up against better equipped, more experienced foes. The one advantage we *might* have is better intel, and we need someone like Arjun who can put patterns together in his head fast."

Kirin hesitated. "All right, but if he says yes, I'm going along."

"Fine."

She stepped out of the way and I approached Arjun, standing across the table from him and waiting until he noticed me. He looked up, staring just past my shoulder. "What is it?"

"Arjun?"

"Oh, hi, Shad. Didn't recognize you."

I was wearing my same coat as always, but maybe my new hat had thrown him. I took it off and held it. "Oh yeah, that's you," Arjun said.

"Have you been following what's going on with phase two?"

Arjun nodded. "Sage keeps sending us video updates. They're very exciting."

"Oh, cool." I hadn't known she was doing that. "Well, there's a big twist about to start and I'm going to need help. We're going directly up against fifteen better-equipped orcs."

"'We' meaning the Mongeese, the Ragtags, and Team Twofeather?"

"Right."

"Ah." Arjun's eyes unfocused a little. "Are these the same orcs you fought before? Or allies?"

"No, this is Existalis. We haven't seen them in action yet."

"No profiles or combat assessments?"

I shook my head. "Nope."

He looked me right in the eyes and grinned. "Oh, this will be fun." He rubbed his hands together. "Start feeding me information and I'll get cracking."

"Unfortunately, we're going to be cut off again in"—I checked my timer—"forty-eight minutes. No communication with the outside world permitted. I'm going to need you to come with me."

His face fell. He turned away from me and hunched in on himself. "No. No way. Sorry, Shad, I can't."

"You have to!" I resisted the urge to grab his shoulders and get him to look at me. Arjun wouldn't respond well to that.

Kirin came at me. "You need to leave—"

"No." I held up my hands. "No. Arjun, we need you. They're better equipped than we are, by a lot. They know the rules of the game, they've played this a million times. The only advantage we have is our people. We need you to tell us how to defeat them. To look at their skills and ours and make a strategy. I need you to tell me how to kill these fuckers."

Arjun shuddered. "I can't go back in there. The spiders . . ."

"No spiders," I said firmly. "We have pirate skeletons and dinosaurs and you'll be inside our outpost. Lots of guns to keep you safe. I swear."

He seemed to hesitate. "You're sure . . . ?"

"Absolutely," I told him. "Believe me. I wouldn't ask if I didn't need you."

Arjun took a deep breath and stood up. "I—I'll try."

At first, I thought I'd stepped through the portal into a different place entirely. Most of our fortifications were gone. The two inner rings had disappeared, and the outer ring was bristling with turrets and towers. I could hear them from here as they shot down the wave of creep approaching our node.

Most of our support structures had been moved closer to the node itself. There was a huge clear area where the defenses had been, and about three hundred people were standing or sitting in the grass there. The ground between them was littered with crafting mats of all descriptions. Baskets full of skins, crates full of metal, barrels and boxes overflowing with glowing gems, enormous bones, twisted branches, curved talons, fruit the size of my head, black-and-orange flowers, and more.

Over by the node itself, the command table had been transformed into a desk setup with three chairs. Juana sat in one, Arjun in another, and in the middle was Sage. They wore headsets like they were about to cast a football game.

Grandpa strolled over to me. "Success?"

"They'll be here in a couple minutes." I gestured around the place. "What's going on?"

"We called in the cavalry." He gestured at the people working in the open space. "Every capable crafter that belongs to us or any of our friendlies. Dwight's directing them now."

"That's a lot of materials."

"Everything we've had stockpiled for phase three. If this doesn't work, we're broke. If it does work, we're going to have to scramble to come up with resources."

I pointed over to the desk. "What's this?"

"We're going to need serious centralized command for this. Veda sent us some presents." He held up a box. It was labeled "All-Seeing Eye: Personal Model." "Here's yours. Go ahead and equip it now."

I took it. The system description read [**All-Seeing Eye. When equipped, allows miners' visual and audio inputs to be transmitted and shared to a central location. Allows two-way voice communication between all wearers. Be careful where you point this thing.**]

I equipped it. "So we're all going to be wearing these, and those three will be watching? Seems like a lot of input."

"It does," Grandpa agreed. "We're just hoping it's enough. They'll be directing squad assignments and tactics."

I looked over at the team sitting at the command table. I felt a little nervous. While I respected each of their abilities, did they really have what it took to direct an operation like this?

Grandpa must have seen my doubt. "Sometimes you've just got to take it on faith that the commanders know what they're doing," he said. "Oftentimes they don't. But we're not going to be able to see the whole picture. Not while we're fighting it. This is a pretty slim chance we've got here. I like the plan we've come up with. But I still think we've only got about a twenty percent shot at pulling it off."

"Well," I said, "guess I'd better go get the briefing."

CHAPTER FORTY-SEVEN

THINGS TO ASK YOUR CATERER: #3: WILL THAT HAVE NUTS?

Veda's personal system chirped to let her know she had yet another message. It wasn't from Team Twofeather or anyone at their outpost, otherwise it would have popped straight up. But it was also classified as important enough to have gotten past her first wave of security.

She glanced at it and swore. Existalis's representative wanted to speak to her. Existalis was backed by Alabaster Sky, one of Proxima's friendly rivals. She hadn't dealt much with that multisystem conglomerate and knew little about them.

As Alabaster Sky's logo filled the screen in front of her, Veda composed herself. It dissolved away into the face of another humanoid who looked like she could have been Veda's sister. She had the same pale skin and stark-white hair, indicating she most likely came from the same origin system as Veda's family.

"Good day to you, Ms. Tvedra," Lakhnar said. "I am Al-Narian Lakhnar, speaking on behalf of Alabaster Sky. Thank you for taking my call."

"What can I do for you?" Veda asked.

"I am here to make a proposal which will benefit us both," Lakhnar said. "You currently are the sponsor behind a team that has a small delta-level outpost in the same sector as one of our affiliates." She glanced down, as though reading information off a screen. "Yes. Team Twofeather. I see. It looks like you've done fairly well here in phase two. Congratulations. You must be proud of yourself. I know Tvedra Corporation was not considered a particularly good bet at the start of this exploit, but it seems as though you have proven some of your detractors wrong."

Lakhnar gave a cold smile. Veda could read her body language perfectly. The woman was being deliberately insulting, perhaps trying to provoke Veda or throw her off guard for what was coming next.

"Yes, and as you know," Veda replied evenly, "your associate's team has challenged mine to a special combat. I'm rather busy right now."

"I don't think you are," Lakhnar said. "They're on their own until it's done. The window to provide advice and supplies has closed."

Veda was happy to let her think that. In actuality, she was working on several backup plans, just in case Team Twofeather somehow changed the rules yet again.

"I am willing to make you a buyout offer on your outpost and your team," Lakhnar said. "This offer will be good for the five minutes it takes you to read over and consider. After that, we will continue with the special event."

"No," Veda said flatly.

"No?" Lakhnar raised her eyebrows. "Ms. Tvedra, you know as well as I do that your team has no chance of winning. Alabaster Sky has sent in the highest level of equipment we can afford. You can't possibly have matched it. Existalis will eliminate your team and their outpost. You will receive the value of the ruined outpost, no more. As we both know, most of the worth of an outpost is in its intact buildings and its setup. Once Existalis is done, you'll be lucky to receive a tenth of what the outpost is worth right now." She tapped her fingers on an unseen desk. "A fiftieth of what we're offering." She sent through a number.

Veda blinked. There were more zeros at the end than she had expected. Despite herself, she did some quick mental math. She could easily pay off the contracts for all of Team Twofeather and their combat miner allies, as well as the crafters she had directly sponsored, like Juana and her family. She'd even be able to contribute toward a buyout fund for the other human miners and still make more of a profit than she had ever expected here.

"In addition," Lakhnar said, "we would be happy to make an endorsement on your license, saying what a delight it has been to work with you. Should you choose to put your name in for the rogue world Reality Engine that we will all be looking forward to exploit here in a few cycles, my bosses will certainly look closely at Tvedra Corp."

There was a temptation. Veda opened the offer, read over it, then looked back at Lakhnar. "Why?"

"Why what?"

"Why bother? As you just said, your team will have to pay a fraction of this in recompense once they're done trashing my outpost. Wait a couple of hours, and this is all moot."

Lakhnar smiled. "As it happens," she said through gritted teeth, "we have been asked by interested parties to extend an olive branch, as it were."

The patriarch of the Church of the Progenitors? Veda couldn't think of anyone else who might interfere. Why would he care? Unless . . . She read through the offer.

This would give Alabaster Sky a first right of refusal clause on Team Twofeather in phase three. Shad and his team wouldn't have to work with Alabaster Sky, but they wouldn't be able to work with anyone else unless Alabaster Sky agreed. Did

the conglomerate want to get Shad and his family on their team or were they trying to keep them out of phase three? Veda looked away from her screens, the offer
still tempting her. How was it that Team Twofeather kept getting her into these
situations?

She checked over her numbers. The reparations from the ruined outpost would
pay for what she had spent, and not much more. It would be tricky to keep the company afloat until the next Reality Engine exploit. Even trickier if she made an enemy
of Alabaster Sky. She was already pretty sure Proxima didn't like her, and the two of
them were heavies in this area. She might have to relocate Tvedra's operations to
another sector entirely, which would again take money she didn't have.

So. Take the money and run. That's what her family would want. It wouldn't
even hurt Team Twofeather that much. Sure, they wouldn't make it to phase three,
but who cared? They'd never manage to claim a share of the Reality Engine anyway. Might as well get out now.

On the other hand, the fact that someone else was so desperate to get rid of
them stoked some little rebellious streak deep inside Veda. Shad and his family
had worked damn hard for her. Their crazy gambles kept paying off. She knew
what they wanted her to do.

She closed her eyes. *What am I getting myself into?* "The answer's still no. Thank
you for it, though. Please convey my regards to your superiors and to whomever
wanted you to make this offer."

Lakhnar looked shocked, her mouth hanging open.

"Oh," Veda couldn't help adding, "and would you care to place a small side
bet on the outcome of this match?" If she was going to burn all of her bridges and
fortunes at the same time, she might as well go out in style. "I'll offer you, say,
five to one odds."

Lakhnar spluttered. "You think there's even one chance in five your team
could win?"

"The other way around." Veda smiled. "I'm betting on Shad."

She cut the feed before Lakhnar could respond. Her system popped up another
notification. *There is someone at your door. She has been knocking for the past two
minutes. I conveyed that you are busy, but she will not go away and says as your sponsor, she has the right to speak to you.*

Veda's eyes flew open. She stood up, feeling a wave of panic. "Sponsor? Who
could it be?" She checked the feed and felt even more surprised at the visitor than
she had at the number Alabaster Sky had offered as buyout.

Mama Grace stood outside her door, holding a covered plate. Veda activated
the voice controls. "Yes? What can I do for you?"

"You can open up and let me have a word with you in private," Mama Grace
said. "I've come all this way. The least you can do is talk to me."

Veda hesitated only a moment before opening her door. Mama Grace stepped in, accompanied by an absolutely delicious odor. Veda sniffed. It couldn't be Kakhnaveri.

Mama Grace held the plate out. Veda hesitantly took it and lifted back the cloth covering. It was an entire plate of Kakhnaveri, smelling just like her grandmother had made it. "How did you even get the ingredients?" she asked.

Mama Grace smiled. "Professional secret, dear," she said. "But it seemed like you could do with a nice home-cooked meal."

Veda set the food down on her desk. She collapsed into her chair, exhaustion settling over her. "I guess I can spare a minute. There's not much more I can do for the team inside the Engine," she said. "Not right now, anyway."

"That's what I wanted to speak with you about," Mama Grace said calmly. "From what Juana told me before she told me to go away and let her work, this is important. Really important. I didn't totally understand why, since she said that we'd all be fine one way or the other. But it matters to her, and it matters to Sage and her brother and their grandpa, so it matters to me."

"To me, too," Veda assured her. "My own fortunes are rather tied up in this mess."

"So, what are you doing to help them?" Mama Grace asked. She looked around. Veda, realizing she had been rude, called up a chair from the room's storage and extruded it. Grace looked somewhat surprised, but she sat down and crossed her legs in front of her.

"I've done what I can," Veda said. "Bought them everything that we could think of that might help, and gave them free rein. And now they're doing what they need to."

"But what else?" Grace prompted. "Let them worry about what's going on in there. What about out here?" She made a gesture around herself, like taking in the entire station.

"Oh." Veda deflated. The scent of the food was really starting to get to her. She picked up her own pair of chopsticks and took a bite of the delicious noodles. They were exquisite, exactly like she remembered her grandmother making years ago when she was a child. She took another bite before she realized what she was doing, swallowed, and then said, "You're right. I've already fielded a call from one group that doesn't have their best interests at heart. I'm afraid we've made enemies of two of the big players."

Mama Grace was nodding. "I get the feeling from Shad that he's kind of a bull in a china shop. But maybe that's what we need here. We didn't ask for any of you folk to barge in and take us away from our lives and our loved ones. We're just doing the best we can."

"I know that," Veda said. "And I'm sympathetic."

Grace held up a hand. "But since we are here, we're going to do our best. Shad and Juana are cooking up some plan that they haven't really shared with me. I'm fine with that. I don't want to be in charge. I want to cook food and make sure everybody's got a full belly and a warm place to sleep. But they're all busy right now, so I'm going to do what I can. You say we've made big enemies?"

Veda nodded. "We have."

"Then we need big friends."

"I suppose that's possible. ConSweGo won't like it if Proxima and Alabaster Sky are in on something together. But we don't have much to offer them. One single delta-level outpost?"

Grace shook her head again. "You're thinking too small, dear. We've got a lot more than that."

"What do you mean?"

"I mean." She smiled. "We've got about four million human miners who've signed a petition I've been circulating."

Veda felt her ears prick up at that. "Oh? Really? What sort of petition?"

Mama Grace sent over the details. As the packet pinged into Veda's system, she pulled it up and started reading. It was straightforward—and beautiful. Veda's trader instincts were intrigued. "This is . . . thorough."

"Mm-hmm. Colonel Ames's been helping me," Grace said. "See the signature count?"

"Is that the right number?" Veda asked. Grace nodded. Her mind was working furiously. "Okay. That might actually get us somewhere. Let me make a few calls." She picked up another bite of Kakhnaveri noodles. The food warmed her insides like Mama Grace's smile. "You're right, we do have things to do."

CHAPTER FORTY-EIGHT

WHAT TO DO WHEN A GREAT OLD ONE MELTS YOUR BRAIN

As the countdown expired, a zone-wide announcement spawned, announcing the arrival of the Great Old One.

[Look upon him and despair. He has arisen from his watery tomb to bring terror upon this world. The team that can take control of him will be able to force him to do their bidding for half an hour. Which team will triumph? There's only one way to know.]

An icon popped up on the mini-map, a giant black-and-white skull. It was just off the coast, at the midpoint that connected our separate islands into a single Y-shaped atoll.

"Right, Jones," Grandpa said. "Get your bird in the air. Let's take a look." We had already dispatched several dozen farming allies to disperse across the island wearing the All-Seeing Eyes. It seemed like cheating to me, but there was nothing in the rules against it, and we needed info about our rivals. As far as we could tell, our enemy had limited themselves to the fifteen combat miners they'd been allowed to bring in. The only advantage we had over these guys was our allies.

Several of our spies were stationed outside their outpost. As the Existalis combat miners emerged, information started to flow back to us. *They all seem to be space orcs. It's hard to tell. They're wearing combat armor, armed to the teeth. A couple of them have shoulder-mounted cannons. No sign of any sort of vehicles or siege weapons.*

Meanwhile, some of our scouts had reached the edge of the lagoon. Juana swore. "What the hell *is* that?"

Sage giggled and shared their feed. The creature had spawned about twenty feet from the shore. It looked like someone had taken an enormous skull and wrapped it in tentacles. It rose up out of the water at least thirty feet into the air.

My eyes couldn't quite get it in focus. The thing just kept wriggling. There was definitely a sensation of empty eye sockets when I stared at it.

Then it lashed one shapeless black appendage toward the beach. Our spy turned and ran, and I couldn't blame him. "I got a remote Eye-Spy off," Sage said happily. "Here are the stats."

She fed them to us, and I boggled. "There's no way we're going to be able to take that thing down. Resistant to water damage. Resistant to electric damage. Resistant to fire damage. Immune to necrotic damage. Immune to disease. What the hell are we supposed to hit it with?"

"Holy damage," Dwight said, not looking up from his work.

"We can get that?" I asked.

"It takes a little bit of effort. Probably pure energy-based damage would work."

"It's resistant to lightning damage."

"Yeah, but I looked at the classifications, and those are two different things."

"If you say so," I grumbled.

Existalis's miners were making straight for the lagoon. "All right, Shad, time to roll out," Grandpa told me.

My team was our vanguard. I was taking a couple of us up to the lagoon now. Bill, Bob, Mitch, and Annie would be coming with me. While I was sleeping, Mongoose had used the last three pairs of spawn point claiming flags to reclaim our points. Now, Juana redirected them into Existalis's path. "Do not engage in combat until we say so," Grandpa reminded me, as though I needed it. "Right now, we're on a fact-finding mission. Hang back and let the spies gather intel."

That didn't sit well with me, but it made sense. We weren't sure yet if the boss could kill our crafters. I assumed it could. Grandpa had warned them all to stay out of range.

Some of our creep wandered past one of our spies just as Existalis's vanguard arrived at the same location. The trio of armored orcs fell on the creep using a combination of weapons and abilities. Too fast for me to follow, but Sage and Arjun started making "Ahh" noises, so they must have gotten some intel from our watcher, who waited until the orcs had finished and then stealthily relocated.

"Right, Suicide Squad, move out," I told my men and Annie, and we set off.

"We're designating these three orcs as Red One, Two, and Three," I heard Sage's voice say in my ear as I led my squad past the army of crafters toward our front gate, which was now sealed against creep. As we approached, it opened. A couple of skeletons tried to get through, but we cut them down on our way out.

"Red team seems to be the vanguards. Moving fast, not as heavily armored as we expect the rest to be. Hit points: between one hundred fifty and one hundred seventy-five." Sage rattled off some values. "The specs we downloaded off Veda's transmission indicate the armor should have weak points, but they're probably not where we think. It may take a couple of shots to locate them. Despite their appearance, the joints are usually reinforced. Common weak points are the shin and forearm."

"What good does that do?" Bill asked me as we went. "I have a feeling these guys can walk off a couple of flesh wounds."

"Their armor is powered up. If you damage one area, it has to reroute power and nanites to reinforce it. That leaves it exposed elsewhere. Damage it enough and you'll be able to get some headshots in." I hoped I had understood the theory well enough that what I was saying was correct.

"Red One has a slowing move," Sage reported. "Analyzing."

"Watch the chatter," Grandpa said over our open comm lines. "Let's tell them what they need to know."

"We have eyes on all of Existalis's miners. They're heading right for Squid Face up there. Nobody's paused long enough to set any traps. They're going for a quick cap," Sage said confidently. "No, they needed to know that, Grandpa. All right, fine." She shut up.

Her chatter was comforting. Even though we had been reassured that Existalis wasn't waiting for us, I still jumped at every noise I heard and felt the hair on the back of my neck stand up.

We proceeded through the jungle. Every few hundred feet, one of our spies popped out of the bush and waved encouragingly at us. I waved back, but I wished they'd let us do our job. "We're starting to put together a nice profile here," Juana said over comms. "I'll be doing most of the controlling of the conversation, unless there's something Arjun and Sage specifically need to say."

Good, I thought. Not that I minded Sage, but Juana was much more laid back. Not to mention easy to listen to. "They've engaged the boss," Juana warned. "Stay back. We'll get you a video feed once you're ready."

We were approaching the edge of the jungle. I stopped just short of the beach, crouching behind a large palm tree to peer past the last few pieces of brush.

Fifteen orcs wearing power armor were running in zigzagging patterns around the great beast. Seeing it with my own eyes didn't help me understand what I was witnessing. It glistened in the sun, writhing, an enormous skull covered in a living oil slick that slithered around its surface, gathering together into clumps and then lashing out with pseudopod limbs. One gnawed tentacle smashed into an orc, knocking her up onto the beach. "Holy shit!" Juana said as the orc got back to her feet. "He didn't die!"

I had started being able to tell male orcs from the females based on some of the symbols on their armor. A diamond pattern along the neckline meant female, while circles meant male.

"She," I said, though it was completely irrelevant. "How much damage did she take?"

"Two hundred and fifty-seven points. Must be one of their heavily armored units. She's got four hundred hit points." Juana sounded disbelieving, and I understood why. None of us had over two hundred health. "That gear is incredible."

The boss spun quickly around, its surface nictating and retracting, then pushing outward. A giant wave of water shot out all around it, knocking the orcs over. Two of them washed up on the beach in a pile of mangled limbs. They vanished. "Did you see that?" I asked.

"Sure did," Sage said excitedly. "That was all water damage, by the way."

Water damage. My hat's set bonus meant that while I was wearing it and the drover's coat both, I was immune to water damage. I mentioned that on comms.

"We know," Sage said. "We were hoping that this boss would do a lot of water damage. It's a big part of our plan. Right now, though, we've got to buy time. Look at its health bar."

I checked. The boss was still green, but it was ticking down fast as the orcs lobbed grenades, filled it with hot plasma, or tossed bright white spells at it. I looked at my team. "Wait until I give the signal," I said. They nodded, their faces wary. This was the worst. Sitting here waiting, watching.

"We've got a profile for almost all of the orcs now," Sage said cheerfully. "Arjun is compiling strats. Just hold tight." I nodded agreement, not that she could see me, and we watched.

Suddenly, the boss gave a loud hooting cry from what orifice I couldn't tell, and a pack of water droplets the size of VW Beetles appeared on the beach. They began to make their way toward the orcs, who turned and fired at them, breaking them into smaller droplets that slithered about, then re-formed.

One of the orcs pulled a rifle the size of a small cannon out of his inventory and fired, shooting a bright white beam at the droplets. Wherever the beam hit, it froze the water droplets. They broke into a dozen small pieces and then dissolved into the sand. "Ice damage," Sage diagnosed.

"I could have guessed that."

"Shut up, Shad. We're keeping the channel open, remember?"

The boss was below sixty percent health now, its health bar yellow. "Okay, so that was probably a health-based move, not time-based," Juana said. "We need to watch as much of this fight as we can."

The boss lashed out with a tentacle and caught one unlucky orc by surprise. The orc was thrown back into the trees. It hit a trunk and sank to the ground with an unhappy thud. "I don't think it liked that," Sage said cheerfully. "Is he dead?"

None of us had eyes on the fallen orc, though I could tell on my mini-map a couple of our spies were crouched not far off, well out of range of the boss monster.

"Yeah, he's dead," Juana said.

"Great." I looked back at the boss. Its health was now below fifty percent. It sent a second wave of water on the orcs fighting it. Another one died, leaving ten to go, but they were making steady progress.

"Hold tight," Juana said. "We want to try to let it get to thirty percent health before we move."

"You hearing this?" I said to my team. They all nodded. Bill and Bob looked almost relaxed, but Mitch and Annie seemed nervous. They didn't have as much experience with this as we did. I tried to smile reassuringly. "We'll make it," I said. "We've got a plan."

The boss monster hit out with its tentacles again. It seemed to have a rhythm there. Spinning, contracting, expanding, thrashing, volley of water. "The tentacles are doing a lot of water-based damage," Juana reported. "Shad, you could probably take one hit, but no more than that."

"It's also got force damage and crushing damage," I said as one tentacle came down right on an orc. He survived, dashing back and draining a health potion before running back into combat and lobbing a grenade. "I'm not immune to those."

"So don't get hit," Sage said helpfully.

"At forty percent and falling; be prepared," Grandpa said. "We've got a battle plan here, but no plan survives contact with the enemy."

"Right," I said. I looked at the enemy orcs, at the boss, and at my team. "We understand." The tension mounted. I felt nervous, more nervous than when I'd been in a middle school play with a walk-on role that I'd managed to flub every time in practice.

The boss ticked down to thirty percent. It gave another call, bringing in a shower of water bubble monsters. The orcs cleaned those up fast.

"Go!" Juana said in our ears and we ran in.

CHAPTER FORTY-NINE

BOSS STRATS: THE BEST, THE WORST, AND THE FAIL

We charged across the sand, spreading out. As soon as we got close, Bob threw out a Babel spell, hitting as many of the orcs as he could with a debuff that would make it harder for them to coordinate.

Two of the orcs turned as they saw us. One lobbed a fist-sized purple ball at us. It exploded on the sand, turning it to sticky tar. I gained a Stuck! debuff, slowing my movement speed by ninety percent.

Bill answered with his Call OSHA ability, which removed the debuff and let us all charge through the tarry mass without any ill impact. Meanwhile, his brother threw out Lost in Translation. The spell hit six of the orcs. I could tell which because they instantly turned on each other, firing their guns madly as the effect forced them to attack whoever was nearest without regard for friend or foe.

I engaged my Fastest Gun in the West to charge into the midst of the fray. I lobbed a couple of grenades at the orcs nearest the boss, blowing them back into the water.

As he got in range, Mitch threw out Spike Their Trunks. The orcs howled in anger as their weapons suddenly began spurting maple syrup everywhere. I couldn't help laughing as the orcs threw them to the ground in disgust, grabbing for backup weapons from their sides or their inventory. Most of them were now wielding swords or short spears, though a couple had handguns.

A pair of spear-wielding orcs charged me. I used Trick Shot to hit one in the hand. She yowled in pain and lunged for me, but I dodged under her spear. The second orc only caught the edge of my coat.

Meanwhile, Annie had raced right past all of the orcs straight to the boss. She used a spell we'd never had a call for before, Hat for Your Rabbit. The ability could only be cast on NPCs. It made them twice as strong, twice as fast, and twice as angry.

The monstrous skull thing grew absolutely enormous, rising up to blot out the sky. It extended long tentacles in every direction. Some of the orcs saw it and shouted, pointing, trying to scramble up the beach, but it was too late. The Great Old One smashed down into the water and the beach. Its body blotted out the sun as it came down on me.

As it smashed me into the ground, my last thought was, *I just hope it wipes their whole party.*

I woke up in limbo. I was hovering in midair right behind Juana's shoulder, about a foot from our respawn point.

"Hey," I said. She turned and looked right through me.

"I hear you, Shad, but I can't see you," she said. "All of you are stuck in the penalty box for the next twenty minutes. The good news is, you guys did it. You took out their whole team. Most of them are out for a full twenty minutes. The next couple are coming up in fifteen or so, but we've got a great profile on all of them. The boss reset. All of its health is back. We're ready to act."

"Glad it was worth it," I said.

Juana smiled. "You just take it easy and enjoy the show while we handle this next part," she said. "We're gonna need you back out there before long."

I wanted to take a look at what was going on, so I tried to move. I could turn in every direction, but I couldn't get more than about a foot in any direction from the respawn point.

Still, I could see the camp bustling. Dwight was moving between aisles of crafters, looking over their work, correcting them, making suggestions. There was an enormous pile of cannonball-sized spheres at one end of the crafting field, and an even bigger pile of fist-sized grenades. A stack of wooden shields were piled about two feet high, and there were a couple of piles of miscellaneous items that I wanted to get a closer look at but couldn't.

"Hey, Dwight," I called. He didn't seem to hear me, so I tried in chat. *How's it going?*

Sorry, can't chat. Too busy. We'll be ready, but we need time.

I felt properly chastised as I turned back to wait out my penalty. I couldn't see any of my dead teammates. Apparently, we really were invisible. I used chat instead. *Nice work, Annie.*

Thanks. I've been wanting to try that. It's only got a twenty-minute cooldown, so we can use it again if we have to.

I shuddered. *Let's not and say we did.*

I'm fine with that.

Grandpa was getting the kill squads ready to go. He had Lara, Ice Spice, and both Smiths as well as Brown from the Mongeese. He was holding Lakshmi, Jones, and Black in reserve. Once the rest of us respawned, he'd be going out with the other dead members of my team.

Grandpa gave them their orders and applied his toned-down War Chief's Aegis buff to them. They stood a little straighter. "Now get out there and knock them dead," Grandpa concluded. The team slipped out.

About halfway through my time out, our spies reported that the first of the Existalis team had respawned and were heading out as a trio. Grandpa chuckled, rubbing his hands. "Excellent," he said, "making it easy for us. Kill squad, first target." He turned to Sage and Arjun. "Give them their marching orders," he said.

Arjun nodded. He had an abacus out in front of him and was working the beads with an intent look. "Should be Red One, Blue Two, Green Three. They're going to be short on intel. None of them have anything that looks like a sensory boosting skill. Take 'em by surprise. Focus on Blue Two. Flashbang to the face, followed by one of your moves, Ice Spice. Lara, lock down Green Three with Time Out."

"Can somebody send me a feed?" I asked.

Juana glanced over her shoulder. "No talking in the group comms," she warned, but flicked her hand to send me the feed.

Now I was looking through one of the spy cams. It took me a minute to decide it was Lara's. She could see everybody else on the team from here, as well as the orcs, who were crashing loudly through the bush. They were making no attempt to hide.

Our team waited until the orcs had gone past their hiding place before leaping out at them. Lara threw Time Out on her chosen target. He froze in place, his rifle pointing skyward. At the same time, Short Smith hurled a flashbang grenade. It exploded in between the other two orcs with a deafening shriek and a bright flash of light.

Ice Spice ran in. He activated one of his kung fu abilities, I couldn't tell which from here, and began striking the orc in the forearm and shin with his hands and feet. Lightning-fast kicks and punches slapped over and over again against the armor's less-enforced spots. I could see the armor failing. The spy cam detected the movement of the nanites as they were routed from other parts of the suit.

"Go for his head now," Juana said, leaning over the command table and speaking directly to Ice Spice.

He lashed out with a whirlwind kick to the head that knocked the orc to the ground. A moment later, the orc was gone, back to the respawn point to wait out his next twenty minutes.

The kill team fell on the orc we'd designated as Red One. She put up a fight, but our team danced in and out as though they'd practiced this.

We had, I realized. We'd spent so long battling creep, picking fights with monsters, even on the farming levels. We knew how to fight. This squad had never worked together as a single unit before. But now, as Arjun and Sage gave Juana strategies, and Juana translated them into easy-to-follow orders, our team performed like a well-oiled machine. I was going to have to make sure I did as good a job of listening when it was my turn up.

They executed the last of the three. "Get out of there," Grandpa ordered. "We don't know what kind of spying devices they might have."

The team disappeared back into the jungle.

The next two orcs who had died during the boss fight were back up. I was sure they would wait for their fellows, but instead they pushed out, moving fast. Our spies told us everything we needed to know. The kill team moved to intercept.

"Why aren't they waiting?" Juana asked aloud.

"They're probably worried that we're taking the boss," I said. "Good. That means they're taking us seriously."

Lara's Time Out was on cooldown, but Ice Spice pulled out a Can't Look Away From These Moves ability which had the pair of orcs standing transfixed as a dozen different copies of my kung fu–obsessed teammate spun around them, kicking, punching, and lashing out with phantom limbs. Meanwhile, the real Ice Spice and the rest of his team came in from behind and smashed through their defenses. The orcs had better weapons and armor than us, by a lot, but if we were coordinated and they weren't, we might pull this off.

"The next wave's the big one," Arjun warned. I checked my own timer. Three minutes left.

"As soon as you're up, we're getting out there," Grandpa told the rest of my team.

"I can help," I said.

"Nope. You've gotta stay alive. Just as soon as we've got the crafting done, we're sending in the kill team." Grandpa grinned, staring at a spot about a foot from where I actually was. "Don't worry. It's gonna take you that long to pick up all of the crafting gear Dwight's made you. Once you respawn, get down there and start filling your inventory. Dwight will tell you what's yours and what goes to Black."

I grumbled, but only under my breath. It was definitely time for Lieutenant Williams to shut up and do what Major Twofeather said.

As soon as we respawned, Grandpa buffed my team and they headed out. Juana was busy giving new instructions. Our spies had Existalis's crew under observation just as soon as they left their base. There were ten of them and ten of us on kill duty, but thankfully, Existalis decided to split up. Probably they were spooked, didn't know where we were, and decided instead of risking walking into some trap to split their forces.

That was exactly what we had hoped they would do. The hunters in the jungle moved in on their prey like a pack of starving wolves.

I, on the other hand, was stuck picking up one hundred and fifty grenades. Could have been worse. Black had four hundred bombs, and they all weighed at least twenty pounds. I was smirking at him when Dwight waved me over.

"And you'll need these," he said.

I stared at where he was pointing in disbelief. "What are those?" They looked like the sparring dummies I'd seen in action movies. Sticks with a padded torso and beanbag head, and wooden poles for arms.

"Those," Dwight said, grinning, "are part of our great strategy. They are, well, take a look. I let Sage name them," he added.

I Inspected. A pop-up appeared.

[Shad Dummies, not to be confused with that dummy, Shad, can be used to replace all attention that Shad has gained from an enemy. Arm before placing in inventory. Will deploy when removed from inventory.]

"Really?" I sighed, armed the first, and put it in my bag.

"Hurry up," Dwight said. "Because after that, you're going to have to come and attune yourself to the taunters."

"The what?" I asked.

He just laughed.

CHAPTER FIFTY

SHOOTING FISH IN A BARREL AND OTHER BAD IDEAS

Veda and Mama Grace smiled at each other across the empty plate of food on Veda's desk. "I think we're ready to make one last call, don't you?" Veda said.

Grace rubbed her hands together as she leaned back into her chair. "I think so. Act fast, we've got a long way to go. I've got to get to work cooking up a victory feast, although I expect they'll be long done before I get back down there." She gave a hesitant sigh. "You'll forgive me if I stay for this one. I really need to see the looks on their faces."

"I'm going to have my algorithms hide you," Veda said. "Just keep this between us sponsors. Nice and clean."

"Fine by me," Grace said as Veda had her systems handle the call.

The patriarch of the Church of the Progenitors picked up himself, not making Veda go through underlings. "What can I do for you, Lady Tvedra?"

"I would like you to arbitrate a phone call between myself, the head of Proxima, and the head of Alabaster Sky," she said without preamble. "I think you will find this call most instructive."

The patriarch raised an eyebrow. "Indeed. As it happens, I have a small amount of time. I am eagerly anticipating hearing the results of your team's actions, Tvedra."

"They'll let me know as soon as they're done," she said. She was certain the patriarch knew exactly what was going on down in Threshold, but she wasn't going to press him to see if he had thoughts.

"One moment." The patriarch looked away, then back. "It seems that both representatives have time for us now. I'll put us all in together, shall I?" A moment later, the holographic heads of both Proxima and Alabaster Sky appeared in the air before Veda.

It was the same woman she had spoken to a few hours ago, Lakhnar, and the familiar Proxima representative, Halithi Dreamwarden, who looked as grumpy as usual. "What's the meaning of this?" Dreamwarden asked. "Have you called to ask our help? We're not interested."

"I told you that offer expired as soon as we got off our call," Lakhnar said.

Veda held up a hand. "I am here with an ultimatum for you both," she said. That got their attention.

Dreamwarden said, "What do you mean, 'ultimatum'?" at the same time as Lakhnar said, "You are in no position to be giving us ultimatums."

"This is on behalf of the Union of Earth Miners," Veda said. "They've asked me to present it to you, as I am the sponsor of the preeminent human mining team in this exploit."

"Human?" Lakhnar's eyebrows raised even higher.

Veda clarified. "The Earthlings. They refer to themselves as 'human,' since that is their species, and they don't really realize that it's not a unique designator."

"Oh, the indigenous." Dreamwarden smirked and tossed his hair. "Go ahead. Several of them have decided to present us demands, have they? This should be good."

Veda looked at the declaration Mama Grace had brought to her. She cleared her throat. "On behalf of the Union of Human Miners, I present this: We state we will be performing no services to any corporation, conglomeration, team, or individual who violates the following.

"First, any contract involving Earth humans may be renegotiated or sold at the behest of the Earth human involved. Current sponsor will sell the contract for a price of twice what was originally negotiated."

"What?" Dreamwarden demanded.

"They want to be able to buy out of contracts," Veda said. "To get rid of exploitive backers, or maybe to join up with other Earthlings, doesn't matter. They're offering to pay back double what their backers paid. You'll keep whatever you've earned off the humans, but they want to be able to buy out."

"That's preposterous," Lakhnar said. "What else?"

"Second, when phase three begins, all farming level claims by Earth humans will be respected. Any outside farm miners who join at that point will need to stake their own claims or make a bargain with the humans who already hold that level."

"That's a matter for the system, not us," the Proxima rep said.

Veda smiled. "Yes, well, I'm sure they've heard stories of all of the ways you get around system restrictions."

"Is that it?"

"One more thing." Veda was truly enjoying herself. Right now, the representatives had no intention of accepting any of these terms, so they were listening with amusement. That would change soon enough. "During phase three, should any human outpost or team be present in phase three, you will agree not to interfere. There will be no assassination attempts on the human miners. There will be no attempts to take their base. If, during the usual flow of gameplay, your miners and their miners come up against each other, then let nature take its course. But no direct interference. You will respect the territory claimed by the indigenous human miners."

Dreamwarden snorted. "All right, then. I take it that's the end?" he said as Veda trailed off. "You can tell them—"

"Wait," Veda said, holding up a hand. "Any party who does not agree to these claims will not receive any goods or services from any human signatory to this agreement. They will not sell you gear. They will not sell you materials. They will not sell you information. They will not work for you in any format."

"Yes, yes." Dreamwarden looked bored. "Very well. We'll have to make do without—"

"The undersigned include the names of over four million Earthling miners. More are signing every hour," Veda said. "Gentlemen, they have seventy percent of all Earthling crafters agreed to this already. They have fifty percent of the miners, and that number is going up with every shift change. You won't be able to buy raw materials. You won't be able to buy the refined goods you need for phase three. May I remind you, there will be severely limited supplies and personnel coming in from outside, especially now that your governments are cutting this exploit short to prepare for the rogue world. I'm transmitting over the agreement along with all the signatures now."

"We'll—we'll send in . . ."

"You'll do what?" Veda asked. "The system will enforce no miner-versus-miner violence here or in Threshold. Inside the Reality Engine levels, they've got the advantage." She smiled. "I'll let you examine the deal, but I'm afraid they have you . . ." She checked. "The human phrase is 'over a barrel.'"

Mama Grace was giggling quietly in her chair. Veda showed her a quick smile. This was going to be worth it.

"Tvedra, this will reflect poorly on your requests for involvement in future exploits," Dreamwarden warned. "The three interstellars—Proxima, Alabaster Sky, and ConSweGo—control most exploits in this section of the galaxy. Are you sure you want to get on our bad side?"

Veda smiled. "Actually," she said, "I've already spoken with ConSweGo. They agreed to all terms and have added an endorsement to my license saying that I am welcome to put in a bid on any Reality Engine exploit that they sponsor in the next ten cycles." She was especially proud of that. Mama Grace had wanted to call up all three major conglomerates at once, but Veda had persuaded her to approach ConSweGo first. They had negotiated a ten percent discount on all services provided by the Earthlings for any ConSweGo-affiliated miner as a way to sweeten the deal.

"ConSweGo signed?" Lakhnar asked.

"Feel free to ask them," Veda said sweetly. "Or check the system. The contract should be registered by now."

Now she had them. If their chief rival had already agreed to these terms, then they had no choice. They would sign, or they would sit the rest of this exploit out. Lakhnar huffed. "We'll see about that," she said. She turned away.

She had silenced her audio, but Veda could still see her face as her expression changed from anger to dismay to horror. "I'm afraid I was telling the truth," Veda said.

Dreamwarden's shoulders slumped. Then he shook his head and laughed. "You win this one, Tvedra," he said. "You're looking to be a sharper dealer than we ever expected. Proxima will sign."

CHAPTER FIFTY-ONE

HOW TO MAKE CTHULHU JERKY, STEP ONE: FIRST, KILL YOUR CTHULHU

As I geared up, I tried hard not to be jealous of my teammates out there in the midst of the action. I kept an eye and an ear on the comms channel. Arjun, Sage, and Juana hunched over the command table, constantly scanning between feeds, working like a well-oiled machine. Our hunter squads implemented their orders instantly. Through the All-Seeing Eye feeds, I saw Grandpa Shadow Step in behind an orc, start into him with a Coup, follow up with a Scalp and then at Sage's quick suggestion, Shadow Step away to the orc's buddy. The first orc, turning to try to get at Grandpa, left his back exposed to Bob and Bill's guandao attack.

All over the island, our kill teams were tearing through their opponents. They avoided any group of more than three and fell on smaller clusters like a pack of ravenous dogs. Arjun fed them strategies, telling them how to target each of the orcs, which skills to use. Every now and then, one of the orcs pulled out an ability we hadn't seen, but we adapted fast.

Our opponents had way more health than we did, but they couldn't match sustained firepower. They didn't have anyone coordinating them. I remembered some comments Mak'gar had made about how a leader needed to be out at the head of his men, that otherwise no one would listen to him. I suspected the orcs had a cultural aversion to taking fighting advice from someone on the sidelines. That seemed like a stupid sort of philosophy to me, but if the orcs were sticking to it, that could save our asses here. Their individual movements were good, but they couldn't seem to work together. By the time another group got word that we were attacking some of their fellows, we had finished and melted back into the jungle.

During a lull, I mentioned my theory to Juana, who thanked me and told me to get off comms. A minute later, she directed Bob to ambush a group of five orcs—more than we'd dared touch so far. He hit them with Babel before the rest of our team stepped in. Sure enough, their minimal coordination dropped to none at all. Grandpa's team slaughtered four, the fifth melting away into the jungle in the confusion

I itched to get out there, and I wasn't the only one. Black kept muttering under his breath as he picked up, armed, and stored each of the bombs in his inventory.

I moved on to what Dwight called the taunters. They were a variety of objects, from maracas to little sparkler fireworks to a repurposed slingshot, all with the ability to gain the attention of a mob or player.

Sage explained our strategy. "You're going to be our tank," she said. "Your job is to make the boss and the orcs, if necessary, focus on you and then to stay alive." To that end, they had given me half a dozen cases of healing potions and assigned Lakshmi to heal me full-time. On top of Lakshmi's own healing abilities, Dwight's crafters were churning out healing wands that would output a stream of positive health when she used them.

Black was the third member of our assault. As soon as the kill squads were done, Mitch would meet up with us to help him out. Those two would be tasked with deploying all the bombs the crafters had just made.

Right now, seven of the orcs were dead, with three minutes until the first of them respawned. The other eight were clumped up near the boss. Grandpa said, "We need better eyes on them. Send in one of the spies."

"We're not sure how far the range is on the Old One," Juana warned.

"Do it," Grandpa said, then hesitated. "We're sure the death rules apply to them, too, right?"

"Absolutely," Juana assured us. "I double-checked."

"Then go."

A minute later, one of our spies stumbled out of his hiding place, running down the beach where the boss was waiting. It still sat out in the water, gently pulsating, its glistening, dark mass oozing across the enormous skull beneath. I saw the boss pulse, then constrict. "It's gonna lash out," I warned.

Just then, the orcs burst out from cover, running to engage it. The boss shot a wave of water onto the beach. "Run!" I yelled, not that our spy could hear me.

But it was too late. The camera feed was a blurry mess as the spy was knocked off his feet and washed into the woods. The feed cut out.

A minute later, Grandpa said, "It's all right. He's back in the respawn box."

I let out a breath I hadn't known I was holding.

"Jones, send in your bird."

Jones flew his drone over the scene. The eight Existalis orcs were once more dancing around the boss, chipping down its health. "Good," Grandpa said.

"Good?" I asked.

"We just made them engage again, and there's still two minutes before any of their allies are back up. We've got this." He called to the kill team. "Get in position. Annie, you're going to suicide in and do that move again. Bill, Bob, if she needs an escort, you're up. Everyone else, stay back. We want you for our boss push. Shad, are you guys ready?"

I picked up the last of my taunters. Black had finished collecting his bombs a couple of minutes ago. "We're ready."

"Then head out. And good luck. I'll be following behind in a minute, but I'll rendezvous with the kill squad. We'll be your backup as planned."

I nodded. "Let's go," I told Black and Lakshmi, and we set off.

When we were about half a mile from the beach, Juana's voice came over the comms channel. "Annie, go now." I resisted the urge to call up a feed and watch. Right now I needed to be alert for traps or ambushes.

As we approached the last line of trees, Juana came back on the comms. "The boss is reset. We took out nine of Existalis."

"We'll play interference from here," Grandpa said. "You get in there and do what has to be done."

I took a deep breath and started pulling the special buff items out of my inventory. Mitch joined us as we approached the beach. I handed him his share. There was a potion tagged **[Lightfeet]**; I drank it, and it gave me two hundred percent increased movement for the next fifteen minutes. Next up was a belt of shielding we'd looted from the treasure room during the special event. That was just for me. It had fifty charges. Each charge could take one direct hit, but there was a fifteen-second cooldown before the next charge was up. Between that and my water resistance, we hoped I'd be able to withstand some of the boss hits. If not, this plan wasn't going to go anywhere.

Mitch and Black drank potions that increased the strength of any explosions they caused. Then Black called up the special inventory item he'd been packing, a suitcase, and handed it off to Mitch. It contained some of the bombs Dwight's team had made and was faster than giving them to Mitch one at a time. "Once you've got the boss's attention, we'll go," Black said to me.

"You stay up on the beach," I told Lakshmi. "As far back as you can while still able to heal me."

"Don't worry. I don't want to get any closer than I have to," she said.

I stepped out onto the beach. The Great Old One took no notice of me until I reached the waterline, when its surface began to swirl once more. I watched the patterns. I'd seen enough of Existalis's attempts to recognize when it was about to launch a wave of water and when it was about to lash out with its tentacles.

I hurled a small metal ball, the first of my taunters, straight at the boss. It exploded in a cloud of bright pink smoke and confetti while letting out a high-pitched shriek. A warning popped up: **[You have attracted the attention of the Great Old One.]** The boss formed a pseudopod, raising it high. One lash of that enormous gooey tentacle would flatten me.

I threw my first Shad Dummy ten feet to my right. It popped up wearing a coat like mine, with a big straw hat on its head. "Over here, you big dope," it called with what I hoped was not my voice.

The boss launched its pseudopod right at the dummy, smashing it into splinters and bits of straw. I tossed another taunter, darted to the side, threw a dummy, avoided a tentacle, and got ready for the longest dance session of my life.

Meanwhile, Black and Mitch were at the water's edge, crouched over an enormous pile of explosives, hooking fuses to each of them. I wasn't going to bug them.

Juana said, "Incoming. Four of Existalis."

"They're on my radar," Jones called on comms. "Kill squad will handle them."

I focused on the boss and my dance. From the patterns rippling through the water, I guessed it was getting ready to throw one of its water waves. "Back up," I warned Mitch and Black. They scrambled up the beach. Lakshmi retreated, too.

I thought I should be able to withstand the water, but I wasn't sure about its force, so I braced myself. A wave exploded out from the Old One. It washed over me like a gentle mist, soaking me but doing no damage. I grinned and threw another taunter.

All right, Reality Engine. If you're behind this, I see how you're tweaking things, I thought. Give me resistance to water and then make sure the monster we faced is water-based? Yeah, it had its thumb on the scales.

I wasn't going to take anything for granted. I was pretty sure this monster still had plenty of ways to beat me. Juana's voice came back in my ear. "The kill squad took out Existalis, but Ice Spice and Brown are down."

"That's no good. We can't lose people."

"You focus on your job, and they'll do theirs," she told me crisply.

I tossed out another Shad Dummy. "Tell Sage I hate the expressions on these things," I said as the Old One smashed the smirk off its face.

"You can do that when you're done here."

Juana's calm was starting to get to me. "Aren't you at all nervous about this?"

"Horribly nervous," she said. "But I'm trying to be professional here, and so should you."

"Right. Fine." I dodged another pseudopod, watching the thing's glistening patterns. Mitch and Black had moved to another point on the beach to start their second cache of explosives. We weren't doing any damage to the boss, so I wasn't expecting it to throw any more of those water droplet minions, but if it did, I'd keep their attention, too.

We got the second cache finished, and the bomb team moved to their third location. Juana spoke up. "I think Existalis is on to us. Six of them have respawned, but there's been no movement out of their outpost yet."

"So they're going to wait until they can make a big push," I said. "They probably figure it'll take us a while to chip the boss down and they'll have time to come in." It wasn't a bad plan. "How long until the last of them is back up?"

"They have fifteen total, like us. The four we just took out have another fifteen minutes to go before respawn, but they could have eight up in—" Juana paused. "Nine and a half minutes."

"Can you get all of the bombs laid in the next nine and a half minutes?" I asked Black.

"We'll try," he said. "Look out!"

I dodged to the side as a pseudopod crashed into the water next to me. I tossed out a dummy and got back into my rhythm.

There was no room for mistakes here. The dance wore on and on and on. "You're a pretty good dancer," Juana observed at the seven-minute mark.

"Thanks, no one's ever said that before."

"Really?"

"No, the girl I asked to the prom turned me down on account of, as she said, she wanted to go with someone who wouldn't step on her feet."

Juana giggled. "Guess it must be the points you put into dexterity."

"Well, if there's ever a dance here, I'll be sure to ask you," I said, tossing out another taunter.

"I'll hold you to that," she said. "And I might just ask my sister to arrange something like that. She's in charge of the morale committee now, you know."

"What?" I almost missed a step, throwing out a Shad Dummy just in time. "We have one of those?"

"Who do you think threw that party last week?"

"I guess I didn't really think about it."

"It's all part of our strategy to keep people focused and happy, which you are most assuredly not right now. Focused, I mean. Pay attention, Shad."

The next wave broke over me. "I am paying attention. Those waves don't hurt me," I said.

"Uh-huh." Juana did not sound convinced.

Black yelled, "It's done! Get into position!"

Finally. "Juana, we're going," I said.

"I'll get everyone else on their marks," she said.

"Tell me when."

A moment later, she said, "Existalis is moving out, a pack of eight together. They'll be here in four minutes, give or take thirty seconds. There are three more respawning in five minutes, and the last four ten minutes from now. You've got to engage the boss now, before they get here."

"Got it," I said. I threw another of the taunters, then backed up toward the first bomb cache. I threw one of the taunters right on it, and then raced off to the side.

The boss's pseudopod smashed down right on the cache, exploding in a gout of fire. Flame seared the oozing black tentacle. It burned to ash, fire racing up it, devouring it, hitting the body of the monster.

The Great Old One shrieked aloud. An answering rain of giant water bubbles appeared, blorping their way along the beach. I threw out handfuls of tiny taunters everywhere, getting the bubbles to focus on me, and then pulled out a freeze grenade Dwight had made me. As the bubbles surrounded me, I tossed it down, locking the water bubbles in place.

The edge of the freeze caught my coat and sent icicles up to my arm. I shook them off harmlessly. They did no damage. I threw a Shad Dummy to the side to buy me time as the boss's outer surface spun and hissed.

"Down to eighty percent," Juana said. "Just like we calculated."

"Good." I moved to the next cache, threw one of my bigger taunts, and waited as the tentacle formed. As it raised its pseudopod high, I left a dummy in my place and scrambled out of the way.

Just like before, the pseudopod smashed into the cache, burst into flames, and carried the fire back to the main body. The boss summoned another wave of droplets. This time, Mitch and Black were close enough to help me with them.

"Forty percent down," Juana said. "Existalis is two minutes out."

"At least it's dumb," Grandpa said in my ear. "Must have been programmed to do the same thing no matter what."

"We're counting on it," I said. We had noticed that behavior in many of the NPCs. I repeated my strategy on the next cache, and then the next. The boss's health dropped in big chunks. It sent out big waves of droplet minions with every explosion, but I had the rhythm now, freezing them and letting Mitch and Black blow them up.

The seconds ticked along. I was in the groove. I could keep this up all day.

The boss was down to twenty percent health as Grandpa said, "We have contact."

I made for the last cache and threw my taunt, but the boss didn't respond as we expected. Instead, it seemed to draw in on itself, shrinking, turning black as night. Existalis hadn't gotten it down this far yet. We didn't know what was going to happen.

"We've got to get these bombs to the boss," I shouted.

"How?" Black asked. "We weren't expecting to move them."

"We need a teleport or some sort of shove ability." I mentally ran through everyone's skill sheets. "The boss won't move, and we can't get the bombs to him. Have we got a . . . trebuchet or . . ." I trailed off as I had a brainwave. "Get Lara up here right away!" I yelled into my comms. "Black, Mitch, get the bombs loaded up in your suitcase or—whatever works, we need them stable just long enough to transport them." I lobbed a taunter at the boss, blessing

Dwight's crafters. They'd gone all out. I still had several dozen taunters and dummies.

"Busy here," Grandpa called back. "Fighting!"

"Get Lara here; I need her!" I threw a Shad Dummy beyond the boss. It was still hunched in on itself and spinning. The dummy hit the water. A spout exploded under it, knocking it thirty feet high.

Lara sprinted out of the jungle. "I'm here!"

"Get Mitch and Black to the boss. Blow it up!" I shouted.

She looked confused. "How—"

"Minivan!"

"Oh, right!" She raced to where the munitions experts were collecting their gear.

"And hurry! Existalis is on our heels!" I could hear the sounds of fighting, not just over the comms but with my own ears.

Lara waved her hands and summoned an actual, literal minivan around the men. The van screeched forward in a cloud of tire smoke, driving right across the top of the water.

The boss writhed. A jet of water began to form under the minivan, but not fast enough.

The minivan crashed into the boss and exploded, blasting the Old One with a burst of fire. It screamed and writhed as flames ate away at its viscous black skin. A plume of smoke and debris engulfed the monster, pushing us back as the monster succumbed to the blaze.

As the smoke cleared and the water settled, I saw an enormous crystal skull, ten feet tall and just as wide, sitting in the middle of the lagoon. The minivan was gone. One tire bounced up onto the beach and rolled toward the jungle.

The box over the massive skull read [**Boss defeated by Misfits Guild. Where would you like to send your agent of primeval destruction?**]

I grinned and mentally selected Existalis's outpost. "Kill 'em all," I said. "Break all their stuff."

And then I lay back on the sand and took my first easy breath of the day, maybe even of the week. There would be more battles, sooner rather than later. But today? Today we had won a fight nobody had expected us to win. One we hadn't asked for.

Not that we'd asked for any of this. Today, we hadn't just outfought them. We'd outthought them. Nobody was going to take Earth for granted anymore. That might not be a good thing, but it was a thing that I had done.

Grandpa's voice sounded in my ear. "Gonna just stay there all day, sleepyhead?"

I got to my feet as the kill squad trooped down onto the beach. "I just thought we'd let him get a head start," I said, pointing to the water where the Old One was forming once more. This time, it took the shape of a midnight-black scintillating squid, lifting its skull high atop a pulsating body.

It crawled to shore on its pseudopods, gaining speed as it went. As it hit the trees, it was going at least thirty miles an hour. It smashed through the brush, leaving only debris in its wake. "Better warn our spies," I said.

"Already on it," Juana said. "A couple of 'em have volunteered to stand watch at Existalis's node, just so we can all enjoy the recording later."

"Get the crew," Grandpa said. "We're going to accompany Cthulhu the whole way, just in case any of them decide to try to take him down. This ain't over till the fat lady sings."

I laughed and reloaded. "Right, so let's finish this."

CHAPTER FIFTY-TWO

HOW NOT TO OVERSTAY YOUR WELCOME

Three days later . . .

Mama Grace's restaurant was packed to the gills. We squeezed in shoulder to shoulder, at least four hundred humans. Those of us who had been most involved in phase two had a couple of long tables at the back of the room, and Mama Grace's assistants served us first.

Grandpa had ordered beer and sangria, with some help to source them from Veda. The barbecued bug ribs were slathered in a solid approximation of Texas sauce. I didn't ask what was in it. The cornbread was fresh and hot, the beans had been cooking for days, and the coleslaw was crisp. I could close my eyes and pretend I was back on Earth, just for a bit.

The crafters were the heroes of the hour. Other coalition members pushed through the crowd to shake their hands and congratulate them. I caught Dwight's eye and raised my beer.

Juana leaned over my shoulder. "Happy birthday, by the way, Shad."

I started. "Wait, what?"

"That's right," Grandpa said. "I checked the date with the system."

"Wow." I sipped my beer, then stared at it. I was twenty-two years old now. We'd been here nearly a year. A huge chunk of my life, and an even bigger part of Sage's. I forced a smile. "You know, they said, 'join the Army, see the world,' but I didn't ever expect this."

"Also," Grandpa said. "Got you a gift. Courtesy of Colonel Ames, but he couldn't make it." He tossed me a small box. I flipped it open. A set of shiny captain's bars stared up at me.

I pulled out one of the linked silver pairs and stared at it. "Wait, really?" I looked up at Grandpa, who nodded.

"You've earned it. Time in grade is a little short, but what we're doing here counts for a lot. Besides, we can't have Earth's finest being led by a mere lieutenant."

"What about you?"

"Ames is working on something. I don't care, but if Waters shows up again it'll make our lives easier."

I went to put the bars back in their box, but Juana grabbed them from me and pinned them to my shirt. "I'm not in uniform!" I protested.

"Yes, you are," she said. "That coat's your uniform now. Besides, I don't think your senior officer is going to mind." She gave me a quick kiss on my cheek and slipped away before I could react. I felt myself getting hot in the face. Grandpa laughed at me and handed me another beer.

"I got you something, too!" Sage said. She pulled a pair of ammo cans out of her inventory. Grunting slightly, she put them down on the table. I flipped open the lids and smiled at the shiny brass cartridges. "More boom rounds, a bunch of frag rounds, and some really fun ones."

"I'll take a look after the party." I pulled the cans into my own inventory and dove back into the plate.

When the feasting had started to slack off a little, Grandpa got up. He pushed his way to the head of the room. Conversation died down as all heads turned to him. I swallowed the last of my food and pushed away my plate. I knew what was coming, and it might be uncomfortable.

"Well done, everyone!" Grandpa said. We all whooped and hollered. "They said it couldn't be done. That indigenous groups never get to phase three. That we didn't have any idea what we were doing. Well, we've shown them."

I raised a fist and cheered with the rest.

"But there's more to come. Phase three will be our biggest challenge yet. We're going to need all of you, and a lot more. We're going to need every human we can get to back this. Together, we have a shot at taking a tiny piece of what ought to be ours back from the assholes who kidnapped us. It's going to be the most important operation in human history. Let that sink in for a minute."

We did, but I heard some shuffling feet and murmurs. I caught the eye of Paul, one of our crafters, and nodded. "Go ahead. Ask him," I mouthed.

Paul raised a hand. "Major Twofeather? I—I'm on board for whatever you're up to, of course. You've steered us right so far. But—why is this such a big deal? I thought we were trying to earn coin to buy out our contracts and go home, but you make this sound way more serious."

Grandpa nodded. "There's something you don't know. Something they've been keeping secret. Something our sponsor told us. I've been wrestling with how or when to tell you all. Well, there's never gonna be a right time, so this is as good as any." He took a deep breath, and I leaned forward, gripping the edge of the table so tight my knuckles went white. I knew what was coming, and this was critical. We might lose some of our people, based on the next couple minutes. But Grandpa was right. They deserved to know.

"We can't go home."

He let that hang there for a moment, then half the crowd was on their feet shouting and the other half still looking shell-shocked.

Sage slipped closer to me. I put an arm around her. She'd already known, but her face was as pale as I'd ever seen it.

"What do you mean, we can't go home?" Dwight shouted.

"The Reality Engine changed us. Really changed us. How do you think we can shoot lightning from our asses and teleport and all that bullshit? It's done something to our bodies, and now we're dependent on it, or another Engine like it."

"So we're trapped here," someone said.

"They've lied to us!" another voice shouted.

"What's the point? I'm done; I'm going to find that safe portal and just sit around doing nothing." That was Phil, one of our best crafters, who had come up with the Shad Dummies plan for our final phase two push. I heard others agreeing with him.

We needed to stop this talk, fast.

I got to my feet. "Of course they lied to us," I said. "They kidnapped and enslaved us. But we weren't even supposed to get here, and we did. We'll find a way. Somehow. There's tech that can let us go back to Earth, at least to visit. Sounds like it's damn expensive. But if we make it in phase three, we can buy anything. Maybe even buy our planet back."

I wanted to convince them, to make everyone take time to think about what this all meant, but my words felt hollow. I wasn't sure I believed them myself. "That's all still a ways down the road, though. Right now, I'm looking at going into phase three and doing what we've been doing all along. Surpassing expectations."

"Hear, hear!" Kirin yelled from a seat in the corner next to Arjun. "I'm with Team Twofeather!"

Mama Grace stood in the kitchen door, drying her hands on her apron. "We're all with you," she shouted. "Anyone who's got cold feet, go ahead and leave, but you'll be losing your friends-and-family discount on your meals!"

That broke the tension. A ripple of laughter swept the room. Most of the crew sat back down.

Grandpa held up his hands. "I'm not going to pretend it'll be easy. Hasn't been so far. But I couldn't ask for a better team to work with. We ain't anything special. They picked us at random, from all over Earth. Well, I'll take our randomly chosen humans over the elite alien teams any day. We're going into phase three, and we are going to make our mark. That's my promise. Not that we win the whole thing. Not that we kick them out and reclaim what's ours. But that we make them remember we were here."

I saw him touch the thong under his shirt where he wore his medicine pouch, with its little pinch of home soil, next to my abuela's medallion, and wondered just what he was thinking about now. His wife? My mother? His ancestors, who had been pushed off their land by more powerful invaders, fighting to keep the memory of who they'd been?

"We can't go home," Grandpa said. It was like he was talking just to me. "But we'll find a way to bring home along with us, wherever we go. As long as we stick together, we haven't lost everything."

I met his gaze and nodded. I didn't know what was coming in phase three, or where we'd go next, but side by side with my family—Sage, Grandpa, and everyone else who had joined us in this fight—I was ready.

Ready to ride for the brand, one more time.

ABOUT THE AUTHOR

M. Talon is the pseudonym of the authors of Not My First (Space?) Rodeo, a sci-fi LitRPG originally released on Royal Road. They are a married couple who live and write in northern Nevada. They also like to go on off-road adventures with their kids and buy really nice hats.

Podium

DISCOVER MORE

STORIES UNBOUND

PodiumEntertainment.com

www.ingramcontent.com/pod-product-compliance
Lightning Source LLC
Chambersburg PA
CBHW031251120726
47906CB00003B/687